the realm of secondhand souls

the realm of secondhand souls

sandra shea

DISCARDED

houghton mifflin company ➤ boston ➤ new york ➤ 2000

For information about permission to reproduce selections from
this book, write to Permissions, Houghton Mifflin Company,
215 Park Avenue South, New York, New York 10003.

Library of Congress Cataloging-in-Publication Data

Shea, Sandra.
The realm of secondhand souls / Sandra Shea.
p.   cm.
ISBN 0-395-83810-X
I. Title.
PS3569.H391256R4   2000
813'.54—dc21   99-43517   CIP

Book design by Anne Chalmers
Typefaces are: Janson, Centaur, Altemus Borders 4

The author is grateful to Todd Lyon, Colleen Mohyde, Caroline Knapp,
Janet Silver, and Zack Stalberg for their extraordinary support during
the writing of this book. The library of Sue Mingus is also
gratefully acknowledged.

Printed in the United States of America
QUM 10 9 8 7 6 5 4 3 2 1

FOR MY FAMILY

Everything that is dead quivers. Not only the things of poetry, stars, moon, wood, flowers, but even a white trouser button glittering out of a puddle in the street....Everything has a secret soul, which is silent more often than it speaks.

— Wassily Kandinsky, *Selbstbetrachtungen*

"Referential mania," Herman Brink had called it. In these very rare cases the patient imagines that everything happening around him is a veiled reference to his personality and existence....Phenomenal nature shadows him wherever he goes. Clouds in the staring sky transmit to one another, by means of slow signs, incredibly detailed information regarding him. His inmost thoughts are discussed at nightfall, in manual alphabet, by darkly gesticulating trees. Pebbles or stains or sun flecks form patterns representing in some awful way messages which he must intercept. Everything is a cipher and of everything he is the theme. Some of the spies are detached observers, such as glass surfaces and still pools; others, such as coats in store windows, are prejudiced witnesses, lynchers at heart; others again (running water, storms) are hysterical to the point of insanity, have a distorted opinion of him, and grotesquely misinterpret his actions.

. . . The silhouettes of his blood corpuscles, magnified a million times, flit over vast plains; and still farther, great mountains of un-bearable solidity and height sum up in terms of granite and groaning firs the ultimate truth of his being.

— Vladimir Nabokov, "Signs and Symbols"

the realm of secondhand souls

chapter 1

NOVENA WAS BORN just as her name would have you picture: surrounded by a halo of candles and eight praying women. It was a hot, still summer night and the hum of prayers sounded like a swarm of cicadas, the buzz that surrounds lawn mowers and tall glasses beaded with sweat.

They were far from lawn mowers, being in the middle of the city, in an ancient apartment that resented the modern age and mournfully released memories of its former glory like a vapor through its rooms: a lingering trace of cigar smoke in deep green drapes, a brief flash of the corner of a rose-colored plush velvet sofa, the ghost of a man in a hat reading the newspapers.

In the bedroom, her about-to-be aunt Quivera was everywhere, fetching ice and blankets, mopping her sister's face, as much in help as in the constant activity of anxiety. Of Catorza's two sisters, Quivera was the practical, antiseptic one, and found the ordeal of birth painful to witness. So much blood. So much mess, and impossible to control. So much heaving and screaming from Catorza, who seemed to be expelling all of her insides. Still, for all the mess, Novena would end up sliding out quietly, almost gracefully, and manage to retain the ability to stay quiet in the midst of chaos until much later in her life.

The other women around the bedside included Catorza's other sister, Elegia, who was praying particularly hard since she thought herself the only sister among them strong enough to withstand the rigors of birth, a stamina she had put to constant practice.

The midwife, Celantra, an old family friend, was called upon whenever the services of a voodoo, healer, or guide were needed, although you needed to occasionally remind her what role the particular moment required, since she was known to bring forceps when a live chicken was more in order, and vice versa. At this moment, she was pawing through a large satchel, trying to remember what she was looking for.

Jakarta, a neighbor who traveled up and down the coast performing in small blues clubs as part of a trio, had just arrived with the other two members of her trio for whatever musical accompaniment the night might require.

Fanning herself furiously in the corner was Margita, Catorza's best friend, a worldly but easily rattled woman who had come by train from a distant city. And finally there was a great-aunt, Annaluna, the only black-veil-wearer among them. She was the one who led the prayers. She was the one who knew all the words, the spotty knowledge of the rest of the women contributing in no small part to the humming sound of their incantations: they were doing a holy version of mouthing the lyrics and humming the melody. Their pinpricks of guilt over the long-forgotten words accounted for the fervor with which they delivered what fragments of prayers they could conjure.

Occasionally, Jakarta and her trio would break out of prayer and into actual song, creating a kind of sanctified scatting: *Our father. Bap bap bap bee boo. Diddlieopti doo. Deliver us from evil. Da wan. Da wan. Amen.*

Annaluna threw them occasional sharp glances, but there was a kind of soothing logic to the music, from which Catorza took some comfort.

Hours rolled by in a salty, undulating tide which had seeped into the room and taken over: screams and pain, calm and breath, heat and dampness. There wasn't a woman in the room who wasn't used to being pulled by rhythmic tidal forces, and on this night they gave themselves up to it. Time was left to sit quietly in the corner, called upon only in short bursts when Catorza's contractions needed measuring.

It was hot, and everyone was sweating. The women had stripped down to their underwear — even Annaluna, whose corset was immense and proud and somehow military in the face of the more dainty, slippery things worn by the younger women. Their dresses formed an airy bundle of color on the floor. When Novena's head finally appeared, Quivera was at the bedside, and in her excitement she bent and grabbed the dress on top of the bundle to wrap her in. It was a cobalt silk owned by Margita, a big, fleshy blonde, who for all her sophisticated flash was the shyest among them and had been the last to peel out of her clothes.

When Margita saw her dress swaddling the bloody, mucus-covered bundle of baby, she started to protest.

"Quivera, my . . . Oh," she gulped, then turned to the others and shrugged.

"Oh well. It was on sale. Loehmann's."

Then she brightened, as the train of her thought moved her from disaster to optimism, a trip she took at least twenty times a day, every degree of which registered on her face. This was what Catorza had always admired most in her.

Now Margita brightened further and said, "Hey, it's luck, isn't it. It'll be my lucky dress from now on. I'll save it for her. She can wear it herself, in sixteen years."

The women had crowded around the bed. Their warm, damp skin stuck to each other. The smell of blood and salt and sweetness, acrid and new, the sounds of their clucking and cooing, their mouths opening and closing like birds, stirred in each of them the sensation of themselves being born.

Catorza, looking down at Novena swaddled in blue, felt a great swell inside her, like the ocean's wave. It rolled in, heavy and wet, built to a gentle crest, then crashed home. As it receded, she knew herself to be different; it was her first moment of motherhood. She became fixed on a picture of Novena at sixteen years, ripe and seductive as she herself had been. Fingering the silk, she looked up and said, "Twenty-one years. And not a minute before."

Novena felt her own small wave cresting and relaxing. She took in the claw-footed sofa, the pile of dresses, the corset of Annaluna, the echoes of the trio's songs, the notes of which were lingering in the corners of the room like cobwebs, and she felt her mother's warm fingers through the blue silk. She looked up at them all and smiled at how familiar it seemed.

➤

Drop an egg into boiling water and the shell will often crack, releasing its albumen in lacy white streams. The same thing happens to a man's heart when he becomes a father: it develops tiny fissures that release the tendrils that tie him to his children. Some men's hearts, though, will stay intact and contained, the threads of protein becoming choked and tangled up in themselves. The children of those fathers usually grow up with similar hearts. They grow up loving solitude with a fierceness that even the best mothers can't alter.

Novena's father, Nick, wasn't a bad man, just a bad father, although like all bad fathers he would never have believed this. And like many bad fathers, he had a multitude of children. Long before he met Catorza, he had married young and his wife had borne him four children in rapid succession, so quickly that by the time he was in his mid-twenties he was already stunned by life. His children confused him, made noises he couldn't understand and demands he couldn't fathom. He wasn't sure what they wanted, but it seemed to be everything. Worse, they showed no signs of giving him anything in return.

"What about me?" he'd yell through the house. "When is it my turn?" and the children would grow still. Even in their baby brains, they knew that to hear these questions from a parent doomed them to become people who would forever try too hard to please.

The thought that he'd been cheated, that he was going to end up empty-handed, gnawed at Nick until one day he stopped going home. He sent money when he could, which wasn't often. He was a musician, which suited him in many ways, but was hardly lucrative enough to support a family.

He met Catorza not long after he'd left, one night when she came to see Jakarta and her trio sing at a small downtown club. Nick was sitting in on piano and saw her sitting at a small table watching him. She liked his big hands; he liked the fact she could sit so calmly at a table by herself. There was a stillness about her that gave him a feeling like homesickness. All he wanted, he told himself, was what was coming to him. Nothing more than what he was entitled to. And Catorza took that shape for him, sitting there calmly in the dark club, watching him. Here was someone who would pay attention to him for a change.

Which she did, for a while. Until the ironic and cynical gods that cursed Nick with fecundity found him again. By the time Novena arrived, he was gone, nothing more than one of the ghosts inhabiting the apartment.

With a new baby, Catorza needed work she could do from home, and began gathering up jobs and taking them in as if they were stray pets. She started typing, mostly immigration documents for a lawyer who had opened a storefront office in the building to capitalize on the hundreds of Vietnamese who were moving into the neighborhood. She did their taxes and helped them improve their rough English so they could start their businesses, teaching them useful phrases like "Thank you, come again" and "Cash or charge?" and, for the women opening nail salons all across the city, "Go pick a color." They stopped going to the lawyer and began coming to her. She started balancing their books, and straightening out their immigration problems, and advising them on the best way to deal with officials. They thought there was nothing she couldn't fix, and she had to convince them to take their sick children and broken appliances elsewhere. They kept coming, some paying her in cash, some with steaming pots of fragrant dishes or boxes of tea, and some with bright bolts of cloth, which she hung in panels around Novena's crib. Novena would lie for hours, watching the play of breeze and light through them.

One day, Xa Ngum, a neighborhood elder, showed up with a daunting stack of letters from the IRS that needed deciphering, and a basket of shirts that needed mending and ironing. Catorza tried to say no to the shirts, but he pretended not to understand and left the basket behind, bowing to her as he went out the door.

She let them sit for a few nights, but the fact was, she found ironing soothing. So one night she took out her iron and lifted a shirt from the basket. The cloth was ancient and beautiful, and it seemed alive under her fingers. As she pressed the hot iron to the shirts, their fragrant breaths were exhaled into the clouds of steam which wrapped around her. With each shirt she pressed, the breaths of the cloth grew stronger, until it seemed as if the shirts were whispering to her. As she mended and pressed, the shirts told her of Xa Ngum's work in the hot wet government offices of the capital, of his escape from invaders through moist rice fields and slow brown rivers. With the next shirt, she saw a green so translucent it nearly blinded her. A green shattering into a thousand greens, the green of parrot, snakes, emeralds, of melon, jade, and new grass. By the time the last shirt was pressed and folded, she sat down, feeling a little drunk.

Xa Ngum showed up a few days later and was delighted with the neat stacks of shirts, which Catorza had bundled and tied with ribbon, like packets of love letters. He began showing up every Wednesday with new piles of shirts. Since he still wore the drab anonymous clothes of the city, she wondered what he did with the shirts, but what did it matter? He paid her well.

Xa Ngum loved Catorza's apartment, especially when the ghosts of its past life wafted through the rooms like sleepwalkers. Mostly, he loved sitting watching her work, a sight he found both soothing and exciting. He would hold Novena in his lap, a cup of green tea by his side, and they would fall asleep to the steady ticking of the sewing machine; the whooshing blast of steam from the iron mingling with the fragrant fumes of the tea would lull them into dreams of warmth and industry.

One night Xa Ngum didn't go home. Catorza welcomed the company of someone in her bed, where he became a young man, by turns ardent and giggling. She began to count on their Wednesday nights.

Months of pleasure and ironing passed. Then, two Wednesdays went by with no Xa Ngum. Catorza felt shy about calling him. She sat with the last batch of his shirts and unwrapped the bundle, inhaling the shirts, hoping to find an answer. But the cloth was silent, having expelled all its secrets under the press of the iron.

The next morning, Xang, one of the neighborhood women, showed up with a note from Ngum, which she offered to translate in exchange for Catorza typing up a stack of liquor permit documents. She insisted the typing be done first. Catorza, not expecting good news, typed slowly. Then she gathered Novena on her lap and Xang opened the letter.

" 'Beautiful iron woman,' " she read. " 'I must go for a while and be with my family.' "

Xang was an old friend of Ngum's and was jealous of Catorza and scandalized by their carrying on. She interrupted her reading to tell her, "His family still in Vietnam. His wife was very beautiful. She's dead now."

Xang continued to read. " 'My son and nephew have been tempted by evil to join the army here, which has returned to killing. This is the army that destroyed us a long time ago. My sister mourns. My family is a field of dry grass that is burning under a too hot sun. I must put out the flames. I ask Xang to take this immediately to you' " — here Xang blushed, since she had deliberately waited two weeks before taking it to Catorza — " 'to let you know I will come back one day.' "

Catorza knew he wouldn't return. As she stroked Novena's hair, she suddenly felt queasy. Something moved in the pit of her stomach like a snake.

Xang grabbed her chin suddenly and looked into her eyes for a long moment.

"You be careful," she said sternly.

Catorza tipped her face up in a question.

"You have something coming," she told Catorza, and quickly gathering up her liquor permits, went out the door.

Ngum, that silly old fool, Xang thought, going down the stairs. She wouldn't tell him. Let him find out for himself.

And so nearly four years after Novena's birth, Catorza was pregnant again. When her time came, she went to the hospital to deliver. Margita, who couldn't get away, sent her a new dress, in what she hoped would become a tradition of stylish receiving blankets. It arrived in a big box from one of the better department stores, swaddled in great mounds of tissue paper. Also in the box were matching shoes and a purse, both in a gay floral print. Their actual purpose in the birthing process Margita hadn't quite thought through, but they matched the dress so perfectly she couldn't resist.

Annaluna didn't trust shoes. In fact, she thought they had the capacity for making their own decisions to conspire against us, and believed they were rendered powerless only if they were on feet or corralled in closets. Her rules were simple:

"Never leave them in hallways; there they can congregate and plot amongst themselves. Never leave them outside, unaccompanied, for they can wander where you don't want them to be. If you see two shoes lying together, imagine the worst."

If she found a shoe in the middle of the sidewalk, which in the city is a not uncommon occurrence, she would bring it home and bury it. Usually they were sneakers, which she considered containers of misfortune rather than instruments of determined evil, unless a pair of them were tied and hanging off a telephone wire, a clear warning that the street had been hexed and was to be avoided. Occasionally, though, she would come home muttering darkly, holding a man's smashed oxford or a woman's bruised high heel, which she had fished out of a gutter amid broken glass and old newspaper. These she would not only bury, but light candles for for three days.

If she had been there when Margita's box arrived, she would have forbidden the shoes from going to the hospital, which as far as she was concerned was like letting the devil vacation in purgatory. A hospital was dangerous enough, but to bring shoes to it could mean nothing good.

She was right. Catorza, in the first few hours of labor, had opened the box, and put the purse and shoes on the nightstand next to her to admire them. A few hours later, when she started giving birth, things took a bad turn. She started bleeding too heavily. The hospital was understaffed, the intern was inexperienced, and when he realized he was losing her called not for another doctor, but for the priest.

The priest arrived with two nuns, who huddled near the intern and, sizing up the seriousness of the situation, directed that the mother be sacrificed to save the baby. Catorza fought, but wouldn't stop bleeding. Rivers of blood flowed from her. But unlike the slow brown rivers of Xa Ngum's escape, this red river moved fast and hard. It bathed the room, spattering the white wimples of the nuns and the starched collar of the priest.

The strong current of this river carried an infant boy, who bobbed and fought for breath as he was pulled and dragged along from his nest. The first breath he took was Catorza's last.

He was alive and his prognosis was good. A baby without a mother, though, has the right to choose otherwise. An hour later, exhausted from his efforts to punch his way into the world, lonely beyond description, he had a final lingering thought of his sister. Then he stopped breathing and joined his mother.

Quivera, Elegia, and Annaluna were in the waiting room, holding each other's hands as they waited for word. When the blood-spattered priest came and told them the news of Catorza's death, they let out a collective wail that shattered the air. They wailed without stopping until an hour later the bad news of the boy was announced. Then they fainted, one by one. As their bodies fell to the floor, their jewelry unclipped, unsnapped, unpinned itself and fell off them, their shoes slid off their feet, their pocketbooks flew across the room. It was as if the pieces of themselves that would now be forever lost without Catorza took shape and fell from them, landing in sad little piles on the hard floor.

Annaluna gathered up the murdering shoes and purse to take home, and vowed to never again speak to Margita. She sat at her kitchen table that night and wept the remainder of the tears she had been allowed in this life. She had spent half of them when her own sister, Catorza's mother, had died. She released a slightly smaller portion of them when she lost her husband, whom she had lost not to death, which would have accounted for considerably fewer tears, but to another woman. Those were the powerful armies of tears; the smaller regiments of everyday hardships, wounds, and sentiment had been exhausted by the time she reached sixty. Now the tears over the loss of Catorza and the baby marched forth freely, leaving in their wake a garden of sodden dis-carded tissues that covered the table like wild roses. After a time, she was finally wrung out, the last reserves of moisture gone, her insides coated with sand and dust.

At midnight, she got up and put the purse and the shoes — safely imprisoned in a box — on the table, considering the dilemma of what to do with them. She considered purses benign, at worst selfish, with a capacity for good that they rarely exerted. She sat, her hand absently opening and closing the clasp on the purse, muttering her options, in a scatting stream reminiscent of Jakarta's trio.

"Mail them back to that wicked . . . no mail, anything can . . . cut them up. Cut them up. Burn. Bury. Too good for 'em."

Suddenly, the idea of disarming the shoes' power receded, and the idea of punishing them started to burn in her. It was a flame that spread quickly through her arid, rainless bones.

As anyone who has tried knows, the punishment of objects is a complex and deceptive science. For example, physical abuse brings only temporary satisfaction: the mute and damaged thing often just lies there, mocking in its lack of remorse, egging you on to further outrage, further violence. The attempt to teach an offending object a lesson with drastic measures like cutting, scarring, or burning doubles its insult to you, as you are left with the scarred, burned, and useless thing. Annaluna, in her intense fury, rejected these options and arrived at the only workable plan of punishing the shoes.

The funeral home was crowded. The first row of chairs was taken up by Quivera, Elegia, and Novena, with an empty chair for Annaluna.

Behind them sat Jakarta; collapsed next to her was the midwife, Celantra, who had thankfully remembered to leave in the car the clumps of sage that she had mistakenly brought with her. The burning-sage ritual was for new houses, to drive out the spirits; there was not enough sage in the world to cover a funeral home. Margita was still in transit.

Novena sat quietly in the metal bamboo funeral home chair, watching her mother sleep a few feet away. A memory stirred, of her mother in bed, of these women surrounding her, of tears and dampness and screams and breathing. Now she heard again the humming drone of incantation.

"Oh Novena, oh Novena," they wept to her, picking her up, holding her in their laps, rocking with her, grieving, using her as a human handkerchief, her calm presence in their laps unleashing fresh sobs and tears.

Jakarta stood to sing. She started with some low, soft hymns until her voice, cracked in sorrow, finally refused to go on. She pulled out her harmonica and moved on to blues, the old-as-dirt kind. She was in the middle of "Motherless Children" when Annaluna arrived.

Annaluna was stooped in her grief, but at the same time seemed taller. She limped to the front of the room, where she stood at Catorza's coffin. She touched her niece's cheek. As she prayed, Quivera nudged Elegia, who looked at Annaluna and let out a little bleating cry that harmonized perfectly with the harmonica's solo moans.

Annaluna had turned and hobbled toward a chair. She was moving as if her feet were bandaged. In a strange way, they were. On her feet were the gaily patterned shoes. They were impossibly large on her tiny feet, but to compensate, she had stuffed the spaces with mounds of her tear-soaked tissues that had collected on her kitchen table the night before.

"Annaluna. What have you done to your feet?" cried Elegia. Annaluna stopped and stared hard at Elegia as if she didn't recognize her. Finally she spoke.

"You see these shoes? These shoes killed Catorza. And now I am going to return the favor," she said.

"I walked here in them, and I am going to walk in them until they no longer exist. If it means I must be buried in them, then bury me in them."

Then she sat down, and someone handed her Novena. Annaluna sat with the child on her lap. Annaluna was calm and dry-eyed, but for one moment wished she had a small reserve of tears left, because it had been a long and painful walk to the funeral home, and her feet were starting to kill her.

chapter 2

AFTER THE FUNERAL DINNER, which had filled the apartment for hours, Quivera, Elegia, and Margita were in the kitchen, putting plastic wrap on an army of bowls and casseroles and dishes and plates that held the remains of the food.

"Is there some grief cookbook I don't know about?" Margita said, wrapping a bowl of pink Jell-O mold. "Have you ever been to a funeral that didn't have Jell-O mold, or pasta salad, or a ham? Why a ham? Why cold cuts? Even those Vietnamese people brought a turkey. There must be a book everyone has that I've never seen."

The idea that everyone else had some critical piece of information that she was missing stirred in Margita a constant hum of anxiety. Then she heard how foolish these words sounded and blushed.

Suddenly, she felt the weight of Catorza's absence, and the bowl of the soft pink mush slipped from her hands and bounced off the table.

The crash of the bowl made the sisters jump. They had been applying deep concentration to laying perfectly sized sheets of plastic film over each bowl and dish, pulling it taut, sealing the edges just so. Grief had exhausted them, and the tedium of domesticity had formed a welcome membrane over their suffering. When they were finished, Elegia surveyed the bowls, thinking they looked like miniature frozen ponds someone could have skated on. Perhaps she was thinking about the icy pond they had to navigate when their cleanup was done: determining the fate of Novena.

There was no question in Elegia's mind that she herself was the best suited to take Novena, but she knew she had to go through the motions of discussion. She had practiced her face of careful and polite listening, which she knew she'd have to affect when she heard Margita make her case. She didn't doubt Margita's devotion to Novena, but she did mistrust her on two grounds: the first minor charge was that Margita had once too often proclaimed that she and Catorza were as close as sisters, a claim Elegia found strangely insulting. The more serious ground of her mistrust was Margita's lipstick: too red, too carefully applied, too suggestive of a mysterious other life that no four-year-old should inhabit. Besides, Annaluna would never allow it.

Quivera was another matter. With her, it was a touchy subject; not only was Quivera the oldest, with the imperious entitlement that comes with rank, but she had no children of her own. Her husband, though devoted to her, was quite old, and her chance of conceiving was quite slim.

To Elegia, her cool, high-strung sister was like a violin slightly out of tune, but picturing her with Novena wasn't completely unimaginable. It was just that no one was better equipped than Elegia herself. And more important, no one had a more compelling need. For Elegia, Novena could be salvation.

Elegia had been born the plainest of the sisters. Her experience of men was limited, and that had suited her fine: she had little understanding of them and even less curiosity. But as she watched her sisters bloom into young women, Elegia had compared her sisters' traits — Catorza's dreamy allure, Quivera's intensity — to her own plodding, unadorned utility. When she turned seventeen, she decided she needed some enhancement, something within her realistic grasp that wouldn't require cosmetic boosters but would at the same time retain her usefulness. A layer of cheer is what she finally decided on, and she grafted it to herself as if pinning a lacy handkerchief to a somber dress. Rather than a graceful enhancement, though, her bustling cheer over the years came off as something strained, more like a permanent wave: tightly wound and increasingly less attractive as time wore it thin.

But in the beginning, it was enough to appeal to Wyn, a thin, slightly morose man who owned a store selling office and art supplies. He found her cheerfulness a manageable counterbalance to his own gloom. After they married, their life had the calm order of brown plaid, until her first pregnancy. Then suddenly, the new chemicals bathing her system — estrogen, progesterone, alpha fetoprotein — had flooded Elegia with an unexpected and delirious sense of joy that almost embarrassed her. For the first time, she felt fancy instead of plain. Her cheerfulness was unstrained. She hummed, she glowed, she beamed, she radiated. She wanted to live her life always pregnant. Wyn, now considerably less morose, did his best to accommodate her.

Her first was a boy, Wyn Jr., followed in close succession by twins, Dexter and Quin, followed, finally and after a longish interval of fifteen months, by Zan. Elegia was so happy in her fertility that Wyn tried to put aside the gnawing concern about the residue of these pregnancies, the little bundles that were heaved out of her, squalling and hungry. He watched Elegia grow less and less enchanted with these beings once they were outside of her, yet she showed no inclination to want to stop making them. It was as if she were getting pregnant to narcotize herself against the actual fact of them. Not that she didn't love her boys, but they clearly overwhelmed her.

Who could blame her? As the boys grew, Elegia's life became a noisy circus of testosterone, boys tumbling out of doorways and cars like clowns and roustabouts. Sometimes the punky aroma of their boyness so cleaved the air, she would lie in bed holding her breath, afraid to breathe in more.

Novena could change all that. She imagined her boys stunned

into shyness in the presence of a girl, the tiny monsters in them gradually tamed into gentle human beings. She imagined they would all start wearing glasses and reading a lot. They would take up the cello, all of them, or maybe form a chamber quartet.

They would no longer flop into the house each night like exhausted fish throwing themselves on the shore, depositing their noise and sweat and dark thoughts throughout the house.

Elegia dreamed of order rising from the swamp of their bedrooms, now complex ecosystems of crusted cereal bowls, tossed records and baseball gloves, with piles of discarded shoes curled up from the sheer dank force of the boys' feet, and fetid socks, dark and watchful from the corners like sea anemones.

With Novena there, the boys would take tiny bites of food and eat with great fastidiousness, instead of slamming into the kitchen for the feeds that meals now were, which amounted to Elegia throwing as much raw meat at the roaring boys as quickly as she could, to douse them into silence. The silence never lasted, though; an hour after dinner, they'd be punching and slapping each other to get to the kitchen, where they'd have eaten the floor tiles and window shades if she didn't lay out a second round of food. They astonished her in their capacity for food, and watching them forage and hunt, she knew that they were powered by forces well beyond their stomachs; she was slightly frightened by the look in their eyes as they roamed the kitchen in search of some more food to put inside of them. How skinny they all were was even more frightening.

She had come to think of herself as a strange species inhabiting a loud planet; Novena would be her ally. Novena would make her cups of tea in the middle of the afternoon, which she would carry carefully, in tiny wobbling girlish steps, her tongue stuck out of the side of her mouth in concentration. Elegia would watch affectionately from where she sat on the sofa with her feet up, as the tea sloshed over into the saucer.

. . .

Elegia heard the kettle whistling now, and looked up with a start from her imaginings. Margita had boiled water and was pouring them mugs of tea. The three sat down with elaborately gentle movements, and each cupped her hand around the mugs.

"Oooh, this tea is nice. And the service was so nice. So many people. So much food." Elegia sighed, trying to lay the tone for their discussion over the table like a cloth. She figured to lead up to the subject slowly. "Anyhoo," she said, rubbing the table with her hand in a soothing gesture.

Quivera, who was lost in thought, looked up at her. "Did Novena eat anything?"

Elegia was annoyed at Quivera for gaining the first points; of course, her first thought should have been for the little girl.

"She didn't eat a thing, although I fixed her a little plate. Poor little thing."

"She's been so stoic," Margita said, her voice trembling. "What happens to the angel, have you figured it out?"

Elegia became nervous; this was moving faster than she had planned.

"Well, dear, have some more tea. Let's be calm about this," Elegia said, patting Margita's hand and struggling to remember how to order her features into her listening face.

"Elegia, I've been thinking," Quivera interrupted.

"Well, I'm sure we all have. I've been thinking of nothing but."

"Well, listen to me. Hear me out. I've given this a great deal of thought."

Of course she has, thought Elegia, probably up all night plotting.

"Now we all know that what's important is what's best for Novena," Quivera continued. "Margita dear, you and Catorza were like sisters."

Here Margita nodded, made a little mewing noise.

"I know we can count on you to be an important aunt. Novena will always look forward to visiting you."

Elegia, now fuming, was forced to give Quivera another set of points, for managing to handle Margita with finesse at the same time she was dismissing her. If she didn't take this conversation back under control, she was going to lose her chance.

"Quivera," she interrupted sharply. "I've been thinking too."

"Elegia," Quivera said in a firm voice. "I think you should take Novena. You've had much more experience raising children than either of us. And I think the boys would be good for her, it would do her good to be around children."

Elegia opened her mouth, then closed it quickly. How had this happened so easily? A tiny crack of doubt entered her mind: this was too fast. With the suspicion of those who rarely win, she now worried that the prize had come so fast, there must be something wrong with it. What was she getting herself into? Had she won, or had she been duped?

"Oh dear," she said, her hand brushing the table faster, rubbing it, petting it. "I don't know. Do you think it would be suitable for her to be around so many boys? And they are a handful," she said, shaking her head. "I mean, you have no idea how much work boys can be."

Elegia believed, as those born to be useful often do, that no one but herself knew how much work was involved to accomplish even the smallest things. Especially her sisters.

She trailed off, and remembered being sixteen, a midwife to the birth of her sisters' social lives. On Friday and Saturday nights, their bedroom became the backstage of a play, with Quivera and Catorza flying around in a frenzy of constant primping for dates, for which she, Elegia, served as wardrobe mistress.

She'd help them get ready, and affect enthusiasm for their outfits, their hairdos, their lipstick. They'd race out of the house, leaving behind clouds of powder and puddles of clothes for Elegia to pick up. Later, her cheer spent, she'd lie in bed, waiting for them to come home, curiosity keeping her awake.

She had little curiosity about the boys in the cars who picked up and deposited her sisters as if they were books that the boys knew were only on loan for the evening but nonetheless would try to keep for their own. But she had great curiosity about her sisters, who always came home from these evenings slightly altered. Lying in the darkness, Elegia would listen to their rustling tiptoeing as they came into the room and quietly stripped off their clothes. The bedsprings would creak softly as they slipped into bed. Then, in the silence of the dark room, she'd feel the atmosphere change into a crackling force field that nearly illuminated the room; it was as if they had come back with electricity clinging to them. Elegia could tell by her sisters' breathing that their eyes remained open for a long time, as if the evening were a wonderful movie that was still running. And try as she might, her own eyes open wide, all she saw — the plain, unadorned, untransformed Elegia — was the familiar darkness.

Now she felt Quivera's and Margita's eyes on her, waiting for her answer.

"Let's see what Annaluna says," she said finally, draining her teacup of the last of its warm sugary dregs.

Annaluna had taken Novena for a walk. Given the state of her feet, she never made it past the stoop, where Annaluna had dropped herself down for a brief rest and hadn't gotten up since. Novena walked up and down the sidewalk in front of her as Annaluna watched.

"Look, I'm walking, A'luna," she would call up to Annaluna as she passed.

"Good girl," Annaluna would answer each time.

Every fifteen minutes, Annaluna said, "Okay, our walk is over."

Novena would say, "Not yet, not yet." Each time, she went a little farther in each direction until she reached the end of the block. She'd stand for a moment, looking around, then go back in the opposite direction. This went on for two hours.

Novena was waiting for her brother to arrive.

Her mother had been promising his arrival for months. She had told Novena he would come when they least expected it, but would be coming soon. Novena knew her mother was somewhere else. "Up in the sky, sleeping with angels, dear," Elegia kept telling her when she asked. But no one had said anything about her brother and she was jittery with anticipation.

Once her mother had held Novena's hand against her belly to feel his kicking, and so she had gotten to know him quite well. Novena had taken to crawling into her mother's bed in the morning, and with her lips on her mother's midsection, would whisper to him as her mother slept. He would talk back in his way, kicking his arms or his legs through his watery nest, and feeling the pressure through her mother's belly, she pictured him as some marvelous underwater creature, one who lived miles away in deep watery caverns and swam to the surface to communicate with her.

"Brother," she would always begin, then go on to tell him about the colors of cloth and the scent of air, the visits from the aunts and the feel of Xa Ngum's bones as she sat on his lap.

She was very anxious about him now, since so much had changed. She had to tell him that Catorza was somewhere else. She was sure he'd arrive very soon; there was a moment just last week when she felt his presence strongly, although she didn't know that it was his last thought of her before he left the world.

She was tired herself, and finally climbed up the steps to sit next to Annaluna, who by now had dozed off, her feet throbbing. Annaluna stirred as she felt Novena lay her head on her lap, and finally roused herself. She knew what they were talking about upstairs, and was in no rush to get up there. She knew she'd be called on to intervene, to make the decision. She was in no rush, because whatever the decision was, it would take Novena from her.

The next day, with the matter decided — although Annaluna favored Quivera, she could offer no reasonable alternative to their plan — Elegia gathered up Novena and a small suitcase of her clothes, and drove carefully out of the city, to the small town of Nile Bay. Novena was asleep in the back seat, a heap of exhausted relief. She was going to live in the house with boys, her aunts had told her, and she was sure her brother would be there waiting for her. As soon as the car stopped, her eyes opened. Elegia took her by the hand, opened the front door and led her through the house.

"Okey-dokey, let's find those boys," Elegia said, her voice rising in a note of wavering bravado that was becoming her only defense against them.

"They'll be so happy . . ." She tripped over a baseball glove that had been expelled from a sweaty hand and left as a trail marker. "Where are my little monsters? WynDexQuinZan!" She called their composite name, which none of them ever answered to.

The boys had nearly torn the curtains off the rod looking out the living room window for them, had gotten bored, and had gone into the kitchen to fill themselves with food. Now they were standing around the kitchen table, their mouths full, chewing with a noisy and concentrated animation, as if the food had been captured live and was putting up a final fight for survival in the dark cavities of their mouths.

"Here you are!" Elegia trilled, banging her shin on a lawn mower engine part that was leaning against the doorjamb. "Ow! Look who's here!"

The boys looked up.

"These are your cousins," Elegia said, giving Novena a little push in their direction. "Boys, say hello to Novena."

Their shirts were smeared with dirt, and their eyes, which had been focused intently on the spread of bread, milk, mayonnaise, and jam before them as if expecting it all to escape, looked like the smug eyes of crocodiles.

Zan made the first sound. He took a deep swallow, and tilting his head up to the ceiling, let out a long deep belch.

"Pig," Wyn muttered.

"Honk," Zan answered him.

"That's oink, moron," Dex said.

"Boink you," Zan said, ramming his head into his brother's stomach for emphasis. "Boink, boink."

"WynDex . . . boys!" Elegia said warningly. She looked down to see how Novena was taking this, putting her hand on her shoulder.

Novena hardly saw them. She was aware of their outlines, and the outlines of the unfamiliar house and its unfamiliar smells. She was aware of the weight of Elegia's hand on her shoulder. But she was most aware that her brother was not among them. In the space of his absence, something dark began taking shape, moving toward her. The knowledge of her mother's death, a slow train which had not completely arrived, was finally pulling into the station with a long mordant wail. She saw it heading right for her. Novena opened her mouth and howled.

"Maaaaaaaaaw!" It was a loud, gulping, sobbing, angry howl that has no equal in the universe, a howl raised up from under the muddy swirls of a riverbed — no, deeper than that, from the river's darkest coldest depths where only blind creatures can live, an evolutionary gasp from life's beginnings. It was the wail of a child who has lost everything.

The boys took a step back, stunned by the depths from which Novena's voice rose, and in the echo of the cry, a moment of silence hung in the air, which the boys used to scatter out of the kitchen and into their rooms, where in their confusion they forgot to put on their loud music, in their nervousness began to pick up the stuff on the floor, and in their fear were silent for maybe the first time in their lives.

For a long time, Novena's wail stayed with them. It hung over their heads, it followed them out of the house, and it haunted the crackling underbrush of their sleep.

It was the only sound she would make for years.

chapter 3

ELEGIA WAS ONLY slightly worried about the fact that eighteen months after she had come to them, Novena still wouldn't speak; she was bright and animated and had quickly developed a serviceable sign language to communicate what she wanted. The truth was, Elegia was calmed by the presence of such a quiet companion, and the slaps and clicks of Novena's fingers against her skin as she pointed or expressed a thought were soothing, like the soft beating of a bird's wing. And it was refreshing to have someone to listen to her finally; in the girl's presence, Elegia found herself unable to stop talking, the words filling up and spilling out of her mouth.

Still, Elegia fretted. What worried her was that the miraculous transformation Novena was to have on her boys had not yet occurred. It seemed that once they had determined that Novena was not food, nor a real threat to their own food source, they treated her neutrally, lacking either hostility or curiosity. They remained uncivilized, tramping in and out of the house. Elegia had long stopped looking to Wyn Sr. to bring the boys into line; he had long ago made it clear that he thought of the boys as nonreturnable gifts he had given to Elegia. He spent most of his time at home in the wood-paneled TV room, his long string-bean limbs poking from the chair in such a way as to suggest he was perched, ready for a quick exit. Elegia had no idea what he thought of Novena.

Wyn Sr. was dismayed the day that Elegia had led Novena into the house. He suspected Elegia of conspiring to find a loophole in their unspoken moratorium on further reproduction, and after ten years she had finally found this one. He winced as he imagined a long parade of children that she might now start delivering to his doorstep.

He was relieved by Novena's silence, although it confounded him too. In the first year or so of Novena's life with them, Wyn had treated her like a trick cigar, or one of those fake cans of peanuts that held a spring-loaded snake — something that any day might detonate in his face. But gradually, this worry evaporated. She seemed to demand nothing; in fact, she was charmingly grateful for any tiny thing she received.

One day, he had brought her home a box of colored pencils from the store; he couldn't sell it because the verdigris and sky blue pencils were missing, but the light in her eyes when she looked at him made him feel suddenly and strangely shy. She treated the pencils as if they were jewels.

He began bringing her small presents: pads of paper, pencils and markers, chunky slabs of kneaded rubber and chalk. He brought her home a notebook whose black and white marbleized cover had been stained and torn, and after that, she was always hunched over it, drawing. He began bringing her more notebooks, always the same type. She carried each one around as if it were a prayer book. And in a way, it was.

Novena had filled up the pages of those first few notebooks with the same image. It was her mother's face, but each page featured a slightly different expression from the one before it. She tried to capture every possible expression, from happy and joyous to sad and sorrowful, so that as Novena thought about her day, she could flip through the pages until she found the expression that corresponded to the one she needed to see. She'd hear Catorza's voice, not in words but as a sound, soothing as music.

Novena, soundless and self-contained, was as happy as a motherless child could be. But still, Elegia fretted. Nothing was going according to plan.

As the boys got older, they seemed to get only wilder, coming home later and later, smelling of dirt and motor oil. As two years passed, Elegia began entertaining darker notions: that the boys might end up actually affecting Novena rather than the other way around. For one thing, nothing seemed to be able to rouse her from her drawing except the presence of one of the boys. When one of them came into the room, Novena would suddenly come to attention. Elegia noticed there would be a watchfulness in her, as if she were waiting for something from him, and Elegia knew that if the boys asked, she would drop everything and follow them.

In defense of the possibility of the boys' influence, Elegia stepped up her tutelage of Novena's femininity. She filled her closet with dresses and taught her to make tea. She bought her dolls and cook sets and ribbons and a toy iron and ironing board, which she set up next to her own.

"I just find ironing so soothing, don't you?" Elegia invariably said on ironing day, although she was often given to manic ironing fits that seemed anything but calm, when she would finish pressing the regular laundry and move on to sheets, towels, hair ribbons, curtains, underwear, and anything else she could find, with curt, jabbing movements that made the iron hiss angrily.

Novena would move her toy iron back and forth on the same piece of linen, remembering her mother pressing Ngum's shirts enveloped by misty clouds of steam. Occasionally, a few fat tears would fall from Novena on her eternally wrinkled scrap of linen. Elegia, chatting away, never noticed.

Twice a week, she sat Novena between her knees to curl her hair.

"A girl's crowning glory," she'd say, pulling the comb through the bramble of Novena's hair; then she'd dip the comb in a glass of warm water and draw it through a section, wrapping the wet strands in pink sponge rollers.

Novena never resisted, although she hated the rivulets of

warm water rolling down her neck, and hated even more the fussy curly mass her hair would become by morning. Although she liked clothes, she found her aunt's wardrobe choices somewhat humiliating — fussy pinafores with frilly socks, sailor dresses, and stiff dotted-swiss poufs. Novena felt like one of her own dolls, and sometimes if she sat still long enough, she became afraid that she would turn into one of them.

To Quivera and Margita, who worried about Novena's silence, Elegia kept up a cloud cover of sunniness.

"Oh, she'll talk when she's ready. Kids are resilient. Believe me, I've raised enough of them," Elegia said cheerily when Quivera called. "And she couldn't be happier, really, so don't you go worrying like you always do. You know what it does for that frown line on your forehead."

"I got her one of those new hair dolls, Hairdo Kathy or something," she told Margita. "You should see her with it. Hours she'll sit with that thing. Well, a girl always loves her dollies."

What she didn't report was that the hair doll, within a day of arriving, had been shorn of its tresses as well as three of its tiny toes. Or the fact that one morning, she found the dolls with their heads popped off and jammed onto different bodies. It gave her an odd feeling, coming across these things. It reminded her of things her boys would do.

Annaluna seemed to be the only one unworried about Novena, and because of this, Elegia allowed herself to confide her own worries to her aunt. She was cautious at first, communicating by ragged sighs and whispered laments, but Annaluna had a way of extracting more and more from Elegia. Annaluna began calling every week. She would listen to Elegia for a while, then, after some thought, ask a battery of questions that sounded as though they were designed to address Elegia's specific complaints, but were in fact bizarrely disconnected. Elegia had no idea how to answer.

"Has she touched something green today? What color sheets

are on her bed? What is she dreaming about? Did you ask her to draw a picture like I asked you?"

Often, Annaluna asked to have her put Novena on the phone. The girl would hold the phone to her ear, listening for a long time, sometimes ten or fifteen minutes. Elegia would see her nodding, sometimes smiling, sometimes swaying with her eyes closed, as if she were being sung to. Elegia was dying to know what Annaluna was telling her. After these calls, Novena would hand the phone to Elegia, and look her in the eye in a curious way that made Elegia feel she herself had been the subject of some deep diagnostic conversation between the two. As if she were the one who was off her rocker. Still, she had to be grateful to Annaluna; Novena seemed to be calmed and happy after the calls.

Elegia was further grateful — God strike her dead for even thinking it — that Annaluna was not mobile enough to be a frequent visitor, presiding over their lives.

But Annaluna was not exactly immobile. She had been forced to make some revisions to her original plan to wear the shoes Margita had sent Catorza until they disintegrated. For one thing, the shoes had fought her in their evil shoelike way, and her plan to walk in them forever was halted by an infection that had blackened her toes, spread through her feet and up her legs, ultimately crippling her. She ended up in a wheelchair, but this only gave her a chance to devise new and complicated punishments for her tormentors.

Since she no longer needed anything to cover her feet, she took all her shoes and transformed them into the basest of household objects. She used them as planters, watering them every day. She stored soap pads and sponges in them, and used the single pair of pumps she owned as hammers. When she ran out of her own shoes, she wheeled through the streets, picking up the vagabond shoes left in gutters and on sidewalks, bringing them home, devising new and humiliating uses for them. She turned a red stiletto into an ashtray, and, to underscore the insult, took up smoking. She got a dog, so she could watch him greedily eat his dinner each night from a heavy black boot. And as for the original offending pair of once gaily printed shoes, she tied them to her wheelchair so that as she moved through her house, they would be forced to confront the debasement of their species.

➤

It was Novena's third summer with Elegia and the boys. Elegia's dimming hopes for a calmer household had finally been all but extinguished, and she had let a neighbor convince her to take a part-time job in his dentist's office, where her sturdy cheer would be put to better use, or at least have a more captive audience. The night she announced the news, she had assembled everyone for dinner, but had kept the food in the kitchen. She knew a bare table would get the boys' attention.

"Now, I have something exciting . . . Zan! Stop that!"

Zan, who was bubbling into his milk glass, emptied most of the contents of his mouth back into the glass, leaving just enough to drool a thin stream down his chin.

"An announcement. I've taken a job, part time, helping out Jack Lerner. Three days a week. For the summer at least, you'll be keeping an eye on Novena."

This last part she said with a rush of words, then said to Wyn Sr., who was hovering in the doorway, "Okay, Wyn, you might as well bring in dinner."

"Yeah, right," Wyn Jr. growled. "Like I'm going to baby-sit. No way."

"Oh, yes you are. You all are," she answered firmly, looking around the table. She saw the rest of the boys shifting in their seats, ready to protest.

"There are four of you: that means if you take turns, you each get less than one day a week of baby-sitting. And if you won't, well, Wyn, you don't have to get your driver's license this winter, do you?"

Elegia waved this trump card almost giddily. Wyn Jr. was turning sixteen in January and was already learning to drive. She knew forcing compliance from him was the key to the rest of the boys.

"Mute-tant," Dex, the first to grasp the inevitable, muttered under his breath. The boys looked at Novena. She felt as if they were seeing her for the first time. She was flushed with a mixture of embarrassment and happiness, and didn't look up from her plate. She even kept her eyes down when Zan, sitting next to her, reached under the table and pinched her leg, hard.

Wyn finished bringing the food to the table, but for the first time that Elegia could remember, the boys ate without enthusiasm and left the table quickly.

Rather than parcel out the baby-sitting according to their mother's plan, the pack of them simply dragged Novena along with them on Elegia's workdays. They set out in the early morning, with Novena trailing a distance behind them. They walked up Nile Bay's Main Street to the luncheonette to buy cigarettes and drink heavily sugared coffee. The place was owned by Check, a burly old man whose wife had long ago left him. Preferring not to deal with females again, he had made the place as dark and unattractive as possible. It smelled of rancid bacon and burnt coffee, and the floors were barely swept; there were fading pinups on the yellowed walls with drawn-in mustaches and their pupils inked in to make them look cross-eyed.

From the booths at Check's, the day would unfold; some days, Wyn would help out behind the counter and the rest of them would sit with coffee for most of the morning. They'd wait for other boys from town to arrive, greeting them with nods and a low utterance of their last names, as in a roll call. Oswiecki. Wherlt. Carabetta. Synott. Meaty names, whose owners seemed to take the slablike shape of their sounds.

On those days, one of the boys would walk Novena to the library across the street. It was clear they expected her to wait for them there. While she found the library pleasant, she was impatient for their company, so after what she thought was a decent interval she would gather up her books and go outside and stand on the corner, waiting for one of them to notice her through Check's greasy plate-glass window and fetch her back across the street. Then she'd sit at a stool on the end of the counter, reading or drawing.

Other days, they would leave the luncheonette quickly, sometimes with friends, sometimes without Wyn, and make their way to the river side of Nile Bay, a dusty backside neighborhood of old brick light-industry factories, now empty and ringed by puddles of oily greenish water, old machine parts, ancient truck imprints in the dirt. A junkyard was next door. Across the road, a thick wood bordered the river.

It was in the woods that Novena noticed that the boys' loud, jumbled-up chaos fell into the calm order of another species — organized, focused, and productive, like foxes or dogs. The boys went into the woods with purpose, as if it were their job. And since the woods require so few words from anyone, a silence would fall over them, which had a way of enclosing Novena in the group. The only sound was the stamping of their feet on the soft sod and the crackle of branches underfoot.

Many summers before, the boys had found a small clearing in the woods that they had claimed as their base of operations. It was a perfectly constructed natural fortress, with a small pile of boulders at its center, surrounded on three sides by a thick stand of old pine and oak trees, whose fallen needles and leaves had created a soft floor. They had dragged some damp and rotting tree trunks to seal off the passageway from view. They had decorated it simply, with the dried shed skins of snakes, a deer's skull, and randomly carved hieroglyphics on the tree trunks. When they were younger, the fortress had been a battle fort, a pirate's cave, and a bomb shelter; now it served as a den, where they smoked for a while, making plans before venturing out for the day's work.

"Stay out here," Dex said to her the first day she accompanied them. "You don't come in here."

"Yeah," Zan said. "No girls."

Novena didn't mind. She could see their outlines and hear their low mumbling, and had quickly found her own nearby rock to sit on. She felt she had the whole woods to herself, which kept her happily occupied while she waited for the boys to come out and roam. In rotting tree trunks, she watched fat white worms crawl through the fine wood dust; she put her cheek down on lichen beds that were like small patches of cut green velvet, and gently unpeeled the layers of bark from white birches to pretend they were paper.

That summer, the boys became devoted to science projects. In keeping with scientific tradition, they favored frogs for their experiments, since they were easiest to catch. They started by tethering a frog to a tree, looping one end of heavy string around its leg, and the other around the trunk. The next day, they found the frog sitting docilely. It didn't move even when they poked it with a stick. A day later, they came back to find only a single webbed foot still tied up in the string; the boys argued all day whether the frog had yanked itself free or had been eaten by a snake.

Next, they buried a frog alive, and dug it up the next day to find it satisfyingly dead. Another day, when Wyn had shown up, they captured a large croaker and, at his suggestion, put it under a pail with a lit firecracker.

Bored with frogs, the boys moved on to cats; the only notable thing they could think of, though, was tossing one on the junkyard's electric fence to watch its spine contort in a panicked spiral. After bouncing to the ground, it ran away. Then they spent a day foraging for detritus — discarded car parts, a pair of men's pants, a stiffened squirrel that had been killed on the road, and once a live snake — then lit a fire to see how each object reacted to the flames.

For all their long-practiced indifference, the boys were always slightly off guard with Novena there. They felt a pressure to be more experimental, or more scientific, than they might have been left to their own devices; frankly, they would have been happy with minor vandalism and stolen beer to fill their afternoons but the audience spurred them to more productive pursuits.

One afternoon, they left the woods and spent all day fishing at the river, off a small concrete bridge that led into town. They fished with dedication, stopping only for the occasional cigarette, and filled two large buckets with shiners and bullheads. At the end of the day, they tipped the contents of both buckets onto the bridge. They paused to take in the vision of the wriggling silvery surface of the bridge, and then ran into the bushes to wait for the first car to drive over.

It was just in time for the six o'clock traffic, and the boys nearly fainted with excitement when they heard the first set of tires crunching the fish-lined concrete. Soon, the line of cars turned the bridge into an ocean of slippery smashed fish guts. By the time traffic died down, cars were skidding over the bridge and the boys were rolling on the ground, howling with laughter.

Novena was a silent witness to it all. The boys rarely talked to her. They simply let her be there, and if they were forced to suddenly remove themselves quickly from the site of their experiments, such as when the police finally showed up to inspect the mysteriously bloodstained, brine-covered bridge, the boys rarely looked behind them to see if she was keeping up.

Still, Novena felt oddly safe in their presence. For one thing, she understood that the boys' experiments were not born of random cruelty, but were more ordered, part of a larger system. It was a system that had its own television station, which Novena watched whenever she could: buzzards picking through the mauled carcass of a felled deer, bears casually ripping flopping salmon apart, snakes breaking the necks of their prey. On one show that gave her nightmares for a week, they explained how crocodiles in rivers in Zaire grabbed goats who were drinking from the banks. They grabbed them in their mighty jaws, dragged them underwater and, unable to chew them, stuffed the animals in caves under the banks until they deteriorated enough to finally be eaten.

This was a system, she learned, based not on violence, but on hunger. Her woods held no peril to her other than the poisons released from certain plants and insects; there might have been a rattler or two, but no bears or crocodiles. But there was hunger in the woods, and it was a live and monstrous thing, snaking through the complex root systems and soft black sod floor, through liverworts and mosses, the veiny undersides of leaves, the swollen stigmas of flowers, up to the very canopy of leaves from the oldest trees. Hunger: that was what the boys recognized and feared, and in their experiments tried to gain a sense of mastery over. Their experiments might have been seen as cruelty, but the boys were just playing nature's own game, with slightly better equipment.

The single-minded focus the boys applied to their projects was impressive, but fortunately for the Nile Bay's wildlife, it wouldn't last. This would be the last summer they would spend together, which probably explained the intensity of their experiments. Wyn Jr., at fifteen, had no business, really, being around anyone younger. But he knew he would be getting his license soon, which was as good as moving to another country, so he didn't mind spending more time with his brothers and Novena than he might have.

It was Zan who seemed more anxious to strike out on his own. He had been spending less time with them, was often absent for dinner, and disappeared late at night; Novena would at times hear him crawling out the window and watch him make his way through the dark streets. He was growing a rough fuzz on his chin, and his appearance seemed slightly altered each day.

One afternoon, the rest of the boys had gone down to the river, leaving Novena in the woods, where she was collecting sticks of equal lengths; she had a pile already amassed near her rock, along with a stack of birch skins, and she was planning to build something. A green heat dappled the woods, and the drone of cicadas in the trees made it seem hotter. She heard footsteps crunching on the path leading toward the fortress. As they came closer, she heard the high pitch of a girl's laugh. Looking up, she was surprised to see Zan, with his arm draped around the shoulders of a short and sturdy blond girl.

Novena stayed crouched, and watched her rock to make sure the girl wouldn't sit on it when Zan went into the fortress. But to Novena's surprise, Zan, with his arm still draped around the girl, guided her past the logs and inside. Novena came closer.

"Ooooh, gross," she heard the girl's voice say.

"On *this*?" Low laughter, giggling. Then they were quiet for a time.

Novena came closer, to a spot she had discovered that allowed her to remain hidden but see through the branches into the fortress. She saw them lying on the rocks, twisted up in an awkward embrace. Zan's mouth was locked onto the girl's, kissing her with desperation, and his hands started moving over her.

"Uh, uh, uh," Zan was saying.

The girl pulled away.

"No! Cut it out!" she cried. She tried to move away from him, but his weight was on her legs.

"Aw, come on," Zan said, his voice hoarse, urgent.

The girl had gotten one leg free. It stuck straight out, with her sneakered foot testing the ground beneath it, as if trying to decide how to help the rest of her to escape. She was wearing shorts, showing her thick heavy legs, the calves and thighs of almost equal size. Her skin was white, the color of a birch branch without its grace.

Novena's face was flushed watching the girl struggle, but she felt calm, as if she was observing her own scientific experiment. As she waited to see what Zan would do next, she thought of a snake breaking the neck of its prey, the harsh swipe of a bear's paw, the hungry jaws of a crocodile.

Zan's hand was moving again, and then he moved himself up so that the whole of his body covered the girl's. She let out a short yelp, which he cut off by covering her mouth with his. Then her leg relaxed, and she stopped struggling. Novena thought for a thrilling instant that she was dead, until she saw the girl's thick fingers grab Zan's head and tangle themselves in his hair as they started kissing again.

A few more times, she heard the girl say no, her voice muffled. Novena, slightly disappointed, went back to her stick-gathering. After a while, she heard them leave.

Novena came closer to the fortress and stood at the log passageway. She hadn't been inside, but now she felt emboldened. Climbing over the logs, she went in.

She took a deep breath and looked around. She had the sense that she was in one of the boys' rooms, in which nature had encroached, as if Dex's or Zan's room had lost its walls and been overgrown by trees and vines and small plants. But there was an order to the space that struck her as slightly odd. As she looked around, she saw things she wouldn't have found in their rooms. An old beer can. Empty cigarette pack. A greasy T-shirt. A small box with a hammer and some screws. The dried snake skin. A magazine, warped and swollen by moisture. Half a bird's nest. A rusted jackknife.

On one of the large flat boulders that served as a wall of the fortress was a collection of sticks, rocks, and skulls that had the appearance of an altar or an arsenal. A row of perfectly ordered rocks and sticks was categorized by size and sharpness, by heft and by potential damage. Tiny pieces of gravel, chunks of quartz, fist-size stones lay beside reeds and sumac and small green elm branches sharpened to points. The animal skulls ranged in size from a bird's to a deer's. She picked up the smallest skull and held it in her hand. It was light as air. She rubbed it, as if petting it. She put it back on the rock.

She picked up the jackknife. It was dull and rusted, but she put it in her pocket. She also pocketed some screws, then lifted the hammer. She held it in her hand, feeling its weight, in such contrast to the tiny cranium. Then she lifted it and brought it down, hard, on the skull. It shattered instantly, and she felt a hot stream of anger and pleasure race through her as she smashed it again and again, and watched the bone become a fine powder that embedded itself in the rock.

chapter 4

BY AUGUST, Novena felt like one of the boys, coming home with twigs in her hair, her hands black with dirt and pine sap.

"You look like something wild, I swear," Elegia would scold, rubbing Novena's hands harshly with a washcloth.

"When I think of all those pretty dresses hanging in your closet . . . God knows the things you're bringing into this house; what bugs are going to be crawling up my legs tonight?"

Unlike the boys, Novena still had the grace to act apologetic, and would give Elegia a calculatedly adorable smile that would usually appease her.

But then Elegia started brooding: a summer at the dentist's office, irrigating the bleeding gums of her fellow townspeople, confronting the startling variety of their bad teeth while standing on her feet all day, was putting her in bad humor, although she was nothing but irritatingly cheerful to all the patients. But standing with the suction wand at Jack Lerner's side, she would start reminding herself of all the cups of tea that she wasn't getting carried to her by a pretty little girl, all the neatly ironed, unused ribbons hanging limply in Novena's pink room, and this brooding would burrow into her, turning over soil that had been untrampled for decades: the hours she would wait for her sisters to come home from their dates, her own efficiency and practicality that she had been forced to tart up like some old whore, the four tiny penises that she had once found so cunning — her own creation! — that had evolved into one large hairy monster of boy. Thoughts such as these seemed fitting accompaniments to the root canals and gum scrapings that now filled her Mondays, Wednesdays, and Fridays.

"Okay, rinse for me!" she sang brightly to Martha Holsta, who, sitting up in the dentist chair looking dazed, leaned over to expel bloody spittle into the little basin next to Elegia; the accompanying flecks of the amalgam filling made little pinging sounds as they hit the metal.

As Martha lay back in the chair, looking as if she had just survived a car wreck, Elegia's brooding turned to Novena's unwillingness to speak. She turned over in her mind the idea that the girl's silence was a personal affront.

"Don't think I don't know what's going on in that brain of yours, miss," Elegia said that night, scrubbing Novena's hands. "Don't think I don't know why it is you won't speak to me."

Novena was stung by Elegia's tone. She had been brooding herself lately. Until recently, the inside of her head had been a room kept clear for the sounds of her mother's voice and the echoes of the watery kicks of her brother, which came to her throughout the day. From the day she had arrived at Elegia's, she had been afraid that if she spoke she would silence these sounds, or at least tarnish their strains. Those sounds, she knew, were all she had of her own. But those echoes had been growing fainter over time, and for the past month she had had a hard time conjuring them at all.

The following week, the boys and Novena spent the day on the river. The boys fished for crayfish, some of which they smashed with rocks, some of which they put down each other's backs. Zan would catch one and while it was still wriggling, dunk it back in the water and hold it there for five minutes. He would then repeat the cycle with another crayfish. Dex, watching him repeat this a few times, finally said, "What are you doing?"

"Drowning 'em," Zan said proudly, convinced he had somehow devised an ingenious new method of torture.

"God, are you stupid," Dex said, slapping Zan's arm. "I ought to drown you."

"Go ahead, try," Zan said bravely. The fact he couldn't swim scared him less than the idea of confronting the angry families of all the fish he had so far drowned.

The sky was turning dark blue, and the boys' stomachs started grumbling. They gathered up their things to start home.

"Hey," said Dex, looking around. "Where's Novena?"

"I dunno," Quin shrugged. "Around, I guess."

They called, but there was no sign of her.

Novena, lying on the riverbank, had fallen asleep under the buzz of mosquitoes that formed a lacy veil over the greenish water. She dreamed of her mother, who was speaking to her, but no sounds came out of her mouth. In the background, Elegia's voice bustled like a broom, sweeping around them. Catorza kept moving to get out of its way, and Novena tried to follow her, but couldn't keep up. A doorway appeared that her mother slipped through, leaving Novena behind. In her dream, Novena made a strangled, choking sound that went on and on and finally woke her. She still heard it, and recognized the mournful croaking of frogs. She heard the river, and the voices of the boys, all moving toward a single sound that grew louder and louder, as if someone were turning up the volume, until the sounds were like stones, crashing around her head.

She had gotten up to move away from it, going into the woods to see if she could find a place where there was quiet. But the woods were even louder, chirping and cawing and rustling, the heavy earthen sound of her feet hitting dirt. It all became amplified, building a pressure in her ears that was now becoming painful. She got deeper into the wood, but there was no relief. She began running. She was off her usual path, running fast and blind into the green.

It was a large tree root that finally stopped her. As she stumbled, her hand reached out and found the trunk of an old beech tree.

Even as she put her palm to its rough trunk, she heard something — not the tree, exactly, and not words, but a kind of sound that was more temperature than noise.

It moved her to climb. Perching herself on a large rock under the first high branch, she dragged herself up. She climbed quickly, each branch under her grasping palm emitting the same heat, up to the tallest branch, where she sat, her breath short and quick, her arms around the trunk.

She felt lightheaded, and her heart felt lifted, raised high up off the floor of the forest, with nothing surrounding her. The pressure in her ears was gradually receding.

Finally, silence. No message, no thoughts, no words in her brain. Her breath slowed. Now, just sensation, crashing into memory. Her weight on the branch, her weight sitting on Ngum's lap, feeling his bones beneath her, hard, like this branch, the steam from her mother's iron heating the room. She had a vision of two of herselves, living in different universes. A world had once existed with one Novena in it; it still must exist, she must still be there, yet here she was.

She realized that she had been all wrong, waiting for her mother and brother to come for her. She knew they were out there, waiting to be found. She could go to them. All it took was letting go, to float gently through the branches and be in the other universe, the one where the other her still lived.

She looked down, considering. It was a thirty-foot drop, although she couldn't see the ground through the leaves. She knew she wouldn't float; she knew the sound she would make when she pushed off into the air, the little cry that would escape her when the air, surprised with her sudden weight, quickly recalculated itself and summoned gravity to grab her. Then, her body crashing through the branches, breaking off small limbs, the sound of leaves dropping to the ground, silent, getting there before she did, and of course, the sound of herself, landing with a sudden, final thud, although a part of her, she knew, would keep going, not be stopped by the ground, would keep falling and falling until she reached some other, more attractive place.

It was a beautiful idea.

Meanwhile the boys had scattered, looking for her. They kept coming back to the rock where they had been fishing, their own panic increasing. It first took form as rage at Novena for keeping them from their dinner, moved to the trouble they would get in for losing her, and grew into something that frightened them more than anything in the woods: the realization that they would die if they didn't find her.

It was Zan who found her finally. He was directly under the tree she was in, calling her name.

The panic in his voice made her alert. Through the branches, she could see a small corner of his striped shirt. While she hadn't given a thought to the boys all afternoon, the thought of them now reminded her of all the hours of their indifference. And the hours of her trailing them, following them, watching them, staying quiet, just to be with them. They never saw that she wanted to be with them, and the thought of her devotion now humiliated her, and made her want to hurt them in some way; not just to injure, but to draw blood, to punish.

But she loved them, on the tense and narrow wire where family love balances, where its members are capable of killing each other, driven by the same hopeless love that ultimately keeps them from doing it. A pitiful and redeeming thing, this love, capable of exhibiting and forgiving the worst kind of betrayals. It allowed Novena to imagine a punishment the boys deserved, and have instant remorse for imagining it.

She didn't know this, being a child, but she felt it, and she heard it now in Zan's bellow.

"No! Ve! Na!" he cried. "Where! are! you!"

Like an animal calling to its far-off herd, she was moved to respond in kind.

She opened her mouth. A tiny sound came forth, no louder than the wind. Tottering on the branch, she broke off a twig and released it, hoping it would fall near enough to get his attention. She watched it float slowly down, landing gently and quietly, nowhere near him.

Zan was turning to leave.

And now, her mouth stretched open, her eyes closed, Novena willed herself to make a sound. When it came, it was an echo of the last sound she had made, like a continuation of that long, desperate, charging wail that had risen up from a small moan and now rose, higher and higher, gathering into it all her months of unspoken words, of unmade sounds.

"Waaaaaaw!"

Her eyes flew open in the shock of the sound. It was so loud, she felt she had split something open, and listened for trees cracking, falling to the ground, the earth collapsing, boulders rolling down the hilly paths. But all she heard was a faint shuddering of leaves, as a few startled birds flew out of the surrounding trees.

And then she heard Zan, climbing up after her.

It took Zan no time to climb that tree, though he was out of breath from the exertion of his panic. He climbed fast, grabbing one limb after another. By the time he reached Novena and held out his arms to her, he was panting, and could hear her own panting breath as she grabbed his arm and began clawing at his sleeve. He lifted her down to the thick forked branch directly under hers where he was standing, and they began making their way down slowly, Zan lifting her down a limb at a time. When they reached the last branch, they sat crouching on it, side by side, resting, measuring the distance to the ground below, not more than eight or nine feet.

She was quivering like a small bird, and as she gripped the sleeve of his shirt, Zan felt his heart open in him, ravenous as a mouth, hungry for what she was giving him, grateful for her dependence on him to save her.

Zan knew hunger — he'd been born hungry, after all. But his had always been hunger caused by emptiness. Not this kind, that was filling him up, expanding a space in him that seemed to keep filling, as if it had no limit.

He began smoothing her hair, patting her back, movements whose tenderness surprised him: he'd never made these gestures before, and he didn't know where they came from. He couldn't remember the last time he had touched her; in fact he wasn't sure he ever had, except for quick pinches under the table. It was as if he had just now become aware of the fact of her, that she even had a body; until now, she had been some vaporous thing always trailing behind him like smoke, and like smoke ready to consume anything — air or space or food — that belonged to him.

But those unused to tenderness are always unprepared for how quickly it turns ferocious. Mothers know it, when they bite their babies, when their mouths seek out the smooth fat pockets of skin at the crook of infants' arms, nibble at the soft apples of their cheeks, their deliciously pudgy ankles. Babies know it too. As soon as they grow teeth, they bite back. This is the love of family: you love them so much, you must consume them.

His hand reached for Novena's shoulder. He squeezed it, wanting to pull her closer to him.

But he felt a tension in her muscles, her body pulling away, going rigid. It was as if her whole body had flinched. And instantly, Zan's fierceness moved to more familiar ground: his hand still on her shoulder, he had the impulse to crush her, to smash each of her bones to fine powder.

But suddenly, she was no longer there.

Novena was falling.

It was not in slow motion as she might have imagined earlier, but fast, as if the ground, impatient, had suddenly risen up to grab her, and she landed on it with a thud. The fall pushed the air out of her chest with a guttural "uggh."

Then a heavier weight was upon her. Zan was on her, holding

her tight, almost smothering, making low animal sounds and patting her back.

Novena was beginning to panic. Her mouth was opening and closing, opening and closing, trying to draw enough air into her lungs. She could find no air, no breath. Black forms — thin lines at odd angles — began taking shape, floating in front of her eyes.

Then she was falling again, falling still, descending into some deep airless space, being drowned by all that surrounded her — the pine needles, the thick moss, the weight and smell of Zan. He smelled of the woods and the river, and the familiar, shocking smell that was almost of herself, of her own blood.

Her mouth opened, and with extreme effort she inhaled, finding a breath, then another.

"Ow! Get off!" she cried.

His weight lifted from her just as the rest of the boys arrived, crashing through the branches, panting. The relief they felt on seeing her made them feel suddenly naked and exposed.

Dex, seeing Zan and Novena lying next to each other on the ground, didn't know why he suddenly wanted to deck his brother, but he did.

"Hey, what're you doin'?" he said. "What's goin' on?"

Zan looked up with a start, and jumped up.

"She fell," he said defensively, moving away from her.

"And she talked," he said almost accusingly.

The boys turned to Novena, who had struggled to her feet, and was now standing, breathing deeply. In their eyes was a wild worry that they were guiltily still trying to stuff back into hiding. It surprised her almost as much as the sound of her voice had.

Her voice made her visible, and she felt suddenly self-conscious. She was there in a way she hadn't been, and felt the outlines of her skin and body and the air against it, giving her a sense of her own shape. It was as if she had been a ghost, and now had taken solid form, solid mass, like a tree rooted in the ground. They were looking at her expectantly. She tried to think of something to say that would convey all this, that would tell them she was here and was one of them. No longer a silent charge following them around like a puppy. Finally, the words took shape.

"Aw nuts, you big babies," she said, in a perfect mimicking of their own language. "Let's get out of here. "

Wyn and Dex grinned in spite of themselves. Quin barked out a laugh, and on their way home, the boys kept her in the middle.

You can imagine all you want about Novena's homecoming that night: Elegia's clasping her hands in delight and running to the phone in triumph; Wyn Sr. stiffly unbending himself from his chair in the den to pat her awkwardly on the head, wearing a grimace of an attempted smile; the boys almost respectful of this monumental change; Novena at the head of the dinner table, wearing a party hat; and all of them caught up in a festive suspension of the normal grim business of nightly food-shoveling. She imagined something like this herself as she and the boys made their way home. She didn't say much, and the boys didn't push. They were wary, as if her newfound voice were a timid animal that could be scared back into hiding.

It was late, an hour past dinner, and there was only a dim light on at home. They opened the door. There was no smell of food, no heat emanating from the kitchen, no sound of Elegia moving around the kitchen, closing cupboards, banging pots, and running water that usually greeted them.

Wyn Sr. was sitting at the kitchen table, alone, a mug of coffee in front of him.

"Hey," he said, getting up when they came in.

He sat down again, looking at his mug, seeming to be exhausted from the effort. "Your mother's working late. There's no dinner ready. We can get a pizza."

"Have Novena call for it," Zan said. "She talks now."

Wyn Sr. looked at Novena and said, "Oh? That so? Good."

And so, initially, her voice simply wove itself into the household, a new and sweeter layer on top of the usual noise. Elegia thought the less fuss made over Novena the better; for one thing, she mistrusted how long Novena's speech would last and feared the girl would find some other surprise to spring on her. She had finally given up on the idea of a pretty, feminine Novena, and had begun to think of her as willful and of herself as betrayed. The sting of it surprised her: that the betrayal came from another female, a source she had been counting on for solace.

In the weeks and months that followed, Novena wasn't bothered by the lack of fuss made over her. She didn't even mind Elegia's growing sharpness with her. She was too preoccupied with measuring the other changes that had come into the house, and wondering if something as small as her voice could have brought them on.

The summer had ended, and at school she was suddenly surrounded by people her own size. She missed the days in the woods with the boys, missed the sense of their bigness surrounding her, like her own private forest of trees. Without them, she felt exposed. And while she had the sense they were growing beyond her, at the same time the sound of them seemed closer, louder. She wondered whether her voice had somehow made her hearing more acute, especially when she began noticing a new note added to the noise of them.

It started out as no more than a small, tremulous vibration that disturbed the air, which Novena registered as a dog might have — with a wary alertness, her ear cocked to the ceiling. Gradually, it grew to a constant thrumming tension that took on the sound and the grinding qualities of an engine. This is when it moved into the pit of her stomach, where her constant agitation and unease led her to believe it was chewing its way through her.

She turned to her usual solace — her mother. Novena gathered all of her notebooks, including the very first she had started drawing in, and one afternoon spread them out in front of her. She leafed through the pages of book after book, studying the progression of faces, and by the time she got to the last book, it struck her that these faces were no longer distinctly her mother's, but over time had taken on the characteristics of other people. They were now a collection of the pleasing but unfamiliar faces of strangers.

No sound, and now no picture, of her mother existed. She had lost her mother completely. And it was her fault. The sound of her own voice had forever extinguished the sound of her mother's, had somehow filled up the room which she had tried to keep intact.

She thought back to the day when she'd been up in that tree, still silent, still feeling the faint trace of her. Then she recalled that sound of herself, that high sharp wail when she had yelled, and the sound that had immediately followed — the rattle of leaves as startled birds flew out of the trees. They had been scared by the sound of her. Novena wished she had paid more attention to those birds. Maybe her mother had taken shape as one of them, flying up from the branches, away from Novena.

Her mother had been beautiful enough to be a bird. Her mother had been beautiful enough to be the queen of birds, and for a moment, a small glimmer of her face flashed before her. Novena closed her eyes, trying to make the picture stay.

It was gone. But she had her pencils and she had a blank sheet in her notebook, and she began to draw it, to capture that face. Unlike the rest of her drawings, though, she didn't stop at the face, but moved on and drew the body. And she moved past that and went on to clothe the body in a beautiful gown, one of feathers and gossamer, an angel's dress, the dress for the highest queen of birds. It had a bodice of soft, green moss, and its sleeves were layers of leaves, stitched together with pine needles. Its huge billowing skirt was made up of feathers, one from every kind of bird in the world, and the hem was trimmed with the thinnest layer of birch bark, which looked just like ermine. And shoes — no, not shoes, but slippers, slippers made from one hundred flower petals laced together with blades of grasses. And finally the wings, growing out from the folds and pleats and tucks in the dress. Not bird's wings, but bee's wings, veined, gossamer, like glass. And not just one, but two sets: wings enough to carry her away to wherever she was going, and wings enough to make sure that wherever she had flown to, she could also come back.

Novena lost herself in the drawing, adding the tiny details — earrings made from slivers of mica, and a bracelet of braided corn silk — hearing in her mind the *caw, caw* that this bird mother might make. She was about to add a small daughter bird flying at her side when something finally broke through her concentration.

The door had slammed downstairs and she heard the heavy thud of footsteps moving through the house.

Before they began climbing up the stairs, she roused herself as if an alarm had gone off, and she quickly leapt up, gathering her pencils and notebooks and sliding them under her bed.

The footsteps moved past her door and pounded down the hallway, their vibration making the little lamp on her dresser tinkle, the floor under her shudder.

Zan was home.

She sat quietly and listened, waiting for the house to start trembling.

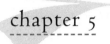

chapter 5

Growing up as the only girl among boys, you need to know one thing. You need to know when to duck.

A house full of boys is a house full of swinging arms, a noisy ring of muffled thuds, of fists against clothes, the sound of skin to skin. It's a comic book picture of a fight, shoes and fists and exclamation points drawn at the edges of some chaotic circle of energy, a tumbleweed, a dust storm.

Elegia had always claimed it wasn't hate that created this storm among the boys, just the force of their physical natures pushing against them from their insides, trying to get out. Novena had come to think of their skirmishes as a loud thing let out of a bottle, like escaping gas, leaking into the house and accumulating in the corners and eaves.

The boys had always kept their fights to themselves. If occasionally they had reached Novena — if, in other words, she forgot to duck — it had always been harmless: little shoves, an occasional hair pull, almost affectionate in nature. But in the past few months, it had become harder to keep out of their reach. Everyone was bigger — the arms and legs sprouting from the boys seemed to fill up the house like extra furniture.

Although he was the youngest, Zan was the biggest. Dex and Quin, who had taken on their father's rawboned leanness rather than their mother's thickness, were still a full head shorter. Zan was nearly as tall as Wyn Jr. and still growing. Except lately he had begun growing oddly, unevenly, as if the irrigation system fertilizing his growth had sprung leaks. His feet were almost dainty, and yet his huge hands hung off him like some deformed, overripe fruit. His ears were tiny dark caves set above the broad open plains of his shoulders. And while his nose and mouth were wide and generous, his eyes were so small in that vast wasteland of a face that overall he had the appearance of a child in the mask of a giant.

Despite his size, he moved fast. But it was a furious speed, as if he were trying to run from any further tricks his body might play on him. He would blow past them, his face a blur from the speed of him, slamming out of the house. Hours later, he'd slam his way back in, smelling of smoke, strange bundles under his arm, filling up the place with yelling and bellowing as he pounded up the stairs.

The house seemed no longer able to absorb the loud thing of him; the walls and floors creaked and shuddered with exhaustion. And although in the months since she had started talking again, she had used her voice sparingly, Novena was afraid, for a time, at the house's ability to accommodate even it.

Lying in bed, or sitting quietly in her room, Novena would listen to the slamming doors, the tremulous vibration of the walls and floors, the rattling of lamps and tables, the occasional shattering of a window, and it seemed as if the wooden frame of the house must be stretching itself painfully around him — the way she lately imagined her own skin to be stretching over her growing bones. She trembled herself, worrying about those beams and posts and shingles bending to their limit and cracking open, forming holes and cavities for any storm raging outside to push its way into the house, and blow it down around them.

It was already well past that, of course. The storm was already in.

Zan started coming home with odd cuts and bruises. He came home limping. One night, he came home with his hair singed into a wiry clump, half of his left eyebrow burned off.

Elegia screeched and wailed whenever she saw him banged up and damaged, demanding to know who he was fighting with, who was doing this to him. He said nothing. And although the rest of his family were repelled at the sight of his embattled body, they were oddly relieved too. Every bruise and burn and cut was a sign that out there, there was someone bigger even than Zan. He was not the largest storm in the universe after all.

One night, walking past his room, Novena saw him sitting on his bed, his head resting on his fists. She thought he was deep in thought, and she started backing away before he saw her. But then she watched as he drew his fist back and began pounding it against the side of his head. *Pound, pound, pound.* She stared, unable to turn away. She wanted to cry out, to make him stop, but something kept her from making a sound. She moved quietly away, and her stomach did an odd little flip as she imagined his fury if he had seen her, watching him. But even that wasn't as frightening as the idea that she had witnessed some secret thing of him. It was not a secret that she could taunt him with, but something strange and confusing, and so disturbing that she wanted to run from it; but like a dream that stays with you because of its utter lack of sense, she kept coming back to it, to this thing: that all of Zan's damage was coming from himself.

Not long afterward, Zan turned his rage away from himself and toward his brothers. The whirling force of him, which had been sucking up everything around him — food and calm and peace and air — now tore gravity up by its roots and took that too, as the sound of Zan became the sound of heavy things falling to the floor — not just chairs and tables and lamps, but Dex and Quin and Wyn Jr.

Theirs were no longer the skirmishes of brothers, no longer the intimate embraces of boxers reeling around the ring, which in most families can go on forever because they are ultimately harmless. Now the boys' scuffles were brutal, and breathtaking in how quickly they began and ended. Zan could slay them in minutes.

The boys quickly gave up trying to fight back, and simply re-treated. Wyn Jr., who had gotten his driver's license the year be-fore, was barely ever home. Dex and Quin withdrew to their room; ironically, they now resembled the quiet, ordered boys that Elegia had once dreamed of having under her roof.

Novena, on the other hand, moved through the house un-touched. So far, Zan had stayed clear of her. So far, her only dan-ger was the house falling on top of her, which she knew was only a matter of time. Meanwhile, she was able to remain invisible.

Although she didn't completely trust it, she felt oddly embold-ened by her invisibility, enough anyway to sometimes steal into the room he shared with Wyn Jr. She didn't do this often, and she never did it without a sense of alarm — not only at the prospect of Zan coming in and finding her there, but at the fact that she was breathing in the same air he did, inhaling his smell, touching his things. She would leave his room feeling slightly stained by being there, and yet she was strangely drawn there. She was looking for something, some clue, maybe, some thing that might explain him. She never found anything beyond his detritus — scraps of paper with phone numbers, cigarette packages, matchbooks, odd keys, nails, and short lengths of wire — although she was too afraid to search beyond the surfaces of things. Sometimes she would take things. Nothing he would miss — loose change, an old, rusted pocketknife, or a pencil. She thought of them as strange inverse charms; as long as she was holding something of his, she would stay invisible. So far it worked. Zan still didn't register her. Or if he did, she was too small to bother with. He was only interested in the things as large as himself; she was too small to even be consid-ered a snack. Yet a part of her waited for the day his eye would turn to her, frightening in its hungry indifference, and she would no longer be safe.

One afternoon, Novena was sitting on the front steps, drawing in her notebook. And then suddenly Zan was there, looming above her. She didn't know why she hadn't heard him approach. She froze, unable to move, although she knew she was blocking his way.

They stared at each other in surprise, and she watched a slow smile crawl over his face. Before she could smile in return, she saw that he wasn't smiling at all, but simply baring his teeth.

Then he growled. "Move."

She quickly slid over on the step, leaving room for him to pass.

But he stood standing, staring at her, not moving.

"No, stupid, I mean why don't you move away from here? Move out. I'll help you pack."

The suggestion was so bizarre and so shocking that she could only stare at him, her mouth open. He shook his head in disgust and made a small hissing sound through his teeth. Then he pounded up the steps and slammed the door into the house.

He began making that hiss every time he saw her: a small whistling exhalation of air blown through his teeth, followed by an exasperated shake of his head. When he spoke to her, it was always the same message, over and over.

"Watch it," he'd mutter, passing her in the hall. "You're only here because I let you be here. We can take you back where you came from, you know. No one will miss you."

She tried to ignore him when he said those things, but she would feel her lip trembling, her face about to collapse. She knew he was trying to be cruel, but she knew it could also be the truth. Who would miss her? Elegia would probably be relieved to have her gone. Maybe they all would.

She had never given much thought to her place here, but now it was all she thought about. She was always alert, wary for the little signs that might tell her she didn't fit, that they were about to get rid of her.

Now it was almost every day Zan mumbled something to her.

"Why don't you go back where you came from?"

But she had no place to go back to. Zan was constantly reminding her that she belonged nowhere.

"I know how to drive, and some night you're going to wake up in the back seat and I'm going to be taking you away from here."

Novena tried to imagine the places she would be brought if she were taken from this house. She could imagine no place, could picture nothing but being dropped into a large, black hole in the world.

"I'm watching you," he'd hiss.

She wouldn't look at him. She would stare hard into space, stare so hard sometimes her eyes would begin to water, waiting for him to disappear.

The rest of the time she was watchful, waiting for him to appear. At night, she fought to stay awake until she heard him come in. Then she would hold her breath as long as it took Zan to climb the stairs, pass her room, and slam the door to his own room. If he took his time or stopped in the kitchen for food, a blackness would appear around her head like a punchy, energetic halo until she gave up, gasping.

Still, the ritual worked; he left her alone. But she knew it was only a matter of time before he'd find her.

If you had seen Novena during this time, you would have been most struck by her eyes. They were cloudy and unfocused, the eyes of some half-blind underwater creature that has been suddenly washed ashore.

In fact, she *was* half blind, stricken by the particular blindness that torments those who have turned to a place inside themselves for solace and found it almost as frightening as the place they are escaping. In this blindness, the sight is turned inward, as if to study that place, to wonder if its terror has somehow been misunderstood. Her eyes no longer looked out, no longer registered the world.

And left to its own devices, the world, only half observed, is free to become as dangerous as it has always dreamed of being. Buildings and bridges will turn to matchsticks, tottering toward collapse. Tree roots that have longed to be poisonous snakes will finally uncurl as vipers. Leaves will spring fingers, become hands, trembling with the weight of weapons. Pictures will jump from the flat planes of the page, looking for someone to tear apart.

These are the things Novena saw, but for a while she was not the only one who had a view of this newly treacherous world. For a while, she had the company of the girls who surrounded her.

Novena and her friends had reached a delicate age of their girlhood. While a boy at this age begins to feel the trembling power of his muscles and joyously begins pushing at the limits of his physicality, a girl at this age feels the stirrings of a single muscle — her heart. Pushing at its limits, she naturally becomes suggestible and moody and overwrought, falling into raptures of despair, happiness, terror, and beauty in the space of a moment.

Novena was able to deliver the spell of her terror to her girlfriends like a gift. For these girls, there was nothing more extreme, more thrillingly delicious, than terror. It was breathtaking how Novena could transform the world into a place filled with danger. She told them stories of girls being stolen, of monstrous creatures that hovered at the edges of their vision, of unspeakable things that went on in the dark. She told them the dreams of her sleepless nights. She brought them into the woods, where they huddled together, listening for the crackling branches, waiting to run. They would clutch each other and moan, and expand their small lungs with their screaming.

For weeks, as Novena's spell held, the small girls of Nile Bay went to bed with their lights on, afraid to look into the dark. Eleven nine-year-olds had stains under their eyes from lack of sleep. Eleven nine-year-olds bore that half-blind look, their eyes at a cloudy half-mast.

But these girls soon grew bored with their constant state of fright; they were moving toward a more refined stage of girlhood, a more delicate, nuanced stage, where they would become a box of swarming kittens, petting each other, licking each other's fur, in love with each other as idealized reflections of their own sensitivity and beauty. Novena could see them pulling away, beckoned by some new idea of grace unreachable by her, and she knew she would be left behind. Forced to inhabit her terror alone, she was sure it was going to be the end of her.

chapter 6

THE TRUE TERROR of storms is not in their relentless pummeling, but in their moments of change, in that white, blank gasp when the atmosphere shifts, the rain suddenly stops, and the wind changes course.

In fact, it was Elegia who changed everything.

She had lately become so altered that even the boys noticed. She no longer screeched and squawked, no longer wailed and wrung her hands over the trials of her household. Now she seemed to float above them serenely, humming to herself. It was as if their mother had disappeared and been replaced by a lighter, less concentrated version.

Even her cheerfulness was different. It was no longer that strained and corny thing that the boys had grown up swatting away, but something more dignified and out of reach, as if she had decided it was no longer meant for them, but something worth keeping for herself.

Somewhere in their hearts, the boys wondered if she had decided that *she* was no longer meant for them, and had somehow removed herself to some out-of-the-way place.

Elegia's transformation was not lost on Novena either, and she might have taken Elegia's remoteness more personally, as another sign of her own peril, if she hadn't noticed the toll it was clearly taking on the boys. She had the sense that Elegia's change was going to have more impact on them than on herself.

Which was only partly right.

The boys were so confused by this new version of their mother that an unspoken truce was temporarily declared, and Wyn, Dex, Quin, and Zan became the single front of boy they had been in the old days.

"Women," muttered Dex one night when the four of them were together. Earlier that night, Elegia had declared a new phase of experimentation in the kitchen, and had made nothing for dinner but a cheese soufflé. The boys were too stunned to do anything but eat it, although they were sure it was a trick designed to make them feel weak and dainty.

They'd left the table hungry and were now lying around the den like formless sacks.

"Old bag must be in menopause," Wyn Jr. declared.

"Yeah," said Zan, although he had no idea what the word meant. He thought Wyn had said "mental pause," which seemed an entirely adequate explanation for his mother's strange indifference.

The fact of the matter was, Elegia had not become indifferent to the boys, nor had she become blind to the turbulence around her. Her eyes had simply been opened to another, more pleasant form of it which she had discovered on her own, two weeks before.

It had been a Wednesday night, at the end of the day at Dr. Jack's office. Elegia had been at the autoclave, sterilizing instruments, when Jack Lerner had come in.

"So. I see Beulah Ratkin's in the book for Friday," he said. "Another crisis?"

"Oh, she probably has a new dress she wants you to see her in," Elegia said, then blushed. It was Elegia's opinion that while Jack Lerner was nothing much to look at, his gentle hands in their mouths kept many women in town a little too happy to keep their dental appointments. This was her private opinion, and now she was mortified that she had let it leak out of her.

She looked up at Jack Lerner and saw that he too was blushing. Somehow, it emboldened her.

"Oh, don't tell me you haven't noticed. They stir up a breeze just batting their eyes at you. It's a good thing you use local and not general. Lord knows what they'd say in their sleep."

"Oh. Well. I don't know what you mean . . ." He laughed nervously. Though she could tell it had never occurred to him, she saw he wasn't displeased at the idea.

After he left, Elegia felt a strange exhilaration. Her heart was pounding and her face still felt hot. "My goodness, what's gotten into me? I'm becoming a flirt," she thought, and try as she might to dredge up some horror in the idea, she couldn't.

On Friday morning, she stepped into Lerner's private office to announce the first patient.

"Dr. Jack? Mrs. Ratkin's here."

He looked up at her.

"And she looks stunning," she said in a stage whisper, and they burst out laughing. Beulah Ratkin was past sixty, and anything but stunning.

For the rest of the day, whenever they caught each other's eye, Elegia and Dr. Jack grinned at each other. After that, they moved naturally into a teasing bantering over the heads of the doped-up, open-mouthed patients.

During their days working side by side, she began noticing the isolated physical parts of him: his arms, his broad shoulders, strong from work — few people realized how physically grueling dentistry could be, the muscular control and strength it required. And she was aware of his scent — a general and familiar male musk, his smudged with pine and soap and a faint, pleasurable sting of nitrous oxide.

But she was fixated on his hands. She stared at them as he worked, those gentle dexterous hands. There was a small patch of dark hair leading from his arm and wrist, which spanned his knuckles and moved down his fingers. She was fixated on this hair, this little patch of his animal nature, looming and uncontained against the starched white of his work smock. She wondered what it felt like brushing up the soft palate of one's mouth, against one's teeth, and would be overcome with the thought of how many mouths that hand had been in, performing miniature and delicate surgeries, or, as in the case of extractions, acts of brutish, bone-cracking strength. The thought could make her weak.

Until one day she realized that there was not a minute she wasn't thinking of him, or so it seemed, since every time she became conscious of her thoughts, he was there. She was petrified that the patients, especially the women, could see the special glances they exchanged, the secret looks that she knew were never really secret, the softening around the edges of her face when they were in the same room. At the same time, she felt superior to these women, almost a little sorry for them as they sat there with their mouths open, their eyes watering from pain, or clamped shut in fear, or wide open from the shock of intrusion, as Dr. Jack performed whatever procedures were required, Elegia at his side with her suction wand.

In fact, Elegia considered Dr. Jack and herself as a kind of king and queen ruling over the teeth of their immensely grateful subjects: draining, pulling, scraping, polishing, drilling, and otherwise perfecting the rickety, rugged patches of their mouths, the states of which, she knew, were symbolic somehow of their very lives.

Dr. Jack for his part signaled his admiration in subtleties, leaving them for her to decipher and unwrap. Looks. A tone of voice. A cough. The subtlety only increased her sense of being adored. It was perfect, this state between them: transcending the roiling sea of sex, elevated to a purer plain, to pure communion without words or action. Oh, there was delight and fulfillment and a certain contained delirium between them — those things, Elegia thought, other people had to resort to sex in order to achieve.

Theirs was a perfect painted miniature portrait of love, neatly framed. Four corners, a square of glass. Hanging there, forever unspoken.

Elegia began wearing lipstick and nicer dresses. She even bought a pair of heels. They gave her walk a wobbly uncertainty until she grew used to them, although she never grew used to their conflicting sensations. In them, she felt tottering and precarious, yet the added height also made her feel powerful, as if she could stride through any place, even her own house.

Especially her own house; in fact, it was amazing how *hers* the house now seemed. She no longer felt herself as a weak outnumbered opponent among an uncivilized herd. The boys had become a distant buzz, like bees at the edges of a lovely garden.

In fact, she even began to see the boys in a new light: they were no longer strange creatures from separate planets, something wrongly ordered and too late to return. Now their mystery and otherness had a perfect logic to it — their noise and appetites and smells seemed to exist to underscore the delicacy of her own. She noticed the hair growing on their arms, and on their faces, and once, when Wyn Jr. walked into the kitchen shirtless, his corduroys drooping off his backside, she became transfixed by a little swirl of dark hair on the small of his back, the vestige, she was sure, of an animal tail. For days afterward, she couldn't look at him or any of the boys without imagining them with long brushy tails, with paws, with thick coats of fur. She couldn't explain why this somehow thrilled her, except didn't she lately imagine herself as sleek and feral, her own tail swishing as she walked — no, stalked — the halls of Dr. Jack's?

Everyone was an animal, she thought, giddy with the strangeness of such a thought.

Or a vegetable, she thought, glancing in at Wyn Sr., hunched in his chair in the den.

·   ·   ·

After the first shock wore off, Wyn, Dex, and Quin finally accommodated themselves to their mother's transformation, and were almost able to shrug it off.

Zan was another story. Zan was confused, then suspicious, and finally affronted at his mother's new behavior. It stung him that he was no longer capable of tormenting her. In some ways, he had come to measure his worth in the decibels of her screeching, his existence in the tense pursing of her lips.

None of these were Zan's words, of course. All of this thinking went on in a part of Zan's brain that he had not yet been formally introduced to, and perhaps never would, for his thoughts had been trained to race past words and translate themselves directly into action.

The action now required was simple. Now that Elegia had abrogated her responsibility as his mother, to bear the cross of him, he was going to have to find someone to replace her. The beauty of it was, he didn't have far to look. Novena was always there at the edges of his vision, waiting.

As a bully, Zan was in transition. He found himself increasingly dissatisfied with the limits of physical force — not because it wasn't effective, but because it had become too easy. He yearned for more. And yet he lacked the acuity, if not the vocabulary, to exploit the full possibilities of mental cruelty. As an unfortunate result of his limitation, he ended up tormenting Novena in the worst possible way: without the right words, he simply stopped speaking to her, and began using sign language instead. Walking past her in the hall, he'd mimic driving, moving his hands as if steering a car. At the dinner table, he'd jingle the ring of keys he kept in his pocket, or pull them out of his pocket and hold them up, staring at her. He'd sometimes remove the setting from her place at the dinner table before she got there, to remind her that she didn't belong.

Novena had given up trying to stay awake and listen for Zan, since he came home so late each night. Given the disturbing quality of her dreams, though, she knew that some part of her registered his arrival each night.

The night Zan finally came for her, she had been sleeping, and she thought she was dreaming the sound of her door opening, but when the light from the hallway spilled into her room, she was instantly awake. She could see the outline of him in the doorway, could smell the stale, yeasty smell of him. She shut her eyes and held her breath.

He was here to take her away, to put her in the car and drive off, to leave her at the side of the road. Her brain traced the familiar path of escape she had outlined for herself. She tensed, waiting for the creak of the floor, the sound of his step coming into her room.

He made no sound, other than the slight wheeze of his breath. He simply stood there.

And as the seconds passed and she lay utterly still, ready to leap up, she felt her body begin to take on a strange sensation of heaviness. It was as if she were being vacuumed of blood, muscle, and bone, and in the hollowed-out places a substance like wet sand was filling her limbs, her head, her chest, and it kept filling her, pushing against her insides, stretching her body, expanding her, like a balloon being blown up, not with air, but with something solid. She was filling the room, but just as she reached the panicked thought that she would never be able to move again, another part of her detached itself from this weight and began rising up from the bed and floating around the room. Now she was no body, just air. Now she was nothing, just atmosphere.

Yet she was conscious enough to register the lack of herself. She was conscious enough to know she could stay out of her body, out of her bed, in this state, as long as her eyes were closed. And she was conscious a moment later, when her door slammed with a sharp crack. Her eyes flew open, and she was back in her bed, back in her body. Her door was shut, and Zan's heavy footsteps were retreating down the hall to his own room.

She lay there, hearing her own breath again, thinking about that place she had just come back from. It frightened her, how foreign it was, yet how quickly she had taken herself there, as if it were a place that was well known to her.

She returned to that place again and again. Each time she opened her eyes and brought herself back from that place, she was shaken at its strangeness, frightened at the darkness and nothingness of it. It was almost as empty and black as that place Zan would take her to.

But when? So far, he hadn't crossed the threshold into her room; sometimes he didn't even open the door, but stood outside, where she could hear him breathing.

She thought of running away, but where would she go? It was an endless and exhausting dilemma. She would end up in the same place whether she stayed or ran away. She would end up nowhere.

In the end, it was Elegia who delivered Novena's salvation. Which was only fair.

While it is possible for love to change us, Elegia was relieved when she found the novelty of her transformation wearing off and her original personality returning. After all, hers was not a temperament built for long-term serenity. The lovely thing was, though, that even though the novelty of her love wore off, something of the actual love remained. Like the higher heels of her new shoes, she simply allowed it to give her a slight lift, without changing the direction of her walk.

But that's not what saved Novena. The occasion of Novena's salvation was Annaluna's birthday. Although everyone had long ago lost track of Annaluna's age, Elegia had always made sure she celebrated her birthday, and each year, she cooked a special dinner for her. Over time, Elegia's preparations had become so elaborate and involved so much roasted meat, wine, and decorative frosting that these meals no longer resembled dinners as much as sacrificial offerings to some god of age and forgetting.

This year was no exception, and after cooking for days, Elegia had driven into the city on the appointed day to bring Annaluna to Nile Bay. Novena was home when she heard the car pull into the driveway, and nearly fell down the stairs in her race to get to her. At the first sight of Annaluna's face, she felt the full weight of everything — terror, anxiety, and doom — instantly fall away. The relief was so unexpected, she burst into tears.

Annaluna had only planned to spend the night and return to the city the next afternoon. But she was so disturbed by Novena's dull unfocused eyes, and the deep shadows under them staining her pale skin like a bruise, she decided to stay on for a few days.

Annaluna took over a spare room downstairs, and that night she lay in bed, breathing in the air around her, trying to measure the size of what was wrong in this house. Something was wrong, and something wrong in a house was like dust and dirt: if you let it accumulate, it would embed itself in the cracks and crevices and would be impossible to remove, no matter how hard you tried.

But the turmoil that she felt lying dense and thick throughout this house was not so complicated to figure out, nor was its source.

"Too much man in here," she muttered to herself, thinking how often this was the cause for anything wrong in a house. "No place for a small girl."

Her thoughts turned to prayer, and out of habit she fingered the small cross that hung from a silver chain around her neck. On the back of the cross was a small plastic window, behind which was a tiny blue speck which was supposed to be the fragment of a garment from one of the saints, though Annaluna had long forgotten which one. Mumbling her familiar incantations, she thought again of the shadows under the girl's eyes, and mumbled more fervently. As if in answer, she felt a soft touch on her cheek.

"Can I come in?" Novena whispered.

Annaluna held out her arms, and Novena crawled into bed beside her.

"So, Beauty," Annaluna said, holding her, her hand smoothing out the furrows that had formed on the girl's forehead. "Tell me a story."

She wanted to hear the story Novena would tell, knowing it

would reveal how troubled she was. But Novena, nestled against the warm bulk of Annaluna, had closed her eyes and was inhaling the smell of her, the soft smell of talc and age, but also something more ancient, a smell that she felt she had known from the beginning of time, and that immediately made her aware of how much she had missed it. She felt in that moment a relief so profound it was a physical sensation, a small fluttering in her throat. This is where she belonged — here, next to Annaluna. This was her place. This was where she came from. If Zan ever were to take her away, she could return, not to some dark space at the side of some deserted road, but here, next to the furnace of Annaluna's warmth.

"Take me home," she whispered. "Take me with you when you go."

Annaluna smoothed the strands of Novena's hair.

"Oh, honey, I can't take care of you," she murmured. "Someday, you can come and live with me, and take care of me. But you have to grow up a little more."

Novena nodded. They lay quietly for a while, and as Annaluna's breath turned into soft snores, her own breath grew slow and heavy as she approached that small bridge that lies between consciousness and sleep. It was a bridge she usually tried to race across, to avoid the dark, chewing beasts that often waited underneath, ready to leap out and follow her into sleep. Now, with the pleasing but distant prospect of life with Annaluna, she relaxed into a heavy and thick contentment. Just as she was about to slide into oblivion, though, one small beast managed to rise up from the swamp of nightmares. In a perfect mimicking of her own voice, she heard it wonder how she would survive the days and months and years that growing up would take.

Annaluna ended up staying for two weeks, during which time Novena barely left her side. They spent what seemed to Elegia to be whole days whispering to each other, drinking endless cups of tea that Novena fixed for Annaluna.

As she watched Novena bringing the wobbling cups to Annaluna's side, her tongue stuck out in concentration, Elegia grew irritated at the memory of the grateful girl she had hoped for, back when she had first brought her here. It was not until the third day that the high-pitched screech of the teakettle finally shattered her equilibrium.

"No more tea!" she yelled. "Get some air! Take a walk!"

Now in the afternoons, they would take long walks through Nile Bay, Novena pushing Annaluna's chair. But the pleasure Annaluna found in these walks — the warm sun pouring over her, and the little breezes from the river that tickled her skin — was only momentary.

Over the years, Annaluna's senses, especially her eyesight, had been growing increasingly dim. This had been so gradual that she had come to believe that the diminishment of her faculties did not stem from her own aging body, but that it was the world which had aged, its own edges dulled and softened by the passage of time.

But here, outside of the city, nothing was dull. The light was harsh and bright. Maybe there was simply too much of it. Unscreened by the city's tall buildings, the immense sky burned a blue that struck Annaluna as inhuman. The sunlight danced maniacally around her, jabbing at her eyes and throwing weird signals and shadows over a landscape that was cartoonish in its greenness. What rattled her most, though, were the strange things she began to see on these walks.

In the city, she wouldn't look twice at the common street detritus or the odd scraps blowing through the gutter, but she was unprepared for the bizarre things she saw as Novena pushed her chair through the streets of Nile Bay. Everything had the appearance of something seen out of the corner of her eye, even when she was staring straight at it.

On that first day outside, for example, she saw thick black snakes sunning themselves in gutters or hanging from trees. A field of grass was strewn with doughnuts. A dog in someone's front yard let out a wail when he saw them, and ran away, upright on its hind legs. Angry red fireflies flashed in front of her, and patterns flashed on her skin that made her think she herself was growing leaves. Things that should have been moving — animals and people — lay dormant as stones, and the things that should have been inanimate — rocks, leaves, bits of metal — seemed, out of her scorched, beleaguered eyes, to fly through the air or run down the street, as if in escape.

What kind of town was this? Annaluna made no comment on these strange things, other than the clucks and whinnies and sharp little exclamations that she couldn't prevent from escaping her; it was no wonder the girl was so disturbed, living in a town like this.

One afternoon, they passed a woman pushing a stroller. The woman was wearing something around her neck that to Annaluna looked exactly like a string of hot dogs. But she was distracted from this by the two loaves of bread that the woman was pushing in the stroller. She could no longer contain herself.

"Did you see what was in that stroller?" she asked Novena when they had passed. "Bread! Two loaves of bread. And what about those hot dogs? What kind of place is this?"

Novena paused, and then she laughed. Annaluna would have been annoyed at being made light of if the sound of Novena's laugh hadn't expanded her heart in sudden relief at hearing it. It was a good sign, the girl laughing.

Maybe it was all meant to be funny, like some kind of circus town. She had lived her whole life in the city; who knew what strange things they had in these small towns?

It took Novena a few days to adjust to these walks too. They were so mundane, so uneventful. Sometimes an hour would pass with no sound other than the chair's pleasant rhythmic click on the sidewalk, or the little clucking or cooing noises Annaluna would make, as if she were delighted with everything she beheld. The world seemed to hold no malice for Annaluna. She rolled through it like a queen, regal and unafraid.

Novena started relaxing. Gradually, the dark holes between

buildings that she always avoided seemed innocuous. The stealthy current of the river, the cracks in the concrete, and the tangle of thorned bushes and branches and lawns that hid bad-smelling horrors began to lose their malice for her. And Annaluna's occasional jokes, while strange, made her feel giddy in their total lack of sense.

Novena thought there was nothing Annaluna wasn't capable of. She had even begun soothing the house. She watched Annaluna wheel through the rooms, patting and caressing the furniture, touching a spot on the wall, as if to measure its temperature, or murmuring to a lamp when she straightened it. Her touch seemed to have the same effect on the house as it had on Novena — it settled around itself like a sigh, no longer tearing itself apart.

It was true that the house was quieter. Zan had been lying low. Day after day, he had been waiting for Annaluna to leave. He felt constricted and rattled in her presence, even though she barely acknowledged him with anything but her strange, evil-eyed stare.

He decided he would put up with it for a few more days. But sooner or later, he might have to do something. Send her a little message, from him to her, about who was boss here.

Maybe he could steal her wheelchair some night. Sneak into the room and roll it away. Who would know? He could sell the thing. He didn't know where he might sell it, but he imagined if he found the right place, such a contraption could bring a fortune.

He liked this idea for about a half hour, until he figured out that without her chair she'd be more helpless, and probably end up staying longer. Besides, the thing scared him. It was metal, and a machine, and he had a fearful respect for both.

He didn't get a chance to do anything until Friday afternoon. He was leaving the house, and pushed open the front door to find Annaluna at the edge of the porch, sitting with her head bent over, softly snoring. Novena wasn't around, but he knew she wouldn't be gone long; she had practically made herself one of the attachments to the chair.

Annaluna hadn't stirred at the sound of the door opening. He approached her slowly. He stood behind her, looking down at the top of her head, slumped in sleep. He could see the pink scalp under her thin white hair. Over the top of her head, he saw the five steps leading down off the porch.

He looked at the five steps to the ground. A little push. It wasn't far. Not far enough to do serious damage. Just enough to scare her.

He put his hands on Annaluna's shoulders, just to get the sense of the grip he'd need and he squeezed them to test their size — they were so tiny he was astonished, because he had seen her forearms, built up from pushing herself around in the chair.

As his eye measured the space from the porch to the ground, something in him registered a similar space, and then, even more oddly, a similar hesitation. Five steps. He suddenly thought of the nights he had stood at Novena's doorway, thinking all he had to do was take five steps, to cross the threshold and reach her. Five steps to get her out of his room, out of his house, to get her to disappear. Without knowing why, he'd so far been unable to take them.

Annaluna had finally begun stirring, and he heard her let out a deep sigh.

"Oh, that feels nice," she said. "Could you rub a little harder?"

He was so startled by her voice that he simply obeyed, and began rubbing her shoulders. He could feel them rise and fall with her breath. She was sighing deeply, making little mews of pleasure, and her head bent lower, her chin touching her chest.

"Oooo, ooo, what a nice touch you have," she cooed.

Zan blushed. No one had ever said that he had a nice anything. His hands felt warm, as a current like electricity traveled into his fingers, into his hands, and up his arms. His fingers were actually tingling. He couldn't break the current, he couldn't stop; if he did, some pleasure that was running through him would stop too. He was confused by that pleasure, but for an instant, he gave himself up to it.

When the door behind him made a small creak, he pulled his hands away. He spun around, but saw no one, although he was sure Novena had been spying, and his face burned in shame. He pushed the door open and as he stepped back into the house to find her, he heard Annaluna cry out.

"Who's there?" she called. "Who's there? Is that you, Novena?"

Zan's first thought was relief; she hadn't even known it had been him. His second was fury: she thought he had been someone else.

His third was defeat: once again, he'd failed.

That night, he stayed out late and broke his own record for beer consumption. When he came home, he went to the kitchen to find food, and knocked over a chair. When he tried to right it, he fell against the table, pushing it against the wall. Finally righting himself, he weaved out of the kitchen and headed upstairs, the steps spongy under his feet as he climbed. He heaved open the door to his bedroom and stumbled into his room, tripping over a box and falling down. He was on the floor, with an overwhelming urge to giggle. He crawled over to his bed, but when he tried to heave himself up onto it, the bed rolled away from him.

Something burst black behind his eyes, and he got to his feet, enraged. He started kicking the bed, kicking it as hard as he could, and from across the room, Wyn Jr. called out, "Cut it out! Shut up!" This enraged him even more, and he started pounding on the floor — pounding with his fist, then his body, then his head. *Pound, pound, pound.* It had been such a long time since he had done that, he had forgotten how much relief it brought. Then he was on the floor again, out cold, snoring like a monster.

The slam of the door when Zan came home had waked Novena. She had gone rigid as she heard him moving into the kitchen, heard the chair tipping over, heard the table moving across the floor, his heavy stomping footsteps.

She lay stiff, unable to move, unable to breathe. She felt herself growing heavy, filling up with that dead weight of terror, a familiar terror which was now laced with an even deeper weight of despair. Her calm, her salvation had disappeared. Chaos had returned; it had been too big for even Annaluna to control. And if it was too big for Annaluna, what would become of Novena when she left?

As that thick darkness engulfed her, she decided she would let it take her, let it drain her of bone and muscle and blood until she was nothing but a stone.

Then Annaluna stirred beside her.

"Listen," Annaluna whispered.

Heavy footsteps pounded the stairs, and then, directly above them, a great thud of something falling that rattled the floor and ceiling.

"Listen to that furniture misbehaving," Annaluna whispered. "Trying to rearrange itself."

Something was being dragged across the floor. A sharp muffled cry was followed by a dull pounding. Annaluna clucked.

"Mine does that all the time. Chairs and sofas hate each other. It's a proven fact. They're always fighting, always trying to get away from each other."

She leaned over and kissed Novena's cheek.

"We'll have to give it a good talking-to in the morning."

And then she fell back to her soft wheezing snore.

Novena felt all the suspended things in her suddenly move again: her blood, her breath, her limbs and something else, something pushing up her throat, so light and feathery she thought it was a laugh, because even though she knew what those noises were, for a single instant, Annaluna had turned Zan into a sofa — a fat, clownish, overstuffed thing with dainty, carved legs tottering under him.

And in the same instant, she had not been Novena. She had not been a chair, or a sofa, or a stone, or even a girl, but someone else, someone like Annaluna, seeing what Annaluna saw — not *what* she saw, but how she saw it. As if she were seeing not with her eyes, but with some other sense, some other organ.

72

It was just a moment, but sensing its possibilities, Novena wondered if she could find some way to hold it to her, some way she could live in it, some way she could become Annaluna.

The next day, and every day thereafter until Annaluna left to go back to the city, Novena would copy her movements. She tried to perfect the fluttering gestures of Annaluna's hands, the slight tip of the head when she was listening, to mimic her low guttural chuckle. She even practiced Annaluna's glare, that hard, cold stare that could wilt even Zan.

And each night, when Annaluna mumbled her prayers, Novena mumbled incantations of her own. Like Annaluna's prayers, they were highly ordered, and like Annaluna's prayers, there was great comfort in their repetition.

She would whisper the names for countries, and the names of people she imagined living there: *Ahari, Babushu, Clindanga, Dyorista, Elpha, Flinghora, Gostina, Hacklocka.* She named new species of animals, plants, and flowers: *Intaylu, Jackarinda, Knu-sanya, Laaxzt, Molynori, Noragh, Ofalanta, Pyweed.* And objects which had never yet been seen, but to which she gave shape and form as she called out their names: *Qintessa, Rati, Shantu, Treehunt, Uytall, Vix, Wyogrist, Xyabu, Yoerna, Zittering.* She went through a new alphabet every night.

After their prayers, when she heard Annaluna begin softly snoring, Novena would wriggle up to lie with her face against her. She got as close as she could, to take Annaluna's breath into her own mouth. The more of her she breathed in, the more quickly she could become her.

Every night, she collected Annaluna's breath. As it filled up her lungs and moved through her body, she would feel herself growing light, but not in the frightening sense, as if she were about to be detached from her body, but with a pleasant, lightheaded dizziness.

Then, lying back, she listened to the sounds of the house. When she heard pounding footsteps, now she imagined long-lost socks skulking back home, stiff with dirt and exhaustion after trips to distant places, and she could picture, at the rattling windows, a menagerie of lonely birds, beating their wings against the glass. She would call forth the ominous shadows that lived in the room, and turn them into gentle folds in the air, like the drape of silk.

The small shimmering things in the room were Novena's eyes, glittering in the dark, no longer blind with torment but shining with a willful blindness, a blindness reflecting only light, seeing only beauty.

By the time Annaluna left, Novena could get drunk on the fumes of her own imagination. Breathing them in, she could leave the world — not into untethered darkness, but into another town, another town of her.

In this town, everything was familiar, yet different. In this other town of her, everything looked like Nile Bay — houses with lawns and sprinklers, and stores lined with linoleum floors, with merchandise on the counter ready for sale. There was a drugstore, a coffee shop with steamed-up windows, a dress shop, and houses.

A girl who looked like Novena guarded the town, watching for trouble arriving. And when it did, she directed people back into their houses, closed their shutters, dispelled their terror with her descriptions of the gorgeous orchestra of the howling dogs, the deep cobalt that stained the sky, the tears of angels that fell from the clouds, weeping in the joy of it all. In this other town of her, the house she herself lived in had very little resemblance to her own.

In this other town of her, Zan disappeared. Zan no longer existed.

Somewhere in his animal heart, Zan knew that she had made him invisible. Most of the time, he didn't think about it. But there were moments when it so filled his heart with blood and fury that he was forced to remind her of his existence, to make himself be seen.

But even when he appeared next to her, and his big hands grabbed her skin and pinched it, Novena would study the blood that rose up to the surface of her skin, blooming on her arm like violets, on the back of her legs like spilled wine.

Each bruise seemed to take on a different character, depending on where he had pinched her. In this other town of her, even these were beautiful, those small violets, the spilled wine, that handful of berries, their juice spreading under the skin. A single small pansy, yellow petals unfolding from a violet-blue center on the upper part of her arm.

By the time Zan had left the house for good, lured by trouble's promise that he could leave a more permanent bruise on the world, Novena barely noticed he was gone. By that time, she had been welcomed back into the fold of her girlfriends, where she felt quite at home preening and mewing with them over their own exquisitely delicate natures. The girls were still in their kitten stage, and their greatest delight was hissing at boys, those smelly drooling dogs with coats like dirty old rugs, who sniffed and galumphed around them.

But even that would change. Everything does.

chapter 7

In these superstitious times [of the fifteenth century] the recipe for
gaining the heart of one's beloved was to capture a toad on a Friday
night "while Venus was shining," dry it, reduce it to powder, put the
powder in a little bag made of soft linen and put the little bag for
three days at the foot of an altar where Mass was celebrated. This
powder was sprinkled on a bouquet of flowers, which was offered to
the girl; she would smell the flowers and inhale the powder, and
would immediately burn with love.

— Mila Contini, *Fashion from Ancient Egypt to the Present Day*

ELEGIA TAUGHT NOVENA to sew when she was twelve. They
made an apron together. Elegia had picked out the fabric, a heavy,
homespun, and somewhat homely calico, too stiff for the many
gathers the apron required. The finished product could practically
stand up by itself. With its exaggerated flounces, its bunched-up
strained cheerfulness, the apron reminded Novena of Elegia —
who wore it for a long time, acting as if Novena had bestowed it on
her as a gift rather than as a discard.

Novena may have rejected the apron but she retained the sewing lesson, and soon she was making most of her clothes, tiny little
skirts and halter tops that were not designed to make her look at
home in a kitchen. By the time she was fourteen, she was coming
home late, always with the stink of boy on her.

Boys took her out in their cars, and she would end up on the edge of a road somewhere, in the back seat, entangled, kissing, the windows fogged and steamy until the mist of their heavy breaths and sighs formed a tent around them. She loved the smell of these boys. Theirs was not the feral stench of her brothers, but the sweet and artificial smell of wooing, the aroma of effort: soap and after-shave, faint medicinal traces of pimple ointments and toothpaste, the slight harshness of newly pressed jeans and shirts. She would bury her nose in the boys' thick wool sweaters, gripping the wool with both hands as if she were lying on the ground peering into a deep hole as she registered their smells changing, becoming more urgent and individual, as if moving along a chromatic scale of desire.

She would go home with their smell in her hair. While it lingered, she would take out one of her black marble notebooks and turn to the page where she recorded each of their scents. She worked like a perfumer-in-reverse, attempting to break down these complex formulas. The title of the list, written in her bold hard-angled hand, was "The Ultimate Smell of Boys." By the time she abandoned it, the list read:

The belly of a salamander
Riverbed, strange grasses that wave at the bottom
Dirt wet by rain, with earthworms crawling in it
Horse flesh, sweaty
Unwashed flannel
Hamburger in the sun too long
Metal shavings
Marbles

She was actually thinking of marbles not as a smell, but as pure sensation, of marbles rolling around her mouth and sliding down her esophagus. Marbles is what she thought of when she was kissing.

Naturally, she had a lot of dates. Elegia acted delighted, and tried to extract what wholesomeness she could out of the parade of surly, awkward, and occasionally beefy suitors who showed up at the door.

"Oh, she's got quite a few knocking on her door," she'd say on the phone, winking as Novena brushed past her. "She's turning a few heads, I'd say. They all come courting, I can hardly keep them straight."

And indeed she couldn't.

"Now, you must be Jack," she'd say, opening the door.

"No, I'm Rick," he would say, shuffling uncomfortably.

"Oh dear, I can hardly keep you boys straight."

Then, realizing her error from Novena's sharp intake of breath, she would roll her eyes a little and say, "Well, I mean, a woman my age faced with a handsome young man, I get a little confused, you understand."

Thinking she had charmed them, she'd say, "Why don't you two stay for supper? I made a nice pie, and we could sit outside."

"Next time; we've got to be somewhere," Novena would say quickly.

And Novena would take Jack or Rick by the arm and lead him out the door, removing her jacket on the walk to the car so he could see the two small wingbones of her back sticking out of her halter top. It was the sight of her frail wingbones that always got to them.

She started collecting their shirts. It took nothing to convince them to take them off, and by the time they dropped her at her door, it was even easier to convince them to give them to her. She'd hang them in her closet. When the smell wore off, so did the boy's appeal. But she wouldn't toss out the shirts, she would cut them up and make things, strange patchwork stuff — small pouches, pillows, handkerchief squares — out of the oxford cloth and heavy cotton jersey. Occasionally, she would bestow these crafts on the new girlfriends of the shirts' original owners.

These objects were first received with confused suspicion, conjuring in the girls stirrings of vague familiarity, although Novena never let on the source of the fabric. A cachet developed quickly, though, when one of the girls started boasting of the luck it brought to her love life.

Sylvie was a flamboyant girl with thick black eyebrows and a chest beyond her years. She was not a bright girl, but she wisely knew the power her endorsement of Novena's handicrafts would bring her: she would forever be known as the source of a legend rather than a mere supplier of its raw materials.

"You know how he treated me. Like dirt," Sylvie's story always began.

Everyone was familiar with the bad treatment of Sylvie. Those untamed eyebrows of hers rightly suggested a too easy compliance that, coupled with a dumb and helpless good nature, had invited bad treatment from every boy she had ever gone out with. Her new boyfriend was no exception, until Novena's bestowal of a patchwork change purse, which Sylvie carried constantly.

"And now? Wrapped!" At this, she'd hold up her little finger, waggling it.

"Lookit these earrings," she said, shaking her head to show them off. "He bought 'em."

The earrings were evidence of her new powers, but not proof. The proof that rang through the halls like a surprise verdict came one cold day in the playground, near the basketball court, when a bloody fight broke out between Sylvie's boyfriend and a joe who had made a crude and joking reference to her generous endowments. It doesn't matter who won; the boyfriend, in fact, took a beating. What mattered was that two boys had fought over Sylvie.

Now the object of courtship rather than seduction, the mooned-over, fought-over receiver of gifts, Sylvie changed. Some thought not for the better. Her compliance took on a slight chill and her good nature became more demanding, flirting, in fact, with greed. If the changes were not exactly good for her soul, they were still very good for love.

The girls started clamoring for Novena's handicrafts. Novena obliged when she could; she felt magnanimous toward the girls, and could afford to, since she not only had the bond of shared boy with them, but had been there first. Soon, drawing on her knowledge of the boy in question, she began embedding into the patchwork little tokens and symbols particular to each boy — beer can tabs, foil from cigarette packs, shells, guitar picks. She would dispense small bits of wisdom with her offerings.

"Take dirt from the football field and wrap some in this. Leave it there for three nights" was one directive.

"Soak this in beer for a day and dry it outside. Then pin it to the inside of your bra" was another.

"Buy a pack of cigarettes. Take one out and turn it around and put it back in the pack, and then wrap the pack in this" was still another.

The girls revered these scraps, and held on to them like precious things, wrapping them in tissue and hiding them in their musical ballerina jewelry boxes or in their underwear drawers, as if they were diaries. Fervent incantations were said over them, many tears were cried into them, and prayers said while clasped in damp and desperate palms. Many girls slept with them.

By summer, it was as if these girls, dewy and ripe as fruit, had been misted lightly with a cloud of voodoo. The boys in question were barely aware of this, although spells were cast in their direction. But the spells were not powerful ones, since the girls were new to this and were shy of the kind of knowledge that would intensify their powers; they felt themselves too young to unleash all the forces that love would demand; all they wanted was a little attention.

Still, the power was effective. Maybe a boy would find himself driving past a girl's house at odd hours, or find himself, having never intended to call a particular girl, dialing her phone number before he could stop himself.

Sometimes a boy would be affected more deeply; he would find himself brooding about a girl even when he and a bunch of his buddies sat on the hoods of cars with pilfered beer in a dark parking lot. While the other boys would talk about sports and rub the stubble of their new beards or the hair sprouting on their legs and arms, this boy would grow suddenly silent, gripped with the worst kind of longing — a longing beyond sex, beyond anything known to him, taking shape as the memory of a patch of skin on the girl's arm, or a few strands of her hair in his fingers, or the sight of her bracelet gently enclosing her tanned wrist.

Once, due to a remarkable confluence, a whole carload of boys who had moments ago been racing through town, whooping from the agitated rinse of hormones and immortality that high speed and beer always created, grew suddenly silent as they one by one became struck with these thoughts. It was like a moment of prayer, a prayer which stirred in each of them a memory, felt, rather than recognized, of Novena. She was, after all, what they all had in common.

It was an odd summer; everyone felt it. The girls felt infected with a low-grade fever that left them dazed and languorous. Some took to weeping. They moved between a sense of jangled distraction and deep rapture over the smallest things: the soft hair on the stem of a flower, the feel of hot asphalt on their bare feet, the salt and silk of their own browning skin. The boys were made even more ardent and tortured by their dreamy-eyed absorption.

The girls' usual highly selective and exclusive formations of friends now unraveled, and took on a casual, accidental quality. Groups of girls who had barely known each other would suddenly find themselves spending hours together, unable to figure out exactly how they had assembled, unable to imagine ever parting from each other, until the next day, when they'd find themselves with another group. The girls, too, would have rambling, disconnected thoughts that often found their way back to Novena.

Novena, although surrounded by friends and confidantes,

always remained at a slight remove from them. She had an influence over them, but she knew it was more than the temporary flames she ignited in the boys or the scraps of them she left for the other girls. They thought that she held some key that would make them complete, and she knew there was potential danger there.

All the dances, the wild rides, the steamed-up cars, the couplings — no matter how much there was, the boys and girls always found ways to keep slamming into each other, looking for something more, some slick residue they could leave as permanent stains on each other. No matter how much they accumulated, Novena had the sense that, with or without her help, it would never be enough.

The routine of the girls' summer weeknights together usually involved loosely knitted groups of them driving around, whizzing past carloads of boys as if they had better places to go. They usually ended up at strange places: they'd forgo the mall and head toward an abandoned shopping center parking lot, or the riverbank, or a small roadside rest stop that had a few picnic tables.

This is where Danielle, Cookie, and Novena found themselves one hot July night. They were smoking cigarettes and lay on top of the picnic tables with their long legs bent at the knees, staring up at the leaves against the darkening sky.

"Where's Sylvie?" Novena said.

"Coming later. Mr. E. drama, part, oh, let's see, seventeen," Danielle said.

"Oh God. Him. I think we should follow her one night and make sure he exists," Cookie said.

Mr. E. was the name they had given to Sylvie's new boyfriend, about whom she was mysteriously silent. She referred to him as "the big guy" and explained, "He's much older. Has his own place. He's a *man*, not one of these boys."

They imagined someone like their fathers, but darker and handsomer, with a large black car.

He had a hold on Sylvie that equaled hers on him. They had huge, magnificent fights, which gave the other girls an almost embarrassingly intimate view of what real love was. Listening to the extremes of their relationship — his possessive hold on Sylvie, Sylvie's torture of him, his rage, her submission — the girls were both ashamed and relieved that their own relationships were still in the baby stages.

"Can you imagine? I mean, do you think we'll ever have boys like that? That we'll ever make someone that crazy?" Cookie said wistfully.

"I certainly hope not," Danielle scoffed.

"I'm worried about her," Novena said suddenly. She had been staring at the moon as a cloud passed over it.

They turned to the sound of tires on the dirt drive. Sylvie's huge car screeched to a stop and she came out, slamming the door.

"Bastard," Sylvie yelled, yelling it again and again as she approached. Her wild hair was snaking out of a corduroy baseball cap with the word BRAT stitched in gold letters.

"Bastard." Sylvie sat down hard on the table. "Somebody give me a cig. It's over. I swear. I'm on my way there now. The bastard. Thanks," she said, lighting up. "I just stopped by for courage. Oh Cookie, I love that sweater on you."

"Thanks," Cookie said, smoothing one of the springy tendrils from Sylvie's face. "Cute hat. So, anyway, do it and come back. We're going to eat."

Sylvie, nettled by the fact that food was taking prominence over her drama, shook her head.

"You guys have no idea. No idea what he's doing to me," she wailed.

"Aw Syl, come on," Novena said. "You don't need him. You're too good for him."

"Yeah, whoever he is," said Danielle dryly.

"You think it's a joke," Sylvie screamed. "Just wait. You'll be surprised."

"Come on, Syl. Do it tomorrow. Stay with us," Novena said. "Don't go."

"No, I have to do it. I'll meet up with you later. Where you going to be?" She had already gotten her keys out of her purse and had smashed her cigarette butt under her foot.

"Daz's. We'll wait for you there."

They watched her walk to her car.

At Daz's, they found a booth and were soon eating french fries as if they were petits fours, with their pinkies raised, and taking noisy gulps of Cokes. Novena kept looking out at the parking lot, watching the steady stream of lights for Sylvie.

Nearly two hours had passed and they were deciding where to go next when the waitress, a sad and heavy girl they knew from school, came to the table and said, "Hey, Sylvie's on the phone for you. You gotta make it quick, though. We're not supposed to let you use the phone here."

Novena slid out of the booth and picked up the phone.

"Syl?"

"Novena? Oh, thank God it's you. He's crazy. He wants to get married. He's out of his mind. I'll humor him for a while and then escape."

"Escape! Sylvie, what's going on?"

Sylvie was laughing hysterically now. "He's going to kidnap me! I don't know what to do."

Now she sounded almost gleeful. "Oh, it's awful." Then she hung up.

Novena went back to the table and announced, "Well, Sylvie says he's going to kidnap her."

"What?" the girls screamed. This was thrilling beyond anything they could imagine.

Ten minutes later, when Sylvie called back, Novena didn't recognize her voice. It was a harsh whisper. "Novena. He's says he's going to take me away. You've got to help me. Call my mother. I don't know what to do."

"Who is it?" Novena said. "Tell me who you're with, Sylvie!"

The phone went dead. Novena called Sylvie's mother and tried to sound casual when she asked if she had heard from Sylvie.

"She's out with that boy," her mother said. "I told her a million times he was no good. Not that I've ever met him," she said sourly.

Novena hung up, intimidated by her bitterness.

"I think we should go look for her," Novena said, coming back to the table.

The girls piled into two cars and drove around with no destination in mind, with no idea what they were looking for, fueled by excitement and purpose. They knew Sylvie would show up the next day with a wild story, and by the following day would act as if she had no memory of anything out of the ordinary. But for the next few hours, they could lose themselves in an event that could surpass anything they had experienced so far. They could pretend to be worried out of their minds, a pretense deliciously tinged with the fact that they actually were slightly worried. They could pretend that Sylvie was in real danger, also deliciously possible. They could pretend that they would find her and rescue her. There had never been a night like this. They were already preparing anecdotes about "the night Sylvie got kidnapped" and imagined themselves screaming with laughter over it.

They drove past parked cars and pulled up to them. They stopped at knots of boys and asked if they had seen Sylvie, their mission allowing them an outrageousness and forwardness in their flirtation that they would never have ventured otherwise. They drove all night, at one point stopping at Sylvie's house, where her mother was worried. But then, she was always worried.

chapter 8

If you have a trophy on your hands, an animal you'll want to mount, don't cut the throat. Don't cut any hair or hide in front of the shoulders. If you're just interested in meat, insert the point of your knife behind the windpipe, push it through, and cut it cleanly in half.

— Norman Strung, *The Hunter's Almanac*

SYLVIE, MEANWHILE, was trying to decide just how worried she should be. It was a new sensation, not knowing, and she liked the novelty of it. Not knowing also helped mask the idea of what was actually happening.

It had been over a year since Sylvie's new status had taken hold and she had become slightly bored with it. She had turned it into a toy and used it to seek out boys, each slightly more dangerous than the last. This one was the most dangerous.

He was a man, compared to the boys in high school, but not nearly someone's father. Just a young man, not long out of high school himself, but with his own place — a shack, really — that he had decorated with pinups of long-haired singers and antlers of the deer he had killed. Until Sylvie had appeared, he had lived in his skin as if it were a dark blanket that never kept him quite warm enough. She had seemed to crawl under it, coaxing out of him new feelings of power and bravery. He had never felt anything as soft as her skin. She had never felt anything as thin as the thread that still remained between her innocence and experience. She played with this thread, as if she were a cat. Or maybe he was the mouse and she was the thread. She teased him with it.

She pushed him, she knew it — professing love, and then doubt, and then surrender, and then doubt of his love for her — and every time she did, he responded in an even more extreme way to show how much he loved her — screaming, throwing things, kicking walls — and naturally she had to keep raising the bar. The rising levels of adrenaline this created in her were exquisite.

That night, Sylvie had arrived at his place and they had fallen at once into a screaming fight. She followed him through the rooms, into the bedroom, where he had grabbed her arm and twisted it, and pushed her down on the mattress he kept on the floor. She felt cold and suddenly absent. He knelt on the floor and started kissing her, saying, "Oh baby, don't leave. You're mine, you're mine," and she felt warm again. This was familiar territory, saying "Yes, honey, yes," and letting herself surrender for a while, until she started reeling herself back in. He usually felt her pulling back and managed to stop. Every level of her surrender was that much more intense and sweet to him, and he was in no rush to push it. Somewhere in his brain he knew that when she finally let herself go completely, it would be total, and she would be completely his.

But tonight, he was different. He'd grown tired of this. Now when she pulled away, he rose onto the bed and pinned her beneath him.

"Get offa me," she yelled. When he finally pulled away, there was something cold in his eyes. He got up and stood over her.

"I've got plans for you," he said. "Get dressed. We're leaving."

"No."

"You wanna go by gunpoint?"

Even this didn't alarm her. She knew his gun. He kept it behind a small glass case and had taken it out and let her hold it once, and she was surprised at how light it felt, how oily the surface of the barrel was. It was pretty too, with an intricately carved forest scene on its butt. He was proud of it, and held it tenderly, like a baby.

She got up. Part of her thought of how much better all of this would have been if there were people around. Like if he had screeched up in his car to Daz's and removed her forcibly from the booth, maybe carrying the rifle. Her mind played out that scene for a while. It seemed a shame all of this was happening with no audience.

"Well, let's go, then. But I've gotta make a call first," she said.

"Forget it," he said.

"Okay, so my mom'll have the police out."

He didn't stop her when she went past him into the kitchen. As she dialed Daz's number, she counted the empty beer cans on the counter. There were eight.

When she hung up, he said, "Get in the truck. We're going."

"Okay," she said, trying to sound as if she was looking forward to it. "But let's take my car. I don't want to ride around in that truck of yours. It hurts my butt." With a tiny sliver of sense, she thought she'd be safer in her own car, somehow. At least her mother knew her license plate number. She threw him the keys and held her breath, seeing if he'd reach for them. He did.

"You go start the car, okay? I've gotta pee."

She listened for the sound of the motor starting and called Daz's again. She hung up quickly when she heard the door slam and his steps coming up the porch, coming to get her.

They drove for a long time. At first she acted mad, screaming "Let me go, you bastard," because she knew it was expected. But she was still excited, and she would have been insulted if he had listened to her.

But they had been driving for more than an hour, and he had long stopped answering her pleas. It was his utter silence that finally unnerved her, her inability to provoke even the slightest response.

"Please," she said softly. "Just tell me what we're doing."

"I'm not bringing you home. I'm driving until we cross the state line. And you know what happens then?"

"No."

"The minute we cross the state line, you're mine. You have no choice. We're married. Automatically. We don't even need a ceremony. Because of your age."

She thought this sounded true. She was barely sixteen. The thought of being married was somehow more frightening than anything.

"You're mine. So just say it."

"No."

"Say it."

"No."

He lifted his arm and she cowered. She curled herself up on her side of the seat and started whimpering. "Take me home now. Please. Come on. Please."

"Too late," he said. "Look."

She looked out the window at the sign announcing the state line. He drove past the sign, then screeched to a halt, pulling up to the side of the road, a foot from the sign.

He looked over at her. He wanted her to be happy, to be excited as he was over the prospect of really belonging to each other. But she wasn't happy; she was crying, with wet heaving sounds that hurt his ears, and for a second he was disgusted by the sound, wanted to be far away from its source. Yet the bleakness of that option — without her, there was more blackness — frightened him, renewing his fury. As he raised his arm again, he felt himself grow larger and larger inside until it seemed she was a small thing on the ground, miles below him. He heard her whimpering his name, and he grew larger inside until he knew the only way he could bring himself back to size was to strike her. His arm came down and the last thing he heard from her before her head slammed back on the door handle was his name. It was a sound contained in the exhalation of a breath, sounding like a whisper between lovers, sounding like something joyous and satisfied. You could hear it yourself by taking a deep breath and expelling it between clenched teeth as you open your mouth. Do it now. Inhale. Exhale. What do you hear? That's right: Zan.

Zan was sitting in the dark on wet grass at the edge of a thick stand of trees, three feet from the car. He was blank, with no memory, nothing. Sylvie was in the car, not moving.

He thought of what to do next. She was just lying there, heavy, like a deer he had brought down. That comforted him somewhat, that thought, since he could order his mind into familiar, methodical territory: rope and knots and equipment.

He thought of the early gray mornings when he went out hunting, with no one else around, the gun as natural and familiar to him as one of his arms. He was always cold out there, until, on those mornings he was lucky, he'd find a deer in his scope and drop it cleanly. He was a pretty good shot, but sometimes his shot would wound the animal instead of killing it instantly. He hated to admit it, but he was always slightly relieved when he came upon it and found it shuddering and scrabbling for its last breath. He'd place his hand on its body and feel its warmth travel into him. He never felt warmer than at those moments, feeling the deer's pulse still pumping feebly inside of it, at the same time its hot sticky blood spread outside, covering his hand. At those moments, Zan believed that some balance had been achieved, as if for an instant the world had righted itself.

He was cold now. He thought of going back into the car, and thought of Sylvie. She hadn't moved and he hadn't touched her.

He hadn't touched her, he told himself.

He started driving again. At one point, he leaned over and rolled Sylvie's window down; maybe fresh air would rouse her. He drove for hours, through the rising light, feeling chilled by the early morning breeze through the window. He kept his eyes straight ahead on the road, driving fast but carefully, watching the outlines of the trees and signs as the road moved from dark shadows to silvery gray. He was far from home, but after a while things started to look familiar again, and he realized he had driven in a large circle and was heading back into Nile Bay.

He drove around town slowly, looking at the buildings and the houses and the stores, concentrating on them, as if he were going to be asked to describe them to a stranger. Finally, he took a turn that led to the river.

He pulled off the road, turned off the car and suddenly felt exhausted. His head fell onto the steering wheel and he fell into a light scratchy sleep, his ears open for the sound of movement next to him. A while later, he woke groggily, and, as if his dreaming had just begun, he turned the ignition back on. He put the car in gear, aimed it straight down the bank, and drove into the river.

It was odd. Everything was the opposite of what it should have been. His foot was hard on the gas pedal, pressed to the floor, but the car was moving slower and slower, floating on the surface of the water, drifting out into the deep part of the river. When his foot went to the brake, that didn't work either: now the car went faster, picked up by the current. He tried to steer, but rather than veering right or left, the car started sinking.

Saving yourself from a sinking car is nearly impossible: if the windows are up and the car is airtight, the water seeps in gradually, and you buy some time. But to do what? Naturally, the great weight of water prevents you from opening the door. And if you roll the window down too quickly, the car fills with water with such speed that you have little chance of negotiating the opening.

As the water began filling the car from Sylvie's open window, Zan was shocked by the instant familiarity of its taste and smell, as the dank soup of mud and plant life and fishes filled his mouth. It brought him back to summers, fishing and smoking, and he remembered when he tried to drown the fish he had caught, and he nearly laughed now with the idea of it, the jerky little boy he had been. It was the thought of himself as a boy that suddenly roused in his brain an instant of panic. He saw a small boy on a riverbank, precarious, about to fall in, and he thought how he might save him. He fought for a second, his arms reaching out, his legs kicking.

Then he was moving, rolling with the pitch of the banking car, toward Sylvie, and the last thing he was aware of was her hand reaching up to him, and he thought with relief, *Oh, she's okay*, as the idea of escape bubbled to his surface. But now her arms, her hair, came floating toward him, to envelop him, languorously, rapturously, in the total sweet submission he had always dreamed of.

He closed his eyes, torn, as we so often are, between survival and surrender.

chapter 9

TIME IS A BEAST uncommonly schooled in the nuances of torture.

A thin-lipped and penurious maiden in the company of happiness, embarrassed at the flounces and flourishes of joy's light heart, time curtly shoos it all out the door as quickly as possible. At these moments, memory often intercedes, with its maddening ability to encase pleasure in amber. As memory's fiercest enemy, time does its best to erode these small fossils of joy, these shiny pellets of delight, these hardening nuggets of rapture.

Time loves only one thing: disaster. In disaster's presence, time becomes expansive, elastic, accommodating. It welcomes it in, makes it feel at home, helps it unpack its bags of grief and sorrow. When disaster arrives, time turns life into a slow, painful dance that never seems to end.

In Sylvie's case, time was exquisitely cruel: it disguised disaster's arrival, so that it appeared as a false moment of bliss. When the truth became known, that moment of bliss would always be recalled with shame.

And so the girls opened their eyes on Sunday morning, still keyed up at their adventure of the night before. They called each other, and were delighted to find that no one had yet heard from Sylvie. This was a gift: an extension to the usual length of such dramas. It was like getting three hours added to curfew.

They used the time well, lying in their beds, poking at the hole in the atmosphere Sylvie had created by her daring departure. They dreamed of transforming their lives. They snapped and snarled at their mothers, who tried to rouse them into the kitchen for healthy breakfasts. They were irritated at any interruption of their morning's work: mentally building perfect little altars at which to worship their new heroine.

By that afternoon, the rumors began: someone had heard from Sylvie. She was in the city with her boyfriend. She was in the city without him. She was alone in her car, heading to California. Each rumor grew more elaborate, so by that evening she was surrounded by a halo of gold and ruled a small country of the left behind.

By Monday morning worry arrived. Not a single gloating phone call from Sylvie had been confirmed. No one believed she could be on a true adventure and keep silent about it. Just as she had moved from humiliated to desired, Sylvie now moved from escaped to something more ominous: disappeared.

Speculation focused on her mystery suitor. Was he real? Did he exist? Many thought not, and still held to the theory that Sylvie had struck off on her own, as a way to get attention. They believed that she wouldn't bother calling until everyone was good and riled up. Sylvie, after all, had her own exquisite sense of timing.

Others believed the worst — that she was shacked up in some sordid place, enjoying herself with a man. Picturing her in a motel room with a stranger, they believed she had simply written the next inevitable chapter of her life, written it boldly as if those thick black eyebrows of hers had become Magic Markers.

Elegia was of this school, for no other reason than that Sylvie's mother, Gloria, was among the more flirtatious of Dr. Jack's patients.

"Poor thing," she said, referring to Sylvie's mother. "But. Does the fruit fall far from the tree? We'll see."

Dr. Jack, to whom she had confided this, had given her a strange look over the set of gums he was at that moment scraping.

Hours passed. The girls — Danielle, Cookie, Novena, and the others who had been drawn into the night's adventure — huddled together, nervously smoking cigarettes, sorting through their growing and knotted skein of worry.

It was Tuesday. Sylvie was gone, and probably not on a glorious adventure, as they had imagined on Sunday. They were afraid, not so much over the harm she might have come to — no one could spend more than an instant imagining those possibilities, and they were young enough to see actual danger as something far in the distance, like age — but over who Sylvie might be when she finally returned to them. It wouldn't be the old Sylvie, they were sure. She'd be smudged and stained with new experience, one whose peril was marked not by actual danger, but by its proximity to the territory usually inhabited by adults, one that they would now have to measure themselves against.

A weight had settled upon them. Not the weight of loss, or grief, but of nostalgia. It seemed like years ago that they had been breathless and excited over Sylvie's departure — egging her on! flirting with boys as they drove around pretending to look for her! delirious with the possibilities! Now they thought, God, we were such babies. That had only been three days ago, and they already missed their innocence. And they were shamed by its loss.

For another thing, they felt a growing distance between themselves and their boyfriends that all of them shared but none of them could quite explain. It wasn't fear, exactly: unlike Sylvie's mystery man who had reached into the night and stolen her, their boys were known, and safely their own age. What's more, since summer's beginning, the boys had been nothing but adoring. The girls had basked in this adoration, had felt their allure expand and bloom into an infinite happiness. But now, overnight, this allure had seemed to shrink and shrivel up into something pinched and small.

On Wednesday afternoon, all these worries were buzzing like flies around Danielle's room, where she, Cookie, Shel, and Jaci had gathered. They were speculating for the hundredth time who Sylvie's mystery boyfriend could be. Danielle had suggested trying to eliminate the possibilities by making a list of all the boys that Sylvie had already gone out with. It was a long list.

"Derek. Remember him?" Danielle said, starting the list with the boy who had started it all, with the fight over her in the schoolyard.

"Oh God, what a geek," Cookie said; it hadn't taken long after being creamed in the fight that Derek's appeal had worn thin for everyone.

"What about Anthony?" Shel said, rolling her eyes.

"Ant Knee. Duh. What was she thinking?"

"Come on," Danielle said. "Let's not dish. This is serious."

"Bo Gant," Cookie said.

"Didn't you always think he was femme?" said Shel. "Oh, sorry, Jaci."

"Yeah, I wouldn't talk," said Jaci, who had been seeing Bo Gant for a few months. "Didn't you go out with LaChapelle? He's more of a girl than we are."

As the list of boys grew, Danielle had unconsciously scribbled their drawbacks next to their names. Now, looking at the list, she pictured a line of boys, a long parade of them in her mind. They all had the same face. She tried to remember her own boyfriend's face, but all she could conjure was his hands, and his tongue, and the sound of his voice in her ear. Even those things, she thought, were indistinguishable from the hands and tongues and sounds she had heard from other boys before him, and — she suddenly knew — from those that she would hear again and again, from even more boys, until she was quite old.

"Come on. It's not like any of us has the ideal perfect boyfriend anyway, when you think about it," she said, an edge to her voice.

Cookie was brooding too. It had been glorious, their power over boys these last months. But who felt qualified to calibrate it? Where were its limits? Especially when its source was some strange voodoo fabric spell, which had until now been harmless, even fun. Maybe, she thought, these spells were more complicated and mysterious than she had thought. Sure, they could make you adored. But they could also make you disappear.

Cookie had never had a thought this big, and she was both frightened and exhilarated by it.

"Huh, huh, huh, oh baby, baby, baby," she moaned in a guttural imitation of boy.

Jaci made a sound like a bark. She pursed up her lips in an exaggerated kiss.

"You're my special thing. You're always in my head, oh don't leave me, oh baby, I never felt like this."

"You're so soft," added Danielle in an exaggerated growl, remembering her own boyfriend's words in her ears. "You feel like cotton or a cloud or sumpthin'."

The girls gasped and squealed, hearing the very words their own boyfriends had said to them, just days ago. Then they had sighed, and had even swooned a little, but that was days ago. Ancient history.

At that moment, the girls felt as if they were all huddled on the same platform of artifice that was shuddering dangerously under them, about to collapse. The room was silent. The girls looked at each other. Something monumental was happening, which had nothing to do with Sylvie. They were all falling out of love at the same moment.

"Oh God," Danielle said, getting up. "I'm supposed to see Jake tonight. I don't want him near me. Those moony eyes of his. Ugh."

She went to her dresser and opened her underwear drawer. She rummaged through it and pulled out a scrap of blue oxford. Sewn into it was a ring from a pull-tab, a small triangle pulled from the lid of a takeout coffee cup, and a picture of a football. It had belonged to Jake.

"Give me a match, someone."

She lit the square and dropped it in the ashtray. The scrap smoldered, and a small flame burst. It burned for a minute, then went out, leaving a twisted clot of black ash and melted plastic.

"You know what?" she said. "I feel so much better."

Cookie pulled her scrap from her purse and added it to the ash-tray. It was a shiny piece of rayon, a swatch from a basketball uniform. She lit it, but it curled up rather than flaming, seeming to implode. Soon, it too had disintegrated.

"That's it," she said, her voice wavering slightly, watching the small plume of smoke trail into the air.

The girls, looking at the small pile of ashes, thought of Novena, who hadn't yet arrived. For an instant, they were fearful. Maybe they had gone too far.

"Who does she think she is, anyway?" said Danielle, not as much reading their minds as being one fifth of a single mind in the room, the part with speech. "Feeding us her scraps. Don't get me wrong. I like her, but isn't this whole Sylvie thing kind of because of her?"

And so, love unraveled in the passing of a moment. One minute a solid mass, the next minute, nothing more than one of a billion dispersed molecules lost in the ether. Love will do this. Girls seem to know it better than boys, or know it earlier. It's what makes them so anxious, makes them look for guarantees, for declarations, for proofs, for commitments. They think they can dry it, press it in a book, keep it. Silly girls.

Boys see love as something larger, heavier, more solid. To them, love is a boulder, perched on a hill, ready to roll down onto them. While a few seek it out because the weight of it gives them comfort, the majority of them do their best to stay out of its path.

And some, like the boyfriends of Danielle and Cookie and Jaci and the rest of them, are distracted and don't see it coming, and so are flattened by it, pancaked, smashed into bits.

Over the next few nights, Rick and Jake and Bo and Rod and the rest of the boys were not happy. Cut off, shut out, they huddled together in dark parking lots, staring out at nothing.

"Stupid bitch," Jake said.

"Who?" Bo said. He knew who, thinking of Jaci, but even saying her name gave him a sharp pain.

"All of 'em," Jake said, drinking deeply from a beer. "Every last one of them."

Novena felt the chill emanating toward her from her friends, and it scraped the ends of her skin. She began to feel some undefinable sense of blame directed at her. And she was also feeling guilty, as if some of that blame was justified. Her friendship with Sylvie had always been complicated. Although outwardly they acted like the best of friends, there was a wariness between them, a boundary between them of giver and receiver. Without Novena and that little scrap of oxford shirt, after all, Sylvie would have remained ill treated. Sylvie had tried to distance herself from that fact, even to the point of being the source of mild gossip about Novena, yet she was a little afraid of her too. Once Sylvie had become flush with her social success, she had given up Novena's talismans, though with such a flourish that Novena had never believed she had let go of them completely. It was this thought that gave Novena an idea of trying to find out who had taken Sylvie away.

On Thursday, Novena went to see Sylvie's mother. She knew she would probably find her alone. Since Sunday, Gloria had been hurling her rage and bitterness from her as if they were plates she was flinging against the wall. Friends and neighbors had been keeping their distance.

When Novena rang the doorbell, she stood waiting, half expecting a stream of objects to fly out at her. She steeled herself. But Gloria's anger had finally exhausted itself and had settled into a thick stupor of terror, which she was trying to keep lubricated with scotch. She heard the doorbell as a faint chime of a clock that marked another hour passed, and stayed in her chair.

Novena pushed the door open and found Gloria sitting with an empty bottle at her side. Novena called out softly.

"Shilvie?" Gloria said, trying to push herself up from the chair.

"No, it's me, Novena." Novena could smell a sharp metallic rot from across the room.

"Uh, Novena. Shilvie's not here." Gloria fell back heavily, her words sounding liquid and limp. "I spilled something."

Novena walked toward her and saw a dried brown bib of scotch on her dress. She looked up at Novena pleadingly, like a starving baby bird.

"Where's my Sylv? Where is she?"

"She'll be home soon," Novena said, feeling as if she were addressing a small lost child. "Let me make you some tea."

She went into the kitchen and took her time with the kettle. By the time she took the tea to her, Sylvie's mother was snoring. Novena put the tea down and sat across from her. She watched her for a while, thinking about what to do.

She knew what to do. She knew what to look for and even where to look, but now, given such a clear opening, she hesitated. Finally, she stood and headed toward the stairs leading to the second floor, to Sylvie's room.

This room always took Novena by surprise. Despite Sylvie's look of someone in constant chaos, her room was neat and orderly. Novena took in the bed, with two stuffed rabbits sitting on its white chenille spread, the small lavender-flowered wallpaper, the neatly placed padded pink jewel box on the bureau, the small framed picture of a meadow with the words of some psalm printed over the grass, the neat row of clothes hanging in the closet. She thought she had never seen anything so sad. She wished it were a chaotic mess, as if a storm of flung sweaters and stuffed animals and papers and shoes could create a force powerful enough to bring Sylvie back.

Novena sat on the bed for a minute, looking around. Then she got up and went to the closet. She ran her hand over the shelf. Nothing. She went to the bureau and opened the top drawer. Neatly folded underwear, nothing else. She opened the jewelry box and lifted the top. A small ballerina popped up, and twirled to a sugary tinkling song. Inside, she found nothing but two charm bracelets and a knot of earrings. The drawer of the wicker vanity, the small bookshelf, the hamper, all yielded nothing. She slipped her hand under the pillow and felt a small mound, figuring it to be Sylvie's nightgown. She pulled it out, fingered soft brown cotton turned gray with wear. Unfolding it, she saw a simple T-shirt, short sleeves, single pocket. On the pocket were two embroidered fish. They were swimming head to tail with each other, forming a circle. Novena stared at the multihued threads, as if to memorize each interlocking stitch. But she already knew them by heart.

She had embroidered them herself, last Christmas, for Zan.

Novena felt everything in her stop. Reason, logic, consciousness — those higher powers so easily thrown overboard at the first sign of trouble, as if they are only cheap adornments, weighing us down — left her. Now she simply moved. She stuffed the T-shirt into her bag and went downstairs and out the door without looking to see if Gloria had awakened. She walked all the way to Zan's, and only when she heard her own breath release in relief at seeing his truck in the driveway was she conscious of the fact that somehow, in the past ten minutes, she had stopped breathing altogether.

She approached his door quietly, listening for the sound of him inside. The overcast sky had darkened into a yellowish gray, and listening, she heard the leaves rattling in a breeze that sounded as if it might suddenly turn cold, despite the earlier heat of the day. Finally she knocked. She waited a long moment, and then pushed the door open. She called out Zan's name, her voice sounding loud and false, and she hesitated before stepping inside, as a vestige of an alarm about entering a place that belonged to him fluttered against her heart like small black wings.

Although she had been here a few times, usually with Elegia, she was immediately struck with the gloom of the place, even after switching on the light. The living room was small and drab, in muddied browns and greens. And although there was a tidiness to the place, a spare order of solitude, it had a mildewy feeling, as if the walls, the furniture, the rugs were getting ready to sprout a thin coat of fur.

She looked in the bedroom, in the small spare room, and headed toward the kitchen. He wasn't here. But his absence didn't mean anything. He could be anywhere. He could be on his way home, right now.

When she flipped on the light in the kitchen, the weak, greenish-yellow glow of the overhead fluorescent illuminated a horrible mess: crusted bowls, forks and knives strewn on the counter, an empty brown paper bag on the floor. A small green bowl sat turned over on the counter, surrounded by eight empty beer cans, and something in their demeanor — protective, yet belligerent — suggested prison guards. She stared at them, and realized what they surrounded wasn't a bowl. It took her a minute to recognize it, and while the edges of the thing became sharper and clearer, in that small moment she thought of how many things she made it out to be — a dish towel, a mound of paper, a small plant — before it finally revealed itself for what it was: Sylvie's green cap.

And still, she waited for it to become something else, willing it to become something else, some harmless thing that had nothing to do with Sylvie.

It didn't belong here. Sylvie didn't belong here.

She wondered how long she had been coming to see Zan in secret. Novena flushed, thinking that Sylvie had probably been here more often than she had. Novena pictured her moving through these rooms, inhabiting this place, and she felt a sudden sharp irritation with her. What had Sylvie been thinking? What was she doing with Zan?

She was sure Sylvie was not serious about him. She knew Sylvie too well, knew she would find an entanglement with Novena's own brother some delicious and perverse trick, one magnified by its secrecy. It would be nothing more than a novelty that would quickly wear off, even quicker than the spell of Zan's T-shirt.

And now Novena grew more annoyed as she thought how Sylvie had used this alchemy to captivate Zan. It felt to Novena like a gauntlet, like some revenge Sylvie had enacted to readjust the power between them. Sylvie had taken something of Novena's — her own work, an innocent embroidery — and corrupted it.

And then, she had taken Zan. Taken him somewhere far, to the point of disappearance. It dawned on Novena that this is what had happened: Sylvie had taken Zan. It was her car that was gone. For some reason, this relieved Novena. Something told her that if Sylvie were driving, they would be back.

She now stared at the counter, willing the arrangement of the beer cans and hat to somehow confirm this. They gave up nothing, though, but a stale yeasty smell that turned her stomach.

Stuffing the hat in her bag, she left the house and began walking home. It was almost dark. There was a storm coming in: the leaves were now rattling against each other furiously, and black clouds were racing over the darkening sky. By the time she reached her street, the light had turned odd, in that eerie moment before a storm when the world is suddenly blanched of all light, all sound. She walked up the stairs in the stillness before the first violent crack of lightning. She went into the house and up to her room. She lay in her bed in the dark, waiting for the sound of thunder.

chapter 10

THE THUNDER CAME that night, with rain that pelted the earth with large spitting drops, quickly turning everything sodden. Hour after hour it poured, into the next morning and afternoon. Trees bowed under the weight of the water, streams of runoff ran down the streets and the river swelled in a muddy churn that turned it a reddish brown and threatened to spill its banks. Right before it did, Sylvie appeared.

Her body suddenly broke the surface of the water, and the strong raging currents pulled it downstream until her thick hair tangled itself around a low branch near shore and held her there, bobbing gently against a boulder. One of the old men who swore the fishing was best in the rain was the first to see her, and by four o'clock, the riverbank was a sea of yellow slickers. She was removed from the water, wrapped in black tarp and taken away in an ambulance. Then the crowd, feeling the second act of some horrid play unfolding, watched as four divers submerged, then surfaced. They had found the car, but it was tough going getting it out. Lines were attached to it, and a heaving pulley which screamed noisily with its effort dragged the car slowly up, until it popped to the surface like a dumb metal creature. The crowd aahed in spite of itself. The car was hoisted onto the bank. Draped with grass and plants and a fine layer of silty mud, it looked exhausted, as if it had swum too many miles.

·   ·   ·

Novena was in the kitchen with Elegia when the call came. Elegia had answered the phone, and after a moment, she turned and looked at Novena as she started saying, over and over, "Oh no."

"Oh no. Oh that poor thing. Oh."

Elegia had turned from her and was listening now, clucking and shaking her head into the phone.

A minute passed before she hung up and moved toward Novena. Her right hand was rapidly patting her chest, near her heart, as if gesturing to the location of this news, the depths from which it was coming.

"Novena, honey, bad news," she said. "It's Sylvie. They found her. In the river. They just pulled her car out."

Novena had been sitting, staring at her, not moving, but suddenly roused herself.

"What else? Tell me. What else?"

"Well, they don't know much at this point. They think she's been there all this time. She must have spun off the road. Driving too fast. You kids think you'll live forever. Her poor mother."

Elegia thought of Gloria, and it moved her to reach for Novena, to put her hands on her shoulders. Imagine losing someone like that. She couldn't bring herself to think about it. Instead, she scanned this disaster, making sure she had no place in it before she allowed herself a common thought of survivors, one which they never admit to having: She's dead, but I'm here. Tragedy happens, but it has passed my house again. I have lived the righteous life that has delivered me again from danger.

"Is that all?" Novena said, jumping at Elegia's touch. "Was anyone with her?"

"With her? Who would be with her? Oh, you mean the kidnapping tale. No, she must have made up that whole story. Well, she was always one for drama, wasn't she?"

The weird choking sound that suddenly came out of Novena startled Elegia; it was so abandoned, it almost sounded, she thought, like a laugh, an exclamation of joy. But Novena had gulped it back in, and now she was making little gasping sounds, as if fighting for breath. As Elegia lifted her hand to smooth Novena's hair, she heard the rawness in the sound, and felt a shameful tremor of joy as she thought, *Now, after all these years of waiting, she finally needs me.*

And Elegia, preparing to bend down, to gather the girl to her tightly, said, "I'm sorry, honey. I know it must be terrible to lose a friend like Sylvie."

Novena brushed her hand away and looked up at Elegia, surprised at the mention of Sylvie. What about Zan? What about her own son?

The phone began ringing again, and Elegia moved to it.

"Oh, Nora, it's you! Did you hear?!"

Novena listened to Elegia's voice rising in excitement, telling the news. She was telling the story of Sylvie. Not the story of Zan. Then Novena remembered: Elegia didn't know that one yet. No one did, except for her.

But in the next phone call, or later tonight, or tomorrow, when they found him too, the story of Zan would come. Zan had drowned with Sylvie.

And she didn't have to scan the face of this disaster to find herself there. She had practically brought them together. Maybe they'd both be alive if it wasn't for her. Now she felt her heart cracking open, and in its opening, it seemed to reveal another smaller heart, and that smaller heart opened to an even smaller one, and now all three of them were thrumming with such wildly chaotic rhythms that she could not catch her breath, and she thought for a moment she might perish.

Blackness was descending, but she was aware of a small white space in the middle of it that held nothing, that was nothing but stillness. And so this is what she focused on to steady her — on white, on nothingness — as she pushed herself up and moved out of the kitchen, up to her room.

She lay on her bed, willing this whiteness to fill her, to spread through her like milk, blotting everything else out. She would lie here until she was nothing but body, nothing but empty space.

A while later, Elegia knocked on her door.

"Novena, honey, here's some tea. Open up," she called.

Novena stirred but made no sound.

"Sweetie, let me in. Some nice tea."

No answer.

"Okay, I'll leave it by the door," Elegia said, now irritated. She had imagined comforting Novena, smoothing her hair back from her tear-stained face, Novena maybe putting her arms around her in gratitude. But as usual, nothing ever happened the way she wanted it to.

On her way back downstairs, she thought there was something wrong in Novena's silence; she should be crying. It would only be natural. She tried to remember the last time she had heard the girl cry. Now she wondered if she ever had.

She paused in the middle of the stairs, considered going back up to her, but then the phone was ringing again, and she ran down to it, eager for more news, eager for another thread of the story that she could then take as her own and weave into the long communal chain stitch of disaster.

Novena, lying on her bed, heard the phone and sat up to listen, as she would for the next few days, alert to the cadences of Elegia's voice, waiting for it to rise in distress, and then higher, into wailing. Each time the phone rang, she would tense up, then wait, then relax.

Six times over the next hour, her muscles contracted and released, waiting for the call.

It never came. Finally, the thought occurred to her that maybe she had been wrong. Maybe they hadn't been together. Maybe she'd gotten it all wrong. Maybe he was home now.

She got up and, creeping downstairs, listened to make sure

Elegia was on the phone. At the front door, she called, "I'm going out," and then she was outside, and running.

It took her seven minutes to get to Zan's.

This time, she didn't call out, but she did pause at the door for a small beat, to make herself ready in case he was in there after all, in case she had gotten the story all wrong. Then she pushed it open and went in.

She knew immediately he wasn't there. The place had a sullen, undisturbed air, and she was surprised that it had not somehow been transformed, for its gloom to be rearranged to reflect Zan's loss. But here it all was, unchanged by either his presence or his absence: the small shelf with a few thin books, mostly outdoor manuals, the antlers mounted on the paneled wall, the tired carpeting, the squat, slatternly chairs.

The gun, with its dully gleaming barrel, was the only thing that suggested anyone actually lived there. The rest of it had such a generic feeling. It was the house of anyone, or of no one, at least no one familiar, no one she recognized as connected to her.

She kept moving, looking for some sign of him, conscious that she was looking for something that would transform her too, for something in her to rearrange itself to reflect his loss. But she was as blank as these rooms. She was having a hard time even picturing his face.

In the bathroom, a white towel hung on its rack, a square of white soap on a chrome dish. A bottle of dandruff shampoo sat on the edge of the bath, and Novena found herself strangely moved by this small intimacy, a confession of an imperfection.

She didn't even go into the spare room; she could see from the doorway it was empty except for some taped-up cardboard boxes.

Finally, she went to his bedroom. Immediately, she felt some stronger trace of him here, in the combination of the atmosphere and a fusty, cooped-up smell, as if he was keeping his essence locked away in this single room. His room.

She switched on a small lamp on his bureau, and a small dish on top glittered with a jumble of coins, nails, and odd keys. She saw the tangled sheets on the bed, and she forced her eyes to slide away.

Then she went to the closet and pulled open the door, and she was almost knocked off balance by a sudden rush of him. It was as if the clothes hanging there — shirts and pants and a few outdoor jackets — had let out a single long, sour breath of Zan.

As the scent of him filled her nostrils, she stepped back, overwhelmed by its familiarity, almost as familiar as her own. It *was* her own, in a way, and she felt she should be able to identify the individual strands of that smell that might belong to her, to each of them — Elegia and Wyn and the boys. And yet, at the same time that the particular and intense smell of Zan pushed at her insistently, she felt a strong impulse to stop breathing, to keep any more of him from reaching her nostrils, and then to run from the room and keep running, away from here.

She stood there, unable to move, confused and wavering, like a plant drawn blindly to light, yet repulsed by some darkness hidden there, under the light. Distinct but disembodied parts and aspects of him were floating up the channels of memory, and began to appear to her: His mouth, with lips that managed to look both grim and greedy. His feet, surprisingly small for his size. His height, his shadow, the way his clothes hung, as if no body inhabited them, despite the bulk underneath.

Then something else came to her. She heard Sylvie's voice, on the phone that night:

He says he's going to kidnap me.

Novena heard her own voice, announcing it to everyone at Daz's: *She says he's taking her away.*

Although the girls had swooned at that thrilling news, no one had really believed it had been anything but one of Sylvie's wild tales, easy to dismiss. Even now, no one believed it. But the minute they found Zan and pulled him from the river, it was going to be the truth.

Zan had taken Sylvie, had stolen her. That would be the story.

He had been born for this kind of trouble, after all. Everyone knew it, knew what he was capable of. It wouldn't matter what really happened that night. It wouldn't matter that Zan had drowned too. In fact, she could imagine a certain relief, a collective delirium at a tragedy made so satisfyingly whole, so complete.

She had a sudden picture of being at home with Elegia and Wyn and the boys, all of them huddled together, trying to grieve for Zan while the people of Nile Bay threw stones at the house, at their windows. She could hear the windows rattling, the dull thud of those stones against the house, could imagine the house trembling under the weight of them, trembling as if it would fall down. This would be the final sound of Zan. A sound of ruin.

There would be no sorrow for him. There would only be blame. There would only be trouble that would stain them all.

She shut the closet door, suddenly overwhelmed with the smell of him, and left the bedroom. She walked through the kitchen, and noticed that the stench of the trash had grown more intense, as if she had unleashed all the bad smells in the place. She pushed open the door and stepped outside. She stood on the porch, taking in the cool night air in a rasping convulsive breath, like a sob.

The light was leaving quickly, and she looked out into the yard, at the shapes of trees and low bushes emerging from the darkness. The hum of insects carved out their own shapes in the dark, and as her eye searched out each punctuating *crick*, she caught sight of Zan's red truck, sitting on a wide patch of dirt.

The idea of escape, the idea of driving fast, out of town, glimmered in front of her. She went back inside and grabbed his keys from the table.

The truck had a nasty smell when she opened the door and slid onto the driver's seat — a feral aroma of blood and fur, thick as paste. An old cap was lying on the seat, and she put it on her head, to hide herself, and turned on the ignition.

As soon as she heard the engine roar up, she realized she didn't know how to drive this thing. She was barely used to driving, and this truck was so foreign, the wheel big and awkward in her small hands, the cab so large, the pedals so far to reach.

Inching the thing forward, she managed to pull out of his driveway, and onto the road. The truck bucked and shimmied as she focused on maneuvering the wheel and pedals and gears, and she knew that she would never be able to go fast, to get the speed she wanted. But still she kept driving, slowly and carefully, and made it to the center of town.

A little more confident, she kept driving. She drove past the river, through the streets lined with neat houses and their smugly lit windows, and then into the back roads that wound up into dark wooded hills, out of the center of town. Up here the roads were narrow, and she pulled over and parked, exhausted with her effort of keeping the truck steady.

She looked around her. The houses were more sparse and pinched, sitting on scratchy lawns, the houses of hard lives. No one she knew lived up here. People Zan knew lived up here. Girls he knew, probably. Not that she had ever seen him with girls — she couldn't even remember when she had seen him last — although she suddenly recalled a heavy blond girl in the woods a long time ago, her legs like the trunk of a birch. She pictured this girl and others — hard, brittle, skinny girls, girls who had been damaged already and would find a kind of familiar solace being with someone like Zan.

Not girls like Sylvie. Not even girls like herself.

It struck her now how little she thought of herself in relation to him. For years, she hadn't had to. Whatever Nile Bay thought of Zan, it had always remained curiously at ease with keeping this separate from what they thought of the rest of his family.

Small towns often make troublemakers their unofficial orphans: they belong to no one; no one is to blame. Plenty of nice families harbor black sheep, troubled souls, bad sorts; it's generally acknowledged that it isn't their fault. Some families appear almost saintly, as if they had been assigned these burdens from God himself.

And while Zan had often flirted with the line between black sheep and something more menacing, to Nile Bay she had always been Novena, taken for herself. But soon she would become Novena, the girl related to Zan, who had taken Sylvie. She would be the girl who had brought them together, and then had kept the fact secret. And she would be the girl to blame for this disaster.

She would become an outcast. All her friends would shun her, and the town would turn against her. She'd be reviled. Just like him.

And then she pictured becoming just like Zan. She pictured moving into his shack, taking over that fusty place, living in his solitude, watching his mildew grow on the walls, the spread of his dirty dishes around her. Sleeping in that bed, with mussed-up sheets, living among that sad furniture. Driving his truck.

She shuddered as she thought, *This* truck.

And then, some recognition of how strange these thoughts were made her flush. She was ashamed at herself, at how small she was being. Zan was dead, and she had not even had a moment of grief for him. All she could think about was herself, and escape.

The recognition shook her. Some part of her she hadn't known about, some monstrous part of her that was removed from grief, from all goodness, had just poked its head above the surface. It had dived deep again, out of sight. But it was enough to make her wary, to think that she was going to have to be alert, to watch herself for signs of it.

She started the truck again, considering where to go next, when she had an unexpected thought of Elegia. She pictured her down there in one of those houses below her, answering the phone, and then collapsing in grief. Novena would be the first person she would reach for, to lean on. It would be terrible to leave Elegia now, when she was about to lose so much.

And so, the idea of escape drained from her, Novena forced the truck, bucking and shimmying, back to Zan's house, where she left it in the driveway and walked home.

By the time she reached her own street, she tried to be prepared for the worst — for Elegia collapsed in hysterics, for Wyn to be sitting in his chair, sunken in and fretting. She pictured the lights blazing, a crowd gathering.

The house looked calm enough; there was no hint of any particular brightness from the lit windows. She noticed that the driveway was empty, and thought it was a good sign that Wyn wasn't home yet.

She stood on the porch for a moment, heard nothing from inside. She took a deep breath and, pushing the front door open, listened, alert for the noise of Elegia.

The noise of Elegia was a whirring motorized sound, which, by the time she reached the kitchen, Novena recognized as the sound of the electric mixer. Elegia was standing facing the counter, steadying a bowl as it revolved around, and she was humming. On the counter next to her were two cakes, still in their pans.

Novena stood for a moment, watching her.

Just wait, she thought. Just wait.

But it was a sad thought, not a mean-spirited one; in fact, something in the slope of Elegia's shoulders moved Novena to go over to her.

At the sound of her step, though, Elegia had whirled around.

"Where have you been?" she cried. "I've been so worried. People have been calling."

"What's going on?" Novena said, forcing her voice to stay calm.

"Gloria's taking it hard. I'm making a cake to take over in the morning."

"Any more news?"

"Well, how much more news do you want for one night?" Elegia said sharply, turning back to her bowl.

At Elegia's sharp tone, Novena almost turned to leave the

kitchen, but then she paused. She moved to Elegia and kissed her cheek and said softly, "Thanks for the tea."

Elegia, who should have been struck delirious by the kiss, felt oddly jangled. It had been a casual little peck, a soft brush of the lips, yet it was so shocking that for the rest of the night, she kept touching the spot on her cheek, as if it had left a stain.

They didn't find Zan on Saturday. Novena went back to his house late in the afternoon and cleaned. She threw the empty beer cans away. She washed encrusted dishes, emptied the trash, cleaned out the refrigerator. She scrubbed counters and windows, and floors, walls, cabinets, and doors. At one point, on her knees scrubbing the bathroom floor, she thought of a saint, washing the feet of sinners or lepers.

They didn't find him on Sunday either. Novena stayed around the house, listening for the phone, which rang constantly but brought no news. Still, she said nothing.

They buried Sylvie on Monday. It had continued to rain on and off for days, and the ground was heavy and swollen. Had Sylvie called for so much water, to remind them all of what she had been lost to? Rivers of it ran down from roofs, poured from gutters, doused windshields. So much water, as if it weren't enough that Sylvie had been filled with it, swelling each subcutaneous layer, warping and distorting her beyond human recognition. She was not pretty in death. Even the undertaker had been ill when they brought her to him.

At the cemetery, the mourners stood in the cold drizzle, Gloria now stunned into a boneless passivity. The girls were weeping. The boys were quiet, staring at the pile of dirt around the grave, unconsciously measuring its height, trying to keep their eyes from measuring the depth of the hole from which it had been dug. At the end of the service a rain of objects was thrown down into the grave: flowers and yearbooks and key chains, a stuffed animal, a locket, a folded-up note. They walked away slowly, each boy and girl, as they threw down their offerings, and then the rain covered it all, and Sylvie was underneath again, underwater, underground.

During the service, and at the reception afterward, Novena had tried to stay in the circle of her girlfriends, holding on to them as if some of their sorrow might be transferred to her. She felt nothing, though, but a desire to be far from the girls, far from the noise of their grief.

As she moved through the hushed, whispering clots of mourners at Gloria's, she was struck by the picture of Sylvie that was floating in fragments around the room like pieces of a torn-up snapshot.

A group of women, Elegia among them, were busy tending the trays of food. They were hissing Sylvie's name among themselves, shaking their heads at the fate of this fast girl, always a worry to her mother, and periodically throwing worried looks to their own daughters in the room.

Another group, mostly men, standing in the back room smoking, were now remembering the hard flash of Sylvie as a softer, shining thing, the light of an angel made alluring in death.

The sons of some of these men remembered that hard flash of her as something even harsher, something greedy that had once consumed them; these were the boys hovering around the food tables, clearing the trays of meat and rolls and cakes, stuffing their pockets with what they couldn't push into themselves.

Novena's own small group of friends were huddled together, holding each other. They seemed to recall nothing of Sylvie but her name, which they would call out in shocked little cries every few minutes, gripping each other's arms so fiercely that when they woke the next morning and saw the small marks on their upper arms, they would stare at them curiously, wondering where they had come from, wondering if they were stigmata of their grief for Sylvie.

But in a far corner of the room, another group of girls were conjuring a more pathetic vision of Sylvie — her younger, more eager-to-please, desperate-for-attention self. With unbecoming triumph, they recalled the girl who had been treated badly by boys. They were whispering that Sylvie's mystery man had never existed. That she had been so desperate she had made him up and then had drowned herself in humiliation.

It was this last thing, whispered to Novena as she was getting ready to leave that she was most struck by — that Sylvie had made up her mystery man. That he didn't exist.

She thought of this as she made her way to Zan's house. She'd been going there every day since Sylvie was found, and today she was especially relieved to have a place to go, away from the noise of the girls' grief. But she also had the idea that this might be the last time she would be in his house. Sylvie's burial had marked some passage, and Novena was going to have to do something about Zan, although she had no idea what. It was already Monday, and there was still no sign of him. He'd been gone now for over a week.

No one in the world knew except for her.

She felt as if the world had shrunk into a tiny thing, a place holding only Zan and Novena. And she had the strangest thought then, that Zan had singled her out to be the only one in the world who knew the truth. That he had wanted it this way, had arranged his absence as a personal thing, something private, something only between them.

She thought again of what the girls said, and it struck her that it was true: Zan didn't exist. Nine days had passed, and no one had noticed he was gone. He was somewhere in the bottom of the river, and no one had even missed him. Everyone had been consumed with Sylvie, and Novena felt a sudden sharp irritation at her. What about Zan?

It dawned on Novena then, how lost he had been, long before this. She couldn't remember the last time Elegia had even mentioned his name. She couldn't even remember the last time she had seen him. And for an instant, Novena felt sorry for herself, for being like everyone else: disappearing him long before he actually vanished. No one, she realized, cared for him at all.

She resolved then to save him. She resolved to be the only one to love him. She would love him as if he were a monster, or the hunchback of Notre Dame, or the Beast loved by Beauty. She would love him as God did, for his tortured, persecuted soul. What love is purer or deeper than that, love that is, in itself, godlike, seeing beyond ugliness to a person's ultimate shining goodness?

She thought of the saints — their mutilations, starvings, gougings of their eyes or other body parts, which led to glorious miracles of salvation. It was something not far from a miracle that she needed, because somehow, before they found him, she was going to have to change him into someone else, separate from Sylvie.

Maybe she could perform a miracle. Why not? Who were saints, anyway, but people who had been touched by love and tried very hard, in all their actions, to be worthy of it?

Surrounded by this halo of almost perfect faith, she turned into his driveway. She stopped and took it in, and she gasped.

What she saw was such a perfect picture of someone at home — the truck next to the house, gleaming red under its mask of rainwater, the lamp she'd left on shining softly behind the drawn curtains — that she had, for an instant, imagined that Zan had come home. She stood for a long time, staring at his house, staring so intently that the outlines of it dropped away, and she was looking into some other place, seeing nothing. It was a familiar emptiness, the same whiteness that she had clutched to herself a few nights ago, willing it to fill her, to steady her. With a small shock, she recognized it for what it was: hope.

She was surprised to feel a vestige of hope, but she was more surprised she had confused it with emptiness.

Then again, as the last thing left, hope always finds itself residing next to nothing. But as the last thing left, hope itself is the opposite of emptiness. It is jammed, like an overstuffed closet, with all those things that it never throws out — fancies and speculation, lies and vanities, the misguided and the worn out, the foolish and the half baked. Because at the very end, anything might be cobbled together — a delusion patched to a tiny shred of faith, taped to a certain blindness — to form a brilliant idea. An idea with wings. An idea to save yourself.

Anyone coming up the driveway would assume Zan was in there, walking around oblivious of everything that had happened, oblivious even of Sylvie. Why wouldn't he be?

Then Novena was moving, across the yard and into the house, where she picked up his keys, took the hat off the peg, and pulled on an old raincoat that was hanging next to it. She left the house, letting the screen slam behind her, and got into the truck.

This time, when she turned the key and the engine roared to life, she felt it in her stomach, in a satisfying surge of power, and so confidently did she shift into reverse, and so smoothly did she drive out onto the road that it might have been Zan driving.

It might have been Zan — she was wearing his clothes, his cap. She was driving his truck — driving fast, with no fear. But it was not with the idea of escape, or even of speed. She was driving through the streets of town — up Main, down Maple, across Elm, across Oak — picturing the truck being seen, being registered, being remarked upon, like a red banner weaving its way throughout Nile Bay: the banner of Zan. A sign that he existed.

She drove by Check's, and although the windows were dark, she had a picture of him, standing at the counter, watching the truck pass.

Then it was tomorrow or the next day, it was someday in the future, when Zan had finally been found, and Check was pouring coffee for the regulars, shaking his head and saying in that stunned bewilderment of the left behind:

"Geez, and I just saw his truck the other night."

She cocked her ear now, as if listening to a story tell itself. A story of Zan, still alive right now, driving his truck. Maybe people noticing him, maybe not. It didn't matter, because tomorrow morning they would find his truck abandoned — parked on the street, in the middle of town, somewhere noticeable — without him. They would notice, then, that he was gone. They would speak his name: There was Zan's truck. Where was he? Where was Zan?

And when finally the river spit him back up and he appeared, the mystery would be solved. Zan had drowned.

There would be no other mystery, though. No mystery to the fact that both Zan and Sylvie had died in the same way, a week or so apart. Just a sad coincidence. After all, Zan and Sylvie didn't even know each other. As far as anyone knew, they had never even met.

This was Zan, driving his truck.

This was Zan, driving all night until it was almost dawn, until the shapes and outlines of the world began emerging into the gray-lavender light.

And this was Zan, driving to the river and finding a spot that was not too conspicuous but not too hidden, parking the truck under a pine tree, then hurling the keys far into the water, watching until the ripples stopped and the water was calm again.

But it was Novena, walking home from the river in the rising light of day, who had been saved. It was Novena who had saved them all.

chapter 11

Here in this body, made up of five elements, what are earth, water, fire, wind and space? Here in this body, made up of five elements, what is hard is earth, what is liquid is water, what is hot is fire, what moves is wind, what is hollow is space. The earth gives support, the water holds the mass together, the fire illuminates, the wind distributes substances and the space provides room. . . .

. . . The head is composed of four sections, with sixteen spaces for teeth on each side, one hundred and seven vulnerable points, one hundred and eighty articulations, nine hundred tendons, seven hundred veins, five hundred marrows, three hundred and sixty bones and forty-five million hairs. The heart weights eight *pala*, the tongue weighs twelve *pala*, there is one *prastha* of bile, an *adhaka* of phlegm, a *kudava* of sperm, two *prastha* of fat and an undetermined amount of urine and excrement, depending on what has been consumed.

— "Upanishad of the Embryo"

WE ARE FINE ACCOUNTANTS of ourselves. Think of the billions of bodies that have been on earth, are on earth now, and consider how few are unaccounted for. Even when our dead are gone, we know precisely where they are — section D, row five, name chiseled in marble, or burned to ash and sitting up there on the mantel or spread over a favorite place, a few floating particles of them even inhaled by mourners, by all who pass through that atmosphere.

There are plenty of people who have disappeared, vanished, gone, escaped, and although their whereabouts may be unknown, they are at least known to be missing, which counts for something. Most eventually turn up, or their bodies do. Fingerprints are matched, if there is skin left; dental records are reviewed, skull shapes, bone lengths are all meticulously recorded, cross-matched, identified.

Of course, there are a few who will never turn up, who will lie forever in an infinity of hiding places: under rocks, in deep water, under deteriorating logs, in caves, in cars, in containers, burned to ash.

The police found Zan's truck the next morning. Rather, they saw Zan's truck, which was not an unusual sight, even seemingly abandoned, with no sign of him anywhere. It wasn't the first time his truck had been seen sitting somewhere it shouldn't have been — in the middle of a supermarket parking lot, at the side of the road, even on the riverbank. Zan would invariably show up a few hours or a day or so later, having been drunk, having been somewhere he shouldn't have been. Somewhere in trouble. So they paid no attention to it. They drove by it ten times that day.

After two days, they finally towed it away, to a lot in the back of the police station. They didn't bother calling Elegia. They had dealt with her hysterics before. It was easier just having the thing towed. They hadn't called her about Zan for years.

Boomer Verley was the only one who paid attention to it.

"Hey, you know this guy never showed up for his truck," he said after it had sat in the lot for two days. The other men waved their hands at him, shrugged, rolled their eyes to each other. Boomer was a rookie. A little soft, they thought. Their slight contempt for him was not because he was a newcomer to Nile Bay. In fact he was worse: a native who had left. He had only recently come back to join the force.

Boomer, who was not only a rookie but a romantic one, offered the possibility to his colleagues that Zan might have been heartbroken over Sylvie's death and thrown himself in the river, but the other men hooted at him, at the idea that someone like Sylvie — who to these men had become even more luscious in death — might be consorting with the likes of Zan. Maybe, Boomer persisted, he was one of the copycat suicides everyone read about.

Nah, the chief told him expansively, he was up to no good somewhere, and would turn up sooner or later in the wrong bed, or the wrong house, or the wrong alley.

On the third day, Boomer called Elegia.

He asked if she had seen Zan lately.

"What's he done now?" she said.

"Nothing, nothing," he said soothingly. "Except we found his truck a few days ago, and he hasn't been back for it since."

"Where was it?"

When he told her, she screeched.

"I've been out of my mind with worry!" She had known something was wrong. She had been trying to reach him for days, she said.

Later, at the station, she insisted they drag the river. They agreed, but reluctantly. The Nile Bay police force, all nine of them, had been jaded by the big doings with Sylvie. The crowds, the scuba divers, the cameras shooting the triumphant car retrieval, all had conferred on them an instant, swaggering expertise in all matters of violent and surprising death. They seriously doubted that they were lucky enough to have, in the short space of two weeks, the drownings of two unrelated people — floaters, they now called them out of the newly twisted-up corners of their mouths, although until two weeks ago, they had never seen one, nor even heard the term — and in fact suspected that there would be a spate of false alarms like this one, as if drowning would become for a while a fashionable parental concern over every child a half hour late to dinner.

But Elegia was hysterical, and so with her standing on the bank, holding tightly to Wyn's arm — Novena had refused to come — the divers went into the river. They turned up nothing. Of course, they didn't look too hard. It was more or less a cut-rate, bargain-basement, lick-and-a-promise dragging of the river.

They came out of the water and told Elegia to go home and get some sleep, he'd turn up, they always do, they were absolutely sure he wasn't there in the river, although they knew very well that the currents and the heavy rains could have dragged his body any-where. They also knew, but didn't say, that by now Zan could even have been dinner for some fish.

Zan eaten by fish would have had a perfect symmetry. It was easy to imagine him jammed under a tree trunk at the bottom of the river, nibbled at by bullheads and crayfish, possibly by a family of crayfish finally getting their revenge for his drowning of their children.

But he hadn't been jammed under a tree trunk. He hadn't gotten stuck under a rock. He hadn't even stayed in the river.

Zan had, in fact, ended up lying on a bed of nails, on a torturous pallet of broken glass and razor blades. This he had felt, rather than seen, since his eyes were closed, but he knew whatever he was lying on had punctured his skin and he had no blood left. All of it had seeped out and now he was a softened sack of unconnected bones and veins dried up and twisted like brambles. He was afraid to look. But he finally opened his eyes. He didn't see the razor blades or nails. He saw instead pine needles and stones. That was all. He closed his eyes again.

It hurt to breathe. He didn't think he would ever move again, which was fine, since he was becoming one with the soil anyway, sinking deeper and deeper into the ground until he would grow roots and be planted there. He hoped it would be soon; he was ex-traordinarily cold, and longed to be blanketed by something, even dirt. Then he fell into blackness again.

How many hours? Time had forgotten him, or had a weak moment of kindness, suspending itself for him. He woke finally, having no idea where he was, or even what he was. He finally opened his eyes, and this time they stayed open. He lay there feeling himself come back to life.

In fact, thirty-six hours had passed from his first broken moment of consciousness to the moment he managed to stand up. It was only when he became upright that some vague memory of being human stirred in him, and he greeted this not with jubilation or relief, but with a slight inner nod, an acknowledgment of classification of species, nothing more. He remembered he could walk, and he started moving.

It was dawn, and as he made his way from the river, things took shape with a watery familiarity, as if he were dreaming: the small run-down houses in the residential neighborhood near the river didn't look familiar, nor was he seeing them for the first time. They were just facts, and he was just a body moving through space, with no memory, no future. He walked slowly through the small quiet streets of houses, passing lawns where a few sprinklers lazily whisked back and forth like palm fronds, and he realized he was thirsty. Parched. He lay on the damp ground in one of the yards and tried to drink, but was only able to dampen his throat.

He reached the main road, which also took on the same character as the houses: he had never been here, but he knew his way around. He walked a few blocks, staying close to the plate-glass windows of the stores, and found an alley right before the very end of a row of stores. He ducked into it and went to the back of the building. He reached for a key hanging on a nail, unlocked a heavy green door, and let himself into Check's.

A few minutes later, he was cramming food into his mouth, bread and cheese and cold bacon. He gulped down some water. He stood in the dark, conscious of nothing but the sound of his bready chewing. He found a brown paper bag and threw in a loaf of bread and some of the contents of the refrigerator — cheese, ham, a few apples — and folded the top down in three neat folds.

On the third fold, he snapped into consciousness. He was standing in Check's in the dark. What was he doing here? What happened? Something terrible was happening. He felt it in his muscles. He was beginning to shiver. His stomach was churning now, grinding its contents. There was something wrong.

He stumbled out of Check's, carrying the bag. He was immediately disoriented. He was now on the side of the road, and two bright lights powered by a monstrous noise cut through the dawn and headed toward him. He fell to the ground and crouched down as it passed, overcome with the danger of these predators with lighted eyes, coming to get him.

He began to run, feeling relief, but not sure if it was because he was running toward something or away from it. Running past the houses and their sprinklers, toward the river, he found himself back in the woods. The scent of pine and the thick furry scent of skunk cabbage were familiar, made him feel safer, but he kept running. Faster and faster he ran, greeting rocks and trees as if they were one of him, an orbit of his friends and acquaintances propelling him forward, pointing his way, and when he reached the small wooden duck blind — nothing more than a wobbly hut perched on a cleared overlook where he and Check had spent many frigid mornings, waiting for ducks — he laughed with relief, as if greeting his family. He stumbled in and fell to the ground, exhausted from his efforts.

The blind was set on a high clearing over the river, with three sides, a roof, and a bench. Under the bench was an old metal cooler where they would store sandwiches to get them through a morning of hunting. Of course it was empty, but next to it, in a plastic bag, Zan found a sheet of foil-backed polyurethane, a space blanket, Check had called it. It barely helped in the autumn mornings and it barely helped now, but at least it was something, and he wrapped the crinkling thing around him and huddled under it, shivering.

He woke a few hours later. His tongue was thick, and he heard a rasping wheeze from the bottom of his lungs when he inhaled. His muscles ached. He was freezing, although his skin was damp with sweat. *Fever,* his conscious mind told him. He felt himself standing on the edge of it, looking in, and suddenly overcome with dizziness, he felt himself falling into it.

For the next two days, Zan rode the sickening waves of fever. Long thrashing cycles of sleep were interrupted by pain and delirium, at times his lungs gurgling as if he were underwater, at other times rasping as if there were nothing but dust in them. His throat was parched, but each time he imagined a glass of clear, cool water, it immediately became brackish, choked with plants and insects, and the image sickened him.

Chaos was roiling inside of him, his insides trying to heave themselves out of him. He was a village besieged: his skin burned in crackling flames, his heart raced through him looking for escape, his muscles pummeled furiously at his skin. His cells screeched horrifically, multiplying themselves, killing themselves off, multiplying again in panicked convulsions. His defeated lungs flapped uselessly, like tattered flags.

Years passed. A lifetime, three lifetimes, an eternity, all of world history, the beginning of time, centuries of darkness, miles of space.

Small pocks had erupted on his skin, like the eyes of potatoes, or the gills of fish. They emitted small moans and whimpers, opening and closing like small mouths, until he realized the only way he could keep them still was to stop breathing.

He held his breath and willed his heart to stop beating, willed his lungs to stop inhaling, for everything to stop.

For a long time he floated, almost serene.

When he opened his eyes again, it was dusk. His first thought was that he was dead, because he felt nothing but a clammy chill. The pain had stopped, and there was a quiet inside of him, as if all his organs had managed to make their noisy escape, leaving him just a shell. Then he heard a steady thudding rhythm coming from the center of his chest. He listened to it for a while. It grew louder and stronger until he realized it was coming from the ground beneath him.

There was a soft crash of branches nearby, and he smelled it first before he saw it: a deer had come through the woods, a medium-size doe, and was standing a few feet away, watching him coolly. They stared at each other, neither of them moving. He thought if he had his gun, he could shoot it and cover his body with the animal's warm carcass. He lifted his hand, pointing his finger at the deer, and whispered "Pow," loud enough to startle the animal. He watched the flip of its white tail disappear.

His gun. He owned a gun. It was the first memory that connected him to himself, and he reached out and grabbed it, holding on tightly. He owned a gun. He forced his brain to conjure its details, and painstakingly, picking through the shards of memory, his mind gave it form and shape. After a few hours, he could see it, could see the intricate carving on the butt, the smooth barrel, could even picture the case where it was now resting, but he couldn't remember where the case was. It was a perfect image floating there in his brain, untethered to anything. But it had been enough to pull him back into full consciousness.

He waited for the rest of his thoughts to line themselves up regimentally, but they began coming back in a jumble. He was alive. He had been sick, terribly sick, but he had pulled himself through, and knew this was an important fact. Something else that had been in him before had been expelled too; he could feel it, or rather, could feel an absence that he couldn't attribute to anything else, a distant memory of something bad. But he owned a gun. And a truck. He remembered he had a girlfriend. His family missed him, and he'd go back there too. His truck was red. His girlfriend was mad at him for some reason. He'd make it up to her, whatever it was.

He tried to sit up and managed to make it halfway, leaning against the side of the bench. He slowly opened the folded-over paper bag from Check's, and took two bites of bread. He held the bag of food on his lap, taking small chunks of bread and cheese, eating slowly, as if learning again. Then, bit by bit, he dragged himself up onto the bench, where he sat for a long time, wondering if he could remember how to stand.

He had never felt so weak, or so helpless, but to his surprise, there was something comforting in this fragility; it made him feel tender with himself, protective of his body. His bulk and massiveness had always given a thick luggishness to his movements, which had transported itself to his very brain, his speech, his beliefs, his heart. But the lightness that now filled his limbs made his movements feel almost elegant. There was air around him now, and in him; he felt hollowed out, pure. Ready to be filled up with something else.

Soon after, it began to rain. He listened to its soft hammering on the roof for a while, listened to it pelting the leaves, falling into the swelling ground. He finally stood up, weaving slightly, and slowly made his way outside, out of the shelter. The rain was light but steady, and he stood under it, letting it wash him. He opened his mouth to it, drank it in and let it stream over his face, and thought of himself being baptized.

Over the next twenty-four hours he felt himself gaining strength, and on Friday afternoon decided to see how far he could walk. He could now picture the details of his house and kept it in mind as he walked downhill, thinking with fondness about the three steps that led up to the screen door, the table in his kitchen, the case that held his gun. He moved carefully, and his step was light on the damp ground. Over him, the canopy of trees was thick, softening the rain so he felt lightly smudged with dampness. He marveled at the greenness of everything around him, shimmering and incandescent facets of green he had never seen before, although he knew these woods almost as well as the animals. He drank it in, astonished at a carpet of moss that lay draped over the massive roots of a giant beech, and thought he could live here quite well if he had to.

He reached cleared and level ground, and the smell of the river filled his nostrils at the same moment he heard a curious drone of machines. He drew closer, and was able to make out the yellow-slickered crowd standing on the banks, a quarter mile away.

They were facing the water, not moving. Staying close to a thick stand of trees, he watched. He watched as the large black car broke the surface like a monster, heaving itself onto the shore. Sylvie's car.

Sylvie's car. Somewhere inside him, the lid of a box flew open, releasing an angry swarm of memories. They stung him, over and over again, paralyzing him at the spot he stood. He had been in that car. He could feel the steering wheel in his hands. No. His foot on the gas pedal, steering the car into the river. No. It wasn't him. Why would he have done that?

Four figures in dark suits now emerged from the water. The crowd moved toward the car, but kept a distance from it, as if afraid the thing would rear up, snarling. Zan was afraid himself, afraid the car would somehow wake up, seek him out, would find him standing there, pointing the crowd to him.

Sylvie had wanted to leave him. That's why he had been in the car. They had both known what that meant: it would have meant the end of him. Yet she had been willing to do it, to end him. Who could blame him for trying to defend himself? So he had hit her. What choice had she given him? No choice. And then she'd stopped moving.

Maybe he had thought the water would rouse her. Maybe he thought they would float away in that big car of hers, float downstream, like a boat. Or maybe he had just given up. He didn't remember turning on the ignition, or aiming the car into the water. He did remember she had been beautiful, as the car descended, weightless — her sitting there as the water filled the car, her hair floating above and around her like a dark halo — and he had had a moment's thought of staying. She was reaching for him, finally wanting him. But even then, he'd known it was too late. It was her final joke on him: she only wanted him when she was beyond wanting anything anymore.

He stopped and leaned against a tree. His insides were spinning. He wanted to vomit, but was afraid of seeing what would come out of him — an infinite sorrow, an endless pain that would take the form of a tiny pathetic baby expelled from his mouth, and he wouldn't be able to look at it, lying there. It would have Sylvie's face.

He took a breath; it was ragged, like a sob, as if pieces of himself were being ripped out of him. He was close to howling.

He began to panic. He had to hold on. If he let go now, he'd end up in a place he wouldn't know how to get out of. He had to hold on. But to what? Something at the edges of his panic winked at him, reached out for him. There it was. Yes. He pounced on it, relieved: he had acted in self-defense. It had been an accident.

No one would believe it; he knew that immediately. He was in trouble. The truth came to him like a coat being held out for him to put on. As he pulled it around him, his familiar shroud, his uniform of disaster, he felt all the air that had been inside him deflate. He would never not be in trouble. He'd been in trouble from the time he was born: this was just a bigger version.

He had almost fooled himself. Had almost tricked himself into believing something different about himself. That he was a new man. Redeemed. Pure. A man who didn't know trouble, who did things right, whose actions bred goodness. Goodness.

He was a nothing, a pansy jerk. He was a moron.

But at least he knew the ground, knew the ground he had to walk. He'd be the pursued, the hunted. He'd be a large dumb animal being stalked in the woods by even dumber creatures. They'd come looking for him. Maybe they already were; maybe they had dogs, who would roam the woods, sniffing him out. He became alert, listening for barking. He turned and made his way back through the woods, back to the blind.

Being pursued didn't scare him. Even losing Sylvie didn't scare him. What scared him was that he had almost let himself get derailed by it. It scared him that he could have been so weak. He wished he had some weapon, something he could use to remind himself what it meant to be weak. He found a good-size rock that overflowed his palm. The weight was good, heavy. He brought it back to the blind and sat on the bench. He leaned over and laid his right hand on the top of the metal cooler. He raised his left hand and brought the rock down, slamming it on his little finger, hard. He heard the bone crack, and the sudden shock of pain exploded behind his eyes. The sting of tears that welled up in his eyes refreshed him. It brought him back to who he really was. A loser. A nothing.

He sat with his finger throbbing, tears streaming down his face, thinking about what to do. He couldn't go home. He couldn't go anywhere. He'd have been better off dead. *That* was someplace to go: dead. There was a glimmer of salvation in that thought, but the thought took a sudden hairpin turn.

As far as anyone knew, he *was* dead. Although he knew that Sylvie had kept quiet about her connection to him — *Don't tell anyone I'm with you. I want you to be my own special secret* she had told him, which at the time had given him a deep arousing thrill — he was sure the public spectacle of her death had laid bare all the private details of her life. For although he hadn't waited to see them pull her from the car, he had no doubt she had been. And as far as they knew, he was still there, underwater.

The idea that he could be thought dead made Zan laugh out loud. As he began to think about it, he felt pleasure, almost happiness. He wondered if they'd already had a funeral for him. He thought of his family around his casket. Elegia screaming, his brothers and Wyn Sr. sunken eyed and guilty, and he didn't know why, but this somehow was extremely pleasant, this idea his brothers would feel guilty about him. Novena he wasn't so sure about; she was hard to read. But he put her with the others in his imagining, sobbing and upset.

Then he remembered that they hadn't yet found his body, and felt momentarily knocked off balance by this. Although maybe they had. Maybe he had no body, maybe he was now reduced to just his spirit, doomed to wander the earth. Which wasn't necessarily a bad thing — he could go wherever he wanted now. The first place he had to go was somewhere else, far away.

That night, Zan went to Check's again, for the last time. He opened the register and took the $84 that was there. He swore to himself that he was not stealing, that he would return it. The food he had taken wouldn't have been missed, but he knew the money would be. He thought about leaving a note, but what would he say?

He went back to the blind and waited for the hours before dawn. He knew they were probably staking out his house, but he knew no other way to get his truck but to sneak back there. He'd be careful, make sure the coast was clear.

He made his way out to the deserted road. A half mile from his own house, he saw headlights coming toward him. He had retained his initial fear of vehicles — this he now took as a confirmation of his spirit status — and crouched down. The lights got closer and as they did, the thing behind them took shape, a shape that Zan knew well. It was a truck like his.

Then, astonished, he saw that it *was* his truck.

And as it slowly passed him, he saw, from the familiar shape of his Deere cap inside the cab, that it was he who was driving it.

It was an odd sensation, becoming untethered from some final single rope anchoring him to the ground as he watched himself drive down the road. Then he remembered: wasn't he dead? Except if he were dead, how could he be driving his truck?

On the other hand, if he was a spirit, why couldn't he fly? Why did he have to walk three miles into the next town, sitting on the chilled bus station bench until the next bus left for the city? This he didn't know, but as his bus pulled out of the lot and he sat back and closed his eyes, he figured it would reveal itself to him. He wasn't sure what limitations this new state would impose, but he supposed he had a long time to find out — possibly forever.

Zan spent the next day walking through the city. He thought he would find comfort in being swallowed up by the anonymity of the city, but it rattled him and frightened him. He felt the outlines of himself being smudged out by the crowds, the unfamiliar noises and the largeness of everything. He longed for the familiar, for someone who knew him; another minute and he was afraid he would be completely obliterated, that if he turned down another unfamiliar street, he would become dust. He had no idea of what he was going to do; escape had made sense, but where would he go? He just needed to rest and think. Who did he know? Who could he see?

Annaluna. He clutched her name to him like a map. She was here, less than ten blocks away. She would know him. He hoped she would know him, anyway. It had been a while since he had seen her, and now, as he walked toward her street, he grew nervous. He would stop by for a short time, then leave.

But twenty minutes later, when she opened the door to him, she not only knew him, she acted as if she had been expecting him — that he was, in fact, almost unpardonably late.

chapter 12

ANNALUNA STILL LIVED in the large first-floor apartment where she had spent most of her years. But for a while now, she had been inhabiting a misty plain of reality, a Moorish, fog-drenched sweep of cranial moss and meadow the soft and surreal color of twilight.

While this fog could have been the natural diminishment of age, it could just as easily have been the accumulated exhalations of all the people who were now sharing the apartment, had they been able to breathe, which was unlikely, since they had long been dead. There were many of them, and although they were phantoms con-jured from her dreams, they were wearing her out.

She had dreamed one night of her mother, and the next morn-ing there she was, standing in the living room, sniffing at the thin film of dust on the mantel. Then, a girlhood friend who had lost her life under the wheels of a car showed up one day, followed by an uncle whom Annaluna had loved as a child. He had died in a bar fight after biting the nose off a drunken soldier. Catorza arrived one day, shivering, and she gave a strange little yelp when she saw the shoes that Annaluna had tied to her chair, the ones which had caused her troubles in the hospital that day.

Annaluna's ghosts, relieved to find welcome, in turn brought their friends. They all milled around her apartment as if attending a noisy chaotic cocktail party. It was as if all the characters in all the books ever written had stepped out of their pages and met in a single room. Conversation on the surface made sense, except it followed no familiar narrative; contexts and histories bumped into each other, staining the rug with their spilled tea.

At first Annaluna welcomed them, as many old people would. Who can blame them? So often neglected by the living, the elderly are forced to turn to the dead for company. Ghosts can be one of the comforts of a long life, as long as you have forgiven them their trespasses against you, which is almost impossible, and one of the reasons you have allowed them in. But Annaluna was becoming exhausted with this traffic.

For one thing, since their arrival, the electricity in her apartment had gone screwy; light bulbs popped and burned, appliances became temperamental, and the very dust in the apartment seemed to have become charged with a life force of its own, creating odd mosaic patterns on the furniture.

For another, while the dead are usually well behaved, they are without exception annoyingly self-absorbed. In fact, the dead's capacity to bore is one of the great surprises of the universe. So astounded are they at their monumental passage, the wrenching, glorious, but exquisitely private transition from corporeal to otherworldly, they act as if no one else has ever experienced what they have. Naturally, they want to be coddled, to be served biscuits and milk with a warm blanket tucked under their chin, as they struggle to put words to an experience that is quite beyond them. Not that it stops them from trying. They talk, endlessly and tediously, into eternity's void. No wonder they have a haunted look; it's their loneliness that does it. No wonder they cling to the living; the living are the only ones who will listen to them.

Despite her growing impatience, there was one ghost whom Annaluna was still waiting for: her husband, Renaldo. She had taken to having conversations in her mind with him, berating him for his usual tardiness. She was furious with him for staying away, but even more furious with herself for wanting him to show up. So when the doorbell rang one afternoon, she knew it was him. Still, she had to take a deep calming breath before opening the door.

There he stood.

All she could do was growl. "Dinner's going to be a while."

She turned and wheeled herself into the living room. Zan stepped inside.

"Well, I don't know where you're going to sleep," she said, suddenly self-conscious.

"The sofa," he mumbled, although he didn't actually see a sofa. His eyes were still taking in the shoe planters.

"You better believe it, the sofa."

He blanched at her reception. She must have heard that he was being hunted, and he felt caged and ready to spring away in escape. A cup of coffee, then he'd leave.

"You better not tell anyone I'm here," he said defensively.

"Don't worry, I won't." Annaluna said. "I'm not so happy about it myself."

"I just want a cup of coffee," he said. "Then I'll leave."

Annaluna snorted and wheeled herself into the kitchen. Typical of him, to have a quick cup of coffee, then run away. She wouldn't have as much time as she thought. She had things to find out. As she poured the coffee, she fought to keep herself from asking about the only thing she was interested in: the other woman, the one who had stolen him from her. She told herself not to ask, not to show interest. But as she brought him the coffee and watched him curl his hands around the mug, she heard herself blurt out, "So what happened to her?"

"What?" he said, startled.

"What happened to your girlfriend?"

"I don't know," he mumbled in the cup. "I guess she died."

He felt his stomach flip actually saying the words. He willed himself to hang on.

"Oh, so you come running back to me."

Annaluna said this not bitterly but with great satisfaction, that she had outlasted someone else. Especially *that* someone else.

"Annaluna, I didn't know where else to go. It's all a big mess. I just need to rest, I'm so tired."

As soon as he said it, the full weight of his exhaustion fell upon him. He felt like a small boy. He felt himself beginning to crack into a million pieces, and suddenly, he was crying.

"Oh, sure, cry now," Annaluna said. "Cry your eyes out. But it won't change anything."

But she felt herself soften toward him. He looked like such a small boy, just as he had looked the night he had left her. And just as she had so wanted to that night, she now reached out and patted his hair. He had always had glorious hair, thick and wavy. It had always been her weakness, Renaldo's hair.

But the minute she put her hand on his head, he stopped crying. He didn't move; she had the feeling he had stopped breathing.

"Okay, look, stay awhile." She relented, pulling her hand back. When he raised his head and looked at her gratefully, she felt a small fluttering in her throat.

Zan spent the night, and the next, and the next. Each night as he lay in the bed she had made up for him in the spare room, he told himself he had to leave tomorrow at the latest. He'd hear Annaluna wheel herself into her bedroom at night, and as he lay in his own darkened room, he'd listen to a strange sound that would start up soon after, a rhythmic, clacking sound that he couldn't identify: a sewing machine? But it couldn't have been, since she wheeled out each morning wearing a dress that looked exactly like the one she had worn the day before, an ancient dress whose seams and frayed patches were being kept together with safety pins.

Her way of dressing was only one of her odd habits. Her entire domestic routine seemed to be one imported from some strange foreign country. She would open a carton of milk, pour it into an old glass orange juice container, then wash and fold the wax carton and wheel it into the pantry, where she had a stack of dozens of perfectly flat cartons just like it. He watched her cook: boiling the daylights out of squash, roasting meat until it resembled tangled and dirty balls of twine, making strange bubbling pots of unpleasant-smelling soup.

She also made pies. She had once been renowned for her pies, but through the years, they had taken on odd distortions. Salt for sugar. Potatoes or parsnips instead of apples. Crusts studded with doughy bullets of suet. She put it all in front of him, and Zan ate. What could he do? His appetite for anything good had left him, and he felt himself shrinking into a normal size.

And then there were those shoes. Some old women had a thousand cats. She had shoes, and her dog, Mamie.

Now he was slowly coming back to health, but he felt an odd reluctance to leave. As much as he tried to think, he had no more idea of where he would go and what he would do than when he arrived.

Besides, he had what he needed here: food, warmth, and even clothes. One morning, Annaluna had wheeled out of her bedroom with her lap full of men's clothes, neatly folded, smelling of mothballs.

"Here's some of your stuff I found," she growled, and the things — pants, heavy cotton shirts, even shoes — fit so perfectly, they felt like they could have been his.

Elegia was still calling Annaluna, but not daily. Her weekly calls now were centered on her worry about Zan, which, as usual, she was reluctant to bring up, but which she felt being drawn out of her by that powerful force Annaluna always exerted on her.

"He'll come back," Annaluna told her with certainty, then stole a glance at Zan. "They always do."

Elegia found comfort in the absolute confidence she heard in her aunt's voice.

Meanwhile, Zan had changed. Something had been leached out of him there underwater. He remembered the schoolbook picture of evolution, of a fish transmuting out of the water into an upright man. He felt himself having gone through a similar process, but in reverse. He had entered the water a man, and had come out something simpler, less complex. He felt he had eyes on the sides of his head, not in front; he felt, walking on his errands for Annaluna, as if he were swimming through brambles and water plants. But he also felt something that was simple but hard to define. Happy. Happy like a dog: fed, warm, rested. Cared for. He in turn took care of her, rubbing her feet, which were two dead things, but at least she was able to feel the warmth of his hands on them.

As for Annaluna, she too was different, more relaxed. It might have been that her phantom guests had stopped showing up so often since his arrival. But also, she liked taking care of him. Before long, they were moving around each other as if they were married. Still, it was different from the marriage she had been used to.

Men, with their genius for simplicity, long for complexity; women, with their complex gifts, long for simplicity. This is why men and women marry, to gain what they long for. But often, it backfires.

A man marries, eager to lay aside his sturdy, quotidian concerns to embark on this rich new life of complex mysteries. But meanwhile, his wife, joyful for her immersion into simplicity, acquires that highly attenuated radar to her mate's every action and breath, trying to translate his desires into the simplest of needs — food, drink, warmth, sleep.

He grows exasperated and impatient with this intense beam of attention to his simple needs, rather than to his complex ones. And he begins to wonder: How did this complex creature become so simple?

She starts to think: Why did such a simple beast insist on being so complicated?

Such had been Annaluna's marriage to Renaldo. And so now she kept waiting for the tone of her husband's exasperation — the familiar sound of her marriage — to make itself heard.

But none of this was coming from him.

He rubbed her feet, he shopped for her, and in the evenings he read her the newspaper. Her sight was blurred now, her eyes having filmed over with a milky opaqueness, which was not entirely unpleasant. Quality of sight is so relative anyway. Who's to say that the intended outlines of things aren't meant to be softly defined and muted? It makes the world less harsh.

But occasionally, unexpected flashes of clarity would flush the milky film from her vision, and she would see the crisp outlines of things with a brutality that was blessedly brief.

One night, she had been laughing over a story about cows he had been reading her, when in the middle of her laugh, she stopped abruptly and stared at him for a long time.

Finally she said, "You're not him."

Zan gulped. He wasn't entirely sure what she meant, but knew it to be true. He wasn't him.

"No," he finally said. "No, I'm not."

She nodded, blinking slowly, as if considering. After a long pause, he went back to reading the newspaper.

Even after that, she didn't stop calling him by name.

Renaldo.

chapter 13

As in most small towns, disaster in Nile Bay tended to remain indoors, limited to private and domesticated griefs. Save for a few scattered hunting mishaps and the usual assortment of car crashes, public and dramatic accidents were almost unheard of. Grown people didn't drown, or go missing.

But it was only Sylvie's tragedy that became a marker people inserted into their lives, to hold their place, to judge everything that came before and after according to which side of the marker it fell on. Zan's disappearance was barely mentioned in public; it was more like a small, almost inaudible sigh at the end of a loud exclamation. He was, after all, one of the worms on Nile Bay's roses, a slug in its garden, sliming out of his dark hole only to make trouble, or to look like he was making trouble, which is all that ever really counts in a small town. He was, in all likelihood, out there in trouble still, trouble so big he had been forced to take it out of town.

The possibility that Zan and Sylvie were somehow connected was dismissed by almost everyone. Those who knew Zan found the possibility that he could have ever been with a girl like Sylvie imponderable. And Check, who believed that Zan felt the same way about women that he himself did, found the idea of him with anyone ludicrous.

But those who knew Sylvie best — her girlfriends — knew she

could have been with practically anyone, and were less quick to dismiss the idea that there was something between Zan and her. In a way, it made perfect sense. It all made sense, and the girls were smug with how clearly they saw the whole thing.

Of course she had been seeing Zan; after all, as an older brother of one of them, he was prize boyfriend material. And of course they had been together when Sylvie's car had ended up in the river. They knew how Sylvie drove — crazily, as if the car were a boy she was trying to keep off balance. She had bragged once about speeding through three stop signs with a police car in pursuit, because she wanted to meet the new officer, who she had heard was cute.

They could picture her that night, showing off, hyped up on her kidnapping lie, laughing about it, speeding through town, Zan beside her. Pulling up to the river. Pretending she was going to drive in, and then something happening, her foot hitting the gas pedal instead of the brake. The car heaving into the water, too late to stop it. Maybe it had been an accident; maybe not.

Only Cookie was confused. "Yeah, but what about his truck? How come it wasn't found till later?"

"It was *found* later," Danielle explained impatiently. "But no one will ever know how long it had been sitting there."

She knew that wasn't entirely true, that her logic was skating on thin ice, and so she let it glide quickly to a less dangerous spot.

"Remember she was out looking for him that night? He was probably out there, sitting in his truck, trying to get away from her, and that's where she found him."

They all now pictured Zan, poor tortured Zan, sitting in his truck in the evening quiet, thinking still, deep thoughts before the overwrought engine of Sylvie's rage screamed up next to him.

"Oooo, maybe he was with another girl," Jaci said. "And Sylvie found them. Threw a scene, made him go with her."

"Hmm," said Danielle. She didn't like other people messing with her theory, but had to admit it was an intriguing twist.

"But who? Who else could he be with?" Cookie was getting

more confused. All of this was far too complicated for her. "Whoever it was would have said something by now, wouldn't she?"

"Well, would you come forward if it had been *you*?" Jaci said. "Imagine, being with a guy and another girl shows up? And it ends up like that? Forget it. I'd die before I said anything."

"Maybe she *did* die," Cookie wailed. "Maybe whoever it was is down there too." They were sitting on a picnic table not far from the one where they had last seen Sylvie, and the three girls now looked out to the river. For a minute, they were mesmerized by its slow, sinister movement, as if it were trying to sneak past them, snaked through with its secrets and horrors.

"Come on, you guys," Danielle said, trying to regain control. "So what do you think? Did Sylvie have an accident, or did she drive in on purpose?"

"Oh my God," Cookie said, near tears. "On *purpose*?"

"Oh Danielle, of course it was an accident," Jaci snapped.

"I'm not so sure. Anyway, we'll never know."

"Poor Zan," sighed Cookie.

"You know, I always thought there was something mysterious about him, something very, I don't know, haunted or something," Danielle said. "Like he always knew it was his fate to die for love."

In point of fact, her actual memory of him was dim — a lumpen male form she would see out of the corner of her eye on her way to Novena's bedroom, or if she was passing Check's. She might have had one conversation with him — although it could have just as easily been Quin or Dex — but her imagination gladly leapt in to fill in whatever outlines of Zan seemed hazy.

She grew dreamy, contemplating this new image of Zan, an image that she was molding from the ashes of her own burned-up heart, from the twisted bits of melted plastic and charred fabric that had filled the ashtray in her bedroom.

A new hero was just what she needed, what they all needed. And Zan, who had never been one of the clean, squeaky puppies that she and the other girls had forsaken, but a darker, more troubled soul, was perfect for the role. A kind of a half man, half beast, almost like a demon, but not. The perfect noble martyr, who had died for all of them. Someone perfect for their new loveless selves to worship.

Zan's elevation might have given great satisfaction to Novena, had she been aware of it. But for weeks, Novena had been aware of nothing but the passage of time.

After leaving Zan's truck by the river, she had arrived home and fallen asleep instantly. She woke hours later feeling such a strange mix of agitation, calm, anticipation, and deliverance that she felt as if her brain had changed in the night, to something suddenly able to accommodate complex new combinations of sensations. But she also felt that these sensations were fitting, given the enormity of what she'd done: she had changed the course of the universe, a change that she imagined was — perhaps this minute — being registered somewhere deep in the earth as the sound of a huge, clanging engine starting up. She spent the remainder of that day listening for its echoes.

But that day passed, and then another, and nothing happened.

Two more days passed in silence. She waited. The idea that she could have altered the universe without the universe even noticing never occurred to her. It rarely, after all, occurs to anyone.

Then, on the fifth day, they finally called with the news that his truck had been found. She had waited three hours for Elegia and Wyn to come back from the dragging of the river. She had waited two and a half minutes from the time she heard the front door open for Elegia to come upstairs with the news: they had found nothing. No Zan. She had waited to feel relieved, or disappointed, but she felt nothing except the need to wait some more.

She woke every morning, wondering if this would be the day that they would get a phone call with news that his body had been recovered. Her heart stopped every time the phone rang, but it was never the call she was waiting for.

Where was he?

Then a month had passed, with no sign of Zan. Novena found herself growing irritated. Where was he? Why hadn't he surfaced? Surely the river wouldn't have held him this long. She wanted him found, recovered, so it would all be over, so all the waiting would be done, the story of Zan told and put to rest.

It occurred to her again that Zan was staying away deliberately, just to taunt her. As if she and Zan were playing some childhood game of hide-and-seek, and rather than coming out when he was supposed to in order for the game to end, he was deliberately staying lost.

Thirty-two days had passed. Sylvie was buried, in a deep plot, under a carved stone, on a sloping hill, next to a tall tree.

Zan, on the other hand, was nowhere.

It had been a rough time for Elegia too. Certainly she was worried about Zan, but like most constantly worried people, she had been primarily worried about herself. How could she lose a son? Or rather, how could she have a son and not know where he was? How could she have a son who was not connected to her, who could leave her like this and not let her know where he was? The idea of her own competence had taken a great blow.

Zan had to be alive. She wanted to believe this as much as she wanted to believe in God. Not that she didn't believe in God, but her faith had always been an effort of will — and to her mind, all the more holy because of how hard she worked at it.

But Zan was gone. She had to face facts. Quivera told her this every time she called, and although her sister tried to be kind, Elegia could tell she was gently trying to steer her to a less optimistic conclusion: that Zan had thrown himself into the river.

"Think, Elegia. Something must have been bothering him."

"But he left no note, nothing. Why would he do such a thing?"

"He hasn't exactly been a cheerful member of society, dear." Quivera could never shake her idea of Elegia's sons: an image that brought to mind some monstrous human vacuum cleaners, roaming over carpets, noisily sucking up everything they encountered. She had not been a fond aunt to her nephews.

"But it just makes no sense. No sense!" Elegia cried, not for the first time.

It made perfect sense, Quivera thought, to anyone who'd spent more than a minute in Zan's sulking presence.

But why now? Elegia had no idea what could have been tormenting him so particularly. She was unnerved by the idea that something as foreign as the dark torment Quivera hinted at was as close to home as her own flesh and blood. The specter of this torment sat there, crouching in the corner like a beast. It was now beginning to creep toward her, a little closer every day. She knew if it got close enough, this dark thing could try to attach itself to her, try to make her believe that it had always been a part of her own self, indelibly staining her crisp whiteness with something dirty.

But what disturbed Elegia the most was that no one, not even Quivera, could tell her what she really wanted to know: What did she do now? How to go through her days? How normal should she be? Her son was a grown man, and his existence hadn't intruded on her daily routine for a long time, so the idea of disrupting it now that he was missing seemed overly dramatic, maybe even melodramatic. Besides, what if he had just gone off to a new life, or some new opportunity, and forgotten to tell her? Not that he ever called anyway. Not that he even cared that she could be beside herself with worry.

Finally, Elegia did the only thing left to do. She took to her bed.

She had always liked the expression "taking to your bed" although there hadn't been a morning in her life that she hadn't opened her eyes at six and bounded out of it, attacking each day as if all it demanded were the right cleaning supplies and some elbow grease. But now Elegia slept and slept. She slept like a stone, and when her eyes opened, she forced them closed again. Wyn Sr., who had been relegated to sleeping in the den, brought her coffee each morning, although she never drank it. He would sit awkwardly at the edge of the bed for a while, watching her, before leaving the house.

Novena brought her tea in the afternoons. She would bring the tea in and set it next to her and Elegia would sit up, saying "Oh, thank you, dear" with a great sigh. She'd hold the cup, sipping and staring into space. Novena would try to busy herself around the room, but there was little to do beyond straightening pillows. Elegia acted as if she weren't even there, and while it was a relief from her usual harping at Novena — over how she was dressed, or who she was with, or where she was going — her distance was also a little unnerving. Novena found herself trying to draw her out, to get her to talk, and she knew there was something perverse in the effort. Had she succeeded, had Elegia started in with her chatter, she knew she would have done everything she could to shut her out.

One afternoon, when Novena arrived home, she knew the minute she opened the door that Elegia had finally left her bed. The house was filled with the abrasive, falsely sweet smell of cleansers — a familiar perfume of furniture polish, ammonia, and laundry soap that can be one of the most comforting smells in the world. But whatever comfort Novena found in the smell as she passed through the living room left her when she saw a new addition to the room: a framed photograph sitting on the mantel, of Zan.

It was a picture of him taken some time ago, after he had come back from one of his fishing expeditions with Check. He had been holding two huge perch in either hand, his arms stretched out to his sides, but the frame, too small for the photo, had cut off the fish, so the image was of Zan standing there, his arms extended into the air, as if, Novena thought, he was about to fly. The photo rattled her; she had the sense that Elegia, in her cleaning, had somehow rearranged the atmosphere in the house.

She entered the kitchen warily.

"Are you sure?" Elegia was saying into the phone. "Okay, then. Well, call me if you hear anything."

Novena looked questioningly at her as she hung up the phone.

"I've been lying in bed for days, thinking that it just doesn't make sense. I feel I should be doing something. There are things here that just don't add up. And I'm going to get to the bottom of it."

"What are you talking about?" Novena said.

"I'm talking about Zan. I'm talking about the fact that no one can tell me what's happened. Grown men just don't go missing. I've been calling some of those people he'd been hanging around with. No one had seen him for weeks before he disappeared. Why didn't anyone say anything? I think something is very fishy here. Maybe I'll hire a private detective. Or that Boomer fellow."

Elegia had blushed imperceptibly at the mention of Boomer's name. It had, in fact, been that Boomer fellow who had started Elegia on her current train of thought. She had been thinking of his handsome face, dwelling on the fact that it was such a nice face for such a nice young man, and it had been from there that her mind had worked itself slowly backward — maybe a little too slowly — until it had reached Zan.

Novena hadn't seen the blush, but she was annoyed at Elegia anyway, for her concern, her cleaning, her photograph of Zan — for everything she'd done that had been too late.

"And when was the last time *you* talked to him?" Novena said sharply. "How long did it take *you* to notice he was gone?"

She turned and left the kitchen before Elegia could answer, and went up to her room, slamming the door behind her.

Once in her room, Novena began to pace. This was not the way the story was supposed to go. The idea of a private detective, or worse, an actual policeman, made her dizzy; she sat on her bed, hoping she might faint as she thought of what could happen next.

She had left her fingerprints on the truck. Her fingerprints were all over his house. Any minute, they were going to haul her into the police station, put her under harsh, glaring lights, and force her to tell everything.

She forced herself to think calmly of what she could be accused of. She'd kept quiet about Sylvie being with Zan. She had distorted the truth, that was all. Cleaned it up a little, moved things around so it looked different. Maybe caused an inconvenience by moving his truck, but how serious could that be? She could explain she was only trying to help Zan. They couldn't do anything to her.

No one really knew anything. No one could know that Zan and Sylvie had been together, or what had happened that night. There were only possibilities. No facts. But she knew that no matter what she told them, they would keep digging and digging at her. She knew they had ways of prying you open, peeling back the layers and layers of truth. And they distorted things, and had ways of making anything look bad.

It struck her that instead of making trouble disappear, she had somehow given it more fertile ground. When it finally appeared, it was going to be monstrous in size.

For the next few days, she stayed in her room as much as possible, looking out the window for the police cruiser that she expected to pull up any minute. Every time she heard a car drive down the street, she stopped breathing, waiting for it to pass.

When she ventured out of the house, and she did see a police car, she would wait for it to pull over, for her name to be called from the window. They'd say they just wanted to have a little talk. She wondered if she would have to ride in the back seat.

But even that waiting came to nothing.

Elegia never went beyond enlisting the services of Celantra to guide her in her search for Zan. Elegia wasn't exactly a believer in Celantra's powers of divination, but she couldn't bear the idea of involving an outsider in family troubles, however handsome he might be.

"You're not serious," Quivera had scoffed when Elegia made the mistake of mentioning her plan on the phone. "Celantra's nothing but the Mrs. Magoo of the spirit world."

Quivera had never had much tolerance for Celantra; it wasn't that she shared Elegia's disdain for the spirit world, but she couldn't abide flibbertigibbets, and in her view, Celantra would surely rule as queen of the world's population of tiddlywinks, were they ever able to stumble their way into a principality.

But Elegia was desperate to do something, and Celantra occupied that peculiar category of "poor dears" among the oldest of family friends — those whom you can call on for anything, while believing it is you bestowing the favor.

Celantra had raced out to Nile Bay the next day, her trunk full of fetishes and icons, herbs and voodoo dolls. She moved through the rooms of Zan's shack, sniffing the air, putting her hands on odd surfaces — the counter in the bathroom, the top of the bureau, the windowsill in the bedroom.

"Are you picking up anything?" Elegia said, following a close distance behind her.

Nothing that you couldn't, Celantra thought, feeling the clean, dust-free surfaces under her fingers.

"He's gone from here, but not dead," Celantra pronounced, opening the refrigerator door. "Someone has been here, taking care of him."

"Taking care of him? Is he sick? Is something wrong with him?"

"Well, his spirit has been very sick," Celantra answered, quickly closing the refrigerator, which had opened to reveal such a smell of rot and soured milk that she had nearly passed out. The smell had conjured an odd picture of Zan tramping through the woods, a similar rotting smell clinging to him.

Elegia nodded, already beginning to tune out Celantra. She didn't believe in sick spirits, thought they were self-inflicted, a bid for attention.

"You're going to have to wait," Celantra said.

Celantra was disinclined to offer any more specific comfort. She knew Elegia had reached out for her in desperation, and had nothing more than a margin of belief in her powers. Besides, she wasn't thrilled with the sense of deep sadness she had gotten in there.

She also knew that Novena, who had left a trace of her own scent in the place, knew more than she was telling, but she'd let Elegia find it out herself. Redemption was something people should have to work on for themselves.

As they left the house, she made a mental note to herself to have a private talk with Novena soon, although the note was promptly lost in the dusty, overstuffed, herb-scented drawers of Celantra's memory.

The last days of summer had finally surrendered to fall.

School had started again, and old routines had been quickly reestablished. The hallways had buzzed with the Sylvie drowning . for a few weeks. One of the younger teachers had tried to get her classes to write poems and draw pictures as a tribute to Sylvie, but she quickly abandoned the idea when she saw some of the results — especially from the boys, who, although not unmoved by Sylvie's death, had goaded one another into writing poems that fixated on the grosser aspects of her drowned body.

Zan was barely mentioned, except within the small circle of Danielle and the other girls.

With the passage of time, the girls had made Zan even more mysterious, more godlike. And they became more like a religious order — like nuns, but with switchblades. They had been gathering at the river every Saturday night, engaging in increasingly strange and noisy rituals, conjuring river gods and other dank spirits in between messy swigs of liquor. They knew better than to ask Novena to attend. As the sister of their god, she should be revered too, but she had lately become so distant.

Novena should have been relieved that they remembered him, that they even seemed to idolize him. Hadn't this been what she wanted? But whenever Danielle or the others broached the subject of Zan, or it became clear that they were leading to some question about him, Novena grew curt with them, changing the subject.

Still, they hovered around her, asking strange questions about what he was like growing up, the things he liked, whether Novena had any pictures of him. She thought she could shut them up once and for all, and had taken the picture of Zan from the mantel and given it to them. Oddly enough, Elegia hadn't even noticed its disappearance.

But rather than making the girls forget, the picture made them more frenzied. They kept talking about him, and Novena grew more and more agitated.

She felt confused, as if she couldn't keep things straight in her head. Everything had turned to its opposite. Two months ago, Zan had been overlooked, forgotten, but now people worshiped him. Two months ago, she had been convinced she had saved herself, had saved them all, but she now felt more precarious than ever. Two months ago, she had put something away, but she had the growing sense she had put it in the wrong place. He was gone, yet it seemed with each day that passed, rather than fading into oblivion, he became a growing presence, buzzing around her. She began feeling it as a jangling current of agitation, as if her nerves had been plugged into a higher voltage.

With it came a sense of hyperalertness that would often, without warning, veer into a jittery sped-up state, when her heart would start racing and her breath would come in short gasps.

One day, she had been in the hardware store on an errand for Elegia, and suddenly felt her heart pounding chaotically. The next thing she remembered was being out on the sidewalk, in a state of dreamy calm. She felt the weight of something in her pocket, and pulled out a small box of carpet tacks. She stared at it for the longest time, unable to imagine where it had come from.

The next time it was two spools of thread from the five and dime. Then a small cork gasket from the auto parts store, a package of shoelaces from the drugstore, and to her eternal shame, a small bottle of rubber cement from Wyn's store.

She worried about being caught, but maybe because she was taking things she didn't even want, things that seemed to simply find their way into her hands, she sensed she didn't need to worry too much. Besides, there was also that state of almost blank calm that would accompany the small new weight of something in her pocket. For a moment, in that blankness, she felt returned to a state when things had made sense, a time that she used to know, a long time ago. It was so distantly familiar, it made her feel nostalgic.

Any reasonable person would naturally assume that Novena wanted to be caught, that she was begging to be taken into the police station, to be grilled under the harsh lights. Truth is a vain creature: it doesn't like to be shrunken down, muffled, or otherwise disguised as something else, and will always manage to break loose, to find a way to make itself known. Truth, in that way, is the king of all monsters.

Yet, as plausible as that theory might be, it would not explain the fact that sometimes Novena would stride into a store, hyped up and chaotic, but for some reason she would find herself at the cash register, paying for the objects that had found their way into her hand. It did not explain how sometimes she would end up in the middle of a store suddenly forgetting completely her reason for being there, and leave empty-handed.

And it did not explain the fact that despite the pile of things she had amassed, Novena hadn't chosen even one of these things; they had all chosen her.

Novena had a more plausible theory: the thread and nails and refrigerator magnets and spools of picture-hanging wire and tiny wire cutters and the felt circles designed to protect the surface of furniture — twenty for $1.59 — the cards of thumbtacks, the lint filters, plug adapters, bobbins, unbreakable combs, eyeglass repair kits, single-edged razors, and all the other tiny tools whose job it is to mend the world's rips and leaks and punctures — these had singled her out to alter their fate. She was their conduit out of the store, out of a life destined for toil, a life that would end prematurely when they were abandoned in the graveyard of a forgotten junk drawer.

She was doing them a great favor, and so they did one for her in return. She took them out of the store, unseen, and they in turn restored her to a state of calm. It was a simple exchange, and she found comfort in it.

There was not much comfort anywhere else. At least not among her friends, whom she now tried to avoid, although she sometimes gave them some of the things she had stolen. But they were neither impressed nor shocked. To her girlfriends, shoplifting was penny-ante stuff. They were committing bigger crimes, crimes of the loveless. Tormenting boys, tempting each other's fathers, flirting with uncles and teachers.

The girls had become what Elegia called rough little numbers. Something had curdled in them, curdled too fast. Novena could not find her place with any of them: she felt as if she moved through school as part of a noisy parade float that moved daily down the hallways; she was part of it, but as a large balloon, hovering overhead, looking down on the crowd below. Filled with bad and stale air.

And so Novena kept going into stores, and things kept finding their way into her pockets, and she walked through Nile Bay, the weight of wire cutters, staplers, and tubes of glue lining her pockets like the weight of secrets.

But you know what happens to secrets. Sooner or later, they spill.

chapter 14

ZAN HAD BEEN OUT running errands for Annaluna one afternoon. Milk, flour, butter. That's all he ever remembered buying, although they were always eating meat and vegetables, canned peaches and hard candy.

He had grown used to the city now, pushing himself to go a little farther each time he went out, and he felt comfortable in the chaos and clatter; he liked the membrane of noise which he felt himself slip through when he reached the sidewalk. He liked the yelling, the sound of people calling to each other, the trails of people's conversations, their intimate overheard half sentences. He was surprised at how much they revealed in these small snatches he caught as he passed them, in their words, the tones of their voices, their gestures.

In the city, people always seemed to be talking about themselves, as if, in the middle of the noise and crowds, they needed to remind themselves they were there.

He had come back with the bags and was standing at the front door, about to go in, when he heard the sound of Annaluna's voice. This was not unusual, since she often talked to herself, but then he heard a sharper, more urgent voice answering her. Someone was with her. He stood perfectly still, listening at the door. Finally, he was able to make out the voice of his aunt Quivera.

She was not his favorite aunt. She never looked at him or his brothers, and whenever she had visited them in Nile Bay, he had always thought of her as a large insect. He knew she would turn him in the second she saw him, and his face flushed with heat at the thought she might be in there, grilling Annaluna right now about her visitor. He quickly backed away from the door and went back outside.

The close call made him feel stupid. He couldn't believe he had taken the risk he had by staying here so long. It was time for him to leave.

For the next three hours, he walked around, waiting for Quivera to leave, thinking about what to do. By the time he returned to Annaluna's, she was alone. They had their dinner, and she said nothing about what had taken him so long, nothing about the butter having melted, nothing about Quivera's visit.

That night, after she wheeled into bed, he lay on the sofa, waiting for an hour to pass, then another. Then he got up and started to prepare.

He didn't know where she kept her money; when she gave him some for shopping, bills would appear from her pocket — sometimes a twenty, sometimes a fifty, sometimes more. She never asked for her change, and in the weeks he had been there, he had accumulated close to a hundred dollars. But he needed more. He got up, and started going through the place, looking for silver, for objects of value. He took a few bowls, some of the silverware. He wished he had thought to find a reason to go into her bedroom before she went to bed, so he could have searched her bureau for jewelry, maybe even find her money.

Finally, having gathered what he could, he thought about what he should leave behind. He folded the clothes she had given him and left a neat stack on the sofa, although he kept one of the shirts and one pair of shoes, because they were good shoes. He put on his own clothes again, and they felt strange on his body, as if they belonged to someone else.

He thought of leaving a note but knew it would be too risky.

He was at the door, looking around, gathering to him the final thing he could: the idea of leaving Annaluna. He knew what he was leaving, and what he was going to: a hardscrabble, patched-together life, of half deals, half promises, things half paid for, half pulled off. Scrapes, close calls, the big ticket, the big chance right around the corner, waiting there until you reached it and saw it was just more trouble, in one of its sly disguises.

His hand reached for the door. He took a deep breath, and stopped. He put down his things and made his way back to her bedroom.

He hadn't ever spent more than two minutes in her bedroom; she always kept the door closed. When he softly pushed the door open, he saw the room was lit with a little porcelain lamp. He stepped back, thinking she was still awake. But he heard the small snores coming from her bed and went in.

He stood there, looking at her.

She was lying on her side, her legs curled up. Her hand was under her pillow, and this made her look like a young girl.

He watched her breathe for a minute, slowly and steadily. The room smelled of talc and mothballs. He saw Mamie in the corner, sleeping. He saw a lit blue clockface on the bedside table. He saw the shine of the glass top of her bureau reflected off the mirror above it. On it, the lamp, a vanity set, a tray, a gleam of something gold.

He hadn't really been searching the room for anything more to take, but the gold was shining so insistently that it was as if it had spoken out loud, telling him he was meant to take it, that it was his. His eyes stayed on Annaluna while his hand reached out for it. His fingers closed on something small and he picked it up and put it in his pocket.

Then he whispered into the room. "I've got to leave, Annaluna."

Her eyes opened immediately. She looked frightened, and started to nod.

"I borrowed some stuff. Take care." He was still whispering.

She nodded again, still looking afraid.

He hesitated, waiting for her to say something.

"Well, okay then," he finally said. "You be good."

He bent down and kissed her cheek. It was so soft and powdery, as if particles of dust had settled there in the night, or had been transported from the surfaces of her furniture. He felt her move a little, and felt her hand moving down his arm. He took the hand in his, and instead of the tight grip he had expected, he felt her slip something from her palm into his. It felt like a damp tissue. She put her hand back under her pillow and closed her eyes.

He backed out of her room. He went back to the living room. Opening his hand, he saw a damp folded-up hundred-dollar bill.

"Okay then," he said to the empty room, where only the ghosts could hear him. "I'll miss you."

Then he left, out into the darkness of the city. As he walked, he thought of Annaluna's face, the feel of her cheek. He could still feel a faint film of talc on his lips. He wondered if she would miss him. He wondered if she had even seen him; her breathing had been so slow, her snoring so regular that he now thought he had only imagined that her eyes had opened.

He was too young to know how lightly sleep lies upon the old. With every year we live, every decade we survive, we learn how futile it is to watch for our death while we're awake. It's in sleep we must remain alert, half awake, the light on, waiting for it to come.

Zan hadn't made any plans beyond packing his things and leaving Annaluna. Only when he found himself out on the street, with nothing but the items he'd taken from her and the money in his pocket, did he think about his options.

He had to get to a pawn shop, but it was not even dawn, and it would be hours before he would find one open. He needed a place to wait, in peace and solace. The faithful have churches for these moments. The fallen have bus stations. That's where Zan went now.

He took a seat on a hard wooden bench and studied the board of departures, waiting for some sign that might tell him where he should go.

For four hours, he had looked at the words posted on the boards. ASHEVILLE. BOWIE. DAYTON. FONTANA. MATAWAN. NITRO. ODESSA. ROCKLAND. SANTEE. They might as well have been pine cones or mathematical equations for all those marks told him.

The last time he had left a place, he had been running away, and the city had seemed to be the only choice. Now he could go anywhere; that's how much freedom he had. But as soon as he chose a destination, he knew he would no longer have even that. So he was in no rush to decide. Anyway, there was no sense making a decision until he knew how much money he'd have from the things he sold.

When morning came, he stood stiffly and went back outside. There was a pawnshop a few doors away. He went in and dumped his knapsack of the cache of things he had taken from Annaluna's onto the counter. Silverware, some old coins, a few small silver bowls and frames.

The man poked at them, then named a price. It was nowhere near what Zan had expected.

He flushed with disappointment and experienced a surge of anger at the items, at their cheapness. He felt as if they had tricked him, or betrayed some confidence about him to this man, and he wanted to pick them up and hurl them across the room, or stamp them under his foot.

The man asked if he had anything else.

Zan shook his head, then remembered the small gold thing he had taken from Annaluna's bureau. He felt in his pockets and pulled it out.

It was a watch, an old-fashioned pocket watch. He studied it for the first time as the man behind the counter waited expectantly.

Zan turned it over. *"R. from A. with love"* was etched in spidery script on the back of it.

He shoved it back into his pocket.

"No. That's it," he said.

He took the money and made his way back to the bus station. The bills felt damp in his hand and he could feel the dirt on them. He wanted to get rid of them fast, to punish them, these crabbed, cheap things. He walked up to the ticket counter.

"Where can I go on this?" he said, laying the bills on the counter. He held his breath, but then, as the ticket man swept up the bills and started counting them, Zan added, "Somewhere south."

The ticket attendant barely looked up. He pushed a ticket toward Zan.

"Boards at gate seven in thirty minutes," he said.

The decision was made, and all that was left was to step onto the bus and leave. Zan took his seat on the bench to wait. He felt his limbs grow dense and heavy, as if his body were already starting to protest the idea of standing again, getting on that bus. He wasn't by nature an adventurous type, not really. He had been born to sit, not to fly; to be not a bird but a tree, some fallen log growing into the forest floor, gaining its density and mass with the rain it soaked up, and the lichen and small plants it sprouted, and the insect colonies that burrowed inside.

He kept himself from looking at the ticket. He wouldn't look until he was about to board. This was the best way to do it, he decided. If he ended up somewhere awful, it wouldn't be his fault. In fact, it would be Annaluna's fault, for the things she owned that had been worth so little.

He thought of her now, remembered the sight of her sleeping, and he felt a place in his chest unfurl with a small flag of forgiveness for anything he might have been ready to blame her for.

This forgiveness expanded him, stirring in him a sense of satisfaction with himself. Enough, anyway, to lift his chin, sit up a little straighter. Enough to give him the courage he needed to stand when he heard his gate being announced and walk toward the open door of his waiting bus.

.   .   .

When he settled into his seat in the back of the bus, Zan closed his eyes as the bus pulled out of the lot and out of the city. He didn't want any goodbye looks.

Once the bus was underway, he took the watch out of his pocket and began winding it. To his surprise, it started ticking. He stared at the inscription again, tracing his finger over the faint lines. *R. from A.* He wondered why he hadn't sold it; it probably would have been worth something. Then he wondered why Annaluna still had it. *With love,* it said. It must have meant something to her. He had an instant of remorse for taking it, but as he stared at the inscription, he reminded himself that as far as she was concerned, he *was* Renaldo. That made the thing his.

Then another thought occurred to him that cheered him even more: as long as he was Renaldo, he would not be Zan.

chapter 15

HOW MUCH DO WE ACCUMULATE in a life? Consider the forks, the place mats, the underwear, the books, the boxes to hold your sentimental ephemera, the photos, the fine leather shoes, the plates and bowls, the window shades and curtains, the sheets and towels, the bits of fluff — doilies if you are so inclined — the notes and cards and letters, pieces of pottery, old prayer books, sleek black ashtrays, metal colanders, rugs, photographs, scraps of lace, soap dishes, buttons, empty perfume bottles, checkerboard linen, old keys, boxes of birthday candles: your stuff. So little can be parted with, each possession tethers you to the idea of yourself as a tasteful and useful inhabitant of the planet. Without them, where would you be? What would you become? Why these objects and not others?

You find these things, or they find you. You bring them home and unwrap them and there they are, completely and immediately at home, balanced precariously on a line that never makes up its mind between utility and desire. You thought you needed them, but actually you chose them. And now they belong to you, each of these objects, and you to them. They are family members, taking on your smells, accommodating your habits, memorizing your rhythms. Is there anything you wouldn't show them? Anything their watchful eyes miss? They are like pieces of your shed skin that have taken new form.

And when you have left the earth, every possession you have accumulated becomes worthless. Not entirely worthless, of course, but seriously reduced in value. They are broken up in job lots or fought over by your relatives, or simply thrown out in the trash heap, burned or buried in the earth, waiting to disintegrate, just like you.

A few will survive, rescued by love or grief or simple need, to become someone else's possessions. They will then go through the same cycle, with fewer survivors each time. What is their survival based on? What determines the life span of household objects?

Novena finally got caught shoplifting. She was in an antiques store. It was a junk shop, really, and she'd been poking around, looking at mismatched bowls and wooden lamp bases, dusty ashtrays and cracked crystal.

She had picked up a heavy brass cigarette case. It was of green enamel, inscribed with elaborate script which read *"Memory of Japan,"* and illustrated with a small picture of Mount Fuji and a tiny map of the country, identifying the cities of Pyongyang, Chitose, Sendai. The case had a built-in lighter unit on its top, which, like most lighters in the world, no longer worked. Although it was not much bigger than her palm, there was a heft to the thing, a pleasing metal weight.

As she moved across the store, it was, in fact, the weight of it which made her conscious of the fact that it was suddenly in her pocket.

She was so surprised at its presence she had stopped, and she was now staring blankly at a piece of crystal, pretending great fascination while she snuck her hand in her pocket to touch it. Suddenly, she felt her elbow grasped.

"I'm glad you saw something you like." The voice was a man's low growl. "A nice prewar artifact. You look a little young to be smoking, though. Or is it a gift for someone?"

Novena wasn't sure she heard him, or what he was saying. She decided to use her confusion to her advantage. She didn't turn right away, processing how it felt, getting caught. She checked her breathing, felt her pulse pounding in her neck before turning to look at him. He hadn't let go of her elbow.

He loomed over her, staring hard behind wire-rimmed glasses. He was about thirty, younger than the gruffness of his voice suggested; his hair was thick and badly cut. She was unnerved by something about him. The breezy and bluffing response that she had practiced for just this event left her brain and all she managed to mumble was "What?"

She hated the fact she sounded nervous.

"Oh, come on," he said, a wincing grin on his face.

"What are you talking about?" Novena said, trying to insert a degree of indignation into her voice. She still could not entirely believe that he'd seen her pocket the thing when she couldn't even remember pocketing it herself.

"Take it out of your pocket," he said, still grasping her elbow.

"Let go of me."

"I'll let go of you when the cops get here."

At the mention of cops, she snapped back to herself, so suddenly that all the blood left her head in a sudden rush. And then, after months of wishing she could faint, she felt her insides dropping to the floor and then her body following, and in the split second before she lost consciousness, she heard herself thinking in surprise, as if she had just accomplished a difficult task, *I'm fainting*.

When she came to, she was not on the floor, but propped up in an old overstuffed chair. The man was crouched at her side, holding her wrists. The case was on the floor.

"Oh God," she whispered, and closed her eyes.

He let go of her wrists and walked away, but a moment later he was standing over her, holding out a glass of water.

She took the glass, her hands trembling, and gulped it down. He looked as if he had been about to say something, but he moved away from her, and she was grateful that he wasn't there to see how she was pouring the water into herself, so thirsty for it that it spilled out of the glass.

She was so thirsty. She wanted more, but she didn't want to move. But then it occurred to her that he had probably gone to call the police. She looked around for him, saw him in the front of the shop, got up unsteadily and made her way to the counter.

His back was to her, and she couldn't see what he was doing, but it didn't look as if he was on the phone.

"I'm sorry," Novena whispered, her throat sore and rasping.

He looked at her over his shoulder.

"You okay?" he said gruffly.

She nodded, her cheeks burning with humiliation.

"I'll pay you," she said. "Don't call the police, okay? I made a mistake."

"I'm not calling anyone," he said, but he didn't turn around.

She was fumbling in her purse when he finally turned to her.

"Here. It's yours," he said, holding out a small wrapped square package. "You wanted this so much, you should own it."

He had gift-wrapped the cigarette case beautifully, in dark red paper.

"Oh my God, I can't take this," she said, fumbling for her wallet. "Look, I'm going to pay you."

"What could you have lost at your age, that you have to replace it with this piece of tin junk?" His voice was now softer, and sad, although his gaze was penetrating, boring into her. "Or with whatever else you've been taking? I'm sure this isn't your first time."

She stared at him dumbly, shocked by his question. The softness of his voice made her want to cry.

"Well, whatever it is," he continued, "if this thing does the trick, it's cheap at the price. Take it."

He came closer to her and put the package in her hand.

"It's bad karma, stealing something," he said. "That's why I'm giving it to you. Maybe some of the damage will reverse itself. I don't know. But you're going to have to find a way to get right with it yourself."

"What do you mean, get right with it?"

In her hand, the package felt heavier than she remembered.

"Restore the balance. You're going to have to figure it out. I hope you do, or it'll suck you dry by the time you're twenty-one."

"How am I going to figure it out?" Novena said, feeling desperate.

"It will tell you. It'll tell you what you need to know. You just have to listen."

She was staring at him, conscious that her mouth was open, and in that moment of consciousness, she also became conscious of wondering why it was that the mouth always chooses to register surprise this way. Then she was conscious of the oddness of this thought, then at the oddness of this consciousness. Everything felt so strange, suddenly. What he was saying made no sense, yet she understood it.

"Go home now," he said. "Just go home. Figure it out."

He didn't say it unkindly, though he sounded weary.

She left the shop, still feeling wobbly, carried the package home and left it on her dresser unopened. For the rest of the day, she tried to listen to it, but the package just sat there dumbly, telling her nothing.

That night she slept fitfully, awakening almost every hour, and although her room was dark, she could feel the package's red presence across the room. But it was still mute.

Every day she listened, occasionally even bending her ear to the package, which made her feel ridiculous. But it told her nothing. At night, she would suddenly wake, and there it would be, glowing red in its corner. It seemed to be nudging her awake at night, only to taunt her with its silence.

For the rest of the week, the package hounded her. Every time she looked at it, she felt her cheeks burn, humiliated at her failure at getting it to communicate. She thought of going back to the shop, to return it, to get it out of her life. But at the same time, she was anxious for the package to do something, to tell her something, as the man said it would.

Every time she came into her room, she would eye it warily. In the mornings, it was the first thing her eyes sought out when she woke. Soon it began to take over her thoughts, inserting itself at odd moments, even when she was nowhere near it.

She was barely sleeping, she had lost her appetite, could focus on nothing else. And still the package told her nothing. It was just as he had said: the thing was sucking her dry.

By the end of the week, the package so consumed her that she began to feel as if there was nothing else in the world but her and it. Her friends were off in their own new world, doing their weird things. Even Elegia wasn't around much anymore, and when she was, she no longer hovered over Novena, but seemed quieter, more removed. Novena missed her and the idea shocked her: she missed Elegia.

And then she suddenly found herself missing everyone. She longed for a familiar touch, and conjured the faces of Margita and Annaluna, even Quivera, with a strange sense of homesickness. They all seemed more than miles away: she was beginning to feel they had never been there to begin with. She even, one night, dreamed of Catorza, or of something or someone who took on that familiar and elusive shape.

Everyone was somewhere else, no longer near her. All she had was the cigarette case.

Had she been a little older, she would have realized that she was feeling nothing more exotic than loneliness. But to a child born for solitude, to a child of an absent father — a father for whom children are nothing but the physical happenstance of a fluid that he can't help but manufacture and occasionally release — there may be nothing more exotic than loneliness.

Solitude is a large, quiet country, each of whose inhabitants rule it utterly. The threat of its invasion comes not from other people so much as the reminder of their absence. That's what loneliness brings when it shoves its way in with all its jarring noises: the reminder of what — and who — you are missing.

Loneliness, the cruel, slightly mad sister of solitude, has no kindness. Its cold touch reminds you that your large and peaceful country is perhaps not so beautiful, but is in fact rather desolate and barren. That maybe you are there by yourself for a reason.

It begins as a sound, loneliness does, a rushing sound, like the beating of wings in your inner ear, the sound of yourself echoing, no one else around to absorb the noise of you. Gradually, your shadow, your breath, the movements you make, the space you take up in the universe, become louder, sharper, more unpredictable, with strange new meanings that have, until now, remained hidden. It's all a distortion, of course, the distorting work of loneliness. This is when dogs sense something odd about you, your belongings start plotting against you, and cigarette cases finally begin to talk.

One night, after the package had been in her room for ten days, she was awakened as usual. Her room was utterly still and silent, but she knew what it was that had waked her, and she nearly sobbed in frustration.

Suddenly, she got up and walked across the room to her dresser. She half expected that the package would give her an electric shock when she touched it. She picked it up and carried it back to bed.

"Okay," she said aloud in the dark. "You win. I surrender."

Her two hands fitted comfortably around it, and she held it for a while, resting it on her chest, feeling the weight of it, imagining the coolness of the metal through the paper. She began feeling calmer, almost sleepy, holding the thing, and after a while as she lay in the dark, Novena's cigarette case began telling her about itself — about a man, a soldier who had found it in a Japanese street stall, bought it, and carried it home as a gift to a woman, because the green reminded him of the green of her eyes, and the lighter part reminded him of the way she held a cigarette when he lit it, bending her head toward him and then looking away quickly as she expelled the smoke, so he would be left staring at her profile, her lips pursed, her eyes half closed. And when the woman opened the present, she read the inscription on it and laughed, saying, "Memory of Japan? I have no memories of Japan. You should keep this yourself."

She left it on the coffee table until the lighter stopped working, and the man stuck it in a drawer. Until years later, now alone, he came across it while looking for a nail or a thumbtack, and the unexpected reminder of the color of her eyes was so startling and so painful that he had to sit down.

This was the journey the case had made: from country to man to woman to drawer to box to shop to Novena's bedroom to her own hand. It was a solid thing in her hand now, and she willed it now to tell her something else, something beyond its own story. Something about herself.

"What else?" she said aloud. She waited.

She played the details of its story over in her mind, and heard the woman's voice again: "I have no memories of Japan."

Except this time, it sounded different. This time, it sounded as if it were her own voice, saying, "I have no memories of Zan."

It was true. For the past ten days, Novena had been so consumed with this package that she had thought about nothing else. She tried to recall the presence of him that had been buzzing around her for the past few months, but the sound had suddenly stopped, as if muffled by thick cotton. Novena nudged at it, cautiously, waiting to remember, waiting to feel her anxiety come awake. But there was just silence. It was as if the past few months didn't exist, only the past of the cigarette case, which seemed to have supplanted her memories with its own.

She brought the package to her lips, to kiss it in gratitude. As she did, she recalled there was one character missing in its story: the man in the shop. It was because of him the lighter was now in her hand.

She thought of what he had said when he put the thing in her hands: he was reversing the damage, by forcing her to take this package as a gift. She smiled to herself in the dark, remembering him placing it in her hand, and she knew that it wasn't the package that was intended as the gift.

It was him. He was the gift.

She held it up to her cheek, inhaling it. She imagined she could smell the shop's mustiness and dust. And something else. It's what the man smelled like, she thought. Definitely not a boy. Not the springy wet wool of boy, but a deeper, more seasoned note. Something with more salt.

She slept well that night, and woke feeling more rested than she had in a while. All day, she imagined the man's eyes following her as she walked down the street, as she walked through the halls of school. And when she was home, in her room, with the cigarette case, it was as if the case were the man and he was there, always looking at her. Now, Novena smiled at it.

But she felt curiously shy about actually confronting him in person. There was a possibility she was wrong, that he had just been humoring her, or playing a joke. Maybe with a day or two to think about it, he might even have changed his mind, and was furious at her for stealing.

She walked past the place for two days, unable to gather the nerve to go in. Finally, on the third day, she pushed the door open and went in. She saw him bent over at the counter, writing something. The sight of him nearly made her turn and walk out. But she took a breath and walked boldly to the counter.

He lifted his eyebrows in acknowledgment, nothing more. She wasn't even sure he recognized her.

"Here," she said, handing him a package. "It's something I made. A peace offering."

She had taken one of her own blouses and cut a small pair of rectangles, which she sewed together to form a crude eyeglasses case. It was not inspired, but it was the only thing she could think of. At least whenever he took his glasses off, he would think of her.

She watched him open the package.

"It's for your glasses," she said quickly. "I would have personalized it, but I didn't know your name."

"It's Whit," he said.

He had taken off his glasses and his face looked slightly distorted, as all faces accustomed to glasses usually look without them, like a naked baby. His eyes were an intense dark blue. She got a better look at his face. He was older than she remembered, but more handsome somehow.

"Thank you," he said, sliding his glasses in and out of the case.

"One gift for another," she said softly, searching his face, looking for a sign that her interpretation had been right.

He just gave her a small smile. It wasn't a large smile, or a particularly meaningful one, but it filled her with a giddy relief anyway.

"So can I come back and visit sometime?" she said.

"Sure," he said, looking surprised. "Come anytime."

"Okay. See you," she said, and on her way out the door, thought, Tomorrow.

When she got home, she went to her room, feeling calm. But after an hour, the surface of her calmness began to wrinkle. She realized that she missed him. But not in the way she missed boys. She knew what that felt like, and she knew missing boys was linked directly to how much they missed her; as if her longing for them was made up entirely of the extra remnants of their ardor for her.

But Whit wasn't a boy. He was a man. She wasn't even in the habit of talking with older men, at least those who weren't the fathers of her friends, and she wondered if somehow the rules were different where they were concerned. Maybe they had another kind of language.

Actually, she had a hard time figuring out exactly how old Whit was. He was a little too young to be her father, but a little too old to be something else.

chapter 16

AT TWENTY-SEVEN, Whit was at the age of nothing: not old enough, not young enough, not wise enough, and not foolish enough.

Whit had reached the age where he had lost the capacity to amuse himself with his own mistakes. He was also losing the ability to tell the difference between inconvenience and disaster. Minor missteps took on the elements of tragedy, and vice versa. It was, he thought, a car crash of an age, a collision of movement and stasis, of decision and indecision, as he waited for his life to appear before him in some recognizable shape and color.

Whit had been married soon after college, and after only a few years his wife had begun cheating on him. A bad year followed, after which she finally left and he began drinking heavily. One night, when he was driving aimlessly, his car had fallen off the road and tumbled down a small embankment. It took an hour to drag himself out of the car. He was unhurt, but by the time he was out, he had the sensation of complete emptiness, as if there was nothing to his body but its shape, nothing to his mind but its void.

He tried to keep that feeling. It was harder than he thought, even after he packed up all his belongings, took them to the dump, and left town in a used car. He drove the car until it died, twenty miles outside of Nile Bay, where he had been heading anyway, to see an uncle he hadn't seen in years. He had settled in the town as if it were a rug he had tripped over, and was too tired to get up.

Empty of anything, of history or connection, Nile Bay was a perfect place, he thought, to be a monk. That was his intention anyway. To be a monk. So far it had been relatively easy.

To keep his mind empty, he meditated every day. To keep his desire for worldly objects at bay, he ran a junk store.

The shop belonged to his uncle, who also had a higher-end antiques shop in a nearby town. Whit welcomed the job. He liked being around this old stuff. There was a mournfulness to it all, to all these rejected objects, that suited his melancholia.

He liked opening the dusty, dirty boxes of people's detritus that they left like babies on the doorstep, as if ashamed, or that they brought in the light of day, affecting an air of largesse, shrugging offhandedly although he could always see their disappointment when he named his price for their belongings.

He especially liked opening the boxes that his uncle brought over from his finer store, the rejected antiques. This was old stuff, not the fine stuff. Not the prissy dowagers of objects, but the squat, homespun, callused survivors of the world — the coal miners and bus drivers and trashmen of objects: old tobacco and flour tins, dried-up fountain pens, speckled mirrors, chipped pottery, wood planes and levels, farm implements, old bottles, musty books. Still here, still on the earth, sitting there in their particular smugness, a thumb-your-nose attitude you could sense a mile away.

They had a right to their smugness. That's what people paid for: the survival of these things against all odds. They had outlasted generations of humans, those old flour tins and Bakelite vanity sets. People reached out for one or another of these as talismans of their own longevity, to the prayer that they, even as ash and dust, would be remembered too, would leave some trace. After all, if a flour tin has lasted for three generations, why not them? Why not you? How could a piece of tin be more important, more lasting, than anything you could ever become, could ever produce?

Whit thought about this, watching the people who came in. Some would scan his merchandise with a quick desperation, as if they had misplaced something, then leave reluctantly. Others stayed for a longer time, and Whit grew adept at figuring out which of them would buy something; he watched for the look of recognition that would pass through their eyes as they picked up a piece of old shredded linen, or a rusty toy sheriff star, or bits of pottery. Sometimes their sense of recognition was so strong, they'd grin helplessly, and yell out, "Hey! Hey! Look at this!"

What did they recognize? It seemed more than a pleasant nostalgia for an unlived time, but a known and concrete memory. But what could they remember about a cracked china cup, or cocktail shaker, or a scrap of quilt that had been on the earth far longer than they had?

As they fumbled for their dollar bills and paid for their finds, Whit was struck with their look of longing and relief, as if some piece of themselves that had been missing would now be filled by the object they now held.

They looked like children who had been lost and frightened, and had finally found a familiar landmark to lead them back home.

The shop was never very busy; he could read and meditate and occasionally sit in the back with an old acoustic guitar, picking out mournful chords.

But this was his third year of retreat, his third year as a monk, and he was lonely too.

Who could he talk to in that place? He didn't make friends easily; he told himself he didn't believe in it. Besides, everyone in this town seemed to be knit together tightly, in lives that had few holes for anyone else to enter. Until the day Novena had come in and stolen something.

He had been struck with her as soon as she entered the shop: she was very pretty, but suffering seemed to illuminate her like a halo, and he had kept his eye on her as she moved around the shop, watching her with pleasure and curiosity. He'd been shocked to see her slip the case into her pocket. It had angered him; he found himself disappointed, as if he had expected more from her. But then her reaction when he had confronted her had made him change his mind again. She had felt weightless in his arms when he had moved to catch her, and when he had held her wrist bones in his hands, he'd been amazed at how frail they were. She had bones like a bird, and he had felt his heart move for whatever had left her so unhappy.

Still, he liked unhappiness in a person. He didn't trust happy people. To his mind, there was a reason misery loved company; it was a more interesting and worthy place to be. Besides, she was pretty. Ripe and scented. And mysterious. What more could you want?

But Whit didn't want. He kept himself carefully from wanting, with the help of a small note tacked to the wall, which he had scrawled for himself years ago. He had written it one night after he had left, while he was on the road. He had been sitting in the dark, crazy with the sudden panic of missing his wife, willing her to come back, although she was long gone.

After hours of sitting there, he stood up, got a piece of paper and wrote down two words: "Stop wanting." Just two words, but the act of writing them brought him an immediate sense of relief. The relief lasted only a short time, but returned every time he repeated the words. He had taken the note with him.

Later, when he landed in Nile Bay and began consuming the books that came into the shop — books that he considered as permanent fixtures of the store, so rarely did people buy them — he was astonished to learn, while reading a tattered, mildewed book about Asia, that he had inadvertently hit upon the chief tenet of Buddhism: Stop desiring. Buddhists, he read, believed that desire was the root of all unhappiness, and was to be transcended. The book mentioned that there were eight steps to do this. The pages outlining these steps were missing. It didn't matter; he was secretly proud he had reached the state without knowing them.

But Whit was not a fool. He knew that his salvation could not have been so simple as two words written with a chewed-up pencil in the middle of an anguished night. He mistrusted things that were too easy. He also mistrusted religion. He thought of religion as an apology for the unknown.

He supposed it could be possible that he was a natural-born Buddhist, that he had been born into his current life occupying an elevated plane of enlightenment. But he knew that if he was there, it had been because of some metaphysical accident, since another part of him found it impossible to accept the idea that you could or should give up desire and all that came with it. He still believed there was joy in wanting, when you actually got what it was that you wanted.

Still, the words brought him relief every time he looked at them. Stop wanting.

They were what had gotten him through the first two years of his retreat, and nine months, twelve days, and five hours into his third.

For while Whit was a man who appreciated old things, like many men, he liked young things too.

Novena began stopping by the shop a few times a week. Sometimes she'd stay briefly, sometimes longer, helping him unpack cartons of newspaper-wrapped merchandise, sorting it and arranging it on tables.

At first, she felt a pleasant sense of virtue helping Whit, as if she was paying him back for the cigarette case. But she also liked being around him. They had quickly fallen into an easy bantering, teasing each other like two lion cubs, swiping harmlessly at each other, without the claws bared. He exaggerated their age difference, playing up his age and her youth, putting himself in the role of a lecherous codger, and rather than feeling more like a grownup being with someone so old, Novena felt younger, somehow unleashed.

Still, she was waiting for something else from him — some sign that he might have a stronger interest in her. She was, like most pretty girls, highly sensitive to such signals, having received them so often from boys, but even after spending weeks together, Whit still kept their bantering light — it was not quite flirtatious, and not quite innocent. He did use endearments, but he exaggerated them, taking the weight and import out of them so they became jokes: Sweetcakes. Honeybear. Googoo cluster.

If his lack of true ardor frustrated her — if, occasionally, she felt a stab of jealousy when she saw him handle with particular fondness a bowl, or a piece of cracked crystal, or an old photograph — she tried not to let it bother her. She was trying hard to keep anything from ruffling the surface of calm that had settled over her.

Winter had arrived, and as the days grew colder, the river had begun to freeze. Every time Novena drove past it, she measured the ice's progress; it was a strange feeling knowing that Zan was being sealed up in there a little more each day. And although it pained her to admit to such a terrible thought, she had to admit she was more relieved each day the ice thickened; she could feel that someplace inside her was being sealed up too, becoming encrusted and inaccessible. She tried to make up for her relief by praying for Zan, but they were bedraggled things, these half-hearted, backhanded petitions, and they shamed her more than the relief she prayed against.

Meanwhile, she spent as much time as possible with Whit at the shop. There was plenty to keep her busy. For one thing, it took a long time just to learn how to sort and arrange the stuff that came in. Whit's shop seemed to be a jumbled-up mess, with things piled randomly on tables and stuffed onto shelves. When she had first suggested organizing the place, Whit had just laughed.

"What do you mean, organize!" he had said in mock horror. "It *is* organized. I've classified everything by species. In fact, I've spent so long perfecting my system that I'm beginning to think of myself as the Darwin of stuff."

He had taken her around the place and explained: one table was reserved for things he imagined would appeal to Hawaiian-shirted tourists, though Nile Bay had few tourists and even fewer who wore Hawaiian shirts: scarves printed with road maps of states, chunky ashtrays from tropical islands, and hand-colored postcards. Whit was derisive about this category, called it all "poi," and priced the stuff high.

Bettys were the household objects, the heavy manual meat grinders that clamped on the edges of tables, egg beaters, boxes of spoons and forks and knives, clogged and mismatched salt and pepper shakers, strainers whose holes were still plugged with dark flecks of some ancient meal, and flour sifters to which ghosts of white powder still clung.

On a table in the back, he had set out the grannies: doilies and gloves and hairnets in their original packages, felt hats with netting, black lisle stockings, rust-stained corsets. Of all Whit's categories — shelves devoted to the seven deadly sins, or the four elements, or chemistry — the grannies was Novena's favorite. She loved the satin bed jackets, the scraps of lace, the tiny hand stitches in the lingerie. She liked the faint aroma of old perfume that still clung to the stuff.

She had a harder time, though, figuring out the appeal of many of the other things that came in. Sometimes, surveying a hideous cracked vase or food-specked tablecloth, she wondered what it was that had possessed someone to save it. So many of these torn, ripped, chipped, cracked, and burned things were beyond purpose or use. Their lives were over. Yet they had been salvaged, wrapped carefully, and delivered here, not to be buried, but to be reborn into second lives.

But she liked being in the shop, watching Whit grow suddenly serious as he unpacked some broken-down thing from its newspaper nest; he'd hold it carefully, moving his hands over it as if he were listening to something, to all of its secrets. She also liked the idea of being around so many things that might have the same ability as the cigarette case to replace her memories with their own. And so she handled as much of the merchandise as she could, hoping its memory might imprint itself on her.

So far, the only thing that she was conscious of picking up was the years' worth of grime and dirt buried in the ridges and grooves of her fingers. Within a month, her hands felt permanently stained with it.

One afternoon, she and Whit were going through a box of children's clothes that had come in. Inside were folded-up baby clothes, a few girls' outfits, and a collection of broken toys.

Whit prided himself on never rejecting anything that came in, no matter how beaten or broken down. This had less to do with his obligation to his uncle than it did with a sense of obligation to the objects themselves. The only thing that bothered him was the broken toys; he felt that toys were the repository of such intensity of love and terror that after leading such short and strenuous lives, they deserved to rest in peace when they were finally cast aside. He put them in a big carton, which he stored in the back room; he was still trying to figure out the right way to dispose of them.

Novena was holding a doll she had pulled from the box. It was a soft cloth doll and its size and weight seemed to fit so well in her hands that she had a hard time letting it go. The doll looked as if it had been pummeled: its patchwork dress was threadbare and torn, its yellow yarn braids were knotted and pilled, and its hard plastic face was defaced with purple ink marks and dented so badly that only a ghost of its original frozen expression was left. Still, there was something in that expression that made it hard for Novena to look away. As she stared, she realized what was so arresting: while dolls' eyes usually stared back at you, the eyes of this one had been painted to look off to the left, and so the doll gave the impression she had achieved not only dignity in the face of her battering, but an utter disregard of it. She looked almost contemptuous, and Novena had a strange impulse to push her finger into the face to make another dent. She shuddered and pushed the doll away from her.

"You know," Whit said, taking the doll from the floor, "I get the sense you don't have much respect for this stuff." She could hear he was trying to keep his voice light, but there was a quiet in it that made her blush.

"I *do*," she said, sounding more defensive than she wanted to. She was stung at how unfairly he'd judged her.

"Listen, kiddo, I'll tell you a trade secret," he said. "The first thing you need to know is that this" — his finger traced the little dents in the doll's face — "this is often where the beauty of a thing is. In its damage."

She wanted to please him. She wanted him to hold her the same way he held some of these things. So she tried. She paid more attention to the tiny fissures, the imperfections, the chips in the china, the forks with bent tines, the rips in the tea towels, the wooden salad bowls and cutting boards with gouges so deep they looked as if they had been bitten.

Novena was soon going to the shop after school a few times a week, and most Saturdays. She became increasingly aware of Whit watching her as she moved around, and she began to feel as if he were constantly testing her somehow, gauging her reaction to things. He still showed her no sign of anything other than a fond but distant affection. She grew a little bolder in her own flirtation, which was a new sensation for her, since she had so rarely needed to make such an effort. But while he always responded with a teasing answer, he maintained his usual reserve.

She began wondering if he even liked her company. She was feeling discouraged. He was probably getting impatient with her failure to appreciate these things. He might even be relieved if she spent less time there. Then she got the idea that he probably wouldn't even notice if she didn't show up. She decided to test this idea, and so the following week she stayed away for four days.

She came in on Saturday. Whit looked up, grinned and said his usual "Hey," and returned to polishing a brass bowl.

Novena felt it like a small slap.

"Hey yourself," she said loudly, her voice surprising her.

"So," she said, walking toward him, feeling bold. "Did you miss me? I bet you did. I bet you were crying until you saw me come in."

"Every minute you're away I'm mis'rable," he drawled, mocking earnestness.

"Well, you should be," she said.

She hated the sharpness she heard in her voice, the stab of disappointment that she felt, and she was shocked to find herself near tears. She moved quickly to the back of the shop before he could read it on her face, and stopped at one of the grannies tables, pretending to straighten the things there. She picked up a teacup, a frail bone china thing with a small spray of violets on its face. There was a small dark crack that ran through the cup, and she was staring at it, trying to calm herself.

But she could find no solace in this thing, and a great hopelessness washed over her. It dawned on her that the essence of these things was lost to her because there was something essential lacking in her, something missing from her core. And Whit could see it. He could see everything in her, he had seen it from the first day when he'd caught her shoplifting. She felt miserably alone; she imagined being very old, drinking from this cup in a dark room, abandoned, all family gone, waiting for nothing. She imagined it so precisely that her mouth filled with the bitter taste of milky, unsugared tea.

It was a tiny moment, but one of such potency that the cup seemed startled by the force of it, and leapt from her hand to the floor, shattering.

"Damn it," she cried, and heard Whit moving from the counter to make his way back to her.

She stooped to pick up the larger shards of the china.

"I'm sorry," she said.

"Don't apologize, for God's sake. Did you cut yourself?" Whit said. "Let me see your hand."

She knew she hadn't cut herself, but she gave him her hand. He inspected it, and then, holding her hand in his, he began rubbing it softly, kneading it between his own. Then, one of his fingers began tracing the lines in her palm, and Novena closed her eyes, thinking of the hairline crack in the china cup, the fissures and cracks in her being smoothed away as warmth spread into her fingers and hand, up her arm. Just as she was going to pull her hand back because she thought she might faint, he raised it to his mouth and lightly kissed her palm.

"No more boo-boo," he said, but his voice was gruff, and had no joke in it.

"Yes," she whispered. "All better."

In the weeks that followed, she had a sense the objects were starting to reveal something of themselves to her. She began seeing dignity, even wisdom in the flour sifters and meat grinders. She found a certain endearing pugnaciousness in the battered, bruised, and stained things. She began imagining the stories behind certain things, the secret lives contained in them. She could lose herself, for example, examining a burn hole in an apron, imagining a woman sitting at a table, waiting for her husband to arrive for dinner, smoking and smoking as the hours passed. And when it was eleven o'clock and dinner was cold and he hadn't yet arrived, her waiting had burned itself into this small charred hole in the gaily embroidered pocket.

Sometimes she shared these stories with Whit, and he in turn would tell her his own. Their stories grew increasingly elaborate, and began encompassing more than a single object, with bowls and lampshades and cups and scissors all interconnected in labyrinthine tales leading to their ultimate demise.

She didn't point out to him that in the hours they spent smoothing and cupping and prodding and holding their hands over the surfaces of things to divine their lives, they had barely touched each other.

He didn't point out to her that all the stories she made up explaining the damage to things always seemed to come down to the same thing: to waiting.

One day, as they were unpacking a box, she saw him unwrap an old terra-cotta jug and hold it for a long time. She waited for him to say something, but he got up and brought it to a shelf behind the counter, where he had a small collection of things — a hand-embroidered linen towel perfectly intact but for a yellow layer of age, an array of small boxes, and a small leather-bound book. It had always struck her as being like a little altar, and because he never talked about it, she had never asked him. Now she was curious.

"What is that stuff?" she said as he walked back to where they were unpacking.

"Oh, some of my favorites. My pets."

"So tell me why they're different from the rest."

"Oh, it's ancient stuff. Stuff with soul."

"Well, what about this?" She was pulling out of the box a square of stained, fleece-backed oilcloth, painted with a profusion of vegetables and fruit. "Soul?"

He took it from her, shook his head. "No."

"This?" She handed him a square plastic salt and pepper shaker set.

"Okay, let Gramps tell you about soul," he said, taking it from her.

"First of all, it's only about seven years old. Look at it. And grime that young is not interesting; it's just dirt. You've got to let this stuff age another decade or two. Then the dirt ages, takes on a mystery, like wine."

She just nodded. He wondered if she thought he was nuts.

He hadn't put words to any of this, even to himself. In fact, he had rarely given much thought to it, until recently. He'd always been able to appreciate certain items based on their aesthetics or simplicity, and there was a small handful that he felt an unnamed affinity toward. When he held them, he could feel something under their skin like a small heartbeat, as if they had something to tell him. Most of the stuff, though, he considered simply a vantage point from which to view human behavior. But lately, since Novena had been coming in, he had found himself becoming more conscious of the things themselves, and the ideas he had been forming about them.

He suddenly realized he had theories, a set of beliefs about these things. And they were not limited to the things with stories to tell in their fissures, cracks, and holes. There were other objects that had something else, something more than just a story. A soul. This soul was in the dirt that covered things, rather than the thing itself. Dirt was on the outside, forming the emotional crust of an object, receiving its sorrow and its happiness, its weariness with use, its imperiousness at its own value. It took time for the dirt to penetrate these objects, to burrow into the cracks and chips, enter the bloodstream — Whit knew they had a circulatory system of sorts, he had felt it under his fingers — and then the dirt would give the object something of second life.

At the same time, he was beginning to wonder about Novena's emotional crust, the dirt that covered her. She was such a little girl in many ways, almost a baby. On the other hand, it seemed she had dirt on her that was older than time itself.

Novena would have been surprised to hear herself characterized like this. In fact, she had never felt lighter, or more relaxed.

In the shop with Whit, surrounded by tea cozies and rusted tools and broken appliances, everything bad had stayed far away. She was covered with a blanket made up of everyone else's history, instead of her own. It was warm there, and safe.

And she wasn't alone. Whit was in there, with her.

She was breathing easier, sleeping better, feeling almost happy, a feeling more reminiscent of summer than the darkness of February. It shocked her to think summer was seven months gone; it seemed further away than that, fully suspended in a thick mantle of ice, thick as the ice that now covered the river. She didn't think about Zan. And she didn't think about spring, or consider what might happen when the thaw came.

And so, as each day passed, stacking itself neatly and quietly upon the day before like the layers of snow gathering outside, she started believing that the more time that passed, the safer she would be.

Of course, it's always just the opposite that's true.

chapter 17

ZAN'S BUS TICKET had taken him down the coast about three hundred miles to a nondescript town that promised nothing. He got off and found a cheap motel room.

Although it was a bright afternoon, the sunlight seemed to have collapsed in exhaustion upon reaching the motel, and mustered only a dim, halfhearted glance into the room. He closed the shades and fell into bed, where the sheets were so thin they had the unpleasant feeling of a stranger's skin against his own.

A few hours later, he woke from a heavy sleep. Or rather, his eyes opened, but it was as if he'd left part of himself in sleep, since he seemed unable to recognize anything in the room. He could identify their names — chair, curtains, ceiling tiles, door — but they were completely foreign. Nothing here belonged to him.

He lay there, taking in the lamps, the rug, the curtains: not his. A canvas bag on the floor, stuffed with clothing: not his. Two shoes on the floor, two leather things: not his. A body on the bed, with weight and mass: not his.

He stared at the two hands that grew from his arms. Two hands. Not his.

He watched them curl into a fist, then fall back on the bed.

He had a terrible thought that the sheets were, in fact, a stranger's skin which had replaced his own, and somehow, he had been given the body of that stranger. He was filled with nothing of his own: no thought, sensation, or memory. All he was conscious of was a hollowness so deep he could hear rumblings from somewhere in his center.

It was, he thought, like being dead.

Suddenly, it dawned on him that he had forgotten something important. He *was* dead.

And while he could feel the tentative, wobbly steps of panic making their way to his brain, his first feeling was one of relief. Being dead explained what he was doing in this strange room, hundreds of miles from anywhere, unable to recognize anything, unable to recall even one thing about himself. He must, he thought, be in limbo. He had always pictured limbo as a white place, not some place done up in brown plaid, filled with tired sunlight.

But then again, how else would limbo be decorated?

Also, he had always thought that limbo was a place devoid of all needs, but it began to dawn on him that the low hollow rumbling coming from his center was hunger. He was ravenous. He kicked the sheets off and stood up.

He put on the unfamiliar clothes and the strange shoes. He packed up the bag on the floor and stood at the door, about to leave. He took a final look around the room, wondering if there was anything else that he could take that he might need.

He saw something gold and gleaming on the table next to the bed. He picked it up and held the ticking thing in his hand, studying the watch's tiny face, the numbers traveling around it endlessly, the spindly hands like the legs of some insect. The script on the back: *"R. from A. with love."*

His watch. His.

He felt a tiny spasm, like a chill, pass through him. The sound had triggered some engine of thought and memory and recognition. He could now recall putting the key in the door to this room, and before that, getting off the bus, and before that, riding on the bus, sitting in the bus station, leaving Annaluna. He tried to push his mind past that point, but at the thought of Annaluna, his mind reared back, refusing to go any further. It fixed itself on her, and he remembered being in her room, staring at her face — so sweet, resting on the pillow, a shadow of blue thrown from the lamp on the bureau.

He whispered her name, over and over, finding solace and pleasure in the repetition of her name, in the small push of breath in the first two syllables, the furling of tongue in the third, the unfurling sigh at the end. *Annaluna*.

His Annaluna. His watch. His.

But now that he had recalled Annaluna, Zan suddenly missed her so much he felt his chest heave up in pain. He wanted to howl with the enormity of it. He wanted to heave this ticking thing from him, to smash it into silence.

But then his stomach growled again, snarling impatiently for his attention. He buried the watch in his bag so he couldn't hear it, and left the room.

He walked around until he found a diner. He took his time eating, filling himself up, then sat on a bench outside the place, watching trucks and cars pull in and out of the parking lot.

He thought about stealing one of the cars. He wondered if he was up to the task. It was a different thing, stealing one far from home, from someone you didn't know, an unfamiliar car that you hadn't seen drive around town for three or four years — almost letting you get used to the feel of it before something told you to slip into the driver's seat and take it.

As he was contemplating this, a man came out of the diner and stood next to the bench. He flipped open a lighter, lit a cigarette, and closed it with a soft metal sigh.

"Evenin'," he said.

"Yeah," Zan said.

"You hitchin'?" he said to Zan.

Zan looked up at him quickly. He was an older, burly fellow wearing a checked shirt. He was staring out into the parking lot —

not anxiously, but perfectly relaxed, as if he were satisfied with it, and with the night, and was now waiting for Zan to join him in his satisfaction.

Zan thought again about the feel of those sheets against him, the brown plaidness of the motel room.

"Yeah," he said. "I'll take a ride."

This is how he traveled for the next two weeks, getting into trucks, moving forward, moving south. During these days, he grabbed sleep when he could and each time he woke, it was with the same sense of dislocation, the same dead weight of himself, connected to nothing. The watch was the only thing that brought him back to something he remembered as his own. It recalled Annaluna to him every time he heard its ticking, as clearly as if it were a photograph, or her voice. He came to rely on its sound like a steady heartbeat, which he thought of as Annaluna's heartbeat, ticking its message — *with love, with love, with love.*

But in those two weeks, its constancy began turning from comfort to pain: as each second reminded him of Annaluna's love, it also reminded him of her absence.

It finally became like his own heartbeat; even as each beat reminded him he was alive, each was also ticking away his time on earth.

chapter 18

According to Naga belief, the human soul is divided into two parts, known in the Wanchu dialect as yaha (the animated aspect) and mio (the spiritual aspect). When a Naga dies, the yaha travels to the land of the dead while the mio remains in the village. Abundant mio is considered beneficial to the prosperity and fertility of the Nagas and their crops, and Nagas zealously preserve the supply of mio in their village. . . . In the past, because Nagas believed that mio resided in the head, the spirit reservoir of the village was augmented by the taking of heads. When a head was brought into a Naga village, the spirit of the slain victim was ritually told that although his relatives no longer cared for him, he should feel welcome among his new friends.

— Stuart Cary Welch, "India: Art and Culture 1300–1900"

HAD SYLVIE DROWNED in February, things might have turned out differently. In the remains of winter, her girlfriends — Danielle, Cookie, Jaci, and the others — would have been forced by the cold to grieve for her indoors, pining alone in their pink and lavender rooms until spring arrived and hope found a place to take root in their wayward hearts. They might not have given Zan a thought; if they had, any interest they might have found in his disappearance would have burned itself out before summer, before they could begin haunting the riverbank at night, undertaking their strange, unholy rituals.

As it was, though, the arid heat of July and August, which had scorched their hearts to dust, had continued into September. That's when they shaved their heads. They took up their shorn hair like sheaves of wheat and burned it as an offering, then rubbed the ashes on their shining skulls.

Once the gray, rainy October had infected their bones with a sudden bleak chill, they took to wearing heavy black boots, ugly steel-toed things. In them, the girls walked as if their boots were storing weapons — although it would be a few months before they actually did. But the most critical feature of their new footwear was the weight imparted by the steel. It grounded them forever to the earth, so much so the taste of it never left their mouths.

By December, they were no longer girls who could flirt with ideas and discard them for the next shiny one that appeared. Any idea they had — like the idea of Zan as their hero — was destined to be hoarded and hung in a dark place until it was dry.

By March, they were wearing it around their necks like a shrunken head.

They began piercing their extremities, and etching themselves with homemade tattoos, on their hands and their ankles. There was one tattoo they all had, made by pricking their skin with a heated pin. They kept this one hidden. Cookie, however, couldn't wait to show hers off, and one afternoon, when she saw Novena in Daz's warming herself over a cup of coffee, she took the seat in the booth next to her.

Novena had grown used to the girls' physical alterations, but she was always slightly shocked to see Cookie. Cookie had always been their pet — naturally sweet but slightly dumb — and her early attempts to appear menacing had struck Novena as nearly heartbreaking. Cookie had, for example, shaved her head like the rest of the girls, but instead of looking crude, her skull quickly turned to a soft peach fuzz, giving her the vulnerability of a new-born. Her thick black eyeliner, rather than giving her the cheap hardness of the others, had rounded her eyes into exaggerated innocence.

Over the months, Cookie's natural sweetness continued to put up a weak struggle with the darker influences Danielle and the others were exerting: for example, a furry pink rabbit's foot still dangled from her key chain, and often, when the girls sat in Daz's sneaking scotch into their Cokes, she would sit among them absentmindedly doodling flowers on the place mat.

But today, Novena saw that Cookie had finally managed to look like the rest of the girls; her hair was chopped haphazardly, and her lips, painted nearly black, fit comfortably around a cigarette. Her eyes were dull under their paint. Now, Novena thought, she just looked stupid, and although she hadn't been close to the girls in months, she felt instantly traitorous at the thought.

"Want to see something cool?" Cookie said.

All winter, the girls had continued to wear jeans hacked off above the knee despite the cold; Cookie had made the winter concession of thick black tights under hers, although they were laddered with rips and tears. She now stuck her finger under one of the holes near her knee, and ripped it open, exposing her right thigh.

"Look," she said. She thought the sight of this tattoo might impress Novena, although mainly she was proud of it because it had been particularly painful to apply, etched in the soft skin on the inside of her thigh. "All the girls have one, but mine's the best."

Novena looked, and saw a blotch of small raised purplish marks. It was just a few days old, and the faint strains of blood under the skin were still visible. She stared hard at it, beginning to make it out. A small circle, enclosing three simple lines, forming the letter Z.

Z, for their hero.

Novena stared at it, unable to speak. It was horrifically ugly.

Cookie's skin looked so tender, so painful, with a yellowish cloud surrounding the bruise, that she wanted to cry.

Cookie, taking Novena's silence as appreciation of the beauty of her tattoo, had leaned forward and was speaking again.

"Nove, I've got to tell you, it's wild. We've been having ceremonies. You should come."

"What do you mean, ceremonies?" Novena said. Her voice sounded as if it were making its way through a long tunnel.

"Well, we call him up. Light candles and stuff. At night. It was Danielle's idea."

"What are you talking about?" Novena said. Her body felt like it was moving away from her, entering the same tunnel as her voice. She shuddered, and hugged her arms around her.

"*You* know." Cookie leaned closer and hissed in a stage whisper. "Zan."

Novena had known she was going to hear it, but she flinched at the sound of his name. But it brought her body back to her — at least her leg, which was beginning to sting, as if the tattoo were imprinting itself there.

"We've been evoking the spirit of him," Cookie continued, speaking with an odd formality that Novena knew was a mimicking of Danielle's words. Cookie would never come up with words like that on her own.

"You're crazy. Why are you doing this?" Novena said harshly.

"Well, he's answered," Cookie said defiantly. "We've seen him."

Novena just stared at her.

"Danielle says she saw him standing by the river one night," Cookie said, leaning forward suddenly, speaking in her old breathless way. "It's so cool. It's like . . . what's his name, that Icky Bob Crane guy."

"Oh, don't worry, he had a head and stuff," Cookie went on, her eyes opening wide. "Zan, I mean. He was just standing there, Danielle said. Right at the place, you know. Where Sylvie went in. Then, when she looked again, he was gone."

She shuddered, thrilled, her eyes closed. "The next day, we got these."

Her eyes drawn back to the tattoo, Novena felt a strange sense of embarrassment, as if her own skin were exposed, and she wanted to reach over and cover up Cookie's leg, but her hands would not move.

For a moment, she thought this was a message for her, for her eyes only. But she was looking at it dumbly, feeling her incomprehension as a large hole in her. Whatever was here, she was inadequate to decipher it. All she could see was its color.

But then she felt anger blooming in her, blooming like another bruise, and she had the sudden urge to slap Cookie. Although there was nothing the girls could actually know about Zan being with Sylvie, somehow the fact that they had fabricated the idea on their own made her unaccountably irritated. They didn't even know him. They didn't know anything.

"God, what's the matter?" Cookie said, taking in Novena's odd, twisted expression. "Don'tcha like it?"

"I've got to go," Novena said, pushing her chair away and getting up quickly. "I'll call you."

"Hey, wait!" Cookie called. She had been getting ready to ask Novena to sell her some of Zan's belongings. The girls had been collecting anything they could of him. Earlier in winter, they had dug under the snow and gathered grass from his front yard, although his house had long been emptied, and had lately been begging Check — who chased them out of the coffee shop — for the mug he always drank out of.

Novena welcomed the rush of air on her face, and she took deep breaths of it as she made her way to the car.

It was a warm day for March, following a string of unseasonably warm days. A constant slow dripping of melting ice had begun last week and icicles had begun detaching themselves from eaves and shattering joyfully onto the pavement. Now the sound of racing water could be heard everywhere, as drains ran, gutters overflowed, and runoff poured from the sides of buildings.

If the thaw continued, it wouldn't be long before the river would overflow its banks. Novena drove there now, the sound of water creating its own strong current that seemed to be sweeping her toward it. She found a spot overlooking the river and parked.

The river's surface was no longer smooth and hard, but mottled with icy patches — thick and white in some places, but thin and black in others — that formed a membrane like crusted lace.

For months, this is where Zan had been, lying quietly in deep and frozen stillness. It had been Novena's private image of him, belonging only to her. But somehow, while she wasn't looking or paying attention, he hadn't remained still and quiet. He had surfaced from the depths onto Cookie's skin as something abstract — like God, or love, or air, something beyond her control. Zan was no longer hers.

She was suddenly frightened about where it all might lead, what other strange, uncontrollable form Zan might mutate into before his body actually appeared. She could picture the girls embellishing their image of him, making him darker, more disturbing. This, she knew, would be the version of him that would become the truth, the part that would stay alive.

But Zan *was* dead, and she reached for the comfort in this fact: he did have a body, and it would have to appear soon. The river had to give him back. But what if it didn't? What if he never appeared? Without his body, he would be nothing more than a ghost in a story. Without his body, the story would never end.

There was something wrong with this idea of Zan, disappeared forever, something terrible about the idea of him never being laid to rest. She shuddered, thinking of him underwater forever, and she wondered if there was something she might do, some alarm that she might raise about him, for someone to look for him. But she knew there was nothing she could say. It was too late.

No one would bother looking for him now. Zan was practically forgotten. Even the girls didn't really remember Zan; they only worshiped his absence, and only because they had dreamed up the idea he might have had something to do with Sylvie.

As Novena considered this, it dawned on her that she might have made a terrible mistake. She thought about all she had done to cover up his connection with Sylvie — moving his truck, cleaning his house — and it struck her that she had separated him from the one thing that could have made him important enough to remember. Sylvie would have elevated Zan. Without her, he hadn't been worth thinking about, or looking for.

If Zan was never found, it would be her fault.

Then an even worse thought occurred to Novena: if she had said something when Zan had first disappeared, there might actually have been time to save him. Maybe her silence had doomed him; she might as well have drowned him herself.

Novena did the only thing she could with this idea. She tried to stop it, to carry it far away, through cell and blood, through bone and muscle, looking for a place to hide it, to bury it, so it would no longer be recognizable. She tried to cover it so deeply, under such weight, that the thing would barely be able to move.

Starting the car, she willed her brain to fill with those important tasks: turning the wheel, backing up, pulling out into the road, and driving fast, away from there, away from the river. She drove blindly for a while, until, out of habit, she headed for Whit's.

But then she changed her mind. Right now, she couldn't bear the idea of Whit's gaze. He had the ability to look at her and see everything, and somehow he'd see the truth. She herself was already picturing it as some grotesque entity, and she could already feel the stirrings of its heart beating inside of her like the fast heart of an animal, an animal wounded but still running, trying to get away, to save itself.

She kept away from Whit's for nearly a week, staying close to home. In those few days, the spring thaw settled in for good, and the mantle of ice lifted completely from the river. The warmer breezes carried the dank perfume of the river, its old history of frogs and silt, rushes and decay, now layered over with new growth. Each day it rolled through town like a fog, and whenever it filled her nostrils, Novena took it as a sign that Zan might soon appear. While she tried to find relief in this, the briny smell hung in the air like an accusation, and began taking shape in her mind as something damp and exhumed, something drenched and hungry making its way toward her.

She began waiting each day for that smell, waiting for Zan to appear. She waited and waited and waited.

She grew to hate the smell. It had a way of clinging to her, and she imagined it seeping into her skin. Her body would feel heavy and lethargic, as if her bones were swelling with its dampness. She returned to Whit's and spent more time there each day, not only to avoid going outside but to avoid going home, where it seemed she was always alone. Elegia and Wyn were never there anymore. They were always off somewhere, no longer around.

Where were they? Where was everybody?

chapter 19

Ask Buddha—he doesn't know.
Nor do Patriarchs.
Beyond our grasp:
Who was born? Who died?
—Unzan,
Zen Poems of China and Japan

ELEGIA WAS BUSY. She'd begun a long resurfacing from the brooding withdrawal that had begun in the fall and, by winter, had settled so thickly and heavily around her that it felt like layers of fat padding, gray and cloudy as suet.

She had kept her job at Dr. Jack's, but had become stiff and pre-occupied, no longer cheerful with the patients. In fact, they sickened her, with their bleeding gums and decaying enamel; she barely paid attention to Dr. Jack himself.

He had fretted over Elegia, not just because he worried about her, but because he missed her attentions. He was a modest man, immune to most attention, even the considerable amount of it that was his due as a widower in a small town. He had noticed when Elegia's beam had flickered on him all those years ago. At first, he hadn't been sure what to do with it, but when he realized it didn't require him to do anything, he had let himself be warmed by it. He'd grown dependent on its small and steady presence, and it had surprised him how desolate he felt at the absence of that warmth.

So he tried his best to rouse her from her funk, trying to jolly her, making his small dental jokes. While they were not particularly funny, he always managed to end each with a horsy chuckle.

One cold day in November, they'd been closing up for the day. She was in the little room where they kept the supplies, his white coats, and the coffee pot. It wasn't a pleasant room; the fumes from the X-ray chemicals stored on the shelves mingled with the many years' worth of sludgy overcooked coffee, permeating the paneling and infusing his white jackets with the smell. Elegia was sitting on a chair, changing into her boots. He tried not to look at her feet; encased in their stockings, they looked like small white paws.

"Oh, sorry. I just came in because I wanted to ask you something. This is a conference I'm thinking about going to," he said, thrusting out a brochure to her.

He had gotten the idea of asking her only ten minutes before, thinking it a perfect way to cheer her up, but he knew if he didn't ask right away, he would chicken out.

"Why don't you come? It's just for the day. Office management stuff. You never know. We might figure out a way to manage those chairs and desks out there, make them work a little harder."

"Oh. Oh, sure." She smiled distractedly at his little joke. "That's fine."

He had picked her up early the morning of the conference and they had driven into the city. The morning sessions were fine, but the afternoon was boring, so they decided to leave early. They found a small bar in the hotel and sat for a few hours. Elegia seemed finally to relax, laughing at his jokes and even showing a little of her old self, making fun of some of the dentists at the conference. They were city dentists, prosperous, slicker than Dr. Jack, or anyway he thought so, with their bow ties and wire glasses. Every time he had reached out to shake one of their hands in greeting, his own hand had looked huge and awkward, reminding him of a farm animal.

He had thought of this again when two hours later he pulled

into Elegia's driveway to drop her off, and she put her hand over his. It was so small in comparison.

"This was fun. Thanks," she said.

He patted her hand, not looking at her.

"No, thank *you*." He wondered if he was blushing.

He gave her a ride home a few nights after that. Then he was taking her home regularly. He always took the long way, finding longer and longer routes, until soon it became their routine to leave a little early and just drive around. She began booking his last appointment on Mondays and Wednesdays at two-fifteen, so they could have more of the afternoon in the car.

She also began wearing lipstick again, he noticed, and some of her nicer dresses.

At first they just drove, stopping at Blackie's, the year-round hot dog stand, where they sat with the engine running, drinking homemade root beer and hot dogs with tart red relish.

"You know, I could take us somewhere nicer, or warmer," he said to her one afternoon, coming back into the car with the pulpy cardboard tray with their hot dogs.

"Oh no! Don't you dare. I love these dogs."

Elegia loved eating hot dogs in winter; it made her feel like a child, like a girl who was being rewarded for being good. Besides, it made her happy to be sitting in the car with him. He was close, but because they sat side by side, it was more relaxing than having to look right into his face.

After they ate, they'd drive some more. In the late winter, they began going to the dam, which sat about four miles outside of town, at the top of a long hilly road. It was a huge artificial mountain of shale and limestone a half mile long, with a paved road on top, ending at a cul-de-sac. It looked as if it had been carefully constructed and then abandoned. Dr. Jack often wondered why the dam had been built. The river hadn't flooded in twenty years. No one was ever in the little station at the entrance, and he had rarely seen a car there, although it was clear from the cheerfully worded signs at the lookout station that the town had hoped the dam would become a bustling tourist attraction.

Every time they took the turnoff and approached it, he would make a little dam joke. The first day he said, "It's a dam nice day."

It's a dam town. It's a dam nuisance. Dam!

At first, reaching the dam meant the end of their drive. He would drive around the cul-de-sac and take her home. Then they started spending more time there, looking at the ravine far below them, at the thin thread of river on either side.

They were mostly silent, staring down below them, but then Dr. Jack would start talking. He would talk without jokes and guffaws. He would talk of his simple and earnest questions about the world, and Elegia would listen, sipping the extra bottle of root beer she would have brought along.

Once, while he was talking, he had a coughing fit, and she passed him the bottle. As he brought it to his lips he saw the pale orange outline of her lipstick around the rim.

He opened his mouth to drink, although it was really to taste the lipstick. It was, he thought, delicious.

Wyn Sr. wasn't a blind man. The lipstick, the dresses, the later and later hours. A man could only take so much. Should only take so much. But he wasn't sure what his limit was. He had always been careful about expecting or asking for too much.

But things were different: his son was gone, his wife was never home, and he was getting mad. And he started nursing his anger as if it were a prizefighter, rubbing its shoulders, patting its back, saying yeah, come on, you can do it, come on. Waiting for the round bell.

One Wednesday afternoon, he left work early and drove to Lerner's office. He waited across the street until they came out, and followed them as they meandered through town. He fixated on Elegia's head, bobbing and bouncing over the bumps. He followed them through town until Lerner finally pulled into their street and into their driveway. Wyn kept driving, conscious of the strange sensation of passing his own house.

He started following them regularly.

He followed them through the streets of Nile Bay. He followed them to Blackie's and watched them get hot dogs. The first few times, Wyn's hunger grew as he watched them eat, giving him a sharp pain in his side. He started bringing his own food along.

After they ate, they would drive some more. The first time they turned onto the hill that led to the dam, Wyn stopped and turned back. He drove back to Dr. Jack's office and sat in the parking lot. He sat there a long time. Whistling softly through his teeth. Thinking.

Did he love his wife? He remembered their early years when she was narcotized by pregnancy, when he had tried to believe it was he who was having that effect on her. He thought of her cheerfulness, which he appreciated all the more for his knowledge of how hard she worked to affect it. He had been scared when she had first withdrawn, and relieved when she had recently shown signs of bouncing back. But now that he knew why, his relief made him feel like a chump.

Foolish woman. Her son was missing, and now she was carrying on with the dentist. Or at least driving around with him. The idea of her actually doing anything more was hard to imagine, but for some reason the fact that she kept driving around made Wyn feel even more betrayed.

In the beginning, when they reached the long road that led up to the dam entrance, Wyn would always turn around and drive back home. Elegia would arrive fifteen minutes later. Then it started taking longer for her to come back, twenty minutes growing to thirty. By spring, it was up to an hour.

Each time, Wyn told himself that he should keep following them up to the dam, but he couldn't make himself. He didn't know why.

One night, he turned off as usual when he saw them make the turn onto the road for the dam. But he didn't go home. He just kept driving. He got on the highway and drove, his eyes staring straight ahead, not conscious of where he was going, but conscious of the fact he was getting farther and farther from home. It excited him a little, and his stomach flipped at the strangeness of being so far away. He rarely ventured this far from home, and almost never by himself. But it was as if he had driven through a curtain, dividing home and the rest of the world. The road actually seemed to shimmer out there, ahead of him. That was when it came to him that he didn't have to go back. His stomach did another little flip, and he kept driving farther away from Nile Bay. He felt good.

He stepped on the gas, and the speed made him feel even better.

Later that night, Wyn called Elegia. When she answered the phone, all he said was, "What are you doing with that dentist?"

"Wyn," she said. But she didn't say anything more.

Her silence threw him off and he couldn't think of what to say. Finally he said, "Well, if that's all you have to say for yourself. I guess I'm going to be away for a while. Tell the boys. Tell Novena. Tell them I'll call."

At first she didn't believe him, but then she panicked.

"Where will you be?" she wailed. "How will I reach you?"

But he had already hung up.

Elegia hung up the phone, her cheeks scorching.

"You fool!" she yelled at the phone. "You damn fool."

She thought of Dr. Jack, and the unpleasant thought dawned on her that she wasn't so much mad as embarrassed. This mortified her even more. Outrage would have been so much easier, and as if to see if she could spark it, she lifted the receiver and slammed it down again.

She could have stood there, her cheeks burning, and grabbed that moment for what it was: to acknowledge her shame, and therefore accept an important new truth about herself, and be transformed. Unalterable change usually happened in such finely nuanced moments. But Elegia wasn't destined for such profound transformation.

And so she turned to her usual defense. She dredged up as much self-pity as she could muster. It wasn't hard, when she thought about it. How could she possibly have lost a husband and a son in just six months? Who was unluckier than her? Comforted by this, she prepared to go upstairs to her room, maybe start a new jag of sleeping. Son gone, husband gone. Already the singsong in her head was starting: Son gone, husband gone. She was looking forward to running freely through this latest scorched meadow of despair.

She began climbing the stairs, taking a step — *Son gone* — and another step — *husband gone* — and another, repeating the chant to herself.

But by the time she reached the top step, another voice inserted itself into her singsong. It was familiar enough that she knew it was her own, although in what part of her it resided, she didn't know.

It said, *Do you even want them back?*

When she heard it, she faltered, her hand gripping the rail, her right foot on the very top step.

She had no idea how to answer.

She went to her room. Instead of taking to her bed, she stood at her mirror for a long time. She looked for the well-groomed trio of mother, wife, and dental assistant that was usually there. Tonight, there was someone else there with them. Someone wronged, misunderstood. Falsely accused.

She hadn't done anything wrong. She hadn't done anything. She had driven around with Dr. Jack, but had only driven around. Nothing more.

The thought made her lift her chin a little in defiance.

It cast her face at a pretty angle.

She hadn't done anything but kiss him.

The voice came to her again. But this time, it actually came out of her mouth. She watched her lips — frosted with Luscious Peach — move in the mirror, forming the words. This time, the voice said, "Well, why not?"

Now she saw someone else in her mirror. Someone with lipstick, and a secret. The thought of it gave her a thrill that even she had the decency to be slightly embarrassed by.

One Wednesday soon afterward, they got into Dr. Jack's car as usual, at three o'clock. But they didn't drive around the small winding roads of town. They didn't stop at Blackie's, or the dam. They didn't go to her house.

That day, and every Monday and Wednesday thereafter, from three until six, they went to his.

Novena was going to Whit's shop every day now and staying until closing. Whit started to wonder. Where were her girlfriends? Where were her boyfriends? She was a pretty girl; he was sure she had plenty of both. Why was she spending so much time with him and all his stuff?

Not that he was complaining. He liked watching her walk around, picking up things, holding them. She had developed a good eye, and reverence for the right things, the same things he had reverence for, and disregard for the same things he had.

He wanted to flatter himself, although it was against his nature, with the idea that she was there for his company. But lately, she had been so remote and preoccupied that he could barely flatter himself with the idea that she saw him at all. Sometimes when he spoke to her, she started, as if she was surprised he was there. If he asked her a question, she'd answer so curtly he'd be stung.

There was another thing that was starting to bother him. Although he saw Novena every day, he knew nothing about her. He had always respected her reserve, but he was growing more curious about what was underneath it. She was as wrapped up as any of the potato mashers, ship lamps, or butter dishes that were delivered to the shop, tied and taped up in newspaper.

· · ·

Whit considered himself well read, but he rarely bothered with newspapers. In Nile Bay, he felt he wasn't missing much by skipping the weekly *Express*. The headlines were the same week after week: COUNCIL PONDERS HIGHWAY BID. SCHOOL VOTE PENDING. LADIES AUXILIARY TO MEET.

They were the opposite of news to him; they were history wrapping history, fitting shrouds to the relics he gathered. Unwrapping a vase or bowl from its newspaper nest, he might read a story that caught his eye, or he might look at a photograph — although all the pictures had a sameness to them too.

He was poking through a box that had been dropped off the night before. It was full of what he guessed was the contents of a girl's bedroom, and thought of leaving it for Novena to unpack. It was mostly clothes, though he found a few sad stuffed animals, some trinkets, and a jewelry box.

It was only because of these things that the word GIRL caught his eye on one of the sheets of wrapping.

LOCAL GIRL DROWNS was the headline. He scanned the story, picking out words: "Plummets into river . . . Mysterious circumstances . . . Car retrieved . . . Survived by mother . . . Services Monday." Above the story was a small photo of a girl who looked to be Novena's age. It was dated nearly a year before.

He nearly forgot about it, but later that afternoon he asked Novena whether she knew the girl.

"Sylvie? Yeah, I knew her."

"It must have been awful," he said, remembering his own car accident, that feeling of spinning, out of control.

"Awful? I guess it was, for her."

He stared at her, surprised. "Wow, that's cruel."

"Sorry." She blushed, sucking her lips into her mouth. "She went to my school. I knew her."

She didn't say anything more. He decided to drop it. There was no species more cruel than teenagers, he thought. Something in him was grateful for the reminder that Novena was a teenager. It made him aware of how rarely he thought about her as one.

"Hey, you know, I almost forgot," he told her. "I've got a present for you."

When she had started spending so much time helping him, Whit had told Novena that anything in the shop was hers for the asking. She rarely took anything but scraps of lace and pieces of old velvet or satin, which she would work into patchwork scarves that she had started making. She also liked the big heavy art books, and she'd pore over any book related to clothing, like old sewing pattern books that sometimes came in with boxes of yarn and tins of buttons. At his uncle's shop, he had found an old history of costume with beautiful color plates, and although the price astonished him, he had bought it for Novena, telling her it had come in with a bunch of other books. She had made such a fuss over it, he started giving her little presents — sometimes pretty things, but just as often joke presents, like a used magic kit with most of the pieces missing, or a hideous poi object, like a garish palm tree brooch or a satin pillowcase with a map of the states.

He now handed her the ballerina jewelry box that had come in that day. He wasn't sure why he had chosen it; he couldn't decide if it was because of the mild joke behind the gift — it was almost a cartoon of a teenage possession and he knew she'd appreciate the fact — or if it was because of the faint vein of sadness he had felt when he had first opened it. Maybe, he thought later, he had wanted to test her, see if she felt it too.

She opened the top, and the ballerina sprang out, twirling around to a tinkly song whose notes sounded warped and dying. Novena's face seemed to collapse, folding into itself as if it were flimsy as cloth.

"What?" Whit said. "What's the matter?"

"Where'd you get this?" she said softly.

"It came in today, with a bunch of other stuff. Look, pick something else out if you don't like it."

She was still staring down at the box. When she lifted her head, he saw her face had changed again. It was composed. Her eyes were cloudy, but he watched them change in an instant into something harder.

"It's cute if I were twelve, maybe," she said, putting the box down.

Whit must have looked crushed, because before he knew what she was doing, she gave him a small kiss on the cheek. And while it had the flavor of a girl indulging her grandfather, it was the first time she'd touched him, their first kiss. The warmth from her lips stayed on Whit's cheek, and her soft, sweet smell stayed in his nostrils for the rest of the day.

Before he closed up that night, he noticed that the jewelry box was missing, and thought with surprise that she must have taken it after all.

The next morning, he looked for the box of stuff that had come in with the jewelry box. It was gone too.

Novena didn't know what had rattled her more: hearing the warped tinkle of the ballerina box, which sounded as shockingly familiar as Sylvie's own voice, or later, when she had looked in the back room and found the box of Sylvie's things on the counter. And while it was like any of the hundreds of boxes that had come into the shop — brown, cardboard, and pedestrian — the sight of it was shocking. It wasn't just the idea that Sylvie's mother had gotten rid of her things, though Novena found that disturbing enough. It was the idea of Whit going through them, figuring things out, that left Novena's throat dry. The box made her think of the bones of something that had been buried, washing up from a flooded ground. She wanted it out of the shop, far away from there. She picked it up and put it in her trunk.

On the drive home, she tried to calm herself. Whit couldn't know anything from this box, just that the things in it might have belonged to someone Novena once knew. But maybe Whit did know something. Maybe he knew everything, and had left the box there as a test, to see what she might say about it.

Novena brought the box upstairs, put it in the middle of the floor, and sat on her bed, looking at it warily, as if it were about to burst into flames or begin hovering there above the carpet.

It was a cardboard box of stuff, like the hundreds that she had helped Whit unpack. But this was different: it was a box of Sylvie, and she stared at it a long time, trying to figure out what it was doing here, in her room, in the world. She couldn't help thinking it had appeared for a reason, that there was a message here, although she was getting weary of always looking for signs. It had been weeks now since she'd been reading signs of Zan everywhere, and yet they all led to nothing.

The ballerina box was resting on top, and she could see a few things peeking out from underneath — the collar of a blouse, the sleeve of a jacket. Novena knew she would recognize them as if they were her own: the cheerful, oversweet, almost chirpy colors and patterns that Sylvie had favored.

Nothing of Zan would be in that box. It was all Sylvie, as if she were reappearing to remind Novena of her importance. As if Sylvie were saying, "I'm the one who matters."

It was always about her, Novena thought irritably. Never Zan.

She stood up, resolved to get the box out of her sight. She intended to push it with her foot into her closet, but she ended up kicking it harder than she intended, and the ballerina box tipped over to the floor.

She couldn't help it. She picked it up, pushed in the clasp and opened it, and immediately the warped tinny sound chirped from the ballerina. Novena couldn't bear to listen to it. She snapped the case shut. She jammed it back down into the box, closed the flaps on the top, pushed it into her closet and shut the door.

That night, though, and for some nights thereafter, she heard the sound in her dreams. But in her dreams, the sound was somehow transformed, from chirpy to slower, more sorrowful. Then a vision of Sylvie would appear, dressed like a ballerina, stiffly twirling round and round. Faster and faster, in a weightless pirouette, she'd sluice through the water, making that sorrowful, slightly metallic tinkling cry, a cry which grew slower and fainter, until finally it died out completely, when Sylvie hit bottom.

Whit started paying more attention to the papers now, scanning for more stories about Sylvie. Two weeks later, unwrapping a box, another headline caught his eye.

LOCAL MAN MISSING, DROWNING RULED OUT.

It didn't say much, it was just a few inches, inside. A man missing, his mother, Elegia, quoted as hysterical with worry. The paper was dated a few weeks after the account of the drowned girl.

He was tempted to ask Novena, but he was cautious. He supposed that if she were another type of girl, she'd be filling his days with breathless accounts of these two dramas. For a town this size, these must have been monumental events. How had he not heard about them? What else didn't he know?

Now he wondered: Who were these people? Who lived in this town? What was he doing here? He just sat and collected their stuff, their castoffs, their archives and relics. He was like the town dump. He should have known the town better than it knew itself. But he knew nothing. He was just a cataloger, a librarian, not even a historian. Occasionally his fingers might feel pleasure moving over the surfaces of some of their things, pleased by their shape, their color, or the minute vibration of something like a pulse, a secret, a promise, a story, but it was all ephemeral, it was all surface. Nothing ever revealed itself.

And here was Novena, flesh and blood before him, revealing even less. He didn't even know her last name. She lived a complete life outside of here, but he had no access to it. Nothing about her was written down. Nothing published, no news stories, no black type that said GIRL DROWNS.

Everything, everyone, he thought, is a mystery until they're dead.

Everyone is a mystery until they have a toothache.

Whit had a screaming one. It woke him in the night, his eyes wide open, and he lay for hours, unable to sleep from the pain of it. Praying for morning, he wondered how toothaches always knew to hit in the middle of the night, in the middle of sleep, when all important messages are delivered — about the unsettled state of your soul, the direction your life has taken, the many hurts you have inflicted on others. Part of its torment is the hint that the agony would evaporate instantly if only you could decipher the message it has been sent to deliver.

Whit wondered what this one was trying to tell him.

Morning finally came crawling to him, and he was out the door and at Dr. Jack's, where within twenty minutes the molar was drilled, filled, and finally quiet. He could have wept with relief.

Now Dr. Jack was poking around in his mouth. Whit was so grateful by then that he opened as wide as he could, offering his gums, his teeth, his imperfect enamel, ready to offer his heart, his liver, his soul to Dr. Jack's probing fingers.

It was suggested that a cleaning might be in order.

"Talk to Elegia out front, she'll make you an appointment," Dr. Jack told him, and Whit said, his mouth still full of small logs of cotton, "Elegia?"

He didn't say anything to her that day, but when he came back the following week, Elegia was waiting for him, wand in hand, ready to clean his teeth. Thirty minutes later, by the time his gums were throbbing with the thirty-two tiny beating hearts she had somehow unearthed in her excavation, he had done his own excavation. With a few polite, interested questions, he learned who Elegia was, who Zan was, who Sylvie was, and how they were all related to Novena.

He turned it all around in his mind. Zan missing, Sylvie drowned. The two unconnected by anything except Novena's strange reticence.

It started to hound him. He tried not to think about it, to clear his mind, but he had a hard time. It even became a mantra when he was meditating. Whenever he closed his eyes, Novena's face floated in front of him. He wanted to know.

His molar might have been quiet, but his mind, which he always strove to keep quiet, nattered and caterwauled. It ran up and down hallways, shaking doors, yelling, "Tell me, tell me."

He asked himself why it was so important. But because his mind was chattering, he couldn't hear the answer to that question. It was probably just as well. It would come to him soon enough. It was a simple answer after all: he was in love.

And love is a brute, a busybody, a nosy-parker. It hates to miss anything, it harps and digs, and like a crone, like a gossip, it never satisfied until it knows everything. All your good, all your bad, all your life, all your secrets.

Whit was watching Novena more closely now as she moved around the shop.

"What are you looking at?" she'd say, catching his glance.

"Nothing."

Standing at the soul table one day, she turned to him and said, "I think I figured something out."

"What, sweetie?"

"Stuff doesn't really come alive until the person that owned it is dead."

"You're so Zen," he said.

He watched her face twist up oddly, as if it were a veil tearing, and he saw her freeze.

"Why did you say that?" she said. "What do you know about Zan?"

"Zen, honey, not Zan."

Or did he say Zan? He couldn't be sure.

"Oh." She relaxed slightly, and he watched her try to compose her features again.

Part of him watched with a detached curiosity at her transformation: seconds ago, she looked more exposed than he had ever seen her, and now the tiniest details in her face — a tiny wrinkle at the corner of her eye, a bottom lip misaligned by a few degrees — told him she wasn't quite successful at totally regaining her composure.

When had he memorized her face so well?

She had moved away from him, over to the grannies, and was straightening the lace. The set of her frail shoulders, her tiny wingbones, her small neck, looked so exposed and vulnerable, that he was moved to touch her. He came up to her and laid his palm on her back, rubbing it softly. He felt her skin open to him, and he thought he felt her move a little, toward him. Her skin was like a petal. He rubbed her shoulders, and she relaxed. He inhaled her hair, filling his nose with the scent of pine and rosemary, lavender and lilac.

"Ah, sweetness," he breathed into her hair.

He heard a little sigh from her. He felt her move closer to him.

What did he want? To love, or to know?

Whit didn't know he had to choose. He was greedy with love, and he wanted it all.

"So," he said softly, "why haven't you ever told me about Zan? Why the big secret?"

Suddenly her muscles were stones, her hair was wire, her skin thorned. She pulled away. When she turned to him, she looked both stricken and frightened. Her mouth was moving, but for a moment no sound came out.

"He's nobody, nothing," she finally said, the words squeezed out of a small space, with no air in them. Then she took an audible breath and said, "I've got to go."

She was moving toward the door. He began following her, and he reached out his hand to touch her shoulder.

She turned and said, "Leave me alone," in a voice that froze everything in him. Then she was gone.

She didn't show up the next day, or the next. A week passed, and he told himself she was probably caught up with graduation, with parties, with friends. That's why she had stopped coming every day.

Two weeks passed. He thought of calling her but finally dismissed it. He had no right, no claim on her. Whit stared at his note, up there on the wall. Now, every time he looked at the words, he had a hard time focusing on the letters. The words seemed to change before his eyes, giving him new messages:

Stop wanting. Stop waiting. Stop wailing.

chapter 20

WHIT WAS RIGHT. Novena was busy. She was getting ready to leave Nile Bay.

She was not, however, packing for college, as many of her friends were. Novena had done nothing all fall and winter about making plans for school, despite Elegia's nagging and the nagging of almost everyone in her life. Her aunt Quivera had taken to calling regularly, barking at Novena about the need to make plans, insisting Catorza would have wanted her to go to school. For months, Celantra had been sending a steady stream of catalogs for small, faraway schools with strange curricula. Margita had even called on a regular basis, urging that Novena consider her own alma mater, where she had studied textiles and design. Even though Novena had loved Margita's idea, she had done nothing about that either.

The only person she hadn't heard from on the subject was Annaluna, but in the end it was Annaluna who came to her rescue.

The rescue — that's how it felt to Novena — came just in time. Even before Wyn Sr.'s departure, she had begun feeling that too many things were coming to an end in Nile Bay. Now that she no longer could find comfort or peace at Whit's, she was afraid to stay any longer, afraid of what else she might lose.

Elegia had been on the phone more than usual, murmuring into it, and while this was not an unusual thing, Novena had begun to hear Annaluna's name mentioned more and more in these whispered conversations. She wanted to ask Elegia about her, but it had been so long since she had talked to Annaluna, she was afraid of what she might hear if she asked. Finally, she put aside her guilt and screwed up her courage to press Elegia for details.

"Oh, I'm so worried about her," Elegia fretted.

"What's the matter?" Novena said, alarmed.

"She's so old, and she's getting so frail. And she can't keep a nurse. She just scares them away."

"Why don't I go stay with her?" Novena said suddenly. "I can take care of her."

"What are you saying?" Elegia said warily; she had in fact been thinking of a way to ask Novena to volunteer, but the way she leapt on the possibility made Elegia suspicious.

"Look, I'm probably going to end up at that school of Margita's anyway, in the city," Novena was saying. "The next semester starts in January. Why don't I just go early?"

"Oh, I don't know," Elegia said. The logic was hard to argue with, although she made a valiant try. "You're kind of young to be out on your own," was all she could think of to offer.

"Come on. I'm not going to be on my own," Novena said, excited now to be making a plan. "I'm going to be with Annaluna."

"Well, we'll see," Elegia said, now finding herself strangely agitated by Novena's haste to leave. It hadn't occurred to her until that moment what her absence would mean — the girl was home so rarely anyway — but now a sudden dread at her leaving had taken hold. Everything was getting away from her. She wanted to take this whole conversation back.

"You'd have to go soon, you know," she said, hoping for even a small crumb of resistance from Novena. "Before the summer starts. As soon as you graduate."

"That's fine," Novena said quickly. "I'll be ready."

It was settled by the next day.

Yet it wasn't her plans that were keeping Novena away from

Whit's. The actual logistics of leaving were simple — she simply had to pack her things.

Novena was struggling with something far more consuming: the pangs and tribulations of love. Maybe all Novena's experience with boys should have prepared her better. But all her time spent with them had told her a lot about boys, but very little about love, how shocking its invasion can be.

As Novena had gotten older, the pleasure that she took from the company of boys had changed. Her appreciation had not necessarily deepened — it is hard, no matter how big or young your own heart, to find many gifts in the heart of an adolescent boy. Nor had her pleasure grown more complex. In fact, being a pretty girl, the pleasure she drew from them had grown much simpler. Like most pretty girls, Novena was used to their attention. It was a particular type of attention, because boys believe they're entitled to everything from a girl, except her prettiness. Even the crudest boys find themselves awed in its presence. Their big hands can't hold it.

And so for most of her girlhood, Novena had been able to inhabit the comfortable and distant room created by the awe of boys. She grew used to the space of it and to the sounds of it: to their harsh fast pantings, their raspy whispers, their sudden yelps of surrender that had all the urgency and confusion of escaping animals.

But Whit was different. He wasn't a boy. He was a man. She couldn't imagine him yelping or panting. She could only imagine him reaching and taking. For months, this thought had filled her with deep pleasure, but then the pleasure had bumped up against panic when he started asking about Sylvie and then about Zan. He had violated some line of safety she had drawn around him and the shop, and while she knew love demanded that this line be crossed, she also knew that, once crossed, he could keep reaching. She was terrified at how deeply he would want to go.

Novena was not the first person who has grappled with the ghastly possibilities of love overstepping its bounds. For nothing wreaks havoc on your demons like love. You always think yours are worse than anyone else's, and in that way, maybe you're a little possessive of the beasts, a little proud of your monsters. You want to keep them as monstrous as possible. But love insists you bring them out into the light of day. And that's when you risk revealing them to be something other than the looming dark shadows of your dreams, revealing that they are in fact rather pathetic, like a bunch of damp, toothless kittens.

But that's not what worried Novena. Her monster was no kitten. To her, it was the genuine article, the real thing. And so her risk was even greater: that love, having seen it, would run screaming from the room.

And so she stayed away. For two weeks, she was torn between wanting to rush into his arms — not that she had ever been there, but she liked the idea of it — and fearful his arms would wrap themselves too tightly around her.

She didn't make up her mind to see him until two days before she was due to leave for the city. She had been sitting on her bed, sorting through her things to pack, and had come across the green cigarette case. She held it to her, breathing it in, and smiled at the memory of kissing it in gratitude that night, when Whit had first given it to her. Remembering the smell of him, the smell of salt. Remembering the gift of him.

He *had* been a gift. Holding the case in her palm, she went cold at the idea she was about to give it up, to walk away without saying goodbye.

She had to see him, right now, before it was too late.

It was nearly five, and he would be closing any minute. She nearly fell down the stairs in her rush out the door, to get there.

But as soon as she reached the door of the shop, she paused, suddenly nervous. Her hand on the doorknob, it occurred to her that this was just like the first time she had come back to the shop, after taking the cigarette case. She had been nervous then too, yet desperate to see him. She had also been worried he'd be angry with her. And she felt the same way now: it had been weeks since she had been in, and she was afraid that he'd be angry. Maybe he'd feel like she had taken something else from him.

She took a breath and pushed open the door, and went in. The lights were on, but Whit wasn't there.

She walked to the back of the shop. He wasn't there either.

There was one place left, the small room off the back where he often disappeared to meditate. She had never been in there, although she had peeked in once when he had been busy at the front counter. It had a small cot where she knew he slept sometimes, and a small rug in the middle of the floor. That was all; there was not even a window.

The door wasn't completely shut and she pushed it open gently. He was sitting on the small rug, with his legs folded and his eyes closed. His glasses were off. She looked at him for a long moment, taking in the sight of him, that sweet, dear face of his, vulnerable without his glasses. She felt her heart turn over.

As if he had heard the sound of it turning, one of his eyes opened and the eyebrow over it arched in question.

She held a finger up to her mouth, saying "Shhhh." She came into the room on tiptoe, and sat on the floor behind him, her back leaning into his. She felt him stiffen at first, but then relax, and she felt his breathing moving her gently with his inhalations and exhalations. She closed her eyes and fell into his rhythm. His warm back to hers, rocking back and forth, the feel of his weight against her. She smiled, her eyes closed. She felt herself grow immensely calm. This is what she wanted, she thought. This is all she wanted, to be rocked like this, back and forth, warm and enveloped.

After a while, she felt him move. She turned at the same time he did, and their arms were around each other, their mouths locked. They sat there, on the floor, kissing, and she wasn't conscious of anything except that they seemed to be moving gracefully into another phase, and another and another. At one point, they moved to the cot, and then she wasn't fully conscious of anything until his grip on her suddenly became ferocious, and he startled her with a sharp exclamation of joy.

Then they lay, not speaking, for a long time, although she was conscious of a thousand words in her head. But they were languorous things, like herself, content to stay where they were, with no urgency to go anywhere.

She heard Whit's breathing slide slowly toward sleep and turned onto her side. His body was next to her, warm. His arm was touching her back. She felt the dampness of him, both on her skin and inside of her — a pool of it, she thought, a lake of him.

Her eyes were open but the darkness of the room was so thick that she had the feeling her eyes were closed.

This is what it's like to be blind, she thought.

She felt him stir. He began rubbing her shoulders and back, softly. His hands stayed on her back, traveling over her spine, feeling deep into her muscles. She wondered how she could ever leave this place.

But for lovers, the secrets of your skin are not enough; the geography of your body is not enough; the mole on your back, the inside of your mouth, the fold of skin at the crook of your elbow — all of these are not enough.

Lovers want to know. They want to know everything. And so Whit called up disaster, in the same way humankind has started trouble from the beginning of time: he started to talk.

He told her what he knew. He said the names of Sylvie and Zan, of Elegia, and of Novena's relationship to them all. He offered it all proudly, cunning lover that he was — that he had learned all this about her, had gathered up these facts of her. He told her this as he rubbed her back, offering his theories, telling her the things he had wondered about in those two unrelated incidents, and his curiosity about Novena's silence about it all.

She tried to catch her breath. She tried to relax. But even though his hands were on the small of her back, she felt strangled by them.

"So tell me," Whit was saying. "Tell me everything. What happened to them? Why don't you ever talk about it?"

She opened her mouth, and closed it. The room was dark, but she stared into it, hoping some words might be floating in the air that she could take for her own. She wasn't sure she could remember how to speak.

"No one knows for sure," she finally said, in a flat voice that didn't sound like hers. "They drowned, that's all."

The words had come from somewhere, and had made it out of her mouth. She was shocked at how calm she sounded.

"What about Zan, though?" Whit persisted. "They never found him, did they?"

Whit had been keeping up. One morning, over coffee at Check's, he had even asked Boomer about it, who seemed eager to talk. No one else on the force would listen to Boomer's theories, and now, having found an audience, he sought Whit out whenever he saw him. And even though Whit had been hungry to hear these theories, to hear whatever he could of this story, Whit had begun feeling guilty for talking about it; he felt strangely like he was betraying Novena, talking behind her back. And so he had stopped sitting at the counter and began getting his coffee to take with him, and giving a slight wave to Boomer as he hurried out the door.

"No, they never found him," Novena was saying now in a small voice.

She was curled up, praying he'd stop talking, feeling every word he spoke was cutting a hole in some heavy blanket that had been keeping her warm. She could feel cold air rushing in against her skin.

Whit was in fact reeling himself back, moved by her reluctance to talk about it. It must be terrible for her, to lose someone, yet never to know, to be unable to grieve, to have such a wound that would never close. But suddenly he was inspired.

"Poor baby. It must be so hard for you," he said, touching her hair. She looked so small there, curled up beside him.

"But you know, anything is possible," he said, trying to comfort her.

"What do you mean?" she said.

"I mean, no one knows what happened. Maybe he didn't drown."

"What are you saying?" she said, this time more urgently.

Poor Whit. He just wanted to offer his solace. Sleep, or love, was making him stupid. It is only one of the ways they resemble each other.

"I don't know," he said hopefully. "Maybe he's out there somewhere. I mean, it's been so long, I'm sure they would have found him by now. Maybe he just ran away, or had an accident and is walking around with amnesia or something. I'm sure he'll turn up.

"It happens all the time," he offered, now feeling ridiculous. As far as he knew, it never happened.

Something in the way she stirred, in the way the sheet moved, made Whit register Novena's surprise almost as a sound, of ripping.

Novena had simply turned her head, to look out into the room. It was already dark, but it seemed to Novena to go even darker, and she had the sensation of everything sliding away into that blackness, until only one thing remained: The idea of Zan, not in the river. Zan, not drowned. Zan, alive.

It was a huge idea, breathtaking in its immensity. The possibility had never occurred to her. But now she saw how possible it could be. So much time had passed, with no sign of him. If he had been in the river, he would have been found months ago, at the first thaw.

Whit's hand was still on the small of her back, and each muscle he touched seemed to burst open, releasing a flood of relief. If Zan wasn't in the river, if Zan didn't drown, it meant she hadn't made a terrible mistake after all. But as Whit kept touching her, she felt another flood of sensations that had been trapped and caged inside her and were now fluttering around, like confused and panicked birds. She could almost feel the brush of their wings against her insides, traces of their feathers, and their tiny fragile bones.

If Zan hadn't drowned that night, where was he? If Zan hadn't drowned, what had happened that night?

What came to Novena then were glimmers and choppy pieces of memory. Sylvie's hat on his counter. *He says he's going to kidnap me.* Zan in trouble, always in trouble.

What had he done to Sylvie?

She tried to relax. She tried to breathe, but she could only take broken jagged breaths. She pulled away from him and struggled off the bed, suddenly furious.

Whit had done this. No: love had done this. Love was a monster, she thought, promising solace, when all it brought you was more terror. Hiding its tricks, waiting for the cruelest moment to bring them out.

Novena was out of bed, gathering her clothes.

Whit cried out, "Where are you going?"

"I'm leaving," she said, and then, to return the cruelty, "I just came here to say goodbye. I'm leaving for the city. I'm moving there."

"When?" Whit asked, surprised at her tone, which was no longer a whisper, but a cold hard thing.

"Tomorrow," she said, thinking it surely must be past midnight.

Whit lay stunned, unable to move or speak. He was thinking what a monster love was, promising solace, when all it brought you was terror. Hiding its tricks, waiting for the cruelest moment to bring them out.

She was dressed, and she turned to look at him, prepared to see him ugly, prepared to take that image away with her.

She wasn't prepared to see him so vulnerable. So dear, so sweet. She felt her heart tumble, and she quickly bent to him, brought her mouth to his forehead, and left a kiss. It was sweet and short, and full of regret.

This is the kiss, and not your first, that you always remember. This is the one that ages you.

Then she was gathering her things. Whit heard her pick up her keys, and heard the door push open, and she was out of the room.

"Novena!" he cried. "*No! Ve! Na!*"

He heard the front door slam.

He cried out her name one last time. But she was gone.

As Whit lay in the dark, feeling the rise of his panic and the sinking of his spirit, he was visited by a specter of his own. It entered the room quietly, almost as a peep, as a chirp, and then there was a cracking sound, and there it was in the room with him. Newly hatched, still wet, its shell broken in pieces all over the floor.

Want.

Whit wanted again. He wanted everything.

chapter 21

THE SOUND OF OUR EXISTENCE is not the first cry we offer as proof of our presence, it is not the rhythm of our breath or the percussion of our feet on the ground. Those are just noises — tongue to palate, breath to teeth, skin to wood — as coarse as belching and farting and bleating and moaning, as pedestrian as a pan falling on the linoleum, or a kettle whistling. The true sound of our existence is more subtle, a sound formed as our molecules — the billion particles of our blood, memory, and destiny, of our experience, desires, and disappointments — meet the atmosphere, bending, refracting, disturbing it, creating something like our own music, which never leaves the earth until we do.

The clattering music of us fills the world, making it almost impossible to distinguish the individual strains of our loved ones. It leaves us to the sad fact that the sound of existence is one most clearly heard by its absence; think of the absolute silence that meets each thought of your dead. We can conjure their face, their voice, their memory, but it is just that: a conjurer's trick. We know it in our bones, in our blood, in our ears when someone is no longer on the earth.

Just as surely as we know when they are.

Propelled from Whit's side, Novena stood on the sidewalk outside the shop, momentarily dazed and squinting in the light. It should have been long past midnight, pitch dark by now, and yet the day was still burning with a hesitant brightness, the sun suspended low in the sky, its light casting an odd mauve stain that gave everything the shiny, sharp look of plastic. She began walking, past the storefront windows that shone like mica, past cars sleek as beasts, past houses glaring yellow and white. There was a stillness over it all, and she had the sensation of walking through a picture, a drawing of a toy town that could be erased or torn up. This was what had become of the world, she thought, with the possibility of Zan in it.

She was arrested by the strangeness of this idea, rather than its actual possibility. The idea was so immense that it was almost abstract, and like the idea of love or death, it didn't necessarily require belief, but it did require a certain recognition. She wanted time and quiet to think about it, away from this irritating brightness, away from this cartoon town. It was then she thought of the woods.

Nile Bay was a small town. It took its name not from a bay, but from an awkward translation of its ancient, original name. And it took its sense of smallness not from its actual physical dimensions or the size of its population, but from its sense of scale: it was set in a low valley and ringed with high wooded hills — old imposing stands of pine, white oak, maple, and beech. It was these woods, a sprawling city of trees that loomed, protective and dominant over the town, that had given Nile Bay its sense of itself as a small thing.

And yet those who knew the woods well — the hunters, the hikers, and a few who actually lived in them — thought of them not as a vast metropolis of trees, but as a series of individual places, like separate towns with their own names: the Flat Rock woods, Lead Mine Grove, the cemetery woods, the River Street woods.

Novena hadn't been in the woods in years. As she found one of the old paths leading into the River Street woods and followed it in, she felt the apprehension of being in a strange place, or a place you have forgotten how to negotiate. She expected things to look dif-

ferent, shrunken down like the rest of the world that you revisit after being away for a long time. But the woods had continued to
live and grow, so the scale was the same as it had been when she
was here as a small girl. Things were just as big, just as looming,
and she began to feel that with each step she was shrinking into a
small girl again.

But with each step, it also felt increasingly familiar. She recalled
that sense, on first entering the woods each day with the boys, of
shutting a door behind her, entering an absolutely quiet room.
Now she was overtaken by its silence, a stillness so profound she
had to stop and adjust her breathing, to adjust her ears, to accus-
tom them to the absence of engines, voices, words; to the sound of
the mad clattering furnace of the world being shut off.

But gradually, in the silence, a million sounds, one by one, began making themselves known: a distant rushing sound of water,
the vibration of insects, the skittering of small animals, the chirping and cricking and rustling of birds. And the smell — of sweet
and constant deterioration layered under the more bitter smell of
new growth — the smell of all of this almost becoming a sound
as well.

This was the sound she was most familiar with, the sound as familiar as her own breath. It was the sound of the woods.

The memory of her days here, trailing behind the boys, began
moving through her like a current, swift and pleasant, carrying her
forward. Up the hilly path, at the top of which was still an old tree
trunk which had fallen directly in the middle of the footpath, now
so overgrown it looked to be sprouting trees of its own. Past a
large emerald patch of moss, which, Novena recalled, had always
made her think of an elbow patch. She moved more quickly, more
surely now, and could almost imagine she was being led by the
small girl of herself.

Although she felt herself shrinking within the vastness of the
place, she now felt a sudden joyous return of something she had
forgotten: how small it all really was. She remembered how she

could carve the woods into a series of spaces as safe and intimate as rooms, finding floors, walls, and ceilings within a circle of birches, or in a nest of boulders, or under a tent of massive felled pine.

Her body was moving to its own memory now, reclaiming this place, so she shouldn't have been surprised to find herself suddenly at the entrance to another room: the boys' old fortress. She was amazed to find there was still an entrance, that it was still intact. She expected it would have been overgrown with years of neglect. It had been a decade since any of them had been there, but she felt a small prickle of unease as she pushed aside the branch covering the entrance and stepped inside.

Looking around her, she was surprised to see that the space looked as if it had been recently occupied. Other boys must have found it, taken possession of the place. The ground was soft and well trodden. A few empty beer cans, crumpled up cigarette packs, an old rag. At the foot of the large rock that served as a seat, the patch of ground was scorched, littered with small charred pieces of wood.

Behind that rock was a larger rock, on whose flat face she now found a neat row of small stones, an assortment of hewn sticks, and a few tiny skulls. She recognized this arrangement, as if she had seen it just a week ago, and knew it not as her brothers' things, but as boys' things. Weapons and armaments. A miniature arsenal whose protective power, she knew, was in its orderliness rather than in the things themselves.

As a small girl, she would collect feathers and ferns, leaves and soft pine needles. Useless, pretty objects. No weapons to speak of.

She thought now that there was something disturbing in the arrangement of skulls and stones and sticks. It had the precision of a language, like a spelled-out message that had been set here, waiting for her to come and decipher it.

She remembered the last time she had been in here and seen this arrangement; it was the afternoon Zan had brought a girl in here. That Zan had allowed this girl into their woods, into their fortress, had been shocking; it had felt to Novena as though something dangerous had arrived.

And then, something in the way Zan's arm draped around the girl's shoulders had suggested the danger was not to them, but to the girl — that he had not allowed the girl here as much as he had lured her here.

Novena had crouched on a rock a distance away, curious and thrilled at this new possibility of danger. She had sat outside listening to them, to the rustle of leaves, the thud of bodies on the ground, to their soft moans.

Novena wondered if she had actually been able to see anything that day; she must have, for she remembered the girl's thick white leg, like the trunk of a birch. She had also seen Zan rising up over the girl, and then lowering himself over her, smothering her with his body.

She had sat waiting and watching; watching them as if it were one of the television shows she had loved, of animals devouring each other.

Novena had been calm, crouched and waiting, thinking of bears mauling fish. Leopards pouncing and ripping apart gazelles. Crocodiles dragging goats underwater, shoving them under rocks until their waterlogged bodies became soft enough to chew.

Then the girl had squealed, a sound that had risen into a sharp cry of fright, then ended in a long silence.

Now she thought, *Sylvie must have squealed.*

Novena started at the thought. She didn't want to think about Sylvie. Sylvie had no place here, in her thoughts about things torn apart, dragged underwater.

But the idea of her was insistent and swarming, as if Novena had lifted a stone and exposed a writhing beetle colony underneath. She couldn't get the sound of Sylvie's voice out of her mind, of that high-pitched, slightly harsh, slightly hysterical cackle that she would use to greet the world.

Sylvie must have laughed just like that, that night with Zan, with the idea she was with him and no one in the world knew. Laughing and laughing, and then crying out, frightened, as they fell into the river and started sinking. Then, silence.

Novena knew what that silence meant. Zan and the boys had taught her. Creating that silence was why they had come here into the woods. They had practiced it here, silencing frogs, fish, small creatures, anything living. Anything was fair game.

Even each other.

Novena shivered, as if a cloud had just moved over a part of her heart, casting a brief shadow inside her. Everything seemed a shade darker, and she looked up, startled to see that the sky through the branches was a deep navy. It was getting late, she thought; darkness would drop its veil soon, and she was alone here, in the woods. And they were not her woods anymore, but a different place. The boys' place. Zan's place.

She had never been in the woods alone, and she felt it like the sudden consciousness of nakedness, so much so she felt her skin prickle. She stood still and alert, listening for some signal of something other than herself out there: footsteps, or a sudden shadow, or the snap of a twig, the rustling of grass. She stopped breathing, straining to listen for the approach of danger.

Novena pushed her way out of the fortress and began walking fast. The warbling and clicking, the crackling, slithering, and scuttling around her seemed amplified by the growing dimness, and more ominous. It was the woods, humming with appetite, growling with hunger. She remembered the exploded frogs, smashed fish, burned-up carcasses left behind by the boys, who had once been so fascinated by this hunger they seemed to consider it their job to see how wide its jaws might open.

Now she felt it following her like an animal. She kept her eyes straight ahead, trying not to think of all the things that might be behind her.

Don't think, she told herself. Don't look. Run.

She was moving through the trees, faster and faster now. Then she was off the path, running fast and blind, into the green.

She had forgotten there was a particular way to run in the woods, a hobbled, cautious gait, feet skimming over the earth to keep from stumbling over stones or limbs, thick tangles of underbrush, the snaky ropes of tree roots.

It was in fact a tree root that finally stopped her, a large root, almost as thick as a trunk, which reached out and grabbed her foot, casting her to the ground. She landed with a hard thud, and the force of it knocked everything out of her — breath, thought, and panic.

As she lay on the ground, inhaling the smell of dirt and pine needles, she slowly rolled onto her back, checking if any part of her was sore, and looked up at the tree whose root had just tripped her. It was a massive red oak. She saw the bottommost branch, thick and knobbed, the succession of more slender branches stretching above her in that familiar inviting staircase, and she was conscious of an old instinct — measuring the tree for how easy it would be to climb. She had climbed so many as a girl, and she remembered how she would assign each a personality according to its bark: some velvet and mysterious, some pocked and melancholy, others crabby and gnarled under her hand, but all cool to the touch, all as familiar as skin.

Now she remembered: she had fallen from the branch of a tree like this one once. She had climbed quickly, pulling herself up, limb by limb, going higher and higher, not stopping until she had almost reached the top, then sitting crouched on a branch. Stuck.

She had been perched on a high branch, and she remembered measuring the distance to the ground, feeling a strange pull, as if the ground were inviting her toward it. But she had been unable to move.

Then Zan had come, crashing through the woods, and then he was there beside her in the high branch, the warmth of him, the smell of him, surrounding her. Together, they had slowly picked their way down through the branches. Resting on the last limb, measuring the distance they'd have to drop. And as they had sat there, resting, Novena remembered feeling the warmth of Zan's hand on her back. She had leaned into it, grateful for its warmth. The promise of comfort was so surprising, that it could have come from him.

She thought of the feel of Whit's hand on her back, hours ago. She had leaned into that too, seeking out its comfort.

The smell of him, the warmth of him, surrounding her.

Then, the sense of falling.

That day, she had been huddled on the branch with Zan one minute, and the next, she had been falling — not in slow motion, but fast, as if the ground had reached up to grab her, to stuff her mouth with dirt.

Everything happened fast after that, and her memory seemed to take on that speed, as she recalled Zan on the ground beside her, scrabbling to his feet when Dex and Quin and Wyn came crashing through the branches, finally finding them. The boys looking at her there on the ground, worry still in their eyes.

Then Zan explaining: "She fell."

Light doesn't leave a forest gradually, but instantly, as if at the moment of day's end, the tallest trees suddenly lean forward and join their arms to close themselves up for the night.

Knowledge comes to us in that way too, often dropping upon us like the swift end of daylight. Or a bird, sweeping from the sky. Or a girl, falling from a tree.

Or a girl, not falling.

She hadn't fallen that day.

Novena, starting to sit up, said it aloud, first tentatively.

"I didn't fall."

She said it again, wonderingly: "I *didn't* fall."

And once more, this time as a statement: "I didn't *fall*."

Then Novena was holding that day in her hands, like an object lost for years and finally retrieved. Except it had come back wrapped up in paper, and while she could trace her fingers over it, and find details that were familiar — the smell of the day, the speed of herself through the woods, her bones trembling on the branch — it kept moving away from her. She moved over the day again, kneading it, poking it, trying to coax it out, looking for that precise spot where she might once again feel Zan's hand on the small of her back, where she might feel the slightest pressure, the smallest movement of his arm — all it would have taken for him to push her from the branch to the ground below.

Anger is always depicted as a fast thing. But it is not always a fast thing. Sometimes it is a slow, syrupy thing, drizzling through the veins, almost pleasurable in its slowness. She stood up, feeling that slipperiness moving through her limbs, up her chest, into her throat. For a moment, there was pleasure in that lubricating thing of her anger and she began walking, her feet hard and precise on the ground, her breath short, like jabs into the air. As it moved in her, she felt this drizzling anger collecting things — images of the half-eaten leg of a frog, the smell of the fried fur of a burned squirrel, the taste of dirt and pine needles in her mouth.

She saw her own small body, falling through space.

She saw Sylvie, falling through water.

And then at the center of everything falling, she saw Zan.

Novena howled, though it was not the wail from some unfathomable deep, but a sharper, more pointed ejaculation. Centered in her throat, it had an almost guttural sound, like a growl.

The woods, surprised at the sound, seemed to suspend themselves for an instant, letting the echo of her howl bounce through the trees, like a skittering animal looking for cover. But unable to find cover, it came back to her, and Novena heard the sound of herself. She was surprised at how loud she sounded, and how much satisfaction she took in hearing it.

Now her fury was running through her fast, like gasoline,

cleansing and astringent. Her insides burned with it. She could almost feel it glowing like a rock inside her — glinting and metallic, smooth and hard. The shine of it reflected in her eyes, and like sun bouncing its light off metal, like light reflecting off ice, it cleared her vision. She saw Zan no longer as an idea, an abstraction, but as flesh and body, somewhere out there, waiting to be found.

She would keep herself open, ready to receive whatever signals of him the universe sent, like radio waves. Something, she was sure, would lead her to him. She could picture him as a ratlike creature, scurrying in the walls and ceilings of the world — never seen, only heard — but gnawing his way through the world, leaving crumbs and small dark trails of himself behind.

And that, she thought, would be how she would find him.

chapter 22

Similar to the living creatures, inanimate objects, whether natural or man-made, can acquire supernatural powers, especially when they achieve a great age. At the end of each year, the Japanese still practice the ritual cleaning of the house (*susuharai*). It is believed that without performing this ritual, tools and instruments become unpure and polluted and eventually may become capable of evil-doing.
— Akira Y. Yamamoto, *Japanese Ghosts and Demons*

As far as Annaluna was concerned, Novena was coming in the nick of time.

She had never really been right since Renaldo had left her, breaking her heart again, leaving it a dried-up biscuit. And with no more tears to lubricate it, she knew it was only a matter of time before it was going to shatter into dust.

Who could she have talked to about this? Who would have believed that Renaldo had returned to her, after all those years, and been so sweet, so attentive? More important, who would have believed that she had a heart that could still be broken? People think the elderly build up that vital muscle, conditioning it with regular workouts of aches and disappointments and betrayals, but it's not true. Old hearts are more frail, not less. That's why so few try love late in life. They know how fatal it can be if it goes wrong.

Although Annaluna had been suffering dreadfully in the months since his departure, the cause of her current pain was not absence — she had finally taken that into her as she might have folded egg whites into the batter of one of her dreadful cakes. The cause of her suffering was worse than absence; it was presence. Her ghosts had returned, and this time, as if miffed at their temporary banishment, they had come back unpacking huge steamer trunks full of grudges, which they flung like laundry throughout the place.

Annaluna had grown accustomed to their petulance, but she couldn't abide the sharp edges of their rudeness. Now they were impossible. They extinguished whatever was possible to burn out — matches, light bulbs, the pilot light on the oven — and hid whatever it was possible to hide — keys, eyeglasses, combs, bills. Then they started hurling things — sending books sliding from tables, cups and forks and knives leaping to the floor, linens nose-diving from high shelves. She was getting worn out, wiping the spills and sweeping up the broken glass that seemed to follow her through the rooms.

"Give me a break," she would mutter, disentangling herself from the latest minor spill or small disaster.

"Cut it out," she'd call to whoever had sent a dish jumping off the counter, shattering on the floor.

She had to fight to keep her voice light, as if she were joking, because the truth was, she was getting a little frightened of these disturbances. While there didn't seem to be anything outwardly hostile in their actions — she hadn't gotten hurt by scissors or broken light bulbs or glasses — on her darker days, Annaluna began to imagine that they had the capacity for it, that there was something more sinister in their intentions than simply getting her attention. Lately, she had taken to spending a good part of the day in her bedroom with the door shut, but she could still hear them; it sounded now as if they had transformed everything in the house into instruments for the orchestra of their endless complaints — pipes banged, dripping water beat against the sink, floorboards groaned deeply, miserably, cellolike, under some unseen weight. Even the dust seemed to chase itself around the house screaming in arias of disappointment.

On the day Novena was due to arrive, Annaluna woke early and, steeling herself, left her bedroom and rolled into the living room. After extricating herself from a ball of twine that had suddenly found itself in the hallway and had tangled itself inextricably in the wheels of her chair like a whiny child wanting to be picked up, Annaluna sat at the window waiting. She was counting on Novena to restore calm to the house, but when Elegia's car pulled up and she saw Novena come bounding up the steps, a forgotten flower of pure joy bloomed in her chest at the sight. By the time Novena had burst through the door, it had pushed its way up her throat, leaving Annaluna unable to make any sound but a small strangled mewing.

Novena was equally overcome at the sight of Annaluna, although her joy was mixed with shock at how drawn and pale Annaluna looked. It had been months since she had seen her, and at the sight of Annaluna as a very old woman, she felt her stomach fluttering oddly.

She was also taken aback at the state of the apartment; she couldn't help thinking it resembled a madwoman in its exhausted dishevelment, its sense of chaos collapsed into itself. As soon as she unpacked, Novena started cleaning. She started in the spare room, now her own, whose fusty, cooped-up smell she doused with detergent. She scrubbed everything, and then she tackled the rest of the apartment, sweeping the floor of its bits of thread and tiny shards of broken glass and pottery, the scraps of paper, twine, crumbs, hairpins, pen caps, and the other small bits of detritus, each of which struck Novena as a testament to Annaluna's decline, as if each were something important Annaluna had shed from herself, like layers of skin. With each shard and scrap Novena swept into the dustpan, she felt another small weight of sadness being hung from her heart.

But within days, both the apartment and Annaluna were nearly restored. A slight bloom had come back to Annaluna's cheeks, and she was sleeping well and feeling energetic. By the end of the first week, they were like girls left alone together, following no order to the household except for what suited them. They could spend hours in an easy, graceful silence, or talk all day about whatever came into their heads: the color of light, or the taste of sadness — they had agreed that pea soup, cheese, and lamb cooked a certain way could be heartbreaking. They'd play cards late into the night, games of their own invention whose only rule demanded the frequent slapping of their palms onto each flipped-over card. They'd eat strange things for dinner if they felt like it — potatoes and peaches, or stacks of cinnamon toast.

Gradually, and in spite of themselves, their days took a firmer shape. They both slept late each morning, though Novena would usually wake first and take Mamie for a walk, bringing back warm bread or bags of fruit for breakfast. By then Annaluna would have risen, and they would spend the remainder of the morning at the table reading the newspaper.

Morning would slide into early afternoon, when Novena would rouse herself to the chores. She had found an old sewing machine in her room, and had begun replacing the tattered and pinned-together dresses Annaluna had worn around the house for years. Rather than throwing them out, though, she had started cutting them up into strips and making patchwork lengths from the scraps, which she incorporated into new dresses or little jackets. She made one for herself, and with the tinier scraps, she made silly hats or collars for Mamie, over which she and Annaluna would giggle helplessly for days.

Annaluna napped in the afternoons, and Novena would make a cup of tea and take it into the living room. She liked that time of day, between three-thirty and four-thirty, when the day itself seemed to pause, to adjust its breath to the slower rhythm of evening. She'd sit in a big stuffed chair, watching the softening of the light, staring at the patterns of shadows on the thick floral rug, the dimming shafts of sunlight dusting the heavy dark furniture, which, she knew from old photographs scattered around the room, hadn't been replaced or even moved in decades. The room at those times was like a cave or a cool, dark church, and she could sit in a chair for that hour, perfectly content not to move.

She began looking forward to that time of four in the afternoon, when she could stare into space, listen to the hollow ticking of the clock as shadows crept into the room, and feel the slowing of herself, the pleasure of a rapturous exhaustion that would often, but not always, lead to sleep.

When she didn't doze, she thought about Zan.

He had taken shape in her mind as something out there, unseen, like the speeding energy of the city's crowds. But she was conscious now of a place inside her she kept reserved for him, a place mapped inside her, like a new organ that worked and breathed and functioned in silent concert with her other organs. All she had to do, she thought, was keep this place open, so she could receive whatever signals or signs of him the universe would send. She had no doubt she would receive them, and that when they came, the signals would be strong as radio waves.

Weeks had passed, though, and nothing was happening. She grew restless, anxious for some sign that at least marked the end of one time and the beginning of another.

One afternoon, Novena was lifting the teacup to her lips, her feet up, listening to the whirring of the glass-domed clock, watching the shadows change in the room. She felt a sudden flash of herself slipping away, an odd feeling of being both conscious and unconscious — conscious of the actions of her body, but unconscious of herself inhabiting that body. She had become someone else at that moment, someone vaguely familiar: an old woman sipping tea from an ancient stained china cup, waiting in a dark living room for nothing. She had felt how heavy the hours of old age were, as if age, in adding weight to everything, could make time itself thicker around the middle.

Then, because this woman seemed so familiar to her, for a

dizzying moment Novena wondered if she *was* that old woman; maybe she had actually been sitting here for decades, and all the years in between had been blanked out, leaving her with only the memory of being young.

She shook herself back into the present, but for the rest of the day the moment nagged her, lingering like the taste of tea in her mouth. The next afternoon while Annaluna napped, Novena stood at the window looking out at the street. As she watched the waves of heat rising up from the sidewalk, the sun blaring its brightness, it struck her that it was odd to be spending the summer indoors. Maybe it was time, she thought, to start getting out of the house.

Because she had wanted to stay close to Annaluna, she hadn't gone outside much beyond her morning errands; in fact, Novena hadn't yet ventured beyond Annaluna's neighborhood. It was as if there were an invisible gate between her neighborhood and the rest of the city, which she hadn't felt inclined to pass through. But the next afternoon, she walked to the end of the block that she considered the boundary of the neighborhood and stood for a moment. Then, as if diving into water, she plunged across the street and kept walking.

Almost immediately, she had an odd recollection of entering the woods in Nile Bay. She could recall the deep silence that would unroll itself into individual sounds, and the city gave her the same sense — of a place she had just entered — although its sound was a single loud cacophonous bray, from which individual sounds unwrapped themselves: engines and trains, car horns and radios, footsteps and sharp bursts of voices.

She took in the smells — the fumes of cooking food mingling with clouds of bus exhaust and the pungent reek of waste in its infinite variety — human, animal, commercial, chemical.

And the people — moving in a sea, breaking like waves around her. There were so many people, it struck her that the whole population of Nile Bay could have passed her on a single block.

In fact, she was astonished at how many familiar faces from Nile Bay she saw that first day, and on the days that followed. Each time, though, just as she was about to rush up to the person, or call out, the face would turn into the face of a stranger, and she would be left standing in the middle of the sidewalk, watching the person walk away, flushed with embarrassment, feeling as if some trick had been played on her.

She stopped looking at faces and began to study clothing instead, taking in everything — misshapen pants, stretched across the bodies of fat men; demure white-piped dresses on middle-aged women; the hard-angled suits of men in hues of putty and a hundred shades of gray; the strange getups of teenagers, with their bright colors and odd hats.

Then she started focusing on smaller and smaller parts of the clothes — the buttons, seams, collars, hems — until she was narrowing in on the weave of the cloth itself. Her eye cataloged it all, instantly and relentlessly.

She was training her eye to miss nothing.

She began looking in the gutters, retrieving bottle caps, coins, keys, buttons, fragments of letters, belt buckles, hairpins, medals, rubber bands, wire insulation, segments of unraveled wool, a doll's head, the heel of a shoe, an umbrella handle, an empty wallet, five links of a chain, empty pill bottles, the occasional photograph.

Sometimes she sent Whit one of these finds, wrapping them beautifully in little nests of tissue paper. His responses to these offerings were sparse and told her nothing. He'd occasionally send objects in return, poi stuff. She would sit with them, trying to decipher their meaning, trying to read any feeling that might be in them.

She had called him when she first got to the city, to apologize for leaving so abruptly. She heard the burr of wound in his voice and no matter how she tried to bring up the lovelier moments of their evening together, he had sounded almost unmoved by her call.

She missed him terribly, and wondered if he ever thought of her. If she had seen him, she might have been able to tell from looking in his mouth. For Whit had reasoned out the perfect way to be near her, yet stay at a safe distance: he had been having his teeth cleaned at Dr. Jack's every six weeks like clockwork, submitting himself to Elegia's ministrations. Elegia was thrilled at his diligence, and thought he set a fine example of dental hygiene to the town, if they would only bother to notice. She wished there were more like him.

Soon a month had passed, into August's steamy heat. Despite the hot air, moist and thick as paste, Novena was spending every afternoon wandering the streets of the city. Though she would have never admitted it to herself, she felt a lightness out there that was increasingly hard to find in Annaluna's dark cave of a place. No matter how much she cleaned, the place seemed crowned by an ever-present halo of dust, and shrouded in an eternal darkness, even on days when the sun blared through the windows. Novena had the increasing sense that some moment of mournfulness — an eternal four o'clock in the afternoon — had been frozen there.

It wasn't that a moment had been frozen, in fact, as much as that one had become liquid again.

While we can usually count on our small daily routines and rituals to inoculate us against the demons of chaos that are always waiting to infect us, Annaluna's were meaner than most. It was in those small routines of the day that her demons had chosen to hide.

As Annaluna's days had once again become familiar — sitting across from someone, drinking coffee and reading the newspaper — she began feeling as if she had returned to a time she had lived before. She would get confused, unsure of whether she was in the past or the present, or somewhere in between. Most of the time, for example, she knew it was Novena sitting across from her, or walking around in the other room, but there were other times, such as when Novena rubbed her feet at night, that Annaluna would sigh and let herself drift through the years, and surrender herself to a pleasantly confused state, imagining it was Renaldo. And later, on those nights when she had wrapped her confusion like a shawl around her, Annaluna would see the thin beam of light under the spare room door, and wonder who was in that room now. Was it that night, or a night nine months ago, or thirty years ago?

What did it matter? It was all the same night, really. It was the same person in the room, with the light on, coming and going at all hours, getting ready to disturb her peace again. Getting ready to leave her.

Each afternoon, under her light cover of sleep, Annaluna would hear footsteps in the hallway, then the soft click of the front door closing. On hearing it, some small engine of recollected longing would start up somewhere inside her. Her eyes would fly open, and she would roll out of her room and position herself at the living room window. The light would fall onto the room, creasing the shadows, and through the yellowed film of the sheer curtains, the waves of heat coming off the street formed a moiré pattern in the air. She could barely make out people moving through it as if underwater. She could barely see anything, in fact. But she didn't have to, to know that he was out there, that he was not far. The heart is a navigational tool more precise than any, and though she knew that of all her muscles, this was her weakest, she tried with all her might to reel him in with it, to make him come closer.

To make him come home.

Alert to receiving her own signs, it took a while for Novena to notice any sign of change in Annaluna. For one thing, Annaluna had been hiding her disturbance from Novena under a hearty appetite.

Although Annaluna had the sweet tooth of a girl, there had always been something animalistic in her ingestion of meals —

dining was not for pleasure, but for storing things for future use, and Annaluna still cleaned her plate at each meal with a sturdy sense of duty, pushing her empty plate away from her with just a tiny snort of completion.

While Novena did sometimes catch Annaluna looking at her as if she couldn't quite place her, and if occasionally Annaluna referred to something they had done together — a radio program they had never listened to, a walk they had taken which Novena knew had never taken place — Novena wasn't worried, nor did she correct her. Annaluna was simply suffering the ravages of age and memory, maybe even losing her mind a little bit, a prospect which disturbed Novena not at all. She respected that gradual diminishment, and knew, from the time she came to stay with Annaluna, that the nicest thing she could do would be to soften its edges, to keep her from realizing it was happening.

Finally, though, you can't live with someone who is waiting, always waiting, without having that rhythm of waiting, that hum of expectation, start imprinting itself on your own bones. Eventually, you will experience your own inability to settle down, to digest your food, to sit still for very long, and you will begin to adjust to the new lightness with which sleep lies upon you.

At that point, though, Novena was only aware of the beginnings of a vague apprehension as she was roaming the streets. A taut, breathless moment of panic would sometimes hit her in the middle of the sidewalk in a strange neighborhood. Crowds would suddenly loom up around her, careening toward her menacingly; vapors rising from grates on the sidewalk would turn sinister and snake around her legs like the hands of spectral beggars.

One afternoon, as she was about to cross the street, she saw an old woman waiting on the opposite corner. Novena's attention had been drawn to the woman's coat: it was an old cloth coat of dull aquamarine blue, but she could tell from a distance how good the wool was. She was studying the shape of its collar when the woman suddenly toppled over backward onto the ground.

It was such a clean movement it seemed almost deliberate, as if the woman had performed a magic trick, and Novena, staring at the space the woman no longer occupied, felt her mind go dumb, as if unable to understand where the woman had gone.

A small circle of people had gathered around the woman to help her up. She tottered off, the crowd dispersed; it was over in moments. Novena walked on, but she couldn't stop replaying the woman's fall in her mind.

She was sure something momentous had happened in that instant the woman had toppled, something as large as the failure of gravity — as if gravity, after years of doing its quiet job, had itself fallen and broken a hip, and was now a hobbling thing, something that couldn't be counted on to remain stable. And even though it had nothing to do with Zan, she took it as a sign, as the first definitive signal from the universe.

It's rarely a good idea to open yourself up to the messages and signals from the universe. Because once the universe senses your interest, it becomes a slut for your attention, lifting its skirts to show you all its secrets underneath.

It's a shameless tart, the universe is. Once you signal you're ready to see what's under its skirts, it never drops them again. And there are a million things under there. There's so much, you could get lost in there. You could lose your way forever.

chapter 23

ZAN HAD BEEN DEAD for fourteen months and twenty-seven days.

Most days, he didn't mind being dead. So far, it was just like life, only longer.

When he finally ran out of money, he settled into another small town, as nondescript as all the others. He lived in a trailer, and found a job helping men assemble complicated machinery whose use he had no curiosity about. The work gave him money to live, to eat. That's all he cared about.

As a result of the hard physical labor of his job, he was growing muscular; not bulked up like before, but harder and leaner. The only soft part on him was his belly, which had swelled from all the beer he drank. Given the hard, well-toned rest of him, this flabby paunch was an odd, distended thing that felt separate from himself, like a pet. When he was in a good mood, he drummed on it, slapped his hands against it, liking the hollow sounds that came from it. But he wasn't in a good mood often. In fact, when he was, it was just that: a mood, which passed quickly. His life — work, food, sleep — was too basic for moods. In other words, he was getting through. That was how you lived in limbo: stacking days on top of one another like boulders.

In the past few months, he felt more and more of his life was being lived in the stranger's skin that had enveloped him in the motel room. He could recall fewer and fewer things of himself, and those he did remember rose up in him in thin watery pictures and quickly sank like stones, forever drowned.

It was as if the act of leaving Annaluna had torn open some place in his own skin from which his past had been steadily bleeding from him, and every day that he rose and moved into the future seemed to erase another day of his past.

By the time he had settled in this town, Nile Bay might have been a place he had seen once in a movie, and on the rare occasions he recalled the faces of his family, or people he had known, the images had the quality of someone else's snapshots. Not his.

He still had his memories of Annaluna, because he still had the watch, and its ticking always brought the image of her to him. But the ticking had grown weaker over time, and one day, as he was winding it, it occurred to him that the thing could one day wear down, and even expire on him.

He stopped winding it every day, and established a new ritual: every Friday night, he let himself wind it. Then the ticking would start up and the few remaining things of her left in his memory would stir and rise — the talc-y residue that had remained on his lips when he kissed her goodbye, the rustle of newspapers over the breakfast table, the feel of her foot in his hands. But lately even these recollections were becoming more sparse; they were like old men, hobbling stiffly around an empty room, with only the hollow echoes of their canes tapping on the floor.

What happened when even these were gone he didn't like to contemplate. He knew it would mean he was truly a dead man. And while the prospect of his mortality was an idea he should have grown used to, the truth was, Zan had always thought that his death was going to be a temporary thing — an episode, a late-Saturday-night, screaming-loud-and-fast adventure that would, like all such episodes in his experience, end with a minor crash and narrow escape from the law. It hadn't occurred to him it might be permanent, that his end could be final.

The concept of our finality never arrives alone. It it always trailed by an entourage of smaller ideas — liberation as well as panic, hubris as well as regret, indifference and remorse, a manic speed accompanied by an increased appreciation for the slowness of time. Had these ideas arrived singly, Zan might have been able to handle them, although remorse and regret might have given him difficulty. But their arrival all at once was too much for Zan. Their warring natures demanded a capacity for contemplation, which even in the best of circumstances he found difficult, but which, in the absence of memories, he found almost impossible.

And so, when finality did arrive, he took its arrival as a harbinger of disaster.

He was right. One Friday night, he picked the watch up from the little nest he had made for it out of the cotton from five bottles of aspirin he had lifted from the drugstore. He held it in his hand, wound it, and closed his eyes, waiting for the image of Annaluna's face to appear, as it always did, lit by the blue shade of her lamp. But just as her features came into his mind, they dissolved again, and he realized that there was no sound coming from the watch. The ticking had stopped.

He gasped, and thought that this might have been his own last breath. This was it: his last moment. Panicked, he shook the watch. It started again, and continued to tick with a mild hollow ping, which to his ears sounded mildly reproachful.

He sat up all that night, drinking in the memories of her, gorging on them, in case they turned out to be his last. By dawn, he felt so drunk he could barely stand.

Now that the watch was on its last legs, he dreaded the coming of Fridays. Now when he wound it, it would start up and falter, start and falter, each time teasing him with little traces of Annaluna, no more than wisps. Which were almost worse than nothing.

Zan was feeling desperate. He stopped eating, so he could attribute his shrinking to this, rather than a larger fading away of himself. Then even his vision started fading, as if his inability to see Annaluna anymore made him unable to see anything. He left the lights off when he was home, preferring to stumble around in the dark rather than confronting all he might be unable to see with them on.

It never occurred to Zan to take the watch to a jewelry store to have it fixed. For him, a jewelry store was not a place to get things repaired, only a place harboring glittering invitations to crimes too ambitious for him. But he did begin to think he was going to have to do something, to take some action, before he was completely lost, before total darkness descended.

Only a few weeks would pass before he got his chance.

chapter 24

NOVENA COULD HARDLY WALK through the city without imagining every tall thing tipping over; she pictured the collapse of buildings and bridges, the ground caving in from the weight of everything on it, people and cars sliding into the huge craters of buckled earth.

Before long, her nervousness had spread beyond the falling bricks from the tall buildings into the more particular dangers of a city like this — crowds pushing you along until before you knew it, you had fallen in front of a train; gangs roaming streets and trains, stripping people of their valuables; men hovering in shadows, ready to pounce. It wasn't hard to imagine these things; she and Annaluna read about them every day in the newspaper. And Elegia often made a point of calling to relate some of the more dramatic disasters she had read about, clicking her tongue to her teeth in a delicious dread.

"I don't know how you can live in that place," she would say to Novena. "I wouldn't be able to sleep a wink. Every night, I'd be sure someone would be coming in to stab me in my bed."

Elegia had a repertory of these brutal fates — stabbings in bed, pushes from high windows, shootings in the back — and although Novena hated listening to them, she would let Elegia go on for a few minutes until her imagination spent itself.

Still, Novena didn't alter her daily routine of roaming through the city; these visions of chaos had become so regular that she found them oddly reassuring.

One afternoon, she had been walking for hours. Her feet were blistering, and she felt the beginning of her jittery anxiety, like a wire inside her somewhere that was being pulled taut. Finding a small park, she collapsed on a bench and closed her eyes, breathing until she felt calm.

She didn't feel like moving ever again. She wondered how long she could sit there, how dangerous it would be to stay after dark. She kept her eyes down, and stared at the shoes of the people walking by.

She usually didn't pay attention to shoes. For her, living among Annaluna's collection, shoes had the mundaneness of grass or pavement. Novena had been thinking lately that she should soon start quietly removing some of them from the apartment; she thought it might soothe Annaluna to be rid of them.

Now she watched the small quick steps of women and the plodding thuds of men. She listened to the scrape of heels, and bouncy thud of sneakers, the grate of oxfords and whish of sandals. She marveled at how flimsy they all seemed, given the hardness of the concrete, the miles they had to carry their heavy human cargo. It was a wonder, she thought, that shoes weren't built more like vehicles, or like equipment, with complicated pulley-and-wheel systems of anodized aluminum or chrome, rather than these precious-looking slips of leather or plastic.

She watched a pair of flat sandals go by. They were unusual, lacing crisscrossed up the legs of a woman, ending at the knee. Gladiator sandals, she thought. She looked up to take in the rest of the woman.

She saw a kimono of dusty-rose rayon, splashed with large orchids and oversize palm leaves, a print that was reminiscent of a faded tropical postcard. The kimono came to just above the woman's knees, and was only slightly longer than its long formal sleeves. She had bound the kimono with a sash of scarlet tulle, tying it in back so it gave a bustle effect. Her hands were covered by a pair of white cotton gloves. Novena stared; she had never seen such a getup. The woman passed her before Novena could take in her face, but she saw that her long hair had been tied in a knot that resembled the knot in the red sash around her waist.

"Wow," Novena breathed.

The woman knew how to walk, rolling her hips in a way that made the long sleeves of the kimono flutter around her like wings. Novena, entranced, stood up and, almost without thinking, started following her.

She was walking slowly, and Novena was grateful; the blisters on her feet burned with each step she took. She was even more relieved when after a few blocks, she saw the kimono turn down a side street, a narrow dark cavern formed by tall buildings on either side. Halfway down the block, the woman stopped in front of a storefront and reached into the sleeve of the kimono for a key. She opened the door and let herself in.

Novena came up to the window of the shop the woman had entered. The glass had been painted black. In fading gold letters that looked as if they had been painted onto the window a century ago were the words GOOD COFFEE SANDWICHES.

Novena pushed open the door and went in.

She shut the door behind her and took a breath. She recognized immediately the bitter smell of age and dust and bodies that lived in old clothes — the smell of time.

Looking around the shop, she didn't see the woman she had followed here, but she did see many versions of her kimono. They were hung from the walls, their arms stretched out like crucifixes. They looked supplicating, as if they had been arrested, caught in some act.

In another far corner, she saw two orange saris draped from the ceiling like bunting. Under them, on the far back wall, were circular racks stuffed with shirts, dresses, and other clothes in more exuberant colors and textures.

Novena was getting dizzy, not knowing where to turn first. As she made her way slowly to the back of the shop, she noticed Thai phasin, polka-dotted house dresses, cheerful chintz aprons, embroidered kimonos, satin hostess gowns, bed jackets, veiled hats. It struck her that she might have entered a museum of clothes of the world, spanning both time and geography, and that it could take her years to make sense of the place.

Novena explored tentatively, picking up hats, stroking the gloves, pulling dresses from a circular rack. Her fingers traced the tiny, exquisite hand stitching, the complicated draping of a bodice, the hand-bound buttonholes of a jacket, and she felt a deep pleasure in these things, in their intricacy. As she lost herself momentarily in these details, she felt the present slipping away from her, another version of time taking its place.

At one of the counters, she began fingering a pile of old silk scarves. She picked one up; it was black and funereal, and seemed to whisper under her fingers, a sadness and melancholy. It flashed away, and she picked up another, this one with salmon-colored polka dots. It too seemed to move under her fingers with some sensation, and she imagined it was about to trill a giggle, when instead she heard it speaking to her.

"How long have you been here?"

Novena, startled, dropped the scarf. She realized the voice was coming from behind the counter, where the woman in the kimono was now standing.

"You've been so quiet!" she was saying. "I didn't hear you out here. Finding anything?"

Novena now saw her face, and it was one of the oddest she had ever seen. It looked as if it had been cracked like a piece of china more than once, and glued back together poorly. There wasn't a scar, but a faint diagonal line seemed to run the length of her face, forming two distinct halves. Looking at her gave Novena the same slightly disoriented feeling she got from being in the shop, as if there was too much represented there.

And yet there was also something else, in her eyes, perhaps, that gave Novena a sense of such familiarity she felt herself almost falling into them.

The woman's lips seemed to hover, confused, for a second before settling themselves into their proper positions for a smile.

"Aren't they delish?" she said. "I've got tons of those if you want to see more."

"Oh, I'm just looking," Novena said.

"Come here, let me see your dress," the woman said.

Novena walked to the counter. She was wearing one of her own creations, a tenty sleeveless dress that she had fashioned from a bias patchwork out of a few of Annaluna's old dresses.

"Total woo-bait," the woman pronounced. "Where'd you get?"

"I made it," Novena said, suddenly feeling shy.

"Hmm," the woman said, fingering it again. "Nice job. Saucy."

"I love your kimono," Novena offered.

"Oh, this old thing? Actually, it *is* pretty old. I decided a few years ago that the geisha thing made sense for me. Kind of like Japanese Venus, rising from the rice paddies, you know? They're so fushi, kimonos are. I think of them as architecture, but lying on a satin chaise longue, eating bonbons, you know? Like, if buildings wore clothes, this is what they'd wear."

Novena felt dizzy, unable to decide whether to keep up with the sudden stream of her words, or her strange ideas, or her face, which seemed to move in a hundred different directions as she spoke.

Novena could only stare.

"Although I've been shopping for a new look lately." The woman paused, adjusting her belt. "These sleeves for one thing. A total hazard."

She stretched her arms out to her side, and the long sleeves hung from her like flags.

"Doorknobs are jealous of how beautiful they are and reach out for them. And I'm tired of dipping them into my food. I get up from the table and half my dinner is on my sleeve. I feel like some Shriner bum with a stained tie, you know?"

"Yes," Novena said, although she was still trying to picture a Japanese Venus, a building wearing clothes, eating bonbons.

"Edo, he's my boyfriend, calls it wabe-slobby. So, anyway, what about you? You shopping for anything in particular?"

Novena was caught short by the sudden shift in her attention.

"No, I was just walking by. It looked like a neat place."

"Well, it's a schleggy neighborhood, but the rent's a song. And everyone who needs to find it, does."

There was a moment of silence, and Novena searched for a reply.

"I have to come back when I have more time," she finally said, suddenly conscious of how long she had been there, and how filthy her hands felt, not from dirt and dust so much as from age and emotion. "This place is pretty amazing. What's the name of it?"

"Good Coffee Sandwiches," the woman said, nodding toward a large free-standing mirror, which reflected back the letters on the front window.

Novena looked at her questioningly, to see if she was joking.

"You don't think it works?"

"No, I just . . . well, you sell clothes?"

"Oh, I didn't have the heart to scrape the letters off the window, and I love the idea of a coffee sandwich, you know? But I may change it. I stare at the letters every day, thinking maybe if I erased just some of them, they might spell out something else that could work. But so far, the only ones I like are Go Co Sand and Good Wiches."

Novena thought Good Wiches suited her.

"Goofee Sandwiches," Novena said, staring at the letters in the mirror. "Or just Goofee." It had slipped out as the perfect description of this woman, and she suddenly blushed, afraid she had insulted her.

"Oh, I love that! It's perfect. How did I miss Goofee? Oh, but it wouldn't work. Look," she said, pointing to the mirror and pouting. "Too much space in the letters. It looks like 'Go offee.' "

"You could just call it Go Off," Novena said, "but I guess that's not exactly welcoming."

"No, but you've inspired me. Here. Take this as a present."

She rummaged in a bin on the counter and handed Novena a scarf, a pale blue silk square dulled and softened with age. It felt as if she were holding a palm full of water.

"Hey, what's your name?" Novena said, suddenly feeling bold, as if the woman had just invited her to come closer.

"I'm Alexia. And you?"

"Novena."

"Well, Novena-san. Come back anytime. And tell your friends to come."

Novena left the shop feeling slightly giddy and disoriented, as if Alexia had adjusted a lens on the world, leaving the familiar details in the foreground blurry, but sharpening the details of odd things in the background.

She tried to recall Alexia's face, but it only came to her in isolated details — her hair, the side of her nose, the right half of her mouth. She could still hear the sound of Alexia's voice in her head, though, like an insistent piece of music that had pushed its way into her brain. She thought of the scarves she had picked up, the little tremors of what had seemed like their own voices talking to her. It made Novena happy to hear these new sounds in her.

She was surprised to find herself almost home; she felt she had floated through the streets, and she was even humming when she pushed open the front door of the apartment. As she walked down the hall, she heard Annaluna calling out with alarm, "Who's there?"

"It's me," Novena said loudly, coming into the living room. Annaluna was sitting at the window.

"Who else would it be?" she said, moving to kiss Annaluna's forehead. "Are you expecting a gentleman caller?"

Novena was used to coming home and finding her here, and she was even getting used to the sense Annaluna was waiting for someone else, not her. But this afternoon, as Annaluna looked up at her, Novena was shaken to see a new expression on Annaluna's face: she seemed disappointed to see it was Novena.

That night, over dinner, Annaluna ate peckishly, pushing the food around on her plate.

"What's the matter, honey?" Novena said, concerned. "Aren't you feeling well?"

Annaluna stared at her, and in a strange burst of bitterness demanded, "Do you have a boyfriend?"

Novena was shocked by Annaluna's harsh tone, but it was the question that rattled her.

"Well, actually," she said, "I don't know."

It was true: she didn't know quite how to think about Whit. She tried to stay in touch, calling him almost every week. But there were many awkward pauses between them, huge craters of silence that almost had a sound of their own, distant buzzes and hums that Novena associated not with the telephone equipment, but with some place deep within herself.

"Well, you're better off not knowing," Annaluna growled. "They always leave. Of course, then they come back too. But you have to be careful when they do."

She made a little sound, something between spitting and hissing. Novena looked at her, alarmed at both the harsh sentiment and the sharpness in her voice. It scared her.

"Who's coming back?" she asked Annaluna carefully. "Who are you waiting for?"

But Annaluna's features had softened again, and she gave Novena one of her sweeter smiles, along with a blank look, as if she hadn't heard her.

Novena went back to the shop a few days later.

"Oh, I'm so glad to see you!" Alexia called as soon as Novena walked in. "What do you think?"

Novena looked at Alexia, wondering what she was supposed to be looking for. Alexia's hair was down, showing off a multitude of shades of red, and she was wearing another kimono, a beautiful purple silk with elaborately embroidered flowers at the border. It was perfect except for the fact that one of the sleeves was missing, and Alexia's single bare arm shone white against it.

Alexia pointed to the window.

"The sign. I fixed it."

Novena looked in the mirror and saw that Alexia had blacked out some of the letters on the window. Now it read GO D OF SAND.

"God of Sand. I like it," Novena said. She wondered what it meant.

"I like it too. God of Sand. It's mysterious in a way, but I like the sound of it. And sand is a good image, it's clean and beige. Inconsequential, but elemental. It all starts with sand, the entire earth. Plus, it's giving me ideas for a new look I want to try, a drapy tenty Bedouin thing. With veils and toe rings. Kohl, too, I think. My eyes need a total overhaul."

Novena just nodded, trying to imagine the transformation.

"Now, we have to have a toast, to the new name," Alexia said. She brought out two small cups and a bottle of wine, and they sat in the overstuffed chairs that formed a little island in the center of the shop — like a hearth, Novena thought, without the fireplace.

"It should be sake. No, it should be whatever they drink in the desert. Which I guess is anything they can."

Novena wanted to draw Alexia out, to urge her to talk, to keep her face moving, as if it might reach some point where she could reach out and grasp it.

But the phone rang, and Alexia jumped up. She didn't come back for a long time, and Novena sat feeling awkward and slightly drunk.

She watched as two women came into the shop and began moving through the store, wandering the aisles, idly fingering a hat or a pair of shoes or a dress. Every few minutes, they would squeal and pounce on something — a suit or a flowered house dress — and hold it up against their bodies, sighing and cooing. This went on for ten minutes as Novena sat, feeling a growing restlessness at Alexia's absence.

Maybe Alexia was waiting for her to leave, she thought. She had been here a long time, and she worried suddenly that she was over-staying her welcome, that maybe she should be looking for something to buy.

She pulled herself up and started moving around, exploring the racks. She had just picked out a cotton short-sleeved button-down blouse, and holding it up, she had a sudden sense of the good-natured laziness of a fat woman, as if a tiny tremor had moved through her. She put down the blouse and moved to the counter, where she found a pair of navy cotton gloves, trimmed in white with small buttons on the cuffs. She picked them up and thought of Easter, and the smell of jonquils. She could picture the woman wearing them; she was standing on a wide green lawn, holding the hand of a little girl. The features of the girl were beginning to emerge when Novena, startled at a sound behind her, dropped the gloves.

"You're good luck, you know," Alexia said, behind her. "I just got the entire inventory of a dress shop that shut down twenty years ago. So, listen, I'm dreaming a gorje idea here. How'd you like to help me for a while? I'm really yazzed anyway and could use the help. I'm way behind on my picking."

"You mean work here?"

"Well, so far, it'd have to be temporary, but you never know. Things have been going great. It's not glamorous, mind you, although I think it will be fun."

"Well, sure." Novena was filled with giddy happiness. "I mean, yes! Do you want to interview me, or anything like that?" she said, suddenly anxious. "I mean, you don't even know me."

"I know you," Alexia said breezily. "We've known each other before. In another life. Don't you think?"

Novena nodded, but was momentarily thrown by this. She

couldn't imagine what other life Alexia was referring to; in fact, all this time, she had been thinking, This *is* my other life.

A little while later, when she stepped out onto the street to go home, she moved to the front window and ran her fingers over the letters of God of Sand, over the black tape covering the rest of the letters hidden underneath, and somehow this small thing filled her with happiness. She went down the street, swaggering a little, as if she had been given a wonderful present, as if the city itself had just opened up for her and admitted her into itself.

For the first time in as long as she could remember, she walked all the way home without once looking over her shoulder.

Outside the apartment, though, she stood on the sidewalk for a moment, hesitating before climbing the steps. Looking up at the window, she saw the light was on, and behind the sheer curtains she could see the shape of Annaluna's head silhouetted in the window.

She felt a sudden sense of something sinking in her, all her buoyancy collapsing. There was something in there she felt unequipped to handle. She pictured herself moving through those rooms, pushing through the dark heavy air. And she could suddenly smell the place, in some ways like the smell at God of Sand, a smell of bodies and time, but in there, in Annaluna's, it was deeper, unleavened. It was time turned unrelenting and rude, each day pushing out a little more sweetness, a little more light, each day collecting up only the odors of spoiled things — ancient cooking fumes, mildew and dirt, the musty smells of decay and sorrow.

And oddly, she thought of the scent of Annaluna herself, of her skin's sweetness moving toward sourness, toward spoilage. She thought of Annaluna's hands, so often crossed on her chest, over her old pinned-together dresses, as if concealing this sourness, keeping it close to her as she sat at the window, watching. Waiting.

She wondered what Annaluna saw out there in her long vigils. She wondered if she saw anything; most of the time, Annaluna's eyes didn't even look as if they were registering the world.

And it struck Novena, or rather it slipped over her, and she could almost feel it envelop her, like a light cloth: there was something in Annaluna's look, in her waiting in the darkness, that she recognized.

You only turned your eyes inward like that when you were watching for a big thing, for some remembered trouble to return.

Like waiting for Zan.

This thought of him was so strange and so strong it was as if he had suddenly appeared. She turned and looked down the street, thinking of that small dark cloud of awareness that was always with her. She thought of all the people she passed on the street every day without looking at them. He could be out there; she could have walked right past him. Maybe she hadn't recognized him, or he had some ability to change his shape and form, or he had in fact changed so drastically that she wouldn't even know him if she saw him.

The idea was enough to propel her up the stairs and into the house.

She pushed open the door and called out, "It's me."

And then, unable to bear the possibility of Annaluna's disappointed look, she called it out again, before she reached the living room.

"It's me, Novena."

chapter 25

The abhorrence of certain colors, and the agreeable sensations produced by others, were much more marked among the excitable Italians than was the case of the St. Vitus's dance with the more phlegmatic Germans. Red colors, which the St. Vitus's dancers detested, they generally liked, so that a patient was seldom seen who did not carry a red handkerchief for his gratification, or greedily feast his eyes on any articles of red clothing worn by the bystanders. . . .

No sooner did the patients obtain a sight of the favorite color than, new as the impression was, they rushed like infuriated animals toward the object, devoured it with their eager looks, kissed and caressed it in every possible way, and gradually resigning themselves to softer sensations, adopted the languishing expression of enamored lovers, and embraced the handkerchief . . . with the most intense ardor, while the tears streamed from their eyes as if they were completely overwhelmed by the inebriating impression on their senses.

— J. F. K. Hecker, *The Dancing Mania*

Novena now inhabited two worlds: Annaluna's house, with its dark heavy furniture and worn carpets, a place frozen in a moment of mournful time, and God of Sand, where time was liquid, ever flowing: a place holding all of time, and therefore no time. Edo had shown up one day and installed a row of clocks on the wall, like the ones in airports for different cities, and Alexia had made labels for them that read *"Mars"* and *"August 23, 1865"* and *"Dinner."*

So far, Novena worked there just a few hours a day, but she was doing almost everything: cleaning, sorting, ironing clothes, repairing seams and ragged holes, running bundles of the fancier clothes to the dry cleaner, hand washing the fragile lingerie and filmy blouses. She liked the domesticity of the tasks; the work brought back pleasant memories of working at Whit's. And she was absorbing everything, from the maintenance of the merchandise to the business itself.

Alexia started taking her on picking expeditions. In addition to haunting estate sales and flea markets, Alexia had standing arrangements with dry cleaners and tailors for unclaimed clothes, and would even paw through boxes of discarded clothes and belongings left on the street — there were a surprising number of these. Alexia overlooked no source. They even went to the large, overlit charity stores in the poorer sections of the city. Novena had been surprised when Alexia had first taken her to one of these places.

"Here?" she had said, wrinkling her nose as she surveyed the sad ugly things of poverty, hardship's overbright colors and mean inferior cloth.

"Listen, this is where I get a lot of good stuff," Alexia said, moving to the racks and beginning to flip through the clothes. She handed Novena an ancient blouse; despite its stain, Novena could see from the fagoting and the lace insets that it had once been beautiful.

"Poor people don't want old stuff," Alexia explained, pulling something else from the rack. "They want new stuff. Shiny stuff. Like this."

She held up another blouse, this one a garish thing, a stiff plaid acetate, all loose threads and burst seams.

"It's a sin. This thing was made to fall apart in two weeks," she said, stuffing it back onto the rack. "Don't get me wrong, though. I don't think the poor have bad taste. They just have bad suppliers."

Of all her tasks at God of Sand, Novena liked these picking expeditions the best. She considered it the archeology of dress, sifting through a vast desert to retrieve a single garment which had waited for five, six, or more decades to serve as a marker for its time.

She was learning from Alexia that this marker could be the width of a waistband, the narrowness of a shoulder, the length of a sleeve. It could be color or pattern: as in the elongated florals and fleurs-de-lis in the muted and mournful palettes of the war era — burgundy and dark green, or gray paired with orchid or yellow, or in the postwar era's chubby prints and dancing abstractions in tomato reds and bright greens.

She listened carefully when Alexia explained how to pinpoint which decade a particular shade of marigold had appeared, or pick out a particular navy crepe from forty years ago, or precisely date a small floral pattern by the brush stroke of a black line that formed the curve of an abstract leaf, or the subtle shading of its ground color, or the symmetry in its half-drop repeat.

But touch was where Novena's focus lay: not so much on color or pattern or details of construction, but on the feel of the cloth itself. She could hear the very breath of fabric, feel its pulse under her fingers: the heartbeats of silkworms carried in silk, the rice paste resist writhing in Chinese batik, the echoes of flax's photosynthetic cataclysm. To Novena, cloth felt like a living creature under her fingers, and it was one of the pleasures in her life that she could touch so much of it.

But just as a lover's touch, in time, will move beyond the surface of a beloved's skin, first finding muscle, then pulse, and then the tiny tremors beneath the pulse, of mood and desire and sometimes, even, of love's end, soon Novena could touch a garment and feel something else under its breath.

She could run her finger down the rows and racks and pull out something — a draped silk chemise, a peplum jacket, a gay gingham blouse — and feel herself sliding into an actual memory of another era for fleeting instants, as if she had inhabited that time herself. Touching a garment twice her age, she would be transported, as if a flap had been sliced into the curtain of the present to let her slip through for a moment to another time, where images of people and their lives seemed to spring fully formed into her mind.

She might, for example, pick up a lime-colored silk surah blouse with French darts and jeweled buttons, and immediately flash on an image of a dark cocktail lounge one late autumn afternoon, seventeen years ago. Holding a man's maroon flannel robe, she would suddenly be in a room, sitting at the edge of a bed, looking out at a gray and hungry day through a grime-covered window. Holding an apron or a pair of gloves, she could feel what had creased the brow of its wearer. She remembered the tremors of these sensations on her first visit to God of Sand, but now all of these images came to her in such specific and concrete detail that she knew the color of the sky that day, she knew if it was a Sunday or a Wednesday, she knew what the wearers had eaten for breakfast and how well it had sat in their stomachs.

None of these sensations astonished her; the moments were still too fleeting, moving through her like a hiccup or a sneeze. Nor did she think these transports odd, for what better receptacles for memory are there but the fibers living next to our skin — spun from living plants and animals — absorbing our sweat and worry, remembering our gestures, adhering to our musculature, breathing with our every breath? Besides, she could see that many of the customers who came to God of Sand fell under similar spells.

She would watch people enter the dressing room, their arms full of chenille bathrobes, flared polka-dotted dresses and cunning felt hats with feathers and nets, two-piece worsted suits and lisle stockings and blouses gaily spattered with lilacs and violets, a jacket of a dusky green, the exact shade of which had not been seen since the month of February, fifty-three years ago.

Then they would emerge from the dressing rooms in the

dresses and hats and blouses, and be altered. Novena would see something — in the shape of their eyes, the set of their mouths, or even the roundness of their calves — that suggested that their modern, contemporary selves had retreated, as if some other person had settled into the body of the wearer. Or as if they were the same person at another time, an earlier version, one twenty, fifty, or a hundred years old.

Novena wondered whether all the people crowding into the shop each day were here to slip into the lives of the bodies that had inhabited the clothes, drawn to all those moments that clung to clothes like lint and were released like plaintive telegrams from their original owners.

On the other hand, they might be searching for the clothes they themselves had worn once, in another lifetime, clothing that contained all their own memories, all their own history.

Novena tried to engage Alexia in such ruminations, but Alexia wasn't interested. She was as hardscrabble as a farmer — uninterested in discussing why people wanted what she toiled so hard to harvest, as long as they bought it. The closest she ever came to theorizing was one busy afternoon, after a few hectic hours of difficult, demanding customers. The last one had finally left, and Alexia was in an exasperated mood.

"You know what they want?" she called out to Novena on her way back to the counter from locking the door.

"All of them are in here looking for the same thing: the dress their mother wore when she was nursing them."

Still, the question dogged Novena: what exactly *were* they looking for? It was more than nostalgia that brought them to God of Sand; nostalgia was just an accessory worn with these things. The more she thought about it, the more she thought there was something odd in the impulse to reach for clothes that had been worn in another time.

As she had pored over the costume and history books Whit had given her, she remembered being struck by the idea that humanity had been content to swathe itself in the same basic designs for much of history. Egyptians had worn the same linen sheaths for three thousand years, and the designs of kimonos, dhotis, saris, and tunics had remained essentially unchanged for eons. But some force of change had blown into the world, as if some mad tailor had suddenly been unleashed, strewing clothing styles over the earth: waistlines were raised, necklines altered; shoes cut higher, then lower; waistlines dropped, then raised again; ruffs, bustles and trains, peplums, pleats and surplices, farthingales, finestrellas, and fichus introduced, altered, expanded, then eliminated.

In the process, fashion had become something sharklike, its survival based on moving only forward, looking only ahead; whatever was left in its wake was instantly dead.

Then something happened. Somewhere in the dense strata of clothing history, a plate had shifted and this momentum had been interrupted. People had suddenly begun reaching back into time's closet. But what is odd was that they now were reaching back not just for the influences of the past — after all, design details had always borrowed from other eras — but for the actual garments. This had never before happened, and it seemed like a retreat born of some panic, a sense that something had gone so wrong, *back there* at some particular moment, that people were compelled to return to it again and again, as to the scene of an auto accident, never able to really undo the disaster, but doomed to approximate the circumstances leading up to it. It was as if donning the clothes could stop the car from crashing.

Novena found it odd that such a cataclysmic moment wasn't written down somewhere, like the account of wars or famine or other disasters. As far as she knew, no one even thought about it, although judging from the volume of business at God of Sand, plenty of people felt compelled to acknowledge it.

Even designers would come to God of Sand to study what was

selling, and magazines would feature the ghostly offspring of the clothes Alexia had sold the year before, which in turn had first been sold thirty years earlier.

It could make Novena's head spin contemplating all this.

But Novena loved the contemplation, and the work, and especially the clothes, although she never actually wore them herself. In fact, ever since her picking expeditions had been bringing her into the dustier, dirtier corners of the city, Novena had taken to wearing big flannel or oxford shirts and shapeless pants which she pulled from the men's racks at God of Sand. She had even found an old pair of men's boots, small enough to fit her, yet still big and heavy. She found she liked wearing these things. They made her feel anonymous and even slightly intimidating, stomping through the streets.

While she wasn't looking for anything of her own in the clothes she found and ironed and sold, sometimes just the sight of something — an old tropical print, or a pairing of two odd colors, or a spray of fat cherries on a white smock trimmed in blue — gave her a sensation that they held something that had once belonged to her. But unlike the specific moments she could imagine from other people's lives, the memories these things triggered in her were disjointed, related to no time or place: a street in the rain, the way light had filled a window once, shining through a bright red curtain, small gold threads woven into the speaker of an old television set, the soft embracing interior of a car. They were so unconnected to any specific moment she could lay claim to that she could barely even consider them memories. They felt like something that would stir in someone during a long, slow return from amnesia.

The same images, and others, kept returning to her, though, even when she was nowhere near God of Sand or the clothes that had triggered them. She would be out on the street or in her room, and she would flash on a place or moment she had experienced as her own, but could not recall.

These tiny but constant flashes of her own memories — if they were, in fact, hers — were strange and backward things, like something she could imagine Alexia dreaming up. Most memories returned to you things you forgot you had; hers brought her to moments she didn't know she had owned. Sometimes at night, replaying these images in her mind, she imagined them as little pieces of her life which had been snipped away, forming a network of small holes in her, lying like a net over her past. She imagined her insides as lace: intricate filigreed threads stretched over nothing, over the empty spaces of all the things she had forgotten.

And yet she longed for the moments they contained, to hold just one in her hands long enough to recognize it. She felt she was chasing something that was always ahead of her, always disappearing around a corner, and now she began to worry that parts of her own past were getting tangled up in other people's. While she had been gathering up the memories from the crepe dresses and delicate slips, the narrow-shouldered suits and pleated blouses at God of Sand, she hadn't ever considered that the clothes might be taking something from her — fragments of her own memories, her own history, her own past.

Poor Novena. She didn't know that memories may fly away from us and wrap themselves around the threads of clothing, worm their way into the bark of a tree, into the cracks in bowls, and hide in the scent of perfume, in the light, in the dark, in a song, in a voice, in the millions and millions of hiding places the world makes for them.

But the past is never far away; sooner or later, it'll have you between its teeth, low growls coming from its throat as it considers how hard to bite you.

Elegia called one morning and Novena heard a tight little bustle in her voice that always made her nervous.

"So," Elegia said. "I've been busy. Cleaning."

There was a pause that struck Novena as ominous.

"Even your room."

"What do you mean, my room?" Novena said sharply.

"Well, I've decided to clear out some of the junk that's been sitting around. I've even been up in the attic. The fire hazards up there! Anyway, I intend to make a clean sweep. It's long overdue."

Novena wanted to yell out, to tell her to stop, to leave everything alone. But she knew how useless it was trying to stop Elegia when she had begun cleaning.

"I've packed up some of your stuff," she was saying. "I'm going to drop it off sometime this week. I want to see Annaluna anyway. She sounds tired. Is she eating?"

Annaluna wasn't, in fact, eating very well.

"She's fine," Novena said.

"*We're* fine," she stressed, hoping it would sound like "Now leave us alone."

A few afternoons later, when she got home, Novena was pleasantly surprised to find Annaluna in the kitchen, rather than at her usual post at the window. She even seemed animated, rolling around the kitchen in fast, short little motions, making dinner.

"Elegia came. You missed her," Annaluna said, increasing the flame under a pot of something thick and brown on the stove that was already burbling violently. "We had coffee."

"What's this?" Novena said, picking up a box on the kitchen table. Lifting the lid, Novena pulled out a cotton house dress spattered with loud and garish flowers.

"Elegia brought it. I told her I don't need any new dresses," Annaluna said bitterly. "She's crazy, that one. Buying dresses for an old lady."

"You're not old," Novena protested, but she thought that Annaluna had never looked older. Although her eyes were clear tonight, the shadows under them had darkened, and she had never seemed tinier.

Novena waited until after dinner before going into her room to see what Elegia had left her. Four cartons were waiting for her, and she sat on the floor and began going through one of the bigger boxes.

They were mostly clothes, stuff she hadn't seen or worn in a long time. It was odd to see these things, her pastel sweaters and little skirts and blouses with their insets of lace from Whit's. She hadn't worn these girlish things in months, and their frilliness almost embarrassed her; it was the wardrobe of a stranger.

She poked idly through the boxes, inspecting them now with a professional eye, wondering if they would sell. They were really too new to appeal to anyone who came into God of Sand, and she wondered how long she would have to store them before they might become desirable.

She turned to one of the smaller boxes, one that looked older than the rest, and pulled open the flaps.

It was the smell that hit her first, that made her want to close the box, get it out of her room.

It was a lemony perfume, sweet as candy, as familiar as her own. But it was mingled with the stale smell of cigarettes, and some other undefinable scent, and she knew it was not hers.

It was Sylvie's.

Here was the box of Sylvie's things which had been sitting on her closet floor for months, forgotten. She hadn't even looked inside when she had brought them home from Whit's, and now Novena's heart was pounding as she pulled out the jewelry box and the fistful of trinkets that were on top, revealing a tangle of clothes underneath. Trembling, she dumped them onto the floor.

Here was a floral print rayon dress. A heavily embroidered denim jacket. A tiny plaid skirt with a shirt that had the same plaid piping on the collar, and two lacy blouses.

Here was her green cap. She remembered unearthing it from her drawer and dropping it into the box, remembered it had carried the unbearable sensation of flinging a flower into a grave.

Here was Sylvie, laid on out on her floor.

She sat for a few minutes, staring at the pile of clothes. They looked collapsed and exhausted, lying on the floor. As if, Novena thought, they had drowned themselves.

Novena knew she wouldn't have to touch them to feel their sadness. She could feel it inside her, uncurling like a snake.

Novena hadn't thought of Sylvie for ages, had been too upset over Zan to even grieve for her, but the nearness of her in these belongings made her feel her absence as a sharp thing in her heart. Sylvie had been her friend. A girl like Danielle, Cookie, like any of them. Like herself. Yet Novena had forgotten her.

Novena was moved by such a sense of sorrow, such tenderness for her, that she was close to weeping. She couldn't bear to look at these things anymore; she wanted to store them away and never see them again. She rose and began gathering up the clothes, putting them back into the box.

They were still stained with the strong scent of Sylvie's perfume, as familiar as her own. It *had* been her own once, since all the girls had landed on the same scent at exactly the same moment, and for months they had all worn it. She remembered going through the halls of school, enveloped in that lemony cloud with the eerie but comforting feeling of being surrounded by herself.

Now she was moving out of the halls, and into the long drowsy days of that strange, languorous summer when the girls had all been enchanted with themselves, with their power over boys. She recalled the smell of those months, the dank perfume of the river mixed with the saltier perfume of desire.

For the moment, Novena was lost in her own memories, moving through the endless days and nights, riding around with the girls, sitting on picnic tables, smoking and waiting. It was where they had been that night, when Sylvie had screamed up in that big car of hers, and then she had left them.

They had spent the summer waiting for Sylvie — at the river, at Daz's, in their rooms. All that summer, while they had waited, Sylvie had been with Zan. Their limbs entwined, holding each other close as secrets, imprinting themselves invisibly onto each other's clothes.

Onto these clothes.

Novena felt a flush spread up her neck and into her face, staining her with a sense of betrayal. The worst thing was that her own stupidity had betrayed her. She should have known it the minute she saw these things. It wasn't Sylvie who had come back in these things. It was Zan.

Zan had come back, clear as a radio signal.

She was holding Sylvie's jacket, and so she shouldn't have been surprised when she sensed that the air and light in the room had shifted slightly. She had a familiar feeling, of the thinnest of fogs descending, and in the split second before letting that flap in time open, letting herself slide away into whatever memory of Sylvie's was held in the jacket, she debated dropping it. But she held on.

What came to her, though, was not what she expected; it had the sensation of memory, but there were no surrounding details — no sky, no color, no place or time. It was just a pure sensation, a single moment, of terror.

There was something else that confused her. She knew it to be Sylvie's memory, but swimming alongside it had been something of her own, some memory that belonged to her.

It was as if for one moment, she and Sylvie had become interchangeable. It was Sylvie's terror, but it had not been wearing Sylvie's clothes. It was wearing her own clothes, speaking in her own voice: *He says he's going to take me away.*

She dropped the jacket into the box, closed the flaps and pushed the box to a corner of her room. But she could still smell the scent of perfume — hers and Sylvie's. Now it struck her as the scent of something gone, lost forever.

Zan wasn't gone, though.

He was here, in the room, in the air, filling up the room. Soon, she thought, he would be everywhere.

chapter 26

The hungry ghosts are typed as: ones with bodies like cauldrons, those with needle-thin throats, vomit-eaters, excrement-eaters, nothing-eaters, eaters of vapors in the air, eaters of the Buddhist dharma, water-drinkers, hopeful and ambitious ones, saliva-eaters, wig-eaters, blood-drinkers, meat-eaters, consumers of incense smoke, disease-dabblers, defecation-watchers, ones that live under the ground, possessors of miraculous powers, intensely burning ones, ones fascinated with colors, inhabitants of the beach, ones with walking-canes, infant-eaters, semen-eaters, demonic ones, fire-eaters, those on filthy streets, wind-eaters, burning coal consumers, poison-eaters, inhabitants of open fields, those living in tombs (and eating ashes), those that live in trees, ones that stay at crossroads, and those that kill themselves.

— William R. Lafleur, "Hungry Ghosts and Hungry People:
Somaticity and Rationality in Medieval Japan"

THE MACHINES ZAN ASSEMBLED were ultimately hoisted onto large trucks and delivered to other, distant places. One day, one of the drivers had called in sick, and Zan overheard someone say that they were looking for a driver to deliver it up north. He volunteered to make the trip.

The minute he got behind the wheel, he was afraid. He was not going to remember how to drive a truck. He would get lost, would forget how to get to the city, or worse, he would not be able to see the road through his fogged-up vision. He was not going to remember how to get to Annaluna's. But he was most afraid that once he found her street, he would remember nothing of it, or of her.

Of course he remembered how to drive. It was easy, and it was actually fun for a while, following in the wake of a hundred other trucks like his, feeling as if he had become part of a nocturnal pack of animals, running over the earth. He imagined the cargoes in these trucks — damp vegetables and steel rods and sheets of leather; machine parts and tanks of liquid and sacks of gravel — all the heavy things whose job it is for men to lift, as they hold up their part of the world.

After his delivery, he managed to find his way to the city, and even found Annaluna's street. He felt crazy and wobbly, driving down her street for the first time in so long. As he came up to her building, he felt suddenly scared and kept driving. Now that he was here, he was afraid to look at it, afraid it would look like any other building. He kept his eyes straight ahead and drove to the end of the street.

He found a place to park the truck and left it. He walked slowly up her street. He still couldn't bring himself to look at her building, and so he stayed on the opposite side of the street, walking up to the end of the block, turning around and walking to the other end. He walked up and down, up and down, four times.

Finally he stopped, and let himself look across the street. His eye moved slowly, up the seven steps that led to the familiar wooden front door, and then he took in the whole building. Finally he looked at her window.

All he saw was the soft yellow light shining through the curtain, but it might as well have been her face — that's how strong the rush of her memory came back to him. He stared up at her window, remembering instantly every detail of his life with her, every inch of the wide expanse of her love.

As far as he was concerned, nothing else had ever happened to him. Annaluna was his only memory. Everything else was a blank. Everything else was just a large black hole.

Zan changed his job so he could start making regular deliveries, and went back to the city as often as he could.

He would stand on her street in the dark and look up at her window, picturing her moving around, at the oven, at the table, rolling across the room. He had never been lonelier, watching what should have been his life being lived behind the drawn curtains of the old apartment. Sometimes, if the light was right, he could actually see two shadows moving past the windows, and he began to imagine it was himself in there, with her. He imagined he had never actually left, or maybe he had left part of himself behind. It gave him pleasure, to think that it could be him in there, still going through the days with Annaluna.

He would close his eyes and recall the taste of the bitter strong coffee they would drink to start their mornings, the little jokes they would share over the newspapers, the errands he would run for her. He imagined himself at her table, eating her stringy balls of stew and the clumpy clots of suet that made up her pie crust. He had never tasted anything so terrible as her food, and he had never been hungrier than he was at these moments, recalling it.

And so he went back to the city whenever he could, watching himself through the shades, imagining this happy life. *His* happy life, as a ghost.

It was such a happy life that a long time passed before it occurred to him to wonder who was actually in there with Annaluna.

chapter 27

HE LIVED IN ANNALUNA NOW like an old sad bird, pecking and pecking away at her. She heard him constantly: in the rattling of the pans in the kitchen, the hard stomp of feet on the floor, the snap of the light in the room, the ticking of the clock on the highboy in the afternoons, marking each second of his absence. When he came in, it was for only one reason: to leave her again.

Even when he stayed, he brought no solace. She had forgotten how unreliable he was, how slippery his presence. His face would appear to her — at breakfast, over dinner, hovering over her bed, leaning over to kiss her goodbye — and before she even had a chance to bring her eyes into focus, he would disappear again.

Sometimes, at the window, a gleam of something shining would catch her eye, and she knew it was him on the sidewalk, holding up one of the silver bowls he had taken from her that night.

She was rarely away from the window now. She hated herself for being unable to stay away, and wished for just one day when she could skip her vigil and know that he would come home anyway. On the other hand, given how tired her bones were, it wasn't unpleasant to sit there in those long afternoons, the warmth of the sun covering her lap like a blanket; she would doze for a while, and wake with a start in the darkened room, shivering — and waiting, for the sound of the key in the door.

Years might have passed. She couldn't tell. Time had left her.

Everything was leaving her: her shoes, her dresses, the nice waxy milk cartons she had been storing for years in the pantry. Every day, something else disappeared — food from the refrigerator, dust from the tables, the very cobwebs above her. She knew that in addition to everything else, he was still robbing her blind. She knew that soon there would be nothing left of her.

That's the danger of your ghosts and demons, the peril of the things that possess us, whatever form they take — living, dead, or somewhere in between. It's not in their ability to remain unseen, to wail eerily in the night, or even to jump out suddenly and frighten you to death. The damage they do is much simpler: they simply wear you down.

Still, whatever else can be said of them, they are our familiars, sometimes the only thing keeping our old and bitter hearts company. The young, unfortunately, don't have such solace, since they so rarely believe in ghosts. Why should they? The young have something far worse to haunt them. They have themselves.

The box of Sylvie's things sat in Novena's room for two days. She felt affronted every time she came into her room and saw the box sitting there as smugly as if Zan were inside, and she had to keep herself from kicking it. On the other hand, they were also Sylvie's things, and she couldn't bear the idea of throwing them out. But then she came up with the perfect place for them, one she thought would have even pleased Sylvie.

She and Alexia had begun salvaging pieces from clothing too worn or stained to sell, patching the pieces together and cutting them into simple dresses. One of these dresses, for example, might contain a lush floral upholstery remnant, a bit of a charmeuse scarf, a long length from an obi, and threadbare squares from two saris. They were odd mixtures, these combinations of old textiles cut and shaped into clean simple lines: they looked modern and ancient at the same time, and people were starting to clamor for them. And so Novena had added the box of Sylvie's clothes to the pile of other clothes, and began cutting them up, incorporating the pieces into these new dresses. She liked the idea of sending pieces of Sylvie out into the world, to be remembered.

Mostly she liked having them out of her sight.

But even with their removal, something of Zan remained. He was never far away, and she started attributing every small disturbance of her own to him: when a moment of dread would move through her like the thrumming of wings, or when she was startled by a movement out of the corner of her eye like a sudden flash of color crossing the sky, or when she felt small, hard, and unblinking eyes following her down the street.

At the same time, Annaluna seemed to be declining even further into some deep funk. Lately, a new hostility had settled into her, a sharp irritation which worried Novena terribly, especially when Annaluna started directing it at her.

One night just before dinner, Annaluna actually growled at her.

"How long you going to be here, anyway?"

"I'm staying in tonight," Novena said, startled. But then she wondered if maybe Annaluna was suggesting she move out altogether. The idea of it made her want to cry.

"Huh. Don't do me any favors," Annaluna said. "I never know when you're coming back. Or if you're coming back."

"Annaluna!" Novena said, alarmed. "I'm always coming back."

Annaluna just sat, pulling absently at the armrest of her chair. She looked like a little girl pouting, Novena thought. She moved toward her, to smooth her hair, to kiss her cheek.

"I thought your girlfriend was dead," Annaluna said, her voice low.

Novena stopped, felt the blood leave her face.

"What?" she whispered, feeling as if she had been slapped.

"I thought she was dead. Have you been seeing her?"

Annaluna had always been able to read her thoughts, and sense what was on her mind, but the accusation in her tone chilled Novena.

"You mean Sylvie?" she asked, her voice nothing but a whisper.

"You never told me her name," Annaluna growled. "Sylvie? Hah."

"Annaluna, what's upsetting you? Are you okay? You're worrying me."

"I just don't have the heart for this anymore," Annaluna grumbled, and wheeled herself into her bedroom. She shut the door behind her and stayed there the rest of the night.

The next morning, Annaluna rolled into the kitchen with a pile of clothes on her lap.

"I suppose you'll be wanting these," she said with a note of petulance, laying the pile on the table.

Five white men's shirts were wrinkled and tangled together as if Annaluna had retrieved them from a laundry basket. As she reached for them, Novena could see they were very old but beautiful, the cotton strong and smooth under her fingers, a sheen of starch and dignity in the threads.

"These are nice, Annaluna," she said, holding one up. "Whose are they?"

"Hah. You're getting old," Annaluna snorted. "Losing your marbles. Like me."

"Annaluna," Novena said calmly, although she was truly alarmed. "Maybe I should stay home today, stay here with you."

"No. Go," Annaluna said, waving her hand. "Just come back."

"Of course I'll come back. "

Before she left the kitchen, Novena turned.

"I love you."

She could not remember ever saying this to Annaluna; she hadn't ever needed to, and Novena felt something had been unalterably changed now the words were there, hanging in the air. But as she turned to leave, Novena saw a pleased little smile on Annaluna's lips, and she was glad, after all, she had spoken.

Then she went out, into the city, into the world, feeling anonymous in her boys' clothes, eating up the hard pavement with her big black boots.

The shirts were still on the table when Novena got home that night, and she took the pile into her bedroom, thinking she might wear one the next day. It would have to be pressed, though, and while she was waiting for the iron to get hot, she held one of the shirts up to her face.

The cotton was smooth and softened with age, and smelled faintly of mothballs and mustiness. She sensed nothing else there, though — no tiny pulse or shuddering breath. She wasn't too surprised — men's clothes spoke to her far less often than women's, and she sometimes wondered if it was because the clothes themselves were stripped of language. Men's clothes had no beautiful poetic names, just words: Shirts. Pants. Ties. Suits. Unlike women's clothes, with fifty different words for a dress, twenty for a skirt, an infinity of names for collars, hems, waistlines, buttonholes — as if women were so full of language, it spilled out onto their clothes.

The iron began hissing for her attention and she laid the collar of the shirt on the board.

Elegia's instructions for the proper way to press a man's shirt — you started with the collar, then moved to the yoke, then the back, the sides, and finally the sleeves and cuffs — had been imprinted in Novena's brain when she was five and had stood next to Elegia, moving her toy iron up and down her tiny square of linen. Novena was always surprised when Elegia's lessons came back to her, since she had always done her best to ignore them.

Now, as she began, the weight of the iron was comforting in her hand, and the simple gliding motions left her feeling pleasantly empty.

The iron was not yet at its hottest point, and so it was not until she started on the back of the shirt that the intense veil of age lifted and she began inhaling the accumulation of dirt and dust, fluids and stains, perfume and smoke which over the years the hungry fibers had swallowed up and retained, and now released back into the clouds of steam that enveloped her.

As she inhaled the old musty aroma, she started thinking that some small thread of sorrow must have been woven into these shirts, after all, because as she ironed, she felt it traveling into her, filling her lungs.

It wasn't until she finished the first shirt and had started on the second that it occurred to Novena to wonder where Annaluna had gotten these shirts.

She knew that Annaluna had been married once, but it had been so long ago. Novena quickly calculated: Annaluna had been alone for twice as long as she herself had been on earth. And yet she had saved these shirts. For over forty years, some small flame must have burned somewhere in Annaluna's heart. Or maybe it was not so small. Did she take these shirts out and look at them? Did she hold them up to her face, inhaling their scent, remembering herself as a young woman, moving around the apartment, waiting for him to come home? Novena knew that while the actual scent of the man would have long disappeared, some memory of him would have remained in the threads, enough to pierce Annaluna's heart.

The idea was enough to pierce Novena's own heart. She thought of the hours Annaluna spent at the window, and wondered, Could this man be who Annaluna was waiting for? Someone she had once loved? But the man was long gone. The shirts were all that was left of him. That young version of Annaluna no longer existed either; now she was so small and frail she seemed to be in the process of disappearing.

Annaluna had been old all of Novena's life, yet she had never pictured a time that Annaluna would not be there. Novena felt a mournful sadness beginning to fill her, rising up from the steam. It shouldn't have surprised her, this idea of Annaluna's end — it was always there; it was, in fact, something contained in the very gloom of the place. Something, she suddenly realized, she had been trying to clean away, day after day. But it kept coming back.

She felt as if the cloud of steam had suddenly turned dark, full of dread, pressing down on her just as she pressed down on the shirt. The iron had grown heavy in her hands, and she was dragging it back and forth across the cloth, staring into space, thinking of Annaluna and these shirts.

She must have stopped moving the iron altogether, because the sound of hissing and a bitter scorched smell brought her to attention. She lifted the iron and saw it had burned its imprint into the cloth, in a triangle of brown marks. The smell was terrible; it was not the clean smell of something burnt, but rather, a bruised smell, a smell of damage, and it made her want to cry.

She was suddenly exhausted and wondered why she was ironing at all, why she had thought wearing these shirts would be a good idea. She didn't even want to touch them now. There was too much sadness in them.

She quickly put away the iron. As she was hanging the pressed shirts in her closet, she had an odd recollection, of the boys' shirts she used to collect when she was younger. She thought of how she would hang them in her closet, storing the essence of all those boys, until some moment when their smell wore off and she would cut the shirts up and give them to other girls. Then her stomach twisted a little, thinking of Sylvie, hoarding Zan's shirt under her pillow.

She thought of the line of shirts she had found hanging in Zan's closet in Nile Bay, when she had gone to his house. They had been sad too, those pathetic empty things hanging there. She wondered where they were now. She couldn't remember if they had been thrown out, or stored in the basement with the rest of his things. Maybe, she thought, Elegia kept them hanging in her own closet, waiting for him. The idea made her shudder.

Then an odd image came to her: she pictured all the closets of the world, filled with the sad, empty shirts of men.

She crawled into bed and lay in the dark, hoping for oblivion. But she was wide awake, thinking how it was that everything — even the ancient shirt of a stranger — always had a way of coming back to Zan. Lately, even her worries over Annaluna led directly to thoughts of Zan. More and more, in fact, they seemed to have gotten tangled up in each other, as if they were connected. She couldn't fathom what the connection might be, but as she started thinking back over the last few weeks and months, it occurred to her that every day, as she had measured the shrinking distance between herself and Zan, she had been registering another small step in Annaluna's decline.

The possibility that they were actually connected had the bizarre quality of something imagined, and yet because it was so perfectly symmetrical, it also had the sour breath of the possible. As Zan was getting closer, Annaluna was disappearing.

She pondered this for a long time. By the time sleep did come, Novena had almost convinced herself that if she could somehow keep Zan away, she could keep Annaluna safe.

Meanwhile, as Novena slept, the shirts hung in her closet. And for most of the night, they did not move.

The air in the room moved, though, in the way it always moves, inhaling and exhaling like a breath. The slight swaying stirred the minute particles — of thread and lint and dust, skin and scent and memory — that the iron's heat had drawn from the shirts. The shirts watched, somewhat wistfully, as these escaped pieces of themselves, joyous with their new freedom, floated around the room.

Gradually, these particles began to settle, drifting slowly into corners and eaves, into the minute pores in the surface of wood, into the hairline cracks in the plaster, into the curtains and the rug, into the blanket and the sheets, and of course into Novena, who, breathing deeply in her sleep, inhaled them.

She inhaled the microscopic particles that we take into us each day: mites, fibers, flakes of skin cells, hair follicles, the fumes from last night's dinner; she inhaled the tiny drops of moisture from the iron's steam, and finally the scents unleashed from the shirts — the bare ancient traces of Renaldo's remaining scent, and the stronger scent of Annaluna, who had in fact gripped the shirts and held them up to her face many times. And Novena took in some of the more recent smells that had been trapped there — the oily residue of her own skin, a minute trace of milk, which had spilled on the table where the shirts had sat all day, and finally, the scent of their most recent wearer, a bullying, insistent smell of pine soap and yeast mixed with a slightly more feral note.

The smell of Zan.

She breathed him in, until the shirts began moving across the room and into her dreams. They were joined there by a whole closetful of men's clothes — suits and jackets and pants and shoes — which were walking around the apartment, sitting in chairs, and sprawled out on the sofa, reading the newspaper. They were in the form and shape of men, but there was no body inhabiting them.

But sometime past the middle of the night, a sound reached her sleep, beginning to wake her. Right before she was delivered to consciousness, Zan had appeared, wearing the clothes. He was standing in the doorway, watching. Waiting for her.

She woke instantly and looked into the darkness of the room. She lay for the longest time, not moving, staring into the darkness. Finally she reached over and turned on the light next to her bed. She searched her room, looking for some halo around the furniture, some force field of strange energy that she might be able to see, like faint dust rings that would be left when something had been moved out of its original place. He felt so close that she had to keep herself from calling out to him.

Every night the shirts moved back into her dreams. Zan was always wearing them. Each night she would be dragged from sleep by the image of him standing in the doorway, waiting for her. She would lie there with her breath coming fast and hard, as if she had been running.

By the end of the week, he had become a noisy thing, living inside her.

Now he was in the shadows against the walls of the apartment, he was in the corner of her eye, he was in the small trembling settling and sighs of the house at night, he was in her skin, a noisy thing, living inside her. He was even out in the street. She saw him a hundred times a week: the back of his head rising above a crowd far ahead of her, or his broad back as he turned a corner a half block away, or his profile through the window of a cab speeding past her. The first few times she saw him, she felt the blood leave her face, pouring like a flood into her rapidly pounding heart. Before long, she grew accustomed to the sight of him, and she would register her instant of shock only by a tiny pulse that throbbed in her neck.

Although by October, Zan was living in both of them, Novena and Annaluna did not acknowledge his presence between them, at least outwardly. But they did in smaller ways: in the stiff and formal way they now moved around each other, and the way they kept half the lights off in the apartment, once darkness came.

They didn't exactly set a place at the table for him, but they might as well have: on those nights Novena came home in time for dinner, a tiny pause would hum over them for a moment, as if they were waiting for him to take a seat.

Naturally, they never talked about him, but sometimes, when Novena was thinking of him, she would meet Annaluna's eyes and there would be a small spark of something, and she had the odd sensation they were sharing the same thought.

Only once did they refer to him out loud. They were sitting in the living room, and Annaluna said, "You miss him, don't you?"

Novena wasn't sure she heard her correctly. She thought Annaluna might have said something about rheumatism. But she was so startled she nodded her head.

"I do too," Annaluna said. "Though he stole my silver, the bastard."

By the end of October, it was a sad fact that Zan had probably never been more alive than he was then. It would have thrilled him to know he was now being kept alive by two women.

But it is another sad fact that two women, no matter who they are or what they mean to each other, will often end up fighting over a man, even the ghost of one.

She and Annaluna began bickering and snapping at each other. Novena chided Annaluna for not eating; Annlauna would sit with her lips clamped shut, occasionally grunting.

Most nights, they retreated to their rooms after dinner, and would barely speak over breakfast. Annaluna barely spoke at all anymore; the only time she seemed to talk was to protest Novena's disposal of some small ancient clump of yarn or paper she had been hoarding. Novena was now cleaning the place with a fury, and she reproached Annaluna for all the small spent things of her that she daily picked off the floor and dumped into the trash, although she swore she was often picking up the same things day after day.

Sometimes, when she was conscious of her harsh, angry movements as she ran the vacuum, or scrubbed down a counter, or ignored Annaluna when she protested Novena's removal of some piece of twine or old shoe, Novena reminded herself of Elegia. She hated herself for her behavior, yet she couldn't stop.

Everything in her felt fast and wound up. Even in bed, she would be jumpy and nervous, listening to the footsteps above her head, the shuddering of the pipes, the screech of the furnace. She had never been conscious of so much noise before. Some nights, it was almost impossible to sleep. Every sound was magnified a hundredfold: truck horns on the street, wailing sirens, harsh echoing footsteps on the sidewalk, dull thuds from the ceiling, the clicking of Mamie's nails in the kitchen, the whistling and creaking and groaning of the building around her.

She would wake in the morning bleary-eyed, her mouth recoiling at the burned bitter coffee, her whole being flinching at the rustle of the newspaper pages, the little clicks of Annaluna's teeth as she chewed her breakfast, the sound of the wheels of her chair rolling on the carpet. There were some mornings Novena could not bear the din. There were some mornings there was nothing inside her but dread, nothing in the world but him.

These were the mornings she found it hard to get out of the house: Doorknobs would catch her sleeve, spools of thread would unravel and reach out to her, tangling her hands as if in a web, a plate would leap off the counter and shatter to the floor when she tried to leave the room.

Then the sharp edges of counters and tables and bookcases began reaching out for her, delivering sharp slaps and bangs to her skin. She would walk through the apartment, feeling everything was lying in wait to trip her, to slam against her shin. No matter how careful she was, they found her. Their strikes and slaps were vicious, although they hadn't yet drawn blood.

Just blood brought to the surface of her skin, in a map of faint black and blue marks on her body. They bloomed on her arm like violets, on the back of her legs like spilled wine.

A single small pansy, yellow petals unfolding from a violet-blue center on the upper part of her arm.

She avoided going home as much as she could. She was able to extend her days at God of Sand by offering to do extra sewing for Alexia, to help keep up with the demand for the new line of dresses. Novena would sew long into the night, kept hypnotized by the steady rhythmic clack of the sewing machine. The sound was like a fast ticking clock, and hours would fall away into neat stitches, into straight lines, into miles of uniformity. Entire nights could be lost, tangled up in thread, leaving her empty and exhausted. She was working so late that she usually ended up having to take a cab home.

She would sink back into the seat and stare out the cab's smeared window as it rattled up the streets, looking for Zan in the dark forms of people — the night's population of bums, beggars, and street people. She would sometimes see him out there, in the huddled bundles of rags on a sidewalk that she knew was a person sleeping, or the dark shadow of a figure crouched in a doorway, or the bent-over form of a man picking through the garbage.

Her cab would pull into her street, up to her building, and she would look out the window, searching out shadows and forms that might be him hovering out there at the thinning edges of the night. She would ask the cab driver to wait until she got inside, but he never paid attention and would squeal away as soon as she got out of the cab. Her heart racing, she would dash up the steps, her key ready to slide into the door. Once inside, she would walk through the rooms, touching things, a lamp, a door frame, Mamie's coat, before she felt entirely alone.

It didn't always work. Flipping on the lights, she would often be struck with the feeling that the room had just emptied of a large crowd. Chairs and tables seemed to blink in the sudden light, as if they were weary party hosts who had just ushered the last guest out and had stopped for a minute to rest their eyes. There would be an intangible sense of rearrangement, as if the dust had shifted slightly, and the air itself would be laced with a strange and sour odor, like the exhaled breath of a sick person. Like Zan's breath.

The smell of him was all around her now.

chapter 28

ZAN WAS AT HIS USUAL POST at Annaluna's, watching the windows from across the street. It was past ten, and he had barely seen a shadow all night. He was about to leave when a cab pulled up and stopped in front of the door.

Zan waited, curious to see who it was.

He heard the door slam, watched the cab squeal away, and then, as he looked at the figure under the streetlight, he felt a strange sense of recognition stirring in him.

It was himself. A smaller version of himself, but he saw his clothes, his hat.

His first thought was that it was a trick of the light, or some vision that he was deciphering incorrectly. But then he was overcome by a memory of a time he thought he had lost forever: It was another night that he had once seen himself — the night he had left Nile Bay, when he had seen his truck driving by, the familiar shape of the Deere cap in the cab. The shape of himself, driving.

He watched as this other version of him turned and looked around, as if scanning the street for something. It was then he saw Novena's face.

Novena. He nearly yelled out to her in the surprise of seeing her. He watched her run up the stairs and open the heavy door of the apartment with a key. He watched the lights go on in the place — the hallway first, then the living room, and by the time he could picture the kitchen light going on, it had dawned on him that Novena was living with Annaluna.

As he thought of the dark moving shapes that he'd been watching for so long, Zan went cold with the feeling that something had been taken from him — some essential thing, like food, or time, or love, had been pulled away from him in the direction of someone else. This feeling was not a new one; it was, in fact, a very old one, so old it had white hair and no teeth. It was so old that he could picture it sitting at the edge of a bed, looking out at a gray and hungry day through a grime-covered window, wearing a maroon flannel robe and crabby with the memory of itself.

Just then, he saw another window light up — the front bedroom. The one facing the street. Not Annaluna's room. His room. *His.*

It was his room, not hers. It was his life, not hers. He was the one who belonged there at Annaluna's, not Novena, dressed up to look like him.

She had taken his place.

He watched the lights snap off in the apartment, one by one, and it seemed to snap something in him, for now it dawned on him with a simplicity that astonished him: it was because of Novena that he was dead. She had stolen his life.

Zan rarely felt flash floods of rage anymore. His riverbank was almost completely dry, and so he no longer felt flash floods of anything. But now he felt a sudden sweeping watery mess of fury that nearly knocked him over. He actually reeled back a little from the force of it.

He could have run up the steps and pounded on the door, broken his way in if he had to, but his instincts, which had once been so pure, had become gluey and clotted with doubt. He could only stand there a dumb thing, unable to move for a long time, feeling everything in him ebbing away.

It wasn't until later, driving home, enshrouded in the protective muffle of the truck cab, that he let himself dwell on what Novena had taken from him, letting small but steady floods of fury lubricate him during his long drive back. There was something deeply luxurious in these small tides of rage dousing him like a baptism. With each swell, he felt the return of his memories, of all the things of himself he had lost, pieces of his life washing up on shore like the shards of rock and broken shells, like the skeletons and carcasses of dead sea animals.

He felt his mind running blindly, reaching out for the surfaces of these memories — the shape of his gun; the curve of a mug of Check's coffee in his hands, the same curve of a deer's heart he had once held in his palm; the smell of the woods, of his truck, of the river. But however welcome the return of these memories, he cast them aside quickly. They were in the way, like underbrush on a path he was hacking, a path that he wanted to lead to only one moment — the one in which Novena had stolen his life from him. He wanted to know when it had happened. He wanted to know how someone so small could have stolen something so big, right from under his nose.

His hand was twitching, as if it had woken up from a long sleep, ready to defend him. He stared at it, watching his fingers flex, as if they were coming alive with their own memory — recalling the feel of the thin little bones of her back under her cotton shirt. Recalling her skin — fragile, like a paper membrane covering her, something that might dissolve or tear under the fingers. Except it never had torn or dissolved, however hard his fingers took hold of it. He could take handfuls of that skin, gather it up into his palm, make a fist around it, twist and squeeze it. No matter what he did, her skin resisted him, keeping him out.

His hand was clenching into a fist, remembering the surprise of her resistance, given how tiny she had been, especially compared to him. Her smallness had always infuriated him; it had always seemed to be an affront to his own size, and had a way of diminishing him.

But it was more than her size that had diminished him, and he felt some furious animal heart in him begin to pound as he remembered something else about her: the way she could look right at him and not seem to register him.

He had watched it happen: he would come upon her, and something in her eyes would retreat, like a curtain falling, taking her somewhere inside herself. She would be standing in front of him and no longer see him. As if he didn't exist. As if she had made him disappear.

Now he recalled the first morning after he had left Annaluna's, waking up in the motel room, unable to recognize himself. He thought it had begun that morning, the draining away of himself. But it had been going on for years; she'd been making him gradually disappear and he just hadn't noticed. And now, he was on his way to becoming nothing.

He was suddenly frightened, and he held up his hand. Was it smaller? In the dark cab, he could barely see its edges. He touched his belly, and found not the usual comforting bulk, but a handful of flannel; his middle had shrunk too. He touched his cheek, tried to imagine the skin dissolving.

He tried to shake himself out of this strange idea that he was losing his body. At least part of him knew he was being irrational, yet that only increased his panic about all the things that were dropping off him like rotting fruit — first his memories, then his instincts, and now rational thought.

It wasn't entirely true that Zan was without instincts. He had exactly one left, the one never relinquished till the very end, the instinct of last resort: to drive as fast as possible.

His truck was empty of cargo, so he gained speed quickly, and soon he was flying down the highway. The speed moved through him like liquid, like something slippery, and he began storming the tiny cars ahead of him, leaning on his horn, watching the drivers cower at his looming. The sight of those tiny cars made him feel better, and it took him a few miles until he realized why. Then he nearly laughed. He was a big thing, powering a giant machine. He brought his foot down on the gas, and he left it there. He let panic slide away, leaving room for breath, for expansion.

By the fifth mile, the roaring under him was not the truck but his own size and strength, momentarily restored. Although he knew better than to count on its permanence, he let himself have a moment of hope. But at that moment, even his hope was big, as wide as the night.

It occurred to him then that maybe he had been looking for the wrong moment. He had been trying to uncover the moment his life had been stolen from him, when he should have been looking for the moment that he could get it back.

The idea excited him; it was almost thrilling in its possibilities. He peered out at the night, through the truck windows, as if that moment might even be out there, standing at the side of the road, waiting to flag him down.

A few miles later, after passing a blaring orchestra of outraged car horns and angrily flickering headlights, he nearly ran it over. At least that's how it felt when it appeared in front of him, in a vision so sudden and startling he nearly slammed on his brakes. He saw how he could reclaim his life. He saw what this moment looked like, how it felt; he had seen it so clearly that he could practically see the color of the sky that day, and what he might eat for breakfast that day, and how well it would fill his stomach. He saw the moment of his salvation so clearly it nearly blinded him.

And yet it was a small thing, really. Not much to ask for. It was all anyone really wants. All anyone needs to get out of limbo, to stop being dead.

Zan wanted to be seen.

chapter 29

Tea is a work of art. . . . Each preparation of the leaves has its individuality, its special affinity with water and heat, its hereditary memories to recall, its own method of telling a story. The truly beautiful must be always in it.

— Kakuzo Okakura, *The Book of Tea*

"I'm worried about you," Alexia said one day. Novena was sewing in the back room of God of Sand.

She looked up, flushing.

"What kind of life are you leading?" Alexia was saying. "You're nonstop work. Your face is so drawn. When was the last time you had any fun?"

"This is fun," Novena said.

"That's not what I mean. You're a young beautiful girl. You should be out there, living. What did you do last weekend?"

"You know what I did. I was here."

"No, I mean at night."

"Well, there's lots to do around here."

"What about the weekend before?"

"Well, I don't remember," Novena said, blushing, suddenly self-conscious. Now, forced to look back on specific days, she had an image of the minutes and hours being fed into the sewing machine, eaten up along with the cloth.

"So why don't you come out with Edo and me tonight?"

The invitation surprised Novena. While Alexia was one of the few people in Novena's life, they spent no time together outside of the shop. In fact, Novena was slightly intimidated by the mysteries of Alexia's life. Most of this intimidation, she realized, centered on Edo. He visited God of Sand regularly, always wearing dark glasses, trailing sharp vapors of turpentine behind him, but he spoke little. She couldn't see or smell or hear anything that told her who he really was.

Now Novena considered the prospect of an evening with them.

"How about tomorrow?" she said. "I'm a mess today."

"Are you brushing me off?"

"No, really. Tomorrow is better. Besides, it'll be the start of the weekend."

The next day, when Edo showed up at closing time, Alexia said, "So, let's get on the iron worm and go to yin-town."

As usual, Alexia's words were like reverse origami: intricate objects that unfolded to reveal the flat, pedestrian plane of paper. Novena had long since stopped trying to translate her speech and usually just waited for it to reveal its meaning.

They ended up taking a long subway ride, arriving at the sprawling Asian district where Novena had not yet ventured; Alexia had told her early on not to bother picking there, since no one in this neighborhood ever sold their clothes.

When they climbed the stairs to the street, Novena was immediately struck with how densely compacted everything was — not only the buildings, but the heat and the smells. There was a smell of things rotting in the street, something organic, like vegetables, although she could see none. The streets were crowded with people, yet there was a curious absence of human sounds. All the noise and chaos belonged to trucks and car horns and the rattle of the trains underground. They passed doors with strange indecipherable lettering, and Novena imagined she could hear the faint echoes of screaming chickens being butchered inside.

They went to a small restaurant, which from the outside looked like nothing. But inside were carved wooden screens and walls hung with brilliant red and gold banners. A small woman wearing a sarong led them past tables of Asian families to a table in the back, where they heard bursts of clatter and yelling from the kitchen whenever a waiter came out bent over from the weight of a tray. Edo ordered them beer, and Novena drank hers quickly, feeling it move through her, smoothing out her bones, making them fluid and relaxed.

When the food was brought to the table — jasmine rice and curries the color of jewels — Novena leaned over and inhaled their scents. She gasped and closed her eyes, and breathed in memories of warmth and industry, of slips of color stirring in the breeze. She felt tiny pinpricks of memory, like something she might pick up from an old blouse or jacket. She was in a room on a street that sounded and smelled like this one. It was in the not-so-distant past, but the room itself had the feeling of an older time. She saw a sofa covered with rose-colored textured cloth, the small horned claw feet that held it up. She saw a patterned rug, dark walls. But the most astonishing thing she saw was herself, in the room. It was a place she had inhabited.

She opened her eyes; Alexia was staring at her.

"I think I was born here," she suddenly blurted out, surprised at how the words had slipped out of her, easy as the truth. But it *was* the truth, she was suddenly sure of it. She looked around her, as if it had been the restaurant she had been referring to instead of the old mournful apartment where she had come into the world.

"Oh, honey," Alexia said, "I think that every time I eat this curry. I get all jungly and feverish."

"No, I mean, I was born in this neighborhood. Somewhere around here, anyway."

She felt dizzy and excited. She looked around her now, half expecting one of the families sitting at the tables to nod in recognition, or someone she had once known to come out of the kitchen.

"This is amazing," Alexia was saying. "Where? Tell us everything."

"Well, there's not much to tell," Novena said, reluctant to stir herself from this cloud of remembering, to let go of the bright flashes of color and the fragrances of her past. Yet she also felt that a giddiness was threatening to waft out of her like the steam from the rice bowl.

"I was born here, and when my mother died, I went to live with my aunt and her four boys. I was very little. I can barely remember the place."

But even as she spoke, she was remembering odd snatches of things. Pots of steaming curry. A window, hung with green velvet, framing a gray day. A soft whirring machine sound, like a sewing machine.

Alexia suddenly broke in.

"And yet here you are," she said. "Fifteen years later, back in the same place. But if you had stayed here then, you would be someplace else now. Like vu-ja dey."

Novena was struck with the oddness of this idea. What if she *had* stayed here, had never lost her mother, had never gone to live with those boys? There would be another, different Novena than she was now, living here among the noise and butchered chickens, among strange writing on the windows of the storefronts. Maybe there was another Novena out there now, the one who belonged to the wispy fragments of memories that she could never remember as her own.

She pictured this other Novena, out there in some nether world, and once again she felt a familiar displacement, another sliding away from the present. She had a dimly glimmering image of herself, at some other time, but it was not the past, or the future, or even the present. It was simply the time of another Novena, who worked at God of Sand and picked through old clothes and sat with her friends in a restaurant, inhaling the warm steam from a bowl of rice.

It was another Novena, without Zan.

"So, tell us more," Alexia was exclaiming. "You never talk about yourself."

But she didn't want to talk. She wanted to stop Alexia's voice. It was dragging her away, and she wanted to stay in the moment she had become that other Novena. She wanted to let it expand until she could crawl into it, to live in it, as if it were a place. A place like this neighborhood, like a whole town that was hers, where Zan couldn't reach her.

"There's nothing much to tell," Novena said slowly.

"Oh, come on," Alexia said. "For one thing, I had no idea you had four cousins. Do you get to see them much? Where are they now?"

"Oh, they're all over. You know . . ." Novena made a vague sweeping gesture with her hand. "Out there, in the world."

She was suddenly aware of a silence over the table, of Alexia and Edo retreating. She saw they were somewhat embarrassed at her reticence. She blushed.

"Hey, let's finish and get out of here," she said, desperate for this conversation to end. She was anxious to get outside, to walk through the neighborhood.

Still, she hated for the meal to end; she wanted to remain there, eating her memories, filling up on them. As it is with all memory, the more she consumed, the more remained to be eaten.

Finally outside, though, she felt hyped up, like a dog straining at its leash. She wanted to break away, to walk fast, to run through these streets, looking at doorways, looking for more flashes of memory, for bolts of cloth, for her mother.

For herself, without Zan.

But she followed Edo and Alexia as they wandered through the streets, maneuvering around crowds of people, peering into darkened windows and stumbling into and out of stores with their strange dank sea smells, their jumbled-up aisles of cookware and food and herbal medicines.

Alexia was delirious, going through the aisles, exclaiming at the colors. "Look at this," she would cry every few minutes, holding up a package of dried seaweed or a jar of paste as scarlet as her hair. "This would be a beautiful color for the walls."

Wandering close behind her, Novena concentrated on the people, scanning their flat-planed faces, looking for familiar ones. All she got back from them were hard, blank looks, and it occurred to her how strange their presence must seem: Alexia in her kimono and her wild red hair, Edo with his dark glasses and long ponytail, and Novena, small between them, in her drab and shapeless boys' clothes.

But still she was giddy, being here, and felt a lightness expand in her as she followed them through the streets. It was not only the lightness of weight, although she did feel the removal of a certain heaviness, but also one of brightness. Everything she saw seemed luminous.

The lightness carried her all the way home: on the train, down her street, into the apartment, and down the hall to the living room. She hesitated at the doorway for a second, looking into the room, expecting it to look somehow changed. As usual, it was shrouded in darkness.

Novena took a deep breath. Annaluna was sitting in a far corner, doing nothing Novena could see but staring into the dark. Novena felt herself wavering, but the taste of the neighborhood still filled her mouth, and it gave her a resolve she hadn't felt in ages. She released her breath, and stepping into the room she felt she was parting a thick curtain of gloom.

"I'm home," she called out in a bright voice. "Are you okay?"

As she moved around the room, turning on lamps, Annaluna's eyes blinked like a baby bird's in the sudden brightness.

Novena bent over to kiss her cheek. Annaluna seemed startled at the contact, but she didn't pull away. Novena felt a little startled too: she couldn't remember the last time she had kissed Annaluna, or even touched her. It made her feel buoyant and slightly giddy.

Novena perched on a chair across from her. She wanted to talk to Annaluna about the night, but felt slightly wary. It had been a long time since they had talked; in fact, it had been days since Annaluna had made much sound at all besides the clicking of her teeth, or little grunts and muttering into her dinner plate.

"Guess where I was tonight," she began, conscious of how loud her voice was. "The old neighborhood, where I was born. You know where I mean?"

Annaluna looked up at her, her stare vacant.

"Do you remember it? Where my mother lived?"

Annaluna blinked slowly, as if to focus her eyes.

"I ate in a restaurant, and then spent an hour walking around there."

She described what she had remembered — the way the light had come in through the window, the scent of curry, the ancient breath of the place — her words coming out in a jumble, in snatches of images and sensations, with no order, or rather, with the order of memory itself. It was, Novena thought, like the kind of conversation she used to have with Annaluna when she had first come here.

Annaluna watched her, and as she talked Novena imagined she was beginning to respond, clicking her teeth against her tongue, craning her neck slightly as if she were listening. After a while, Annaluna began fumbling around at the side of her chair. She pulled out one of the old remnants of shoes that she had not let Novena take from her, although there was barely anything left to this one, just the remainder of a spike heel. She held it in her hand, rubbing her palm against it, her eyes closed slightly.

Her expression was so odd that Novena couldn't read it, but she had the sense Annaluna was signaling the conversation was over.

"Well, it's a beautiful place anyway," Novena said, rising. "I'm going to go back tomorrow. See if I can find anything."

She went back to the neighborhood the next night. It was almost dark by the time she got off the train and came up the steps into the dense noise of the place.

She walked slowly, looking into the darkening storefronts, the lit-up restaurants, the curtained windows of apartments above them. There was nothing exactly familiar, and yet it was all somehow familiar — the absence of human sounds, the indecipherable words on store and street signs, with odd hooks and curves dangling off the characters, and the smells of meat and steam and rotting things. Like seaweed, she thought — a green smell.

All day at God of Sand, she had pictured going back to the neighborhood, finding it shining, with pieces of her past strewn in the gutters like flowers, waiting for her to come and gather them up. She had even entertained a vague notion of looking for the actual house where she had been born, but put it aside. She knew it would be impossible to find without asking Elegia for the address. And she could hear Elegia dismissing her, saying, "Oh, why bring up all that old stuff?"

"Because this is where I was born," Novena now whispered to herself, and there was such pleasure in those words that she repeated them to herself as she walked, expecting that any moment, more memories of this place, of her place, would rise up in her. But she had already spent a half hour exploring the small side streets and their complex maze of tiny alleys, and so far the only memories she had of this place were the memories of being here last night.

She began whispering the words as a chant, willing them to bring her back to that room she had inhabited, the place where she had been born, where her mother was.

But nothing was coming back to her, and now the maze of narrow little streets was starting to confuse her, and she was getting tangled up and lost. The rows and rows of brick buildings, anonymous doorways, and tidy little houses set above their own staircases all had a closed-up, secretive look. She felt her pleasure and certainty slowly draining away, and she began to think that maybe she was in the wrong place, that she had simply dreamed last night.

So she began looking for the restaurant. She covered three busy streets, each lined with all the restaurants of the world except the one she had been in last night. She had been walking for nearly an hour when it started raining, a cold and sudden downpour.

Shivering and soaked, she ducked into the first restaurant she found, sat at the counter and ordered tea.

"Green tea?" said the woman behind the counter.

Novena nodded. Everything was green here. It struck her that this was the only solid thing she had grasped all night — the color of the place.

She had been trying to hold off her disappointment, but waiting for the tea to arrive, she began to fret. She was no longer sure she was in the right neighborhood. Maybe she had imagined everything, all the slips of color, all the memories that had stirred in her last night.

It now struck her as ludicrous that she had spent the last hour wandering around a strange neighborhood, brought here by nothing but the smell of curry. She felt foolish and miserable, shivering there on the stool.

The woman appeared with a small ceramic pot, which she put on the counter in front of Novena. She didn't move away, though, but stood there, as if waiting for something. Novena, confused, thought the woman was waiting for her to pour the tea and give her approval. So she reached for it, but just as she was about to grasp the handle, the woman pushed her hand away, and put her own protectively over the small lid of the teapot.

"Not yet," she said sternly.

A full minute passed, and then, as if receiving some invisible signal, the woman lifted the pot. After tipping it gently from side to side, she poured a small stream into Novena's cup. She gave a little nod and moved away.

The tea was not the green that Novena had expected, but a muddy amber, tinged with olive. Her hands circled the cup instinctively, and the heat so instantly warmed the whole of her that she felt grateful for whoever it was who had invented the cup, who had thought to give it this shape, for the hands to enclose its warmth.

Novena brought the cup to her mouth and took a sip. The tea slid into her mouth at the same moment she registered its fragrance, and it struck her how perfectly balanced its smell and taste were: a delicate but deep essence, vaporous yet dense, like wood smoke and earth.

She took another sip. The tea was slightly bitter on her tongue, but as she held it in her mouth, it changed to a sweeter afternote, like the tender leaves of a rare plant. She swallowed, and she felt it coating her insides like the thick nap of green velvet.

The next sip brought more green, shattering into a thousand greens, the green of parrots, snakes, emeralds, of melon, jade, and new grass, greens so translucent they nearly blinded her. Yet all of these were greens she knew, all of them in a place she knew — the same room, with dark wood walls, a pink sofa, the nap of green velvet again, this time between her fingers. She saw the colored lengths of fabric hung at her windows, recalled the scent of tea and curry and the low murmur of women's voices in late afternoon.

Memory was rising in her like steam, steam and the smell of slightly scorched cloth, of warmth and industry.

Novena breathed all of this in, took this pleasure into her, swallowing it, holding each sip of tea in her mouth like a gift, and even after releasing it into her throat, her mouth was still filled with the flavor of her past.

And warmth. She felt enveloped in warmth, like someone holding her, hands enclosing her like a cup. Like her mother's hands. She saw Catorza's face more clearly than she had remembered it for years.

She felt an immense happiness expanding in her, so immense that her eyes were filling with tears. But they were strange tears, not of sorrow or sadness, but of some deeper, more complex thing hovering there behind the simple pleasure of her mother's face. It was tantalizingly distant, a feeling she couldn't name, yet so full it was pushing its way up her throat, as if on its way to her mouth, as if on its way to becoming words to describe itself, when she was startled by a voice.

"You want order?"

She opened her eyes and the woman at the counter was staring at her coldly.

Novena smiled weakly, and shook her head.

"Just tea," she said.

"Beautiful tea," she added.

The woman slapped her check on the counter and moved away.

There was something in the woman's movement, or her voice, that stirred something else in Novena. She suddenly recalled the face of a man, an old man with gnarled hands that reminded her of the bark of a tree, circling her. The bony legs of his lap, like the limbs of trees. The bitter smell of him, like rotting leaves.

Then she remembered the low joyful groans of her mother's voice coming from her bedroom, mingling with his.

She went to pour the last of the tea, but the pot was empty. Looking around for the woman, Novena saw the restaurant was empty too, and she realized they were probably waiting for her to leave so they could close.

Novena left the restaurant and headed toward the train. She was passing one of the bright, overlit grocery stores Alexia had dragged them into the night before, and on an impulse she went in. Wandering the aisles, she found a shelf full of tea in tins and bright boxes. She found a box of green tea and bought it, and had the package open by the time she stepped outside.

The rain had finally stopped, and the street was now shining, and skitters of colors bounced off the neon and sliced up the street into colored shards. The windows and glass storefronts looked clean, as if they had been unshuttered and washed, and the buildings no longer had a closed-up, secretive look. The place, she thought, looked beautiful. It looked like hers — a whole town of her.

She opened the box and tipped a little of the tea into her palm, studying the soft little leaves and tiny branches and sticks, and she brought it to her face and inhaled. The smell of green filled her, and she suddenly wanted to stain the world with it. She flung it from her palm, heaving the tea into the air. She wanted to see it carried in the breeze, to have the rain carry it through the gutters and sewer drains, into the rest of the city. She wanted the wind to carry it upward, to tint the sky with a million different greens.

She was enchanted with the idea of a green sky, wondering why it was that no one had ever thought of it before, why the sky appeared only as lavender or scarlet, orange or blue, yellow or gray, but never jade, never emerald, never the shining green of a lizard's back. Annaluna might know. Novena hurried home, grateful for the first time in ages that Annaluna was waiting.

Novena brewed a cup of the tea for Annaluna, letting it steep in a pot and tipping it gently back and forth a little before pouring, just as the woman had done. She watched Annaluna's face as she drank, curious to see if the tea would have a similar effect on her.

Annaluna made a sour little face and looked at her, as if surprised, but she kept sipping it.

"Do you like it?" Novena said. "It's past-life tea. Good memories will come back if you drink it."

Annaluna looked at her, smiling slightly.

"I went back to the old neighborhood again. It's so green there," Novena continued. "Mysterious. Like this tea."

Annaluna kept sipping, her eyes closing against the steam as she raised the cup.

"I spent an hour walking around. I thought about finding the house, but I knew I wouldn't. Do you think I should ask Elegia? No, I guess not. You know how she gets. But I remembered other things. Like my mother, holding me. And a man who came to see her. Oh, and a machine. Like a sewing machine. Did my mother sew?"

Novena described the images that had come to her, in the same fast jumble of words as the night before. She liked filling the room with these moments and images of her childhood, as if she were moving them from the old neighborhood to live there, in their rightful place.

As Novena talked, it seemed to her that Annaluna was actually smiling slightly. In fact, the heat from the tea had brought small patches of color to her cheeks. They were like rough little roses — past their prime, dull in color and browning at the edges, but still alive.

That night, Novena brought a cup of the tea to bed with her, placing it by her bedside so she could inhale its fragrance. Covered with a blanket of her memories, she was drawn into a contented sleep. That night, for the first time in ages, she slept free of dreams, free of Zan.

chapter 30

AT HEART, THE PAST is a weak old thing, cranky with the limitations its age imposes. And when it finds itself sitting in the dark, as forgotten and neglected as a grandmother, it relies on the same thing yours will when she senses your indifference: it will dredge up the old days and force you to reminisce.

But the past does not love you as a grandmother does. It evokes memories only to get your attention, hurling them randomly like stones, pelting you with recollections of pleasure as well as humiliation, your shining moments along with your most shameful ones.

Sometimes it will tease you, sending you only the shards of memories. These fragments of moments, jagged and incomplete, bring terror without explanation, sorrow without reason, pleasure without satisfaction.

These are the worst of all, the past at its cruelest: promising more than it ever delivered. Reminding us of just how much we have forgotten, of how much we have lost.

Novena was going back to the neighborhood every night now, always stopping first at the restaurant for a pot of tea. Then she'd wander the streets, waiting for pieces of her past to unfold to her a moment at a time. But no matter how much tea she drank, or how many hours she spent walking, Novena seemed to be caught in the same continuous loop of memories: her mother's face, the pink sofa, the heavy green drapes of the apartment, the colored lengths of fabric hung at her windows, the scent of tea and curry and the smell of the steam iron, and the pleasant but irregular company of the old man.

It was like having the same dream, over and over. In fact, they were a lot like dreams, these remnants of memories. They were just as disordered, just as random, carrying the same portentous weight, the same demand for attention and interpretation. And yet, as far as Novena could see, there seemed to be no purpose in her recollections beyond the pleasure of their possession.

The pleasure was complicated, though: walking through the streets, she felt the same bewildering emotion that had risen in her the night she had discovered the tea — a happiness that expanded not into fullness, but into longing, like a sweetness in the mouth that dissolved into a sour aftertaste of something incomplete, unreachable.

She sometimes imagined that another version of herself was hiding somewhere in this neighborhood, hoarding her past like coal, watching her from the dark shapes between buildings, following her in the fumes from the restaurants and the steam rising up from the grates like mysterious whispers.

Novena wondered if she would live her entire life being followed.

But at least it was no longer Zan following her. Although she still felt his presence in the rest of the city, she never had the sense he even existed when she was in this neighborhood.

Night after night, she traveled up one street and down another, tugged by a combination of pleasure and loss that left her feeling full and empty at the same time. The strangest thing was that this too had the sensation of memory.

➤

Annaluna's pleasure was much simpler, now that she and Novena had begun a new nightly ritual.

Each night, Annaluna would listen for the sound of Novena at the door, and would roll away from the window to wait in the kitchen for her to come in. Novena would make a pot of the tea, and sit with Annaluna. As they filled themselves with the taste of green, Novena would tell her stories of the neighborhood.

Her stories always began in the room with the claw-footed sofa, and the green drapes. She would describe the nights the old man visited, Catorza waiting for him to arrive with his arms full of white flowers or bolts of cloth wrapped up in ribbons. She told how the joyous muffled sounds from her mother's room sounded, how sometimes Novena would lie there with her mother when he left in the morning, their arms wrapped around each other, hands on each other's faces.

Given how limited her actual recollections were, Novena soon began embellishing. To fill in the gaps of her own memory, she began borrowing the shreds of lives from the clothes from God of Sand, embroidering the hours of her mother's waiting with the moments Novena had picked up in a scarf, or a man's felt hat, an old fur, or silk dress.

She embellished a little more with each telling, and each night, the old man grew a little younger, until his skin became smooth and shining, his clothes more finely cut. And each night, he visited a little more often, until he was leaving every morning and coming back every night, his arms filled with increasingly elaborate gifts. Each night, the sounds from her mother's room grew louder and more joyous.

It was a pleasure to sit with Annaluna again, talking to her, watching her face soften in the pleasure of listening. But Novena was getting more and more frustrated going back to the neighborhood night after night. She would hurtle into it, ready to gather all her happy memories, yet was still unable to recall anything more than the usual snatches and traces and threads of things. Confronted by as many blank holes as actual memories, she began wondering if there was anything there for her after all.

Soon a shadow of sadness was following her through the neighborhood — an undercurrent of melancholy and rue that infected her bones, made her weary. She was worried now that there were pieces of herself that were lost forever, parts of her she'd never be able to retrieve.

As she sat with Annaluna, embroidering and embellishing her past as if it were a hat, with the feathers and seed pearls, the flourishes and flounces of other lives, she sometimes wished she hadn't found the place. The small tastes of those moments were worse than none at all. She began to think that maybe she should give up, stop going back to the neighborhood, stop bringing it back into the house each night.

On the other hand, how could she stop? Annaluna was rarely at the window now, rarely in the dark, and the constant gloom of the place had lifted into nothing more than a vague, dusty patina of occasional melancholy. Whenever she came in, Annaluna's face would be so expectant, opening like a flower at the sight of her. Novena would bring her a cup of tea and settle at her feet, resting her head against her legs.

"Which story do you want to hear, Annaluna?"

She always asked the question, although of course Annaluna never answered her. She always told the same story anyway, or a variation: always Catorza, waiting for the moment he arrived.

"The radio is on, and she's humming," she began one night. "Tonight she's thinking of wearing the white sundress, with the little lace stole. He's going to be wearing that blue serge, you know the one. She always teases him that it smells of mothballs and apricots."

This was a detail Novena had picked up just that day from one of the suits at God of Sand.

"I wonder sometimes whether she would notice if he ever skipped a night," she continued. "Because even when he wasn't with her she saw him everywhere. She saw his face in her dreams, and she saw him on the streets when she shopped. He even rose up in the steam while she ironed. That's how much he was a part of her."

On this night, Novena was growing sleepy and leaned her head against Annaluna's knees and patted her feet, the story so familiar she felt it begin telling itself.

"In fact, she's ironing right now, waiting for him. She's thinking about him as she's ironing, and she can't wait to see him. He's late tonight, though. Twenty minutes late. Then a half hour. She's getting a little nervous. She's tired of looking out the window, and she finally goes outside and stands in the doorway, looking up and down the street for him. She's searching the crowds for the shape of him coming toward her, and she thinks she sees him a hundred times. But it's never him."

Novena paused. Although the story was still familiar in its details, she suddenly had the feeling it was about to change, to become something else, veering off in some strange, disturbing direction.

"She's beginning to wonder if she's made him up. Maybe he doesn't even exist. Maybe he never existed anywhere but in her imagination."

She thought she should stop telling this story before it got away from her and took over its own telling. She looked up at Annaluna, who seemed to be dozing. Novena wondered if she had even been listening.

Annaluna suddenly gave a little snort and her eyes fluttered open a little.

Novena took a breath, and with her voice almost a whisper, she went on.

"And then she saw him. Walking toward her. She knew he would come. She knew, because he would always come back. He would always come back to her.

"He'd never stay away."

For a moment, she wondered whose story she was telling. For a moment, it had sounded like her own.

Of course Annaluna had been listening. Annaluna always listened.

Night after night, she had been taking in these stories, making small accommodations in her sorrow, pushing aside her disappointment and bitterness in order to make room for them. Each night, she had taken these borrowed threads of other lives and had woven them seamlessly over the threadbare and unreliable patches of her own memories, until they had become her own. Her own story.

And before long, while Annaluna was listening, Renaldo had been undergoing a miraculous transformation. The shape of him that she had held in her mind for decades had been shifting and changing, becoming something else. Renaldo was becoming another man: not a man who spent his whole life leaving her each day, but a man who loved her so much that he had spent his whole life coming back to her.

But the real miracle was this: from the dark root cellar of her life — that dank, mildewed pit overgrown with grief and sorrow, with anger and regret — Annaluna had retrieved her memory of love.

How else can we save ourselves?

However faint or distorted or ancient, however sparsely it came or harshly it was delivered to us — in our mother's arms, from the strong, soothing hands of our father, in the deep drowning kisses of our lovers — we never lose our memory of love.

Even after we lose everything else, we never lose this. Because in the end, our memory of love is the only thing that can save us from its loss.

And so tonight had been like all the other nights — Annaluna listening, smiling to herself, sinking into the warmth of the story, into the warmth of the girl's hands on her feet.

That's right: the girl's hands. She knew there was a girl with her. And not just any girl — this girl. How could she not know her? Hadn't she shared her life with her? Didn't she know her as well as she knew herself? Hadn't she walked in her shoes? It was the girl she adored, the one who would always come back to her:

Catorza.

chapter 31

A FEW NIGHTS LATER, Annaluna was on the beach. She had stooped over to pick up a conch shell, and as she cupped it in her hand, its spiral unfurled into two magnificent birds, one the mottled white of the shell's exterior, one the shining burnished orange of its interior. They hovered in the air before her, flapping their massive wings in a slow easy rhythm that matched her own sleeping breath.

It was the sound of their flapping wings that woke her, but as she came out of sleep, they were changing their shape again. By the time her eyes opened, they had become two of the nightgowns which, fifty years ago, had made up her trousseau — one a peach satin, the other a snowy cotton with smocking on the bodice. She recognized them instantly, and remembered with a small shock that she still owned them.

It took her three days to unearth their actual location from her memory, and another two to get her hands on them, since it had required clever but painstaking poking with a broomstick before she could dislodge the bundle from a high shelf in the hall closet. Unwrapping them from their layers of tissue paper, she felt as if she were also unwrapping them from layers of the long-forgotten pleasure associated with them, and she almost blushed. The white cotton gown was now beige with age, but the lace edging the neck and cuffs was still beautiful. The peach satin one had a million tiny hand stitches hardly discernible to the eye, but her fingers found them and traced them with happiness before she brought the whole soft thing to her cheek with a sigh.

It took her another day to summon her nerve to try them on. Although they were frail, and stained with mysterious spots of age not unlike her own, they seemed to be intact. Finally, with much struggle, she managed to pull the satin gown over her head. She got her arms through it, and she pulled it down over herself. She was trembling slightly with the effort, and sat for a minute catching her breath. Then she rolled over to the mirror. Staring at the image of herself, she felt her breath leave her again when she saw how well it fitted her.

When had her body shrunk down into such a small thing?

As she stared at herself in the glass, she had an even more unsettling realization: while she had been struggling to get the gown on, she hadn't given a thought to how she would ever remove it.

But it didn't matter, really. Her intention all along was to wear this pretty thing to bed. Because that was where he was finally going to come to her. And this time, she was not going to let him leave without her.

She decided she would not even bother trying to take the gown off. She'd wear it under her thick flannel one. The nights were colder now anyway, and she'd freeze to death in this little slip of a thing before he'd even had a chance to arrive.

At least it was next to her skin. That's what counted.

One night soon afterward, while she was drifting through sleep, Annaluna heard someone calling her name, and while she was conscious that the sound had been in her brain, it had been so loud and distinct that it had waked her with a start. She lay there, her heart fluttering wildly, her eyes shut, waiting for his soft breath on her cheek. But none came. She opened her eyes, and looked around the room. Empty. But she knew he was there, somewhere.

With only the tiniest prick of annoyance, she got up to look for him. She walked through her rooms, astonished at the crowd that had gathered: all the ghosts that had left with Novena's arrival were now back, and they seemed to have brought all their friends. She recoiled a bit, waiting to see if they had also brought their hostility, but as they turned their faces to her, she saw that their expressions were welcoming, as if they were happy to see her. They began clamoring for her attention, which made it hard for her to focus on finding Renaldo. The room was so crowded she could barely see anything.

She stood there, looking around wildly, beginning to panic at the idea he might leave without her, when she realized something: she was not in her wheelchair. She was standing, walking around. She looked down and saw her feet, and for an instant felt the ground under her give way, felt herself tottering above it.

To fall would be a disaster. She knew all the stories of women her age, perfectly sound one minute, gone the next because of a simple fall.

"Broken hip," people would whisper about them, shaking their heads sorrowfully, which had always infuriated Annaluna. Did they think she was a child? She knew "broken hip" was a code for something far more sinister. As if you could lose your life over a simple broken bone, when you broke far more by simply lasting this long.

But still, in that instant of knowing she was standing, unaided, she had a dark, cold dread of that fall. She felt precarious, as if she were about to be pushed from a great distance into a long eternal descent.

And it suddenly came to her: she had been all wrong. He hadn't changed. He hadn't come back for her love. He had come back to trick her, to lure her out here, to bring her to some harm. He was behind her now, ready to push her down.

Her arms went out in the darkness, reaching for something to hold on to. But there was nothing but empty space around her. Her hands flapped wildly, grasping at air.

What good were family and friends if you could not call upon them for help in times like this? And so Annaluna called out their names — Catorza, and her father, and her mother, and her uncle, and her childhood girlfriend, and all the other visitors in the crowd, all of whom seemed to be filling every space in the room but the one around her.

She felt minutes pass as she stood there, her arms outstretched in the darkness, her voice faintly calling their names, waiting for them to come forward. But she had forgotten how selfish and self-absorbed these creatures were. There were cowards, all of them. And she was a fool.

Suddenly, she felt something: not a hand in hers, but a kind of weight against her, heat and strength supporting her waist, and she leaned against it. She made her way slowly back through the living room, down the long hallway, into her bedroom, and then she was lying in her bed, panting slightly.

The small porcelain lamp was not lit, and Mamie, unaccustomed to the dark, started whimpering and leapt up onto the bed. But Annaluna, lying in darkness, was not afraid. She was calm again. Her loss of faith had only been momentary: an old habit. He had not come to harm her, after all. He had come to gather her to himself, to take her with him. And so she closed her eyes, and with everything that remained in her, Annaluna summoned the effort of will that love always requires — for in the end it is not a thing to be waited for, but to be reached for, to be leapt toward — and she raised her arms and held them out for him.

And with her arms around him — or around Mamie, she couldn't tell which, and what difference did it make anyway? — Annaluna, for the first time in years, welcomed sleep with delicious anticipation, with joyous abandon, with the ardency of a lover, as she fell into its soft and welcoming arms for the last time.

➤

Novena overslept by nearly an hour that morning, but she woke instantly, her eyes snapping open as if she had been shocked out of sleep by the lateness of the hour. It was strange she had slept this long, and she lay there, wondering what was different, what was missing.

There were no sounds coming from the kitchen, but that wasn't unusual; although Annaluna was rising very early these days, she was always quiet in the morning. Usually, by the time Novena woke, the only trace of her was the bitter fumes of the coffee Annaluna insisted on boiling into a thick grainy sludge.

Then it dawned on Novena what was missing: that smell, of coffee.

Novena got up and made coffee as quietly as possible so she wouldn't disturb Annaluna. She sat drinking it slowly despite the fact that she was late, waiting for Annaluna to stir. She wondered if she should wake her, wondered if she should be worried. Finally, she got up and stood at the door to her room, listening. She heard nothing.

Just before she pushed the door open, she had a strange thought, of how large the silence was, as if the world had suddenly been removed of all sound.

Mamie was lying quietly on the bed. Annaluna was curled up, her face on the pillow looking sweet, like a small girl. She was smiling slightly.

Novena didn't think she had ever seen her smile in her sleep, and she moved to her, touched her cheek, and felt its coldness.

"Annaluna!" she cried.

Annaluna didn't stir.

Annaluna was gone.

Her mind seized up, frozen and blank, and she sank down on the edge of the bed. Annaluna was lying on her side, her left hand under her head, her right hand out in front of her, palm facing the bed, fingers curling inward. It was such a tiny hand, and Novena didn't know what else to do but take it between her own and begin stroking it, trying to bring the warmth back into it. She had no idea how long she sat there rubbing Annaluna's hand, but no warmth came; the hand stayed cold. It was for this coldness that Novena finally collapsed onto the bed next to Annaluna and wept.

She wept for a long time, a soft kind of weeping that was more exhausted surrender than anything else.

When she stopped, she lay huddled at the edge of the bed, her back to Annaluna's bulk. Novena thought of how often she had curled into her as a child. Sitting on her lap, her back fitting into the contours of Annaluna's body, she would look out at the world from that shelter knowing what substance there was behind her.

But it was no longer Annaluna's bulk, no longer familiar. Annaluna's body was closed down, self-contained, no longer the factory that steadily manufactured warmth and comfort.

Novena lay there for a while, listening to her own breath; it sounded so loud. She thought of all the air that had filled these rooms, the air that she and Annaluna had shared — inhaling, exhaling the same molecules, breathing each other's breath. Now for the first time, the air Novena was taking into her lungs did not include anything of Annaluna; it was just her own breath, pushed out into the room, drawn back into herself, pushed out again, as if her lungs were rejecting it for being found so wanting. She was overwhelmed with the sadness of this, and felt that sadness spreading out, including all the other things they had shared — hours and days, meals and jokes, a language, an entire country of themselves. Now it was all reduced to nothing, to only herself.

Compared to the sturdier realms of love or anger, which can last a lifetime, grief is a more delicate thing, built for intensity, not duration. It is more like the fine china of emotions, brought out for solemn and momentous occasions, to be wrapped up and put away again.

Grief's pain can be shattering. Still, the hardest part of grief is not its pain, but the moment it begins to expand and attach itself to anything it can, hoping to stave off its diminishment. It worms its way into our failings and inadequacies, it embraces our regrets.

Novena's grief now began multiplying to include all the things she hadn't done with Annaluna, all the other things they could have shared but hadn't.

She grieved for all the afternoons she had spent at God of Sand, away from Annaluna. She grieved for her impatience with her, for the fact that she had never insisted on taking Annaluna outside. She could have pushed her chair, maybe even taken her to the old neighborhood, to see if she remembered anything. Annaluna might have enjoyed going back; she'd known the place even better than Novena. It was odd to realize this: Novena had thought of it as a place only she had inhabited, but only a tiny part of her own life had been there.

She thought of all the years she had spent in Nile Bay as wasted years, years she could have been living with Annaluna, taking care of her. She grieved for the fact that she'd been sent to Elegia's instead. One day, she'd been living in the apartment with her mother, surrounded by all that was hers, and the next, she'd been standing in a strange kitchen, surrounded by boys.

Somewhere in between, before Elegia had taken her home that day, Novena had spent her last day with Annaluna. They'd gone for a walk, although it was actually Novena who had done the walking. Annaluna had sat on a nearby stoop, watching her as she had walked up and down the street. Novena could recall the heat of the sun, the precise places it had hit the sidewalk, how it glinted off the chrome and sleek metal of the cars parked on the street as she'd walked past them with a child's sturdy steps.

Up and down that street she'd walked, for hours, waiting for something. When she reached the end of the street, she had paused, and then turned and made her way back to the other end. Up and down, past her house, past Annaluna, who called out to her as Novena passed.

Thinking of that small girl walking up and down the hot street, alone and motherless, Novena felt the worst kind of sorrow — a sorrow for herself that moved through her like a sharp thing, taking her breath away.

She recalled that moment in Elegia's kitchen again, when she had stood alone, the understanding that she had lost her mother taking shape as a dark thing moving toward her, like a slow train pulling into a station. Now Novena could feel that train bearing down on her again, and she turned herself around to face Annaluna.

She grasped the sleeve of her flannel gown, to have something to hold on to, not only to keep Annaluna from leaving her that alone again. She began crying, in deep gulping sobs, pulling Annaluna's sleeve into her mouth, biting down on it, until she finally let it go and wailed.

It was a long, mordant wail that even as Novena heard it ripping itself out of her to tear up the air, she thought was the saddest sound she had ever heard, this sound of herself, once again registering everything she had lost.

Novena lay still for a long time, unable to move. She thought she would never get up again. Maybe she would just lie here with Annaluna forever, under this heavy blanket of grief.

But slowly she was becoming conscious that time, which had left the room with its head bowed, had crept back into the room, and was now ticking softly away in the bedside clock. Novena listened to the ticking, listened to the hollow echo of her heart beating against the mattress, and she began looking around her, at the lamp on the bureau, the rug on the floor, the curtains on the window. She noticed a thin veil of dust on the bureau, streaks on the mirror, little dustballs on the floor in the corner, and despite herself, she began to enumerate them, to take in these small details.

We might perish from grief if it were not for these details — the dust to be removed, breakfast to be cooked, trash to be emptied, clothes to be washed — all those things that demand our constant vigilance, our continual attention, the unceasing pull on our leashes that moves us forward, from one day into the next.

But it is the dead themselves who finally call us out of the deepest grief, at least for a while, by demanding our ministrations. No one needs us more than the dead; they are as helpless as infants, waiting for us to clean and swaddle them.

And so Novena stirred herself and got out of bed, because Annaluna was waiting.

Novena stood and smoothed Annaluna's flannel nightgown, adjusted her blanket, and bent down to kiss her cheek. But she wasn't quite ready to leave her yet. She went to the closet and opened the door, running her hand across the sparse row of Annaluna's dresses. She went to the dresser, picking up the small things of her — the old perfume bottle with its ancient netted bulb, the little painted ceramic dish that held her hairpins, the box of her dusting powder. Novena smiled slightly as she picked up each one. In that moment, she loved each of these things as if it were Annaluna. She was grateful to them, these mute objects, gathered and kept for just these moments: to hold what remains of us. To stand for us in our absence.

Then she went into the kitchen, picked up the phone and began making calls.

chapter 32

"O clothe thyself in peace! Put thou on thy apparel in peace! May Tatet put on apparel in peace! Hail, Eye of Horus, in Tep, in peace! Hail, Eye of Horus, in the houses of Nit, in peace. Receive thou white apparel. . . ."

— *The Egyptian Book of the Dead*

NOVENA CALLED Elegia first.

"Elegia, bad news. It's Annaluna."

She paused to take a breath, so her voice wouldn't crack. Elegia was strangely silent in the pause, as if she already knew.

"She's gone."

"No. No. No, don't tell me this," Elegia cried. "Oh, call Quivera, oh, I have to . . . Oh, Novena! We'll have to bring her here, I have to, oh . . . I'll come now."

But Elegia didn't show up for close to two hours. By then, Novena had cleaned the house, fed Mamie, and called Quivera, then the undertaker in Nile Bay — who couldn't come right away, it would be later today or tomorrow, he couldn't say when — and had gathered up candles and brought them into Annaluna's bedroom. Each time she went into the room, to set up another candle, or to lay another blanket over her, Novena talked to Annaluna, as if it were another ordinary day together. She talked softly, things of no importance, and then she talked to her about what kind of plans she should make, what kind of service Annaluna should have. It made her happy to be taking care of her like this. She started to sing to her, first a soft humming, then some of the old songs she remembered from Jakarta's trio, what Elegia always referred to dismissively as swamp music. Novena had never realized how beautiful they were, nor how much of them she had recalled, until she heard the words coming out of her own mouth. She was starting in on "Lay My Burden Down," when Elegia arrived.

She swept Novena into a hug, dropped a handful of shopping bags, and went into Annaluna's room, where Novena heard her wailing for a long time.

She finally came out, her eyes swollen and red.

"I don't know if I'll ever get over this," Elegia proclaimed. "I swear I don't think I will." She snuffled and blew her nose.

"What's in there?" Novena said, pointing to the shopping bags.

"Oh, it's something I stopped for, to have her buried in. I don't know what I was thinking, it just came to me as I was driving over that she needed something new to be buried in, something pretty."

Elegia took a pale pink dress out of its bag and held it up. It was a sturdy double-knit of some spun chemical or another, with only the vaguest leaning toward prettiness. If it weren't for its color — a dim pink that covered the cloth only grudgingly — and a small, tumorous-looking neck ruffle, it would have looked like a uniform. It had the same utility and durability. It was the type of dress in which many old women dragged to churches and parties stumble around in, looking like disposable dolls. They are humiliated into wearing these, because no one makes pretty dresses with them in mind — dresses designed to set off the beauty of their frail bones, rather than wrapping them up as if they were burst pipes needing splinting.

Novena wrinkled up her nose at it.

"Oh, and I bought some matching shoes," Elegia said, rummaging through another bag, lifting out a pair of ugly pumps which didn't even muster the effort to be pretty.

"Bone," Elegia said. "Neutral, so they'll go with anything."

"Oh come on, Elegia, she would never have worn that dress in a million years. And you know how she feels about shoes," Novena said.

She had, in her hours alone with her, become possessive of how Annaluna would be leaving the earth. She definitely thought she should not be wearing shoes.

Elegia's face caved in and she started snuffling again.

Novena sat her down, made her tea, and told her, "Look, you're much too upset. Why don't you just not think about anything. I'll handle it all."

Elegia looked up at her gratefully. Grief had made her more pliable than usual. She felt that all her guideposts had been shorn down in some tumultuous climatic disturbance, like a tornado.

"Do you want to try to take a nap?" Novena asked. "We can talk about the details when Quivera gets here."

"Oh, I'll never sleep again," Elegia said. "Maybe I'll just go sit with her for a little bit. It's chilly in here. I want to put another blanket over her."

Elegia drifted out of the kitchen.

A half hour later, Quivera arrived. She and Elegia moved into each other's arms, and for a long time they stood crushed together, swaying slightly but oddly silent. It struck Novena that she had never seen Quivera and Elegia embrace; in fact, she had never seen Quivera in a moment of weakness, and it made her feel suddenly and strangely old.

A while later, the three of them were sitting quietly at the kitchen table, when the undertaker unexpectedly showed up.

"Oh!" Novena said, answering the door to him. "I thought you weren't coming."

"I got a cancellation," he mumbled, "so I was able to come sooner than I thought."

Novena had gotten used to the idea of Annaluna spending her last night in her own bed, in her own house, with her, and had half a mind to turn him away, but Quivera had appeared behind her and ushered him in.

And so, before dusk, Annaluna left her apartment for the last time. They kissed her cheek a hundred times each; then, when they heard the door close behind the undertaker and his charge, all three of them gathered in the kitchen and wept, Mamie howling along with them.

"Well," Elegia said, snuffling, "we might as well be heading back home. Novena, honey, you'll have to drive. I'm not up to it."

Novena looked up, startled. She hadn't thought of going back to Nile Bay; she didn't want to leave the apartment. She felt as if Annaluna would want her here tonight.

"I'm going to stay here. I'll come out tomorrow and help you set up," she said, and saw Elegia's features begin to quiver.

"I feel like I should clean up," she explained, trying to keep her voice soothing. "And Mamie needs to be taken care of. I'll come out tomorrow."

In the instant of silence that followed the door shutting behind them, Novena felt the full weight of the apartment's emptiness, saw the long hours unfolding before her, and nearly cried out, to call them back. What was she going to do here alone? Without Annaluna? She felt a little spiral of panic unwinding itself in her. She felt the edges of darkness threatening to spread out in her again, and she was dizzy with the memory of herself falling through it.

She ran to the living room and went to the window. She pulled the curtain back, to look outside, to see if Elegia's car was still out there. The street was dark; there was nothing out there.

Everyone's gone, Novena thought. *Everything's gone.*

She dropped the curtain and, turning from the window, she felt her foot catching on something. She looked down and saw a deep groove in the rug. She stared at it, wondering at the oddness of it.

She saw another similar indentation and it occurred to her that this was where Annaluna had been sitting, day after day, staring out of this window, for so long that the wheels of her chair had left impressions on the rug.

She felt her heart break open at the thought of how much time Annaluna had spent sitting in the dark, waiting for someone who had never come back. Now Annaluna was gone, all her waiting done.

As she moved from the window into the room, the dim glow from the small table lamp seemed almost furtive, and the room's darkness had an inexplicable quality of movement and noise, as if it were a live thing. She wanted light, as much as possible. She moved across the living room, switching on lamps. Then she made her way through the apartment, switching on all the lights in the place.

She began tidying up — adjusting the doilies, straightening the photographs, the books, the small figurines and bowls on the tables. She was doing this as much from habit as from the need for her hands to be touching Annaluna's things, all these things that stored her memories.

The new pink dress that Elegia had bought was still on the dining room table, and Novena pulled it out of the bag, shuddering at its harsh chemical feel under her fingers. She resolved to find something suitable for Annaluna to wear, something lovely and familiar.

She went to Annaluna's closet and surveyed the row of dresses, the shelves holding gloves and aprons, scarves and sweaters, things Annaluna hadn't worn in years, and Novena had a sudden picture of them sitting on a counter in God of Sand, being picked up and held in the hands of customers. Novena couldn't bear the idea of strangers touching them, seeing that look sliding over their eyes, of something of their own remembered.

She found nothing of beauty in Annaluna's closet, but then she hadn't expected to; Annaluna had loved all of her dresses to rags. They were full of safety pins, split seams, crude patches.

Then Novena had an idea — she would make something. She went to her own closet, where she stored the fabric she had accumulated, pulling out a length of white silk and another of linen, her mind leaping around shapes and forms, thinking of what to construct. It had to be beautiful, but simple. Not a dress, exactly, but more than a robe. She thought about a tunic, but finally settled on a modified kimono, long rectangles that would be easy to cut. She made some rough sketches, including a wide border of linen on the sleeves and hem, and then cut the cloth quickly. She cut up some of Annaluna's old dresses, and patched them together to make a lining for the robe, so she would feel the cloth she had loved near her.

It took her no time to construct the finished garment, which was plain and elegant — but it seemed almost too elegant, too impersonal. Novena embroidered a simple chain stitch along the neck. As she imagined Annaluna's hands at work, she added a row of hands along the sleeves. Her mind searched for other images, and she added a tiny figure of Mamie. Although she was using her machine for the more complicated embroidery, it was taking a long time, so she started going through Annaluna's jewelry box.

Novena was surprised at the amount of jewelry Annaluna had acquired; she couldn't remember her wearing any of it. She took two long strands of pearls and a handful of other necklaces, which she applied to the cuffs and hem of the garment. She gathered up other small trinkets, beads and brooches, and worked them into the garment.

Then she started going through the rest of the apartment, looking for other bits she could incorporate into the robe. She went through drawers and cabinets and closets, pulling out tins and boxes, packets and felt pouches — of buttons and greeting cards, handkerchiefs and silverware. In the china cabinet, she found some fine old linen napkins and a damask tablecloth wrapped in tissue, small pieces of which she snipped and appliquéd onto the sides and back.

Novena worked into the night, cutting and stitching, binding and embroidering. She should have been tired, but as each hour passed she grew happier and happier with her work, with the lightness that came into her heart when she thought of another figure or element to add to the robe, and when she imagined how Annaluna would look, surrounded by everything that meant something to her.

She was nearly done, and took a last walk through the place to make sure she hadn't overlooked anything. In the pantry, she found Annaluna's cookbooks resting on a shelf, and thought about attaching one of the recipes to the robe. One of the books had a plain unprinted spine, and pulling it off the shelf, Novena was surprised to find that it was not a cookbook, but a scrapbook of photos. She took it to the table and began leafing through it, pulling out a few snapshots to apply to the lining in gold thread.

They were images she had never seen before — very old ones, of Annaluna as a girl, and of Quivera, Elegia, and Catorza as very young women; her heart stopped at one of Catorza at the age Novena was now; she was astonished at how much she looked like her mother.

On the bottom of the page, she was arrested by another snapshot of Catorza, sitting on a sofa, a sly smile on her face, her hands around her stomach swollen with pregnancy. Novena stared at the image for a long time, taking in the room, the familiar sofa, the patterned rug, and, emerging from the right edge of the frame, a pair of high-heeled feet crossed at the ankles — Quivera's, she thought, without knowing why. Finally, as if she had been focusing on those other details only to prepare herself, she turned her gaze to her mother's body — to herself, in this picture, but unseen. She studied it as if she might see some essence of her unborn self. Catorza was wearing a gingham maternity dress, with smocking on the bodice and oversize decorative pockets, and although the photo was black and white, Novena could immediately conjure the exact shade of red of the gingham checks.

She felt transported to the small room of memory where her mother resided. She knew that dress — knew the texture of the fabric, its weight, the sweet, warm smell of it; it filled her like a flavor. She marveled at how such small details could be so deeply imprinted onto memory, at how powerful those small things were at collapsing the bigness of time.

Yet there was something jarring in her recollection, as illogical as the ghosts of her memories rising from the clothes at God of Sand. She thought of Alexia, moving through the shop, saying, "They're all here, looking for the dress their mother nursed them in."

Novena wondered how she could remember this dress if her mother had been wearing it before she was born.

She found the answer on the next page. It was a photograph so similar to the first that it had to have been taken on the same day. Catorza was wearing the same dress, sitting on the same sofa. Except in this one, sitting next to her, leaning against her with a four-year-old's small hand on her mother's belly, was Novena herself.

It felt like a window had been thrown open in that strange room of memory, letting in a gust of wind that blew through her with such force Novena felt everything in her being rearranged, like furniture.

She felt as if she'd been delivered to a different room, where she remembered lying in bed with her mother, her face pressed against her mother's belly. A floppy wet sound, like the echo of her own heartbeat, had drummed against the mattress. She was listening to the watery kicks of a marvelous underwater creature who had swum up from long tunnels to greet her, whispering to him, as if he were a secret between them.

With a wave of strange, shocked pleasure, she remembered her baby brother. But remembering him was like retrieving a handful of air or light. He had barely existed; he'd really only lived in her imagination. In fact, all she could actually remember of him was herself, waiting for his arrival.

That's who she had been waiting for that day in the old neighborhood, Annaluna watching her from the stoop: her baby brother. She had been walking up and down that street for hours, looking for him, convinced he was going to show up any minute. She'd been so sure she was going to see him that day. And she hadn't given up. Even after the long drive to Elegia's, she had expected him to be there too, waiting for her in the kitchen.

He hadn't been there. He had never arrived, and since no one had ever said a word about him, she must have only imagined him after all.

Except here was proof he'd been real, that she hadn't imagined him. She felt a wave of pleasure at his return washing over her. But the wave receded quickly into loss. It was such a strange combination, holding both pleasure and loss in her at once. Like being full and empty at the same time, or being homesick for a place she had never been.

It was familiar, though: the same combination of pleasure and loss had filled her all those nights in the last month, when she had been going back to the neighborhood. She'd had the same expectation she'd find some missing piece of herself. It occurred to Novena that all this time, she must still have been waiting for him. Still traipsing up and down the same sidewalk, still expecting her brother to arrive.

Now she had found him. She closed her eyes, waiting for that retrieved piece of her to slide in and take its rightful place in her. She waited to feel restored to something, to feel whole. To feel the lacy holes in her filled in, rewoven into whole cloth.

A minute passed. Then another. How long would it take? She was trying to focus only on the space inside her, but her attention was increasingly drawn to the ticking of the clock on the china cabinet. She tried to block it out, but the hollow metallic sound filled the room, and the more she tried not to hear it, the louder it became. Her focus was sliding away from her as she was sucked into that ticking sound, of time eating up the present, chewing it up, pushing itself forward, never looking back. It was demanding she pay attention to it, and she began thinking of all its clichés — picturing time flying and marching forward, slipping away, not waiting for anyone; time always moving, like an acrobat.

Whit had once told her, when he'd been explaining his own theory of déjà vu, that you had to think of time as a wide, immense river that flowed in both directions, that had no beginning or end.

She had remembered this when she'd begun spending days at God of Sand, watching people trying on clothes as if they were donning baptismal robes, ready to dive out of the present and submerge themselves in a different place in time's river. Every one of them, though, would be drawn by some swift current back to the same place they'd gone in, resurfacing in front of the cash register at God of Sand, still empty-handed. Whatever they'd gone in to find was irretrievable. And yet they'd kept coming back, to don the robes, to dive back in.

She had been diving into that river too, swimming through it, looking for things to fill her, and had kept coming back empty. There was nothing in there to retrieve, nothing to fill her.

Sitting there, the sound of the clock now pecking at her skin, Novena knew Whit had been wrong. Time wasn't immense. Time was not a river. It was just a thin trickle, measuring out your life in slow, torturous drips.

She hadn't found her brother, only a tiny moment of him, frozen on a piece of paper. Nothing was ever going to fill her but the knowledge of his loss. That's all he was: someone else she had lost, an absence she'd tried to make solid. He was something else the past had lured her with, but had no intention of ever delivering.

She'd spent her life returning to the same place, looking for the same thing. She'd spent her life waiting for someone who didn't exist, hoping for the arrival of a creature who had been lost forever underwater.

Just like Zan.

Novena felt the collapse of some tense wire that had been coiled up in her for months. All that time, looking for Zan in signs and signals, in dreams and in dust, feeling his presence behind her, expecting him to move out from the shadows, to reach out for her. But she'd only imagined him, too.

All those missing pieces in her, all those losses she'd kept returning to find, really all came down to one thing. It was all absence, just taking different shapes. Just wearing different clothes.

Zan wasn't out there, roaming the streets. He was somewhere at the bottom of the river with Sylvie, drowned. Another creature lost underwater forever.

Zan was dead.

She expelled a long breath. It came from such a deep place in her that she felt she might empty herself of whatever might remain of Zan, half expecting her breath to contain solid things — scraps of paper, small threads, dust particles, coins, the motes of a larger thing.

She stared at those things strewn across the table in front of her — the beads and scraps of linen and damask, the photos and silver and thread spools — as if they might have come from somewhere in her. They were foreign objects, no longer Annaluna's things, but some tired rubble from another time, not her own.

Novena was suddenly sick of the past, of breathing its fumes. She'd never realized what a tiresome, repetitive place it was. She'd never seen it for what it really was: not a collection of distinct moments, random notes waiting to be ordered into a glorious piece of music, but a broken record, playing the same note over and over again.

Novena sat for a little while longer, utterly drained, staring at nothing, sensing the beginnings of a gradual shift of light. It was still a few hours before dawn when she finally stirred and stumbled toward her bedroom.

Moving down the hall, she thought of her own clean bed

waiting for her, thought of the whiteness of those sheets, cool and blank and empty as next week. She thought of Annaluna's room, the air still thick and sodden with the years of her. Novena hesitated at the door.

Just one more night, Novena thought, and opened the door to Annaluna's room. She collapsed onto Annaluna's bed, burrowed into the pillow, and fell into sleep.

While she slept, Annaluna's robe lay on the dining room table, draped and preening in the darkness. It almost glowed, as if the jewels, small photos, medals, scraps of clothes and the small fragments of things knew they had been selected above all others to be lifted from their mundane settings, to become something else. Something whole.

Well, almost whole. There was still one thing missing: Renaldo.

But that's the risk of keeping your love secret. You can take it with you up to the grave, but not, unfortunately, into it.

Even if it is the thing that finally drove you there.

chapter 33

THREE WEEKS HAD PASSED, but imagine them as three years. That's how long it had felt to Zan as he waited for another delivery to take him back north, to Annaluna's. Every day as he waited, he cautiously monitored his body, searching for further signs of diminishment. Once he began keeping track, he was astonished at how much of himself he had left behind. He counted the hairs in the sink, measured the sweat seeping out of his skin and the saliva from his mouth, scrutinized his eliminations, even studied the flecks of food that he excavated from the tiny caves in his teeth and the deep blistering pockets in the back of his throat. He read these emissions like tea leaves, which some actually resembled, looking for a particular alignment of them that might spell out the date he would finally disappear.

By the tenth day, he began waking every morning calibrating the exquisitely strained thread from which his existence hung: the longer he had to wait for a delivery, the less of him there would be for Annaluna to see. He imagined himself finally arriving at her door as nothing but a huge rubbish heap of his own effluvia.

When the delivery job finally came through, he was so relieved that he drove all night without stopping. It was four in the morning when he reached the city, and Annaluna's street. He parked in his usual spot and made his way to the house; standing outside, it occurred to him that he should have come up with a plan, besides simply seeing Annaluna. Or rather, her seeing him.

He had given surprisingly little thought to Novena; in fact, he had imagined that once Annaluna had seen him, once his life with her had been restored, it would be Novena who would vanish instantly. Now he wondered whether he should wait until Novena had left for the day before going in. But he dismissed the idea. He was here now, and had no patience for waiting.

When he had been here, living his rightful life, he had always left his key under the doormat. He prayed it was still there. It was; in fact, it seemed not to have moved from the last time he had used it. When he picked it up, it left a rusted outline of itself on the concrete. Which probably meant that Novena kept her own key with her. Like she owned the place, he thought bitterly.

His hand was trembling as he slid the key into the lock and pushed the heavy front door open.

He stood at the doorway and swooned as the smell of the place rushed up to him, as if it had a tail wagging in joy at his arrival. He was weaving slightly, overcome by the smell of heat, of hand lotion and furniture polish, of curtains laced with years of dust, of the cabbagey sourness of ancient cooking: everything he knew of happiness was contained in these homely smells.

His hands outstretched in the dark to guide him, he moved into the living room, felt for the sofa, and gently lowered himself into it. His body must have immediately recalled itself, unbending its muscles into this familiar shape on this particular spot on the sofa, because they released a new rush of pleasure in Zan. He stood and moved to another chair, and felt the same giddy sensation. He nearly giggled, and moved back to the sofa. He sat heavily into the cushions, rubbing his palm against the small rises and indentations of the damask, inhaling the room.

As he breathed in the familiar air, he was able to recall his life there in such detail that he imagined it was all still there: the old, expelled breaths of his contentment, the particles of ancient laughter, all the other residue of the long afternoons of his happiness still filling the corners of the room.

But as he sat, breathing, he grew conscious of some alteration to the atmosphere. Whether it was something added to the place or missing from it, he couldn't immediately tell, but he felt a small twinge of anxiety. He searched out the shapes of furniture rising up out of the darkness like boulders, and wondered if they had been rearranged in his absence. But the rearrangement was something more elusive, and it finally hit him when he inhaled again: a sharp astringency in the air. Clean.

That's what it was — the place had been cleaned. And it struck him then that whatever had remained of him there was long gone.

Zan had a strange thought, that moment, of dying. But this idea of dying was different from the idea of death that he had lived with every day, which he had come to treat rather like a chronic but low-grade condition. This thought of dying seemed more complex — something more ominous and irreversible.

He sat up, alert. He felt the place had grown suddenly dangerous, as if something perilous was closing in on him in the darkness. He was almost unnerved enough to turn on a light. As he sat, unmoving, it began to dawn on him that maybe there was nothing here for him after all. Maybe he had made a mistake, coming here.

Zan considered himself an expert in dangerous ideas, but the truth was, his ideas were only schemes, and their danger was only measured by their damage to others, never himself. He had never entertained the supremely dangerous idea that he was capable of making a mistake.

Like all those born to trouble, Zan aimed for toughness; mistakes were soft things, big pillows stuffed thick with regret. And Zan, like all those born to trouble, managed to avoid regret, because Zan never looked back.

When trouble loves you, it loves you completely. You never have to look for it. It's always there behind you, like a shark, nudging and pushing and prodding you forward. Never letting you look back. Never letting you see it coming.

Sitting there in the darkness, Zan felt the strange taste of regret filling his mouth. It was strange, not only because it was foreign, but because it was as yet unconnected to anything specific. This regret simply filled his mouth, letting him feel its shape, its bitter taste. He chewed on it awhile, getting used to its flavor, waiting for it to dissolve. Instead of dissolving, though, it was expanding in him, filling him up.

He looked into the dark corners of the room, felt a flutter of panic, as if some reproach that had been waiting for him here had stepped out of the shadows and was bearing down on him.

An idea came to him, something between a premonition and a memory, that somewhere along the line, he had done something terribly wrong. As if he'd taken something from Annaluna. Not the money, or the silver items that had bought his bus ticket. Not even the watch. Something more irreplaceable.

A flash of heat stung his cheeks, as if he'd been slapped, and he felt the heat spreading inside him. It was a feeling more foreign, and far worse, than regret or remorse. It was sticky and hot, like blood, but prickly, like the pinch of dried grass on bare skin.

That was Zan's first impression of shame.

By the time he registered his second impression — that shame could move you faster than outrage, more urgently than desire — he was off the sofa and halfway across the room. He had to get out of this room. He had to get to Annaluna, now.

He moved down the hall as quickly as he could without making a sound. He tried to make his feet land as lightly as possible, but he'd only moved a few feet before he hit a weak spot on a floor-board, and could not lift his foot fast enough to keep it from creaking. He stopped, not breathing, listening for the sound of someone stirring.

As he stood listening, he panicked at the idea of Novena coming out and seeing him first. Sweat was seeping from him — his shirt was wet, his hands damp, and tiny rivulets were beginning to rise on his temples. It shocked him, how acrid it smelled. It reminded him of a fire.

He was a few feet from the bathroom door, which was slightly ajar, and he stepped in, to get his bearings. A small night light was on, and he was grateful for its dim light. He moved to the towel rack to wipe his hands. Gathering up a towel, Zan held it against his face, feeling the soft yet slightly rough loops of the terry cloth. As he inhaled, he had the strange thought that it could have been Annaluna's wrinkled cheek. This could have been Annaluna's skin. He felt himself sliding backward, ready to lose himself in that re-called sweetness, in its fragrance. But he could feel something mixed in with that pleasure, that same sense of regret which had returned to occupy him, as if it had followed him down the hall.

What had he done? He was thinking of Annaluna's face, cupped in his hands. That sweet sleeping face, the last night he'd seen her. The night he'd left her behind.

Zan felt something aching and precarious, pressing at his in-sides, wanting release.

He was still holding the towel to his face, conscious that some-thing else was stirring in him, something else remembered in the softness of the towel, its sweet scent.

This was not just Annaluna's scent in the towel; somehow, it had gotten mingled with some other scent — a fragrance he knew, one that had always drawn him in, so deeply he had gotten lost.

It was Sylvie's. He knew he should drop the towel and run, but he wanted to breathe it in again. He wanted to put it into his mouth and eat it.

He inhaled deeply, and Sylvie's essence flooded through him, bringing him such pleasure that he closed his eyes, bathed in the remembrance of her — the cackle of her voice, her crooked smirk, her thick black eyebrows.

He'd been plunged into some deep cold water of memory, and was falling now, deep and deeper. Thinking of her tangled mass of hair, her soft arms. A great weight was pressing against his chest, and he couldn't breathe. Zan was drowning in the remembrance of her, which was also a remembrance of drowning itself.

He'd been surprised at how quiet it had all been that night: the car sliding down the bank, how it had slipped into the river almost gracefully, as if it had wanted nothing but a cooling dip in the water. And initially, the current had swept them out in a way that had made it still seem as if the car were swimming in long graceful strokes.

But then had come the shock of the water's taste filling his mouth, and the further shock of its coldness, its darkness, and the out-of-control movement of sinking. He hadn't known how to order those shocks, which had come all at once, even before anything else, even before panic. Yet there had seemed to be no rush to sort these sensations out — time had somehow dissolved in the water, because floating through the dark silence, it felt like they had been sinking for days. For years. It had been like falling endlessly through a cold, black sky.

But then, suddenly, panic had come. Zan had begun losing himself, his internal systems shutting down, like switches being flicked off one by one — sight, sound, taste, all gone. Breathing, thinking — gone; then cold, heat, fear, panic, all shut off, just at the last moment before drowning. Just at the moment Sylvie's white arms had reached out to envelop him.

At the remembrance of her arms, Zan felt Sylvie's absence so sharply he gasped. The realization of himself, without her, howled in him like a monster.

He let go of the towel and staggered backward slightly, leaning against the opposite wall, breathing hard. He had to keep himself from sliding down to the floor; he knew he would never get up from it again.

He also knew he had to pull himself back from this, had to bring his focus back to where he was, right now. He began jabbing his temples with his fingers, jabbing and pounding the side of his head to force his concentration to the present, to what was in front of him. Not to what he'd left behind, but what he'd come for.

It hurt just enough to work. He drew himself up, pushed himself away from the wall, out of the bathroom and into the hall.

Finally, staggering slightly, he made his way to Annaluna's room.

Standing in Annaluna's doorway, it struck Zan that there was something different here, too. He wondered what it could be, what had altered from his memory. Then he realized what it was: the door was open. Annaluna's door had always been closed.

But there was another thing: the room was completely dark. It had never been dark; a soft light had always shone from under the door. He was slightly thrown by this alteration, unsure how to interpret it.

He could not see into the room, but he could sense her, could feel emanations from her body. He listened for the sound of her soft snoring, for the soft push of her breath. He wondered whether to whisper her name, or if he should just walk in.

Still, he hesitated at the doorway. It seemed like cheating, to go in there and wake her, or to make any sound at all.

Then he knew what was really bothering him. It wasn't the darkness of the room, or the fact that her door was open. What was wrong was that Annaluna should have known he was coming.

That's what he had really wanted: she should have sensed his approach. She should have known of his presence, been sitting in the living room waiting for him, as she had done every day when he had come back from the shopping.

But she was sleeping, oblivious to him, as the apartment was now oblivious to his existence. He was nothing to her. Annaluna had forgotten him.

Zan stood in the doorway, completely unable to figure out what to do, utterly helpless. He couldn't move. In fact, he didn't even exist; in that moment, he was not a man in a doorway, he was not even a body — he was just a decision hovering someplace between going and staying.

It was a place he knew, a place he'd been before.

He'd been submerged, underwater with Sylvie, just at that

moment before drowning, when all his systems had switched off. Only one small switch had remained lit — dim, but just bright enough to lead him back up to the surface. It was the moment he'd had to decide: survive or surrender.

Now it dawned on him that the moment of his death had nothing to do with Novena or Annaluna. It was when he had followed the light, and left Sylvie behind. That had been the moment of his death, he thought: the moment he had survived.

He took a few steps back, ready to turn and get out of there. His life was not here. He was in the wrong place after all. He belonged somewhere else. He knew where; he knew it so well he could taste it, that dank cold soup of it, where Sylvie was waiting.

It was the first time in his life he knew exactly where he belonged.

Did Zan understand the irony? Like the rest of us, he must have had at least a glimmer of it. But when he heard the soft rustle of Annaluna's sheet moving, the slight groan of the bed, he froze and turned back toward the room. He felt his heart leap up in him, to grab for whatever final sliver of hope might still exist: that maybe what he'd come for might be here, after all. That Annaluna could give him his life back. She could save him.

Then he heard the low growl of her voice.

It would not be for another four days — Zan's last day on earth — that it would occur to him that hers had been the last human sound he would ever hear.

At the moment that he stood in the doorway, though — before he got out of there, found his truck, and got back onto the road — the voice sounded anything but human. It was as ugly as a sin, a harsh croaking sound that hit him like a physical blow.

But what the voice told him — that's what really killed him.

chapter 34

SOUNDS OF CREAKING AND GROANING, of ticking and rustling, were inserting themselves into Novena's dreams. In her dreams, she turned these sounds into hands, since they had the effect of pulling her up from a long tunnel of sleep; she tried to push them away from her, to burrow back down in the deep folds of unconsciousness, but they were strong and persistent, pounding against her brain and growing louder and louder. Then, suddenly, they stopped, and she fell back into oblivion.

But sleep is an unreliable oblivion. Some time later, she was wakened again; this time it was as if someone had leaned into her ear and told her in a firm strong voice to wake up.

It was nearly five o'clock, the small shard of time between night and dawn. Novena's eyes were open, but she was in her own in-between state, a groggy stupor that felt as if sleep had turned itself inside out, like a shirt on laundry day, with consciousness left behind in her dreams, and her dreams dragged into consciousness.

The room was dark, although slivers of charcoal gray light pushed at the edges of the window, trying to get in. Just enough light for her to make out the dark shapes in the room: Dresser and chair.

Mirror and lamp.

And the shape of a man, standing in the doorway.

· · ·

You may be surprised to learn, if you haven't already, that your first reaction to the appearance of a ghost — or any spirit that has long haunted you — will rarely be fright, but rather a serene calmness. This serenity may last quite a long time, as it had for Annaluna, or it may disintegrate immediately into more predictable reactions like alarm or terror. That odd suspended moment of calm is, in fact, a form of communion — a tiny breath you are given to acknowledge each other's presence.

Or rather, for you to acknowledge his. The fact is, he's already acknowledged your presence, simply by appearing before you.

Novena's calm lasted only a moment before she reacted. She actually had two reactions. Her first was surprise, because she recognized instantly who was standing there. It was the specter of the man Annaluna had been waiting for all this time. Annaluna's lost love, whose shirts she had held to her heart, as she had sat at the window waiting for him.

Her second reaction was annoyance. At another time, Novena might have welcomed him. But of all the nights for him to appear, it infuriated her that he had chosen this one. She thought of Annaluna, sitting in her chair, disappearing a little each day that he hadn't come back. He had made her wait for so long, and when he had finally gotten around to showing up, it was too late.

Still, Novena's outrage was muffled by her extreme exhaustion. She only had the energy for a deep, weary exasperation as she called out to him.

"You're too late."

Her voice surprised her, how much it sounded like Annaluna's.

"Get out of here," she growled. "You don't even exist."

Then she closed her eyes, and burrowing under the covers, banished him from her sight.

Novena woke a few hours later to the doorbell. She stumbled to the door and was shocked to see Alexia; Novena had forgotten she had called her the day before.

She was more shocked when she opened the door and saw that Alexia had changed out of her kimono, and was wearing a beautifully tailored suit — a new one, not one from God of Sand. Somehow, the lines of the suit seemed to throw her face into a strange balance, and she looked striking; she looked like another woman.

"Sweetie," she said, seeing Novena's astonishment. "There are few things I dress for. But you have to dress for death."

"I figured you'd be alone," she said, stepping in and holding Novena in a long embrace. Novena rested her head on her shoulder, feeling small and grateful — like a bird held in someone's palm, she thought.

"I've closed up for the day," Alexia said, patting her back. "I've brought breakfast. You eat, and then we'll go to Nile Bay."

As Novena ate, Alexia inspected Annaluna's robe. She fingered the delicate embroidery, felt each of the stones, traced the shapes of the faces in the photographs, and although she had never met Annaluna, she cried at the loss of her as she surveyed each detail in the robe.

"Oh, honey, it's gorje. It's so holy," Alexia said, wiping her eyes. "I want one. You have to promise to make me one when it's time."

Then Alexia shooed her into the shower and went through the apartment, sweeping up the scraps and threads, the loose beads and pins, the rest of the detritus from Novena's night, knowing it would be painful for her to come home to this. She packed a bag for Novena and took Mamie to a neighbor's for safekeeping. Then they headed for Nile Bay.

Novena leaned her head against the car window, half dozing, as Alexia drove. It was strange to see Alexia behind the wheel of a car; it was strange, too, how silent and contemplative she seemed as she drove. It was as if the suit she was wearing had muted her.

They were entering Nile Bay when Alexia finally spoke.

"You want to drop the robe off at the funeral home first, right?" Novena nodded.

"You know, I've been thinking," Alexia said. "How nice it would be if other people knew something like Annaluna's robe was available."

"What are you talking about?" Novena said, rousing herself.

"I mean I've been thinking that you could make similar things for other people. I know people who would pay a lot to know they had such a beautiful thing to wear when, you know, it was time for them to need it."

"Alexia. Forget it. I think it would be morbid and gross," Novena said. "I can't believe you."

"Oh come on," Alexia pressed. "Think about it. We plan what we're going to wear tomorrow and the next day and when we're going to church or on vacation, or a job interview, but when we're about to get dressed for eternity, do we give our clothes any thought? No. It's left to our grieving relatives, who are going to drop off some schleggy suit or skanky dress in a paper bag at the undertaker on their way to the caterer."

As if she had timed her speech precisely, they had just pulled up to Belvay's funeral home.

"Believe me," Alexia said, getting out and pushing the car door closed with her hip. "The last person you want to pick out an outfit for you is someone who can't even see through their tears."

Novena laughed in spite of herself, thinking of Elegia's hideous pink dress.

"Don't forget the bone pumps," she said, trailing Alexia up the sidewalk.

Alexia snorted. "Pumps for bones."

Inside, Novena gave instructions. She insisted that Annaluna not be wearing shoes. It was Alexia's idea to have Annaluna buried with her purse. She had tucked into it a small dog biscuit, "For when Mamie meets her on the other side."

At the house, they found Elegia in the kitchen, covered in flour and surrounded by the residue of baking.

"Thank heavens you're here. Nothing is coming out right," she wailed. "All these people coming to pay their respects, and I'll have nothing to feed them."

Her cake had refused to rise, her custard was curdled, and her pie crust had become crumbly as dust.

Novena left Alexia to help Elegia and went upstairs to take a nap.

She fell heavily into her old bed, and found sleep waiting for her impatiently. Hours later, she woke, feeling as though tentacles of exhaustion were still wrapped around her. She could hear the footsteps and murmurs of people downstairs, and she listened for familiar voices.

It was a shame funerals were so public, she thought. She would have liked to have Annaluna's all to herself. To concoct some elaborate but private ritual of departure instead of having to make her way through a crowd of mourning faces, a crowd which would, she knew, end up in the living room after the service, balancing plates on their laps. She wondered why grief made people particularly hungry; maybe, she decided, eating was a natural response to losing someone, an attempt to take something in, to fill up the space.

The wake was held that night, and Annaluna was resplendent. She looked beautiful. The garment lay upon her like a splendid royal robe.

Even Elegia had to admit it was beautiful, although Quivera commented that it looked "a little pagan, don't you think?"

"And what are you, some kind of saint?" Celantra scoffed. Celantra was in a bad mood; in addition to her grief over Annaluna's passing, she was irritated she hadn't known about it until minutes before Novena had called her.

By eight o'clock, Novena was already dazed by the crowd. As she greeted people she hadn't seen in ages, Novena tried to keep her balance between their almost cheerful buoyancy and the sad undertow of the occasion.

Quin was across the country and had been unable to get away, but Wyn Jr. and Dex were there. Novena was surprised at how glad she was to see them.

Quin and Wyn Jr. had grown up to look much as they always had, becoming simply older versions of themselves, but Dex looked different. His hair was to his shoulders, pulled back in a messy ponytail, and Novena couldn't stop looking at his face, jarred by how unfamiliar it seemed.

When she saw Dex edging his way across the room to head outside, she followed him. They stood together on the porch as he smoked cigarette after cigarette. He didn't speak, but she saw he was agitated, as if he were carrying on some strained internal dialogue. His disturbance struck Novena as odd, since as far as she knew, none of the boys had been that close to Annaluna.

"Dex, are you okay?" she finally asked.

"I don't know, Novena. It's weird. I keep thinking that this is someone else's funeral, or a funeral we should have had a while ago."

"What do you mean?" she asked, startled.

"You know. Zan's."

She felt him look at her, as if to gauge her reaction. The sound had given her a small shock.

"Do you ever think about him?" he asked, but he didn't wait for her answer.

"I do. Especially lately, I don't know why," he went on. "It's been almost two years. No one ever talks about him. It makes me crazy sometimes. Like I never had this brother. Just gone, into thin air.

"Poof," he said, snapping his fingers.

"I had no idea you were thinking about all this," Novena said.

She was not used to thinking about Zan in relation to other people. In fact, it shocked her to realize that anyone had been thinking about him at all. She felt heat rising in her face, ashamed to think how much she knew, and how long she'd been keeping it to herself.

She'd made Zan such a small, private thing. But Zan was not a private thing — he was an enormous thing. She flushed, wondering how she could possibly tell anyone now what she knew. What words would she use? And worse, how would she explain why she'd said nothing before now? Sometimes she could barely remember herself. She considered blurting it all out to Dex, to tell him everything.

She hesitated. Dex looked so lost, that she found herself reaching out and touching his shoulder instead.

The contact seemed to open up something in him, and he said in a rush of words, "I came home a couple of months ago. I just wanted to sleep in that room. That room of his, which he hadn't been in for years, I know. But it had been really haunting me. The next day, I went to the basement, and went through his boxes."

"God, Dex." The idea of him pawing through those things made her want to cry.

"I know. Elegia had a fit. But I wanted something. So I took a few things of his. A shirt, one of his hunting books. That old trophy that he stole in high school. And this."

He reached into his jacket pocket and pulled out a small rumpled brown bag. He pulled something from it and held it out to Novena.

"Crazy. It's one of his fishing reels," he said, dropping it into her palm. "I was thinking of using it myself, but I couldn't."

The reel rested cool and heavy in her hand. It was such a small thing, really, a few inches in diameter, with a mile of filament wound around itself. It brought to mind an elusive fish leaping from the water then diving in, leaping and diving, as Zan had leapt and dived in and out of her consciousness for nearly two years. Now this reel had dragged him to the surface, long enough to hold him in her hand.

This was Zan, as solid as he would ever become.

She shuddered and handed the reel back to Dex. Her empty palm was still slightly curled from its shape.

"So I have this idea," Dex was saying, putting it back in the bag. "I want to put it in with Annaluna. Have her buried with it. Somehow it will make it seem like we're burying him. Do you think that's totally twisted? I've got to do something, though. It's just not right, not to have done something for him."

"I think it's fine, Dex. Why don't you do that?"

She had said it to comfort him, although she was appalled at the idea of Zan occupying the same space as Annaluna. That was the strangeness of death, she thought: suddenly, you had to accept conditions that never would have occurred naturally in life.

She heard the soft push of Dex's breath as he exhaled the last of his cigarette.

"Although I wouldn't put it past him to be out there, watching us," he said, flicking the remains of the cigarette off the porch.

Novena watched the small arc of burning tip sweep into the darkness.

"The bastard," Dex said, and went inside.

Novena stayed on the porch. Behind her, she heard the low murmuring of the crowd, a sound that now seemed so familiar and comforting that she felt she could almost lean against it. In front of her was silence, dark, empty, and cold. She stared out into it, considering the enormity of Zan. She wanted to think about how she might put it all into words.

But she couldn't get her mind off Dex. She was struck with how upset he'd been, how desperately he must have pawed through Zan's belongings to reach for something to fill the loss of him. It was strange, how lost Dex seemed without him. But then it had been such a long time since she'd thought about Dex, Quin, Wyn, and Zan as an interlocking set, of brothers connected to one another.

She thought back to that noisy pack of them, that roaming, snorting herd of boy, thrashing through the woods, with her trailing behind like a mute shepherd. Or rather, like a sheep — a black sheep. She'd always been outside their circle, that chaotic circle of their energy. She recalled their yelps and wails, the noisy ring of their swinging arms and muffled thuds, the sound of skin to skin. A turbulent storm, with Zan always at its center.

She recalled Quin, with a black eye. Wyn, his shirt ripped.

A nasty egg over Dex's eye, from where his head had hit a wall; the indentation was still there, in the upstairs hallway, a small, hollowed-out curve, like the palm of a cupped hand.

Remembering all this, it struck her as odd, how deeply grieved Dex was at Zan's disappearance.

But it occurred to her that what was odder was how little it had upset her. She'd been consumed by panic when Zan first disappeared, and later, so possessed by his absence that it had become a presence, but she couldn't remember actually feeling sorry over Zan's loss. She hadn't grieved for him once, not in the beginning, and not even when it came to her, finally, that he was dead.

She wondered if she had kept the idea of him alive for so long because she'd been waiting for that moment of grief to come. But sorrow for him was frozen somewhere in her, lodged in her like a small shard of ice.

Suddenly, she could picture this shard — smooth and hard and glinting. It lay in her like a small, cold heart at the center of all her own memories of him: of the sound of him, pounding up the stairs, herself frozen in her room, waiting for the house to collapse. The small bruises he'd left blooming on her skin. And the hours she'd lain huddled in her bed, waiting for Zan to come and stand in her doorway with his stale yeasty breath, waiting for the moment he could reach for her, take her away and get rid of her. She had nearly drowned in the terror of those moments, when he'd take her and drop her into some dark hole in the world.

But though she hadn't recognized it then, there'd really been nothing to be afraid of. Because by the time she'd arrived at Elegia's, she'd already been dropped into that darkness. She'd already been living there, in that dark hole made by everything she had already lost.

Novena shuddered, pulling her jacket around her, conscious that the temperature had been steadily dropping, even in the short time she'd been out there. Now there was a sharp edge to the air, and she looked up at the sky, looking for signs of snow.

Before turning away to go back inside, she looked out at the broad sweep before her, scanning the darkness, but only out of habit; she wasn't expecting to see the figure emerging out of the darkness, now coming up the walk. She gasped at the familiar shape, instantly conjuring the sound of him, the smell of him and the warmth of him surrounding her.

"Whit," she whispered, and then she was off the porch, running to him.

chapter 35

The ambiguity . . . inherent in all social situations, is embodied in the materials with which spirits are wrapped: Combinations of soft and hard materials like cloth and sticks, trees and stones, cores and bark, trunks and leafy branches, analogs of shrouds and corpses, tombs and bodies, the bones and flesh of human beings, both female and male. The interconnections of these different materials, and their transformations back and forth in time between fragile and more enduring states, is the root of Malagasy burial rites. In their transformations, they are commentaries on the complex composition of human beings and of human relations, especially relations of domination and subordination that call for silence as well as speech, concealment as well as open confrontation.

    — Gillian Feeley-Harnik,
      "Cloth and the Creation of Ancestors in Madagascar"

THEY BURIED ANNALUNA the next morning, accompanied by a memento of Renaldo after all.

They had to use heavy machines to open the earth, because the ground was so hard from the cold. The mourners stood and watched, weeping softly as they heard the first shovelfuls full of dirt fall down onto her. It took them forever to cover her, but no one was surprised. Annaluna had left a hole in the world that was much too big to fill quickly.

· · ·

A small crowd of mourners went back to Elegia's, where for a few hours they filled the house with their soft chewing sounds, the tinny click of silver against plates, a drone of low murmurs occasionally pierced by a harsh guffaw. By three, the last of them had disappeared, leaving behind Elegia, Quivera, Margita, Celantra, and Novena. They found themselves drifting around the house aimlessly until they ended up in the kitchen. But even here, they seemed unable to settle themselves, to figure out what to do next.

"Well, she lived a full life," Elegia sighed, wiping a counter for the third time in an hour. "That's all I can say."

"That's all you've been saying all day," Quivera said, but even her snappish tone had a dull edge to it.

"Well," Celantra announced, looking around her. "I'm going to take a nap."

This struck all of them as a good idea, and the women drifted out of the kitchen, falling into beds and chairs and sofas, until the house curled itself up in a dreamy, late afternoon silence.

They rose at dusk — Elegia first, then Quivera and Margita, then Celantra — all but Novena. They gathered in the dining room, pouring wine, picking at the crumbs and melted wax embedded in the tablecloth from the afternoon. Although they were here to mark the passing of Annaluna, it occurred to each of them, although no one said it aloud, that after almost twenty years, they had once again gathered to wait for Novena's arrival.

Few remnants remained from that evening, nineteen years before, when Novena had slid gracefully into the world. For one thing, it was not a hot, still summer night, but a snappish cold evening in early winter. There were no lit candles, no ghostly vapors moving through the rooms, no scatting trio — although they would arrive later — no Catorza, and of course no Annaluna. Just these four women, who had retained only a few remnants of themselves since that long-ago evening.

Quivera, having buried her very old husband, had taken up with a very young man who had fulfilled in her whatever need of mothering she had ever had; although her personality had retained its sharpness, her features were softer and rounder, complemented by new blond streaks in her hair.

Margita's blondness had faded over the years, but the rest of her hadn't; she had grown ever larger, with dimpled thighs and a huge backside, both of which she stoically disregarded, and with a seductive hoarse whiskey rasp she had cultivated to compensate for any physical shortcomings. She had moved from the city and was now living in a small shoreline town in a bramble-covered cottage where minor domestic disasters — squirrel nests in the attic, exploding pipes, mysterious wall stains of no known origins — untethered whatever sense of placidity she thought she affected to the outside world.

Celantra had spent years fighting to retain her already limited gifts of divination against an onslaught of accidents and obstacles that would have daunted God himself — unfortunate aerosol explosions of Money House Blessing Spray, disastrous herbal healing remedies that led only to rashes, infections, and blistering eruptions, and one magnificent conflagration with a sage smudging stick that had nearly leveled the house of a client. Not long ago, though, in one of her arm-wrestles with the higher planes of consciousness, Celantra had taken a blow to the head that had triggered in her authentic abilities in the visionary department. She was so astonished at her newfound clairvoyance that she now affected an air of vaguely startled serenity.

Elegia believed herself to be the most unchanged of all the women. The truth was something else, of course, but her genius for remaining blind to it was one of the few things she'd retained.

She had lost more than most, but it was not her losses that had transformed her. For one thing, she had not found a place in her mind to put Zan, and so he was rarely anywhere near it; for another, though Wyn Sr. had left, he still appeared occasionally, circling her heart like a distant planet; and although she'd loved her aunt like a mother, she had the idea, without knowing why, that Annaluna had come to the end of some long period of suffering.

What had changed Elegia was love. In her case, it was the first true gift she'd ever been given. She felt as if Dr. Jack had been picked out with only her in mind. And he fit perfectly.

It was the first time in her life she'd felt satisfied by someone other than herself. She had grown so calm that she'd become prone to occasional bursts of serenity. Even Quivera noticed the change in her, though she didn't know how to explain it, for Elegia had still never spoken to anyone about her involvement with Dr. Jack, and believed that no one knew, although there is no house in any town more carefully watched than that of a widower. But the subterranean scandal had given Elegia a patina of glamour, which, although she was innocent of its source, became her. What we hide may ultimately ruin our digestion, but it often does wonders for the complexion.

As Novena lay waking from her nap, she felt as if a whole town inside her had collapsed, house after house after house, blown down. Gone. There was nothing in her left standing.

And now that she believed she had turned away from everything in her past — though it always grows back, usually returning at twice its original size — Novena was trying to keep herself looking only forward, her view focused on the clean empty lines of the future. So far, though, she could see no shapes, no colors, nothing but a great white empty space before her. It was not, at that moment anyway, a promising blankness, but a bleak one. That was one thing that kept you tied to the past, she thought; at least all the pictures were familiar.

The noises of the women downstairs had been drifting up to her, then the strong aroma of coffee began pressing against her more insistently. She rose and made her way downstairs.

When she came into the dining room, the women were on their second glass of wine. They were not exactly festive, but they were rested, at least, and talking softly.

"We just made coffee but you're only allowed to drink wine," Quivera told her as she took a seat. "We're trying not to get maudlin," she continued, giving a hard stare to Margita, who, she suspected, couldn't wait to begin weeping into her wine.

"Poor Annaluna," Margita sighed, ignoring Quivera's stare. "She was always there, for all of us. What will we do without her?

"Although she scared me to death sometimes," she blurted out, and embarrassed, she took a deep swallow of wine.

"You should have seen her when we were girls," Elegia said. "She terrified us into learning how to cook. The three of us used to spend every Saturday in that apartment of hers. Remember, Quivera, how Catorza would always try to sneak away?"

They lapsed into silence at the mention of Catorza, trying to keep their eyes from sliding to Novena.

Novena was staring into her wine, barely listening. She was dwelling on the fact that if they didn't know what they would do without Annaluna, she might be in worse shape than she thought.

"We've all lost so much," Elegia sighed, moving her hand over the tablecloth. "Sometimes I think if I ever stopped to think about it . . ."

No one mentioned Zan, but he hovered there for a moment until Quivera swatted him away.

"You know, she was so happy when you came to stay with her," she said to Novena. "I think she had spent too many years by herself."

"She wasn't always alone, though," Novena said, stirring herself. "Wasn't she married once? What ever happened to him?"

"Oh, him. A rat," Quivera said. "He was long gone. I don't know if I met him more than once."

"Poor thing," Margita said. "He must have broken her heart."

"Oh, Annaluna was a tough old bird," Quivera said. "Once he left, I don't think she gave him another thought."

"But, Quivera, she had gotten so frail," Elegia said, her voice quavering. "You didn't see her as much as I did, at the end. She had gotten to be such a little thing."

Celantra looked at Novena, who had receded again into some

other place. But then she noticed that Novena's face had begun moving, looking as if it were fighting to keep from collapsing. She reached over and touched Novena's hand.

"Your robe was gorgeous, honey," she said. "Annaluna looked beautiful."

The women nodded, and began talking of the beauty of Annaluna as she lay there, remembering the pieces of the robe; as they called up each snippet of photograph or damask tea towel or bead, they were moved to yet another remembrance of Annaluna: her mysterious habits, her deep cackle, the way she ruled everyone with a fierce protective force. As they recalled another story, another memory, their hands moved to each other, touching skin lightly. Wine spilled over words, words spilled over each other, stories got interrupted and taken up by someone else, until the women were grasping each other, grasping hands, rubbing arms, stroking hair, and soon Novena felt herself pulled into them, her hands touched and stroked, her fingers entwined in other fingers.

She felt drunk and swaddled, with hands and limbs and hair and voices weaving together. Like warp and weft, she thought. Like a cloth of women.

More than an hour had passed, and the women had been debating the points of Annaluna's cooking prowess, one that was best preserved only in the longest memory, when they began to recognize hunger. They went to the kitchen, and soon they were moving easily in the choreography of preparing food, at the counter, at the oven, at the refrigerator, in a dance that was as precise and graceful as the *mudra* of a beautiful Indian goddess.

The women had only been drinking wine for two hours, but they had drunk it deeply and thirstily, and it had begun sloshing onto everything. Elegia sent Novena down to the cellar to bring up more.

Quivera started taking bowls out of the refrigerator.

Elegia and Margita began uncovering them to bring them out to the table.

"Fifteen years," Margita said, with a sigh.

Elegia and Quivera knew what she was referring to. The last time they had all been in a kitchen together was after Catorza's funeral. It had been a hushed kitchen curtained with their grief, and they had been carefully laying sheets of wrap over the bowls of food, deciding Novena's fate. Then, Elegia thought, they had sealed the bowls as if the girl's fate were contained in them. Now they began uncovering them, anxious to see what was inside.

"Are you glad you took her?" Quivera said, low, to Elegia.

"Are *you* glad I did?" Elegia answered.

"You've done a good job," Quivera said, touching her shoulder.

Elegia flushed, unused to kind words from her sister, and to the large amount of wine she had just consumed. She had a strange sensation of wanting to fall, to collapse into Quivera, to lean against her so her shoulder could be patted, like a child.

Instead, she pulled herself up and sighed, "Oh, it's been hard. You have no idea."

As she said it, she realized just how hard it had been.

Raising a girl was so different from raising boys. Boys were so easy, even hers. They always let you know what they wanted, and then they took it from you gladly — even more if they could get it.

Girls never did. Even if they capitulated and told you what they wanted, which you had to fight out of them — even then, you could never be sure of their accepting anything from you. Why was it so hard? Why did girls fight their mothers?

"I'll never stop worrying about her," Elegia said, actually thinking, *I'll never stop wishing she showed me more kindness.*

"But I have to say," she quickly amended, "she's a good girl."

"The *best*," said Margita, bringing another bowl to the counter. "That girl is a little genius. An artist. What an eye for clothes. I often wonder if she had come to live with me . . ."

Margita stopped, her face stretched open in an expression that looked like horror. "Oh!" she screeched. "Speaking of clothes . . ."

She dropped the bowl on the counter and ran from the room.

Quivera and Elegia exchanged a glance, rolling their eyes.

Margita came back into the kitchen bearing a large box.

"I almost forgot. Where is she?" she said. "Where's Novena?"

"Novena!" she called out, and then, to the women, "I can't believe I almost forgot."

"Here she is," Elegia said as Novena came into the kitchen. "Novena, Margita brought you a present."

"A present?" Novena said, putting down the wine and taking the box from Margita. "Why are you giving me a present?"

"It's not really a present," Margita said. "It already belongs to you."

Novena sat at the table and undid the paper carefully. The women came close to watch as she opened the lid.

She pushed back a cloud of tissue paper and lifted a cloud of blue silk from the box.

She held up a dress, inspecting it wonderingly. She could tell it was not new; she could judge from the shade of cobalt and the style that it was about twenty years old.

There was a pause in the kitchen as the women stared.

"Oh Margita, it's the *dress*!" Elegia cried, the first to comprehend.

The women started exclaiming.

"I can't believe you saved it," Quivera said.

"Oh, I'll never forget that dress," Elegia said.

Novena looked at them all and said, "What? Tell me! What is it?"

"You came into the world, juices and fluids and goop all over you," Elegia explained. "This is your receiving blanket. It's the first thing that we wrapped you in."

"I wrapped her in it, remember?" Quivera said.

"And Catorza said, 'Don't let her wear it till she's eighteen,' " Celantra said.

"Actually she said twenty-one," Quivera said, remembering. But looking at Novena, she thought, *She seems years older than that now.*

"It was my lucky dress after that, although I haven't worn it since," Margita said, flushed with the success of her present, although she had a guilty thought about Annaluna, imagining the force of her scowl had she been here.

"So," Elegia said to Novena. "Aren't you going to try it on?"

Novena stood, dizzy from the wine, and took the box upstairs.

When she took the dress out of the box, it felt lighter than air, a shimmering ball of cobalt. The fabric itself was substantial, though, and her fingers appraised it as a silk crepe, a heavy four-ply. She felt the fabric move under her fingers as she lifted it over her head and slipped it on, and the dress floated over her and made its way back to earth, falling around her perfectly.

Novena looked in the mirror, and she saw her mother there, in the dress. It made her want to weep — but not from the loss of her, not from her absence, but from a joyful recognition of her presence.

There is never a right time to lose your mother. But the worst can be to lose her, as Novena did, just as memory itself is being formed, just as it is learning how to remember. Imagine if your recollection of a favorite coat was reduced to nothing more than the shape and color of the button on its sleeve. This had been Novena's memory of her mother: sharp and strong, but fragmentary.

But now her mother appeared to Novena whole, so whole she seemed to fill the room. It was as if the dress had been lined with a layer of her mother's breath, of her whispers and sighs that had been waiting only until Novena could put it on for them to be exhaled. As Novena moved across the room, they now surrounded her with memories of the night she was born: with the scents of the salt and tears and fluids of her birth; with the slowness of time in the corner, forgotten; with the sounds of the trio scatting; with the sight of the bundle of the women's clothes on the floor — a pile anchored on the bottom with Annaluna's black dress, and this very dress she now wore resting on the top.

And it was not just her mother in the dress, it was all of them —

all the women who had witnessed her birth, all of whose essences had been secreted in there, stored in the pockets, in the darts, in the fold of the hem. All her mothers.

Her heart felt clean and light. For one beautiful moment, Novena felt completely full.

Novena ran her hand down the cloth, and noticed a small dark stain at the hem. She fingered it, wondering at it, and then her heart opened further with the realization that this was probably her — this small stain had been some part of herself that had settled into the cloth that hot summer night nineteen years ago, and had refused to be removed.

Staring at the little flower of a bruise on the dress, she saw it not as a stain, or a bruise, not as something marring the dress, but as something that had made it more beautiful. It was a piece of herself that was here, that had endured.

"This is me," she said out loud, to the reflection of herself and to the rest of the world that stared back at her in the glass. "This is me, Novena."

She glided downstairs, and as she came back into the dining room, she heard the women's chattering stop, and heard their collective intake of breath as they took in the sight of her, of Novena, swathed again in cobalt. But it wasn't just Novena they were seeing walk into the room. It was Novena as the image of Catorza.

They watched Novena parade around the room, modeling the dress. The women looked at her with wonder at the idea that their own hands had delivered this creature into the world.

Then Novena took her place at the table, and they began eating. The women ate fully, their eyes closing in pleasure at the flavors, astonished again at what they had been able to create with their hands.

Novena was suddenly ravenous, and ate more than she had ever remembered. For the first time in a long time, she ate until she was full.

. . .

Conspiring with the wine, the dress took Novena to Whit's later that night, and when he opened the door, the dress put its arms around him, engulfing him in a cloud of perfumed blue. The bitter sweat of his longing, and the sweeter essence of his relief at the sight of her immediately imprinted itself onto the dress, so in an instant, he too became part of the fabric, mingling with the scents of everything else there.

By the time he stepped back to take her in, he was a lost man.

They spent the next few hours in the pleasure of losing themselves. They were easy hours, of love reengaged.

A little later, they lay in the dark. Whit's hand was in her hair, wrapping it around his fingers.

"So, little girl," he said. "It's been a long time."

"Yes."

She paused, braced for an onslaught of his questions, expecting him to pick up the thread of the conversation where they'd left it when they'd last been together in the dark. Then, she'd been so panicked when he'd begun asking about Zan that she'd run away. Now, though, she was ready to stay put, to tell Whit anything he wanted to know.

She almost looked forward to it, being forced to say the words "Zan and Sylvie" out loud. She wondered what it would sound like. She wondered what else would come as that long story began unspooling itself. She wondered, in fact, how long the story was. It might take years to tell.

So Novena hovered there, at the edge of speaking the truth, waiting for Whit's questions.

But it's only new love that chatters and prods, jumps up and down like a frisky dog, wanting to know everything. Love that's been aged by obstacles and travails just wants to sit quietly, basking itself in warmth, gathering its strength.

"So, what have you found out there in the big, bad world?" he asked, his voice drowsy.

Novena was surprised by his question.

"Nothing," Novena said. "Everything."

A long pause, and she waited for more.

But Whit was mute; he'd taken a strand of her hair and put it in his mouth, and seemed content to nibble on it, letting his mouth fill with this instead of with more words. His mouth then moved to her ear, and she felt his breath shifting into a slower rhythm.

She was surprised at his lack of curiosity, but she said nothing. It made her wonder, though, whether something in him had moved on in their time apart, passing her by. Maybe she had missed it, like a train that had passed a station without her on it. It was gone now.

Whit, lying there, had the feeling that whatever it was that she had been so protective of, whatever horrible thing had been burning inside her, might have been doused somewhere along the way. Maybe in her, maybe in him, for he was surprised that he wasn't that interested anymore in knowing what it was. He wondered if it was a good sign, or a bad one. He wondered if he should worry about it.

Before he could think any more about it, she moved over him and made him forget everything, so quickly, in fact, the speed of it took his breath away. Somewhere far in the back of his mind, where all the laziest and most useless thoughts live, he wondered where she had learned so much about pleasure.

It was early in the morning when Novena woke. Whit looked beautiful, sleeping next to her. She wanted to stay in bed with him, never to move from here. But she knew Elegia would have a fit, not knowing where she was. So she kissed his forehead and stole out of bed, full of energy and yet dazed at the same time.

It was dark gray dawn, miserably cold and wet. She got thoroughly soaked on the way to the car, and in its closed-up warmth, the damp dress released faint traces of its perfume of dirt and age. She inhaled deeply.

She began driving slowly through town. It felt so strange to be in Nile Bay again, driving through these streets, past Check's, and

Whit's shop, the smug little houses, where now a few lights were being snapped on to greet the day. It looked different, not like her town at all. Yet all her life was here, she thought, pieces of it scattered all around.

She came to the river and found herself slowing down, to take it in; it was silvery gray with ice, and a thick mist was rising from it like smoke.

Zan was somewhere in that river.

She paused, waiting to see if the sight of it might stir anything in her.

But whatever grief she might have for him was still frozen. It remained in the river, with him.

It occurred to her that she'd be driving away from Nile Bay in a few days, leaving it all behind to go back to the city. It would be a shame to leave without somehow marking the end of Zan. Maybe she could have her own ritual, to bury Zan as Dex had done.

Her headlights had broken through the mist, and she noticed for the first time a tree sticking out of the middle of the river.

It wasn't a tree, it was a bush.

She peered out through the fogged-up window, and realized it wasn't a bush, it was a man.

A man, standing on the ice.

It was so dark, and she was cloudy with love, so filled with it that she knew it could really have been anything out there. But she took this to be a vision of Zan, one that she had conjured for herself, to allow her to lay him to rest, to say goodbye. It made perfect sense. Here was the most fitting place for her burial ritual — in the river, with Sylvie.

So, barely slowing down, she closed her eyes for an instant and she whispered goodbye.

And when she opened her eyes again and looked in the rearview mirror, a thin veil of moisture had condensed there. Sure enough, the mirror was blank. The vision of Zan was gone.

chapter 36

AFTER LEAVING Annaluna's, Zan had driven south, back home. It was going to be a quick trip — just long enough to pack his things and drop off the truck before heading back to Nile Bay.

He was proud of himself for deciding to leave the truck behind. For once, he was going to leave a place with only the things that belonged to him. But by the time he pulled into his driveway and had pondered the actual logistics of getting out of town, he was already reconsidering.

He owned so little, it took him no time to pack — a pair of boots, some shirts, a pair of jeans, socks and underwear. Annaluna's watch was the only thing that gave him pause. He held it in his hand, considering: did it belong to him or not?

He decided that even though it probably did, he would leave it behind, like a sacrifice. Or better, an exchange: he'd take the truck instead. Putting the watch carefully back into its little cotton nest, he left the house.

He swung back up into the cab and started the truck. But the watch nagged at him; he could almost hear it in there, its faint ticking muffled even more by the cotton. He knew he would hear that sound in his brain during the whole drive, reproaching him for leaving it behind. So he got out, went back into the house, and retrieved it. He tossed it on the dashboard, to show it how much he resented it, and pulled out.

Finally he was heading north, back to Nile Bay. Back to Sylvie.

Zan drove numbly for a while, until the monotony of the highway settled into him.

After the third hour of driving, Zan began to feel his eyelids growing heavy. He should have taken a nap before he left — he hadn't slept in days. He rolled down the window and hit the gas, hoping the speed and the air might keep him awake.

The air rushing into the cab of the truck was bracing, and he felt not just his body waking, but a part of his brain too. He could actually feel it as little pulsing waves moving through his head, like strings of tiny lights being switched on, one by one. The sound of the truck, of the road underneath him, of his own breath, grew louder and more distinct. The edges of things seemed sharper, even his own edges. It was as if he'd lost consciousness when he'd left Annaluna's, or most of it anyway, and now he felt himself slowly coming to, becoming aware of where he was, what he was doing.

He was on his way to Nile Bay, to Sylvie. Zan leaned forward, suddenly anxious, impatient to get there. Why wasn't he there now? Why hadn't he gone there directly from Annaluna's? He could not remember what it was that had made him go back for his things. He'd driven all that way, for a bunch of old clothes he would no longer need.

He looked at the fat lumpy sack of them huddled on the floor. They annoyed him, cowering there. They might as well have been a bag of boulders. Ever since Annaluna's, he'd been conscious of the great weight of all the things he'd left behind. Now, though, he felt there was a much heavier weight in these things — all the things he was taking with him.

The watch was sitting on the dashboard, noisily vibrating in a nervous dance from the shuddering momentum of the truck. He reached over and picked it up. He closed his palm over it, so tightly he imagined he could feel the small indentations of the inscription imprinting themselves onto his palm. He squeezed his fist around it; then, drawing his arm back, he hurled the watch out the window.

It's hard to throw things well from a moving vehicle. You might imagine the thing you throw will match your speed, will climb in a long high arc where it will hover for a moment before starting a dramatic descent, gaining force and speed until it shatters to the ground.

But instead, velocity is against you, and so the thing you throw skips straight across the air like a stone on water, and lands with an ungracious thud a puny few feet away.

On leaving Zan's hand, the watch skidded to a halt at the edge of a bush at the side of the road. At least it had the grace to land with the inscription facing up, so a few hours later, when the moon climbed to a particular point in the sky, the gold was caught briefly in its light. And for one small moment each night, until the loose dirt and stones and twigs that circled it slowly like a curious tribe finally smothered it, Annaluna's watch shimmered.

By the time the watch landed, Zan had already reached down and brought his knapsack up to the seat beside him. He reached in and pulled out a shirt and as he shook it out, could smell its rankness. These were not his clothes — they were his laundry. He held the shirt out the window, and then he let go.

But he was driving too fast, or hadn't been holding the shirt out far enough, because it fell back against the side of the truck where it flattened itself — as if it were desperate, holding on to the truck for its life. It almost made Zan laugh to see this. He slowed down until the shirt released itself and flapped away into the air like a bird.

He reached into his bag for another shirt, and flung it out the window. He flung all his shirts, one by one, feeling lighter and lighter as they left his hands. A small bark of glee escaped from him; it was a sound that was more animal than human, slightly strangled at his efforts to contain it. He had the idea if he started laughing, he'd never be able to stop.

He hurled his jeans next. He could see them in his rearview mirror, lying in the middle of the highway, looking hapless and ridiculous.

Now he pulled out three pairs of rolled-up socks, lobbing them out the window like baseballs.

He was wheezing now, beginning to feel helpless under a great molten eruption of laughter that was rising in him. He flung his underwear next; it was shocking and marvelous: his underwear, released into the night.

It felt like he was stripping. In fact, for a moment, he considered taking off the clothes he was wearing and tossing them too, driving the rest of the way naked, with nothing but the air against his skin.

Only his boots were left. He heaved one, then the other. As soon as the second one left his hand, he saw it heading for a car that was passing him in the next lane. He watched the boot hit the car's roof — could hear the suprisingly loud thwanging thud of it — and Zan finally exploded, howling with laughter as he watched it bounce off the roof, onto the road. As he pulled ahead, he saw the car swerving wildly behind him, the driver looking startled and frightened. Zan could hardly breathe, he was laughing so hard.

For a while, it felt like one of the best nights in his life.

After that, though, the trip turned miserable. A while later, the truck began making horrible grinding sounds, then started heaving crazily. Zan nursed it along for a while, unable to get it to move beyond a slow, bucking crawl. He finally pulled off the highway into the parking lot of a diner. He sat there, considering what to do.

He closed his eyes to think, and almost immediately fell asleep. Waking a while later in the darkness, he watched the headlights of cars moving smoothly into and out of the parking lot. Finally, an old idea came to him. He got out of the truck. Moving along a row of cars, he found one whose hood was still warm. He slid in, got it started and drove out of there, fast.

All told, it took him three days to get back to Nile Bay.

By the time he reached the first traffic light leading into town, the gray dawn had turned white with snow.

Although for the last eight hours he had thought of little else but his destination, he was unprepared for the actual fact of it, for his first sight of Nile Bay. How familiar it was, how much it belonged to him, like his bones, or his blood. It shocked him as much as if the place had sprung out in front of him to startle him.

It was such an unsettling sensation driving through town, past the river, past all that was familiar, that he simply drove straight through without stopping. It took no time at all, but he was trembling by the time he reached the town limits. Still, he didn't wait before turning around and heading back, toward the river.

He parked the car in a lot where he knew it wouldn't be noticed for a while, and began walking the half mile to the riverbank. Tiny razors of freezing rain were falling now, stinging his cheeks.

When he reached the river he stood on the bank, looking out over the wide expanse of it. It was covered with ice, barely recognizable.

He had imagined himself walking straight into the water, diving in and swimming out. He hadn't counted on having to maneuver a hard icy surface. Still, confronting that icy coating gave him a momentary tremor of something — some weak flutter between hope and despair. Maybe Sylvie didn't want him. Maybe the river had grown this thick membrane to keep him out.

A small seizure of sorrow brought him dangerously close to sobbing.

This is where he belonged.

Zan stepped onto the ice.

. . .

He started walking, very carefully. The ice made hardly a sound as he moved across. But as he got farther out, he was conscious of patches that began groaning when he tested his weight on them.

He was also conscious of his caution, which in the circumstances he found curious. But he continued to walk carefully, almost daintily, and with each step he let his weight down slower, feeling for how strong the ice underneath him might be, listening for that high-pitched cracking sound.

He'd been out there for ten minutes, in utter silence. He was not more than a third of the way out when he took a step and felt the icy sting of water filling his right shoe. And suddenly he was straddling an odd place: his left foot behind him was on solid ice, and his right foot in front was beginning to push through a thinner patch, where he could actually see the current running underneath.

As he stood considering what to do, how to move, he heard something droning in the distance. A car shot over the curve, its headlights cutting through the gray.

It came so unexpectedly that Zan didn't think. He turned and looked behind him, toward the light. The minute shifting of his weight was enough, and he heard a sharp crack. The last thing he heard, though, was the sigh of the river, although it might have been from himself, giving up, surrendering. Then the river engulfed him like the arms of a woman, the arms of Sylvie.

chapter 37

Everything is fabric, clothing to the very end. Everything turns to
dust, but dust is still an extreme covering; it envelops everything.
— Mario Perniola, "Between Clothing and Nudity"

IT WAS FORTUNATE they buried Annaluna when they did. Two
nights after her interment, Nile Bay was hit with a freezing rain-
storm, and by the next morning a mantle of cruelly shimmering
diamonds encrusted trees, pipes, tracks, houses, and power lines.
Electricity was lost for twenty-seven hours, plunging everything
into darkness, although Novena and Whit, who were already huddled together, barely noticed.

The harshest winter in memory began with that storm, but
there is still no agreement on which day it ended. Most people declared winter's end on the last weekend in March, when the first
thaw came and sent a heaving, mucky flood of mud and water
through the streets. But for a few in Nile Bay, the official end of
the winter came more than a week later, on the Wednesday the
river finally overflowed its banks and spit up Zan.

He was actually found two miles downriver, by two boys who
had been lobbing large stones at the dark floating mass they had
spied, caught between a rock and a floe of ice twenty feet from

shore; eventually their tireless pelting had shifted his body around until Zan's face suddenly turned to them, so grotesque it was like a reproach. Had Zan been alive, he would have been thrilled with the terrified howls he elicited from the two boys.

The small crew of men who showed up to retrieve him were confronted with an enormously complicated task. The current was swift and dangerous, and it was going to be dark soon. They had to deliberate over whether or not he was far enough out to use a boat; they ended up tethering a large raft with heavy rope and sent two men out to retrieve him. His body was too heavy to lift into the raft, so they had to wrap the rope around him and drag him into shore. On the way to the morgue, someone joked that they should take bets on how long it would take to fully defrost him.

The Nile Bay morgue was a small room in the basement of the police station. It was so rarely used that it had served occasional double duty as a nap-and-breakfast room. On the metal table where they put Zan's body lay a small spray of crumbs and pow-dered sugar from the doughnuts and the elaborately sweet baked experiments regularly sent in by the chief's wife.

It was the dinner hour when they brought him in, and Boomer Verley was alone in the station. Although he hadn't immediately recognized Zan, he later claimed that some strange premonition had come to him the instant before he had flipped open the wallet and seen Zan's name on his license.

"I just knew this wasn't any ordinary drowning victim," Boomer would tell anyone who would listen for weeks afterward. He was still not hardened enough to use the term "floater."

Boomer held off calling anyone right away. He could barely understand why, but he wanted some time alone with Zan. Pulling up a metal chair next to the table, he sat for a while, staring at him.

It was the damnedest thing, the biggest mystery Boomer's brain had ever had to grapple with. For although he knew it couldn't be possible, it was like Zan had been down there, underwater, all this time, eating, sleeping, working, aging. It was as if he had lived an entire secret life down there, for nearly two years, and only now, for reasons unknown to anyone, he had finally come up for air.

➤

The thick, earnest planes of his face, and the apologetic slope of Boomer Verley's wide shoulders made him one of the few policemen in the world who could show up at someone's door in the evening without causing alarm.

In fact, when Elegia opened the door and saw him, she was only conscious of the blush she felt crawling up her neck and staining her cheeks. It wouldn't be until hours later that she would muster enough grace to be ashamed that her first instinct at the sight of him had been pleasure instead of trepidation.

"Oh!" she cried. "How are you?"

She stood dumbly, holding the door slightly ajar, a move that was oddly mirrored by her mouth, which was also slightly ajar in a small but welcoming smile.

Boomer made a vague little gesture with his hand, and she opened the door wider and began backing up into the house as he came in, her eyes fixed on him, her smile now a little confused.

"It's Zan," he said softly. "They found him this afternoon."

"Zan?" she said.

She was still backing up as he came into the house, and she careened into the edge of a table. It was as if the meaning of the word "Zan" had hit her at the same moment she hit the table. Boomer saw her face instantly rearrange itself into shock, her hand covering her mouth as if to take back the memory of her smile.

Boomer took her arm and led her to a seat in the living room. He knelt down and took her hand.

"They found him in the river," he said quietly.

"Thank God," she said, her eyes closing.

He was afraid he had confused her, had somehow made her think they had found him alive.

"I'm so sorry about this," he said. "You'll have to come down and identify the, um, remains."

374

"I knew he was there, I told you he was there," she said, pulling her hand from his, sounding both angry and triumphant. "If you knew the suffering you people have caused because you couldn't find him before now."

Boomer didn't take offense, nor was he shocked by her reaction. He had been with the police long enough to know that it was not his job to administer the town's laws as much as it was to administer its fate. He also knew that as fate's deputy, he was the most logical receptacle for the rage of its victims.

"Where is he?" Elegia demanded, pushing herself up from the chair. "I want to see him. Take me to him."

She was quiet in the car, making only the soft skin sound of her hands kneading each other, a sound which, by the time they reached the station, he was finding embarrassing in its intimacy. He went ahead of her into the room where Zan was waiting, to pull the sheet from his face, folding it neatly under his chin. Then he brought her in.

Elegia let out a small moan and clutched Boomer's arm. She stood shaking her head slowly back and forth, but saying nothing. Then she reached out and touched Zan's face.

"He's so cold," she said. "Don't you have a blanket or something?"

"Sure, I'll get one," Boomer said, moving toward the door.

"No, wait! Don't go," Elegia cried, suddenly unable to bear the idea of being alone with Zan. She was afraid she might disappear, or forget to breathe without the presence of a breathing, live being near her.

Boomer moved quickly to her side. He moved his arm to curve around her shoulders in case she collapsed, yet at the last moment felt it would be presumptuous to touch her. Instead, he let his stretched-out arm hover a few inches from her back, his fingers not quite grazing her shoulder.

"He looks good," she said, reassured by Boomer's proximity. "I'm a little surprised. I would have thought after two years . . ."

She shuddered at what the rest of the thought conjured: her son nothing but fleshless bone, eaten away by fish or other animals.

"Elegia, I'm not so sure he's been there that long."

It had come to Boomer as he had sat staring at his body that his odd notion of Zan having lived underwater had been a strangely hopeful one — he had somehow pictured Zan happy, living down there. He knew from the condition of the body that it was unlikely he had been underwater all this time.

"What are you talking about?" Elegia said. "It's been two years."

"Well, I'm not sure he's been in the river for the whole time, is all I'm saying."

"Oh, that's ridiculous," she scoffed. "Where else would he have been?"

She moved a little closer to the table, as if to shield Zan from such foolish ideas. Who knew a son better than his own mother? This was her Zan. Drowned two years ago. Finally found. End of story.

Boomer didn't push it. He didn't see the point. He knew that just as there is a love that wants to know everything, there is a love that wants to know nothing at all. In his experience, that was usually the one reserved for mothers.

Back home, Elegia called the boys, then Quivera and then Celantra. She had left Novena for last. She thought the extra practice saying the words would help her keep her own equilibrium when she talked to Novena, who had a way of challenging it, whatever the subject of conversation.

By the third call, though, Elegia was surprised at how calmly she was able to impart the news, as though she were telling an old story, something that had happened sometime in the past. It *had* happened a long time ago, after all, except it was also happening now. She had the dizzying sense that time was being mischievous, botching up her thoughts. In fact, when she finally dialed Novena's number, which she still thought of as Annaluna's, she was momentarily rattled when she heard Novena answer, and realized she had been expecting to hear the old woman's voice.

"Oh! Novena," she said. She took a breath. "Are you sitting down?"

"What?"

"They finally found him."

Novena knew from her voice, high and strained, that she was talking about Zan.

"Tell me."

"In the river," Elegia said. "They pulled him out this afternoon. I just got back from the morgue."

Novena was listening to Elegia, but she was also marking the things around her, surprised at how conscious she was of the light in the kitchen, of the chairs and the table and the gleaming white of the refrigerator, the oven and its four black burners, the tiny hint of blue flame under each. She was taking in these details as if they were important elements of what Elegia was telling her, or as if they might rearrange themselves if she wasn't paying attention.

"Do they know how long . . . ?" Novena said, inspecting the tiny gullies between the tiles of the counter. "I mean, was he there —"

"All this time," Elegia interrupted. "I *knew* he was there. Wyn thought he would come back someday. But I knew he was down there all this time. I knew he was close. A mother knows where her own children are. Of course, no one believed *me*. No one ever takes me seriously."

"Are you okay?" Novena said. "It'll take me a few hours to get there."

"Oh, don't bother coming tonight," Elegia said. "There's nothing to be done here."

Novena leaned against the counter after Elegia hung up, waiting for the news to catch up to with her, to feel herself changed by it. She had the feeling it was going to crash onto her head, yet she also felt curiously blank and distant from it, as if she were nothing but an onlooker to some immense disaster that ultimately had nothing to do with her.

Zan still did occasionally rise to the surface of her thoughts, despite her ritual of bidding him goodbye at the river that wintry morning months ago. Sometimes she'd wake in the middle of the night, and ponder for the thousandth time whether she should tell someone the story of what she knew. But she would reason that too much time had passed; if she said anything now, she'd look foolish, or even worse, suspicious. Besides, she was sure some moment would come that would finally demand the truth from her, although the more time passed, the more distant it seemed.

Sometimes on those nights, she fretted about what she must be lacking as a person, to have kept this enormous thing to herself. Although she knew exactly what was missing: her distance from any grief, any sadness over Zan. She knew, too, that this absence was probably at the heart of her silence.

There were times during those nights she would turn to Whit lying beside her, ready to nudge him awake, to tell him everything. But the sound of his sleeping breath or the warmth of his body would bring her back to the present, and she'd decide once again to leave everything in the past where it belonged.

Whit had moved in with Novena as soon as he was able to close up the shop in Nile Bay. Their life had settled instantly into a pleasant and not unfamiliar routine, which often — especially in the mornings, over coffee in the kitchen — reminded Novena of her life with Annaluna. But she recalled those moments with pleasure, and sometimes imagined that the three of them were occupying the house. It was easy to imagine Annaluna and Whit getting along.

At the moment, though, Novena was glad that Whit wasn't home yet; she wanted more time with this news. She left the kitchen and began drifting through the rooms, touching Annaluna's things, which she always did when she was feeling unsettled.

"They found Zan," she whispered to a frosted blue vase that always sat empty. "They found him."

It struck her that it was an odd way to describe it: it made it sound as if someone had been looking for him.

She was still waiting for the impact to come as she drifted into the bedroom and sat on the edge of her bed. She tried to picture him, tried to imagine what it would be like to see him. Novena could not imagine seeing him; she could not even remember what he looked like, and as her thoughts drifted in and out, it was like watching a movie, picturing the funeral home, picturing Elegia wailing, and the boys huddled and silent. She wondered what her reaction would be. She tried to picture Zan laid out at the head of the room, waiting to see if anyone would show up to mourn him.

Then, thinking of Annaluna's robe, she wondered what he would be wearing. Out of curiosity, she began imagining what such a robe for Zan might look like, what objects it might contain.

She recalled his house, and as she took herself through the rooms of that crabbed, mildewy shack, she couldn't remember a single personal thing of his, other than the ring of beer cans on the counter, his gun in the case, a bottle of dandruff shampoo on the ledge of the bath. She thought of his clothes and other things, which were stored in boxes in Elegia's basement, but all she could bring to mind was tired plaid flannel, worn corduroys, and thin towels, all of them unappealing.

She thought suddenly of the small things she used to steal from his room when she was a girl. Even then, she had never found anything of consequence — a pocketknife, a book of matches, links from a chain, a few dirty coins. She thought of herself, squirreling those things of his away, hiding them in her own room, and now she wondered, with a little tremor of sadness, if maybe she had just been hungry for something of him to hold in her hands, something to bring him closer to her. She had looked to these things for some clue to him, but they had never revealed themselves, never given themselves up to be anything but pedestrian.

Now he was gone. She thought how typical it was of Zan, to leave nothing of beauty behind.

➤

One funeral home was more than adequate to handle a town the size of Nile Bay. Belvay's took up the first two floors of a large Victorian house near the center of town. No one remembered who the original occupants of the house had been, or when it had been made over to become a funeral home, but from the outside it looked as if it had served this role for centuries; the white paint had faded to a dull gray, the shingles were peeling, a few shutters were loose. Yet its proprietors seemed disinclined to rush into fixing it up. Indeed, while the Belvay family was respectful in every other way to the formalities of grief demanded of their occupation, a perverse logic seemed to have taken hold in their ideas about the outside of the place: they must have thought it wasn't a bad thing for a house of the dead to have a slightly haunted appearance.

The small letters on the metal awning that led to its front door had also seen better days, and as she approached the place the next afternoon, Novena noticed that the letters now spelled BEL A 'S FUN   HOME.

Novena had gone directly to Belvay's when she arrived in Nile Bay. She had no idea how she'd react to the actual sight of Zan, and she wanted some time alone with him, before being swept into the contagion of grief of Elegia and the boys.

When Ardita Belvay answered her ring, she was clearly rattled to see Novena, and seemed astonished that anyone would come to the front entrance at any time but an hour published in the newspaper.

"Calling hours aren't until five," she said nervously, clutching at the collar of her flowered house dress, as if embarrassed to be caught wearing something so cheerful.

Novena told her she had just come in from the city, and wanted to see Zan.

"I'll have to check. Come in and take a seat and I'll see where things stand."

She led Novena into one of the parlors, filled with rows of empty chairs. Novena took a seat in the back.

As she waited, Novena looked around her. In all the times she'd been here, it had never struck her what an ugly place it was. There was little left of the gracious proportions or details of the original Victorian architecture. Cheap pine paneling had been applied to the walls, and the ceilings had been dropped; fluorescent tubes buzzed in the quiet. The room was filled with rows of metal folding chairs. Boxes of tissues rested on metal radiator covers. It all had a stale smell, of cigarettes and grief.

She looked around her, and Novena couldn't help wondering what she might do if the design of such a place was left to her. Something beautiful — the walls and ceilings draped in silk, and instead of these hard chairs, maybe pillows on the floor, for people to lie languorous in their grief.

She was thinking through a palette of rose shades that she might choose when a tall man in a dark suit came into the room.

"I'm sorry for your loss," Victor Belvay intoned softly.

Tall, bony, and dark, Victor Belvay was the perfect picture of an undertaker, a picture he carefully enhanced with his somber suits, softly modulated voice, and generally joyless life. But within the arrangement of his facial features were a few unfortunate quirks — a certain crook of the left eyebrow, a twist at the corner of his mouth — that in combination gave the impression of a constant leer. Female mourners who encountered him were often given to an inexplicable shudder which they could not always attribute to their grief.

"It's going to take a little while," he said, barely above a whisper. "A suit was dropped off this morning. We're about to finish up. Meanwhile, there are some, er, effects. I wonder if you would like to have them."

As he held out a parcel to her, Novena had the strange sense he was offering her flowers and candy.

It was instead a paper bag, which Novena noticed was from the local grocery store, its top carefully folded down.

Victor was saying she could wait a little longer or come back later, "perhaps during calling hours."

It was clear he preferred she leave, but Novena said she'd wait.

After he'd slid out of the room, Novena emptied the bag onto the chair beside her. She found a small pile of clothes — a shirt, a pair of pants, a pair of rolled-up socks — and she felt her throat catch as she realized they must be the clothes they had found him in.

They'd been washed and carefully folded, the socks sitting on top. Zan's socks. They looked so helpless. For some reason, they made her think of sleeping babies, of curled-up embryos, and her throat clenched again. She touched them tentatively, surprised at how these small things could move her to such sudden tenderness.

But it was the strangeness of the sensation — this tenderness for Zan — that shocked her. It was something she couldn't remember ever feeling for him.

That wasn't true. After Sylvie was buried, when Novena had realized no one had noticed Zan was missing, she had decided, in a grand gesture of resolve, to be the only one who cared. To love him as a saint might, as God himself might.

That was her only memory of tenderness for him, ever. And even that had been nothing but some fleeting, romantic idea, moved mostly by pity.

But it *had* been the moment she had decided to save him.

It was extraordinary now to think of the lengths she had gone to clean all evidence of him away, to bury his secrets — moving his truck, cleaning his house, keeping silent. All that effort, because she'd been afraid of what people might think if they'd known Zan had been with Sylvie. She had imagined a swarm of angry people pelting the house with stones, Elegia and the rest of them huddled inside. She had imagined Zan never being mourned.

That part was almost true, Novena thought, but it was only she who was unable to mourn him. Something more extraordinary occurred to her then: that maybe she'd been afraid not for Zan, but for herself. Afraid she'd be delivered to a day like this one, right now, when she would be the one to look upon the remains of him and feel nothing. Unable to grieve over his loss. Wanting to pelt his house with stones.

She felt her heart, which had opened in tenderness, now closing like a fist. It had suddenly become a cold muscle, curling tightly inside her, as she remembered him, alive. The storm of him, shaking the house. The stealth of him, standing in her doorway at night, or coming up behind her, sneaking up to leave his marks on her — pinches, harsh twists to her skin, stinging slaps, shoves.

Taken individually, they had been almost harmless, like a series of small car accidents — the nicks and dents and scratches of childhood. No serious damage. But even as a child, Novena had known how to add them up, to see the sum of them as something far more threatening: the threat to extinguish her, to make her one of the burned-up carcasses Zan was always leaving behind in the woods.

But she had learned how to keep herself safe. There was a place she could retreat to, an entire town in her where Zan never appeared, where she no longer saw him.

No wonder she'd been unable to find any sorrow for him. She had made him disappear, long before he actually had. By the time he'd reached the river with Sylvie, as far as Novena was concerned, he'd already been dead for years.

It wasn't his secret that she'd been keeping all this time, but her own. She hadn't been trying to save him. She'd been trying to save herself.

Just then, a soft knock on the door made Novena jump, and Victor Belvay came into the room.

"Whenever you're ready, I'd be happy to take you in," he murmured.

"Okay." Novena got up more unsteadily than she expected. She suddenly felt nervous.

He took Novena's arm in a vaguely courtly gesture, and led her into another parlor, similar to the one she had just left, although this one was filled with an almost blinding yellow light from the sun streaming through the windows. Victor hurried around the room, pulling down the metal blinds, then disappeared.

There was Zan, lying twenty feet away. Novena approached him slowly, her throat dry.

Finally, she was standing above him, looking down at his face. She felt the instant shock felt by the living confronting the dead.

He was wearing a suit, an ugly, ill-fitting pale gray suit, with sleeves that were too short. He had never worn a suit in her memory, and it made him look like a small boy, dressed up to look like a man.

Even his hands, crossed low on his stomach, looked like those of a child.

She felt her face twisting up as the thought came to her:

He's so small.

Much smaller than her memory of him. Much smaller than the space he had taken up in her all these years.

She knelt weakly in front of him, overcome. She studied his torn and ragged fingernails, the hard little knobs of his wrist bones exposed by the short sleeves of his suit, and the faint trace of a purplish bruise on his right cheek.

He was nothing but a boy, she thought.

But she knew there was more to him than this. Because so much is contained in the body, even in its remains: the way eyebrows will curve down in a protective hood over the eyes; how the edges of the mouth will set in a grim crease, the lips tucked away; the way shoulders will narrow and slope in defeat. She felt the corners of her own mouth tremble as it came to her that Zan's real story was in the collapsed, unthreatening body he had left behind: he had lived and died an unloved creature.

She felt her heart cracking into small fissures, thinking how helpless he must have felt. Not monstrous, but frightened. Not violent, but desperate to reach out, to be enfolded, enclosed, in other hands.

It's a sad day when you look down upon your monsters with pity, when you see how small they have become. It'll age you forever.

Novena was trembling when she reached over to him and touched one of the small bruises on Zan's face. She knew she should have expected him to be cold, but the actual fact of it shocked her, and she pulled her hand back.

She forced herself to touch him again.

And even though his skin was cold, the touch had the force of heat against ice. Inside her, years of thick blue ice began cracking, shattering into smaller and smaller pieces, allowing a strong current underneath to swell and flood, which Novena felt as a huge shuddering wave of grief that moved up from her center and ended in a shuddering rapture of sorrow.

And then she was weeping, finally, in true grief for the loss of him. Because she was finally seeing him, for the last time. Because her heart had finally cracked open, and in its center was another, smaller heart, one that had loved him. Loved him like a monster, as Beauty loved the Beast.

It was such a helpless love, the love that stumbles blindly around the house, banging into things, walking into walls, the love that bumps against furniture in its blindness, the love that gives you bruises, the love that you must have in you in order to survive, despite its attempt to eat you alive.

The helpless love of family that binds us all.

Hearing Novena's sobs, the Belvays closed the door softly behind her, relieved now that things had been restored to their proper place: someone in one of their rooms, where the thick drapes hung on the windows, muffling the sounds of grief that were now piercing the air.

This is where Elegia found her, twenty minutes later, still kneeling in front of him, calmer now, but wrung out.

Elegia kissed the top of Novena's head and knelt down beside her.

"I always knew he'd show up. Poor thing," she said, reaching over and patting Zan's hand. "You know, I was so young when I had the boys, I didn't know what I was doing. They put me in such a dreamy state. I felt . . ."

Elegia hesitated. It wasn't that she didn't know the word she wanted to use, but she was shy about saying it out loud.

"They made me feel . . ." She wondered what made her think suddenly of Dr. Jack.

"I felt beautiful," she said. Then, registering Novena's surprised glance, she hurriedly went on. "But once they were born, they were such hard work. And poor Zan. Always so troubled. I always worried about him. But what could I do? I never knew what he wanted. They never tell you anything."

She rose and half stood, leaning over him, making little adjustments in the lapel of his suit, in the sleeves, in his tie. Bending lower, she kissed his cheek. Then she sank to her knees again and said mournfully, her voice cracking, "He would never have let me do that if he was alive."

Then she started weeping, and Novena, moved, had no choice but to join her.

And so in Zan's last hours on earth, or at least in his last hours above the earth and not under it, a small measure of love finally found its way to him, in time to redeem him.

If you think it was too late, that his moment of grace and salvation missed him by a few months, you'd be wrong.

It's almost never too late. Even if you don't believe we leave this life to return to the realm of souls, where we wait to be reborn, consider all the things we leave behind: the dusty tracks of slough, the gummy trails of our deposits; the stains and particles and molecules of all we've shed — breath, skin, tears, possessions.

So even by the time his body was put under ground the next day, much of Zan still remained, scattered throughout the world — hair and skin, boots and shirts, even underwear.

Consider, for example, that last shirt he tossed from his truck, the one that had taken flight, borne by a breeze that carried it as far as the branches of a low bush, where, an hour later, a man who had pulled to the side of the road to check a map found it. He took it home, and his wife cut it into rags, and for months she used it to clean the surfaces of her furniture, wiping away dust — which is nothing but flakes and shards of our skin, shed from our bodies — mingling this dust with particles of Zan's own shed skin.

And that was just a shirt. Imagine all the other things he shed from himself, a country of things he left behind. Enough so that even now, somewhere, a smudge of Zan might still remain, floating in the air like a tiny piece of ash, a speck of soot, a mote of grit. So small as to be almost inconsequential.

But just big enough to be seen.